VIPERS AND THE GODS

THE ORIGINS OF CYLLA

BOOK TWO

HARLEIGH KNIGHT

Identifiers
ISBN:978-1-963934-02-1 (eBook)
ISBN:978-1-963934-03-8 (paperback)

TRIGGER WARNING

This book may discuss topics that are not suitable for everyone and may be difficult for some readers. This book includes mentions of parental neglect, emotional abuse, infant death, dismemberment, physical abuse, panic attacks, forced infertility, child death, sex slavery, sex trafficking, and attempted sexual assault. This is a story about deities with loose inspiration from mythology. If topics of violence and death are too much for you, put the book aside and take care of your mental health first.

AUTHOR NOTES

Book Two is set in another realm with another sister. I know it may feel jarring at first as you ease back into the story, but it all connects in the end.
I hope you enjoy reading it as much as I enjoyed writing it.

CHAPTER ONE
THE PLAN

SHIVANI

One harsh truth I've learned about the world is the futility of trust. You cannot have it, not in the god that abandoned us nor in the child loitering outside the shops with their sad eyes. You don't accept anyone's words as truth unless you're prepared to pay for it. Honesty is a rare commodity, and those who possess it don't survive for long. A moment of mercy can cost you everything. The world is cruel, but I can be worse.

At least, that's what my mom taught me. I wonder if she's repeating that to the keeper of the under realm.

Before my time, in an era I'm not sure I believe ever existed, the Goddess of the Moon and her sister, the Goddess of Starlight, crafted our realm. The Goddess of Starlight grew envious of her sister after she wed the God of the Sun. Our realm flourished for a brief period until the news of a child to be born from the Goddess of the Moon spread. In a fit of jealousy, the Goddess of Starlight slew the God of the Sun and imprisoned her sister, the Goddess of the Moon, within a tree. The Goddess of Starlight took her sister and departed our realm, leaving the other gods behind, too. They continued their rule in a state of perpetual anger.

Our king now calls himself a god-king. He claims he has the blood of the gods in his veins and that he is the last remaining line to speak to them. All the kings have the same name and enraged temper, even with different faces. Not many of us believe him; there's no trace of Gods left. No trace of humanity, either.

The only ones who disagree live inside the lines that separate our fates. I live on the outside of those lines. I've been a burden since I was old enough to remember. My father left to look for a woman who could bear him better fruit from his seed, fruit with more use, and my mother only kept me so I could earn her coin. It's easy for me to see the king's lies, but he keeps us so low that there's nothing we can do. We spend all of our time worrying about the next meal. No one has the means to revolt.

Besides the stories of our god-king, we were told tales about demons and how their price was always high. We had better deny them if they showed up. I was already paying a high price for life with nothing to show for it. I was already walking the line of death every day. There was no price higher for me. When he offered me blood magic and a chance to hurt my mother the way she hurt me, I agreed without hesitation.

When he told me all he wanted in return was my soul, that price was not higher to me than the overwhelming wave of relief and joy that washed over me when I pulled every drop of blood from my mother's body and heard her heart stop. It was a fair price because with it came the ability to listen to her last thoughts while she left the realm of the living. I adjusted to hearing many thoughts from strangers that I couldn't before the deal.

Today, when the sun woke and the sky shifted from oranges to gold, I killed for the second time. I drained the blood of a girl from a land far away while she slept at the inn.

I took every belonging she had with her before I buried her body underneath the most beautiful rose bushes. I sat her small silver, jewel-filled headdress over my red hair after I braided it. I covered myself with her veil and hid my eyes. I wore her red gown filled with delicately designed embroidery, and I took the hand of her coachman. I sat in the seat she would have been placed in and commanded the man to make haste on our journey.

I did my best to slow my breathing. I heard the man's thoughts. He ignored my presence entirely. He forgot I was present at all, and instead, he spent his time moaning and groaning about how he didn't want to be up so early. He considered if he could nap while the horse took us on the correct path. I still could not fully ease my anxiety. I took my time to learn every detail I could of this girl before I killed her. I made sure we looked as similar as we could have. I sifted through the fine details of killing her and where to hide her.

I picked to leave her under the roses our village coveted because it was against the law to dig them up. Claiming to have grown one set of flowers was impressive. Having a row of bushes became part of the town's prized possessions.

She was selected to be one of the girls sent to the castle to be picked for new staffing. I wasn't born into a wealthy family or a position of power, but with a strong sense of will and an even stronger sense of motivation, I was confident I could make up for it. That's more powerful in the end. There were multiple positions to fill. Two that mattered, two for marriage to the princes and common staff. I was going to take the position that mattered. The one of the Queen and nothing less. I spent enough of my life as a maid or worse. I was ready to promote myself.

I took two of my fingers and gently lifted the carriage curtain to look outside. We were already nearing the border of my homeland, Askia, and close to entering Vesper, the kingdom that held the royals. Vesper held a smaller compound of royals who would never rule. They lived without need there. Royal blood was blessed blood, as the king would say. Inbred filth is what most outside the walls would say. Never out loud. Never in mixed company. Our king liked to get creative with punishments. I never knew if the day would bring news of burning, boiling, or becoming food for the crows. I didn't care how they bred themselves out as long as I got into their company.

I knew I'd face one of his creative punishments if caught, but I refused to dwell on the thought. My soul, my afterlife, was sold and done. As long as I ended the god-king line before I was caught, that's all that mattered to me. I would become queen and kill him, regardless of anything else. I would make sure the lesser city children ate instead of going to bed in pain.

Outside the carriage, the landscape was covered in browns and reds. Fall was greeting us quickly. A warning winter wasn't far behind. I hoped to hold the crown with a dead king by my side before next winter. I had been able to make it twenty-two winters so far. Another would pass quickly. With how much I had to do, it would. I woke up today as Shivani, but I would go to sleep tonight as the nameless veiled beauty for only the king's eyes.

The carriage stopped, and with it, my heart dropped into my stomach. I knew we were not at the castle yet, but we would have at least half a day's ride if the horse kept up speed. My mind raced at the thought of the coachman receiving a bird that detailed what I had done. I was prepared to get into that castle and participate in selection no matter how many lives I had to take, but I had hoped my third kill would be the king.

A hand rested on the door to the carriage, and I moved my thumb over the button I kept between my fingers, small and hidden; one press and the dagger I kept strapped to my wrist would release into my hand. I was a young child when I watched a girl do the same to protect herself, and I knew it would also be my first line of defense. If I were to need more, I kept others hidden in different places of my body, too.

The door opened, and my thumb ached to press down. My hand begged to grip the dagger, but my mind told me to wait. I must keep my head level and hold it until the last moment. I practiced slow, deep breathing to keep my presence emotionless. A man was on the other side. He greeted me with a smile that did not meet his eyes. A smile that told me he was no happier being here than I was to have him. I tried to enter his mind, but there was nothing. Not a thought about even the frigid air. He didn't speak to himself of the tacky purple velvet covering the inside of the carriage. Nothing. It meant I couldn't get a glimpse of him to ease my nervousness.

"Please, feel free to pretend I'm not here." He nodded in my direction before he moved the curtains to watch the scenery in the same way I had before his arrival.

I didn't know his name, but I knew from the black and gold trim on his clothing that he had to be part of the royals. The best our lands had to offer was theirs to take. From the silks to the healers, they owned it. The rest of us only existed to serve. How he looked at me with his chiseled jaw was the last indication I needed to solidify my assumption. He looked at me as if I were below him. His eyes ran over me, but the veil that was covering all except my lips made it hard for him to take me in fully; it was still enough for him to begin judgment. I was disgusted with him, too. His privileged scent was leaking into every space around us.

"I didn't mean to startle you," he said.

I wanted to say that his voice made it hard to pretend he wasn't in my carriage. I wanted to remind him that he permitted me to ignore him, and speaking again was making that hard. What I wanted to do was release my dagger. What I did was give a small laugh like all the well-mannered girls I had watched come in and out of my village, like we were a sight to gawk at.

"It's my fault, sir. I startle easy," I smiled.

"Your nerves must be high. I should have left a note letting you know I'd be joining for the final stretch to Vesper," he said.

His voice was rough, as if he had spent days yelling or talking more than his vocal cords wanted. He had medium-length white hair and the brightest golden eyes I had ever seen. The contrast between the brightness of his hair and the darkness of his skin was beautiful in the sun.

His presence outside of his looks could have been more impressive. He had the body of a man who fought often but the demand of a lonely barman drunk and drooling on himself while everyone complained of his scent. I left the smile on my face regardless. It helped me stay in character. Adding the softness to my voice was harder.

"Please, sir. There's no need to worry. This carriage, the horse, it's all yours after all," I said as I lowered my head.

"You can call me Fennic. There's no need to keep saying, sir. You're making me uncomfortable now," he said, his lips turned down.

"I apologize again, Sir," I answered.

He sighed and crossed his arms. "So, what's your skill, then? Do you cook, sow?"

Our eyes lingered on each other momentarily while I considered my answer. There was no way he could see through my veil, but it felt as if he could all the same. I knew I did my work well when I picked this girl. I knew I didn't miss anything I needed to know. I also wasn't stupid enough to think the palace and the royal guard didn't do their home-work. My palms gathered moisture again, just as I had convinced them to stop.

"I can play many instruments," I responded.

He nodded. "I thought with your over-the-top manners, it would have been your family ties that got you in. I suppose something so simple makes sense, too."

I ground my teeth through my smile before answering.

"No, Sir. My family ties didn't hand me everything, so I could do nothing and still benefit."

A smirk grew on one side of his face, but I still saw no teeth behind his lips.

"So, then you know who I am?" he asked.

"I do not, sir. I can only assume by your attire that you belong within the ranks of the royal family," I said.

The other side of his lips finally lifted and turned his smirk into a smile.

"So, then, we may as well gossip while we wait for our arrival. Whom did you come for? The king or one of the princes? Do you care? The prospect of an easy life makes it worth the risk, right?" He leaned forward, resting an elbow on his knee.

I wanted to laugh at how easily he thought I would enjoy engaging in this line of questioning. I didn't need to know who he was or read his mind to know my answer would sign my death sooner than I wanted it. His eyes were still locked on mine, and he looked so deep into me that I wondered if he could also read minds.

"I am here to do my duty as it's given to me, Sir," I answered.

"Oh, come on, it's just us. I heard rumors while I was in Askia that the king was a blood-hungry demon. The princes had become his food bags, and the princesses were his breeding stock. What do you think?" he asked.

Blood dropped off my hand from how hard I was digging my nail into the button between my fingers. There was only one way to get blood magic; if I used it so soon, it would set all of my planning and patience back. I could kill him with my dagger. I could kill him and the coachman and claim it was bandits. I could get away with it. I would talk down Askia and embellish its crime rate. I would claim creatures attacked us; there were any number of options I could toss around to make his death seem believable.

"Nonsense rumors from starved mouths," I said.

He tossed himself back in his seat. "You're probably right, but knowing your answer would have been fun so I could place bets on how close you get."

I didn't answer him because I had hopes that if he were not entertained any further, he would shut his useless mouth. I was looking forward to this ride being quiet—my last line of peace before the games began. He was making the trip insufferable. I didn't realize I had slipped out of my newly formed image and was contorting my face until I caught his lifted brow aimed at me.

"Am I disturbing your peace?" he asked, dripping sarcasm.

He was interrupting it as well as a rat interrupts a feast.

"No, Sir. Your presence is driving away the loneliness of travel," I answered.

"You may survive in the palace," he said. "I'll place my bets that you at least meet one prince before you die."

"Thank you for your blessings, Sir," I said.

Our carriage finally stopped after what felt like hours, and the coachman yelled something I couldn't make out from inside. His eyes rolled over me one last time before the door came open, and a woman stood outside. She was hardly older than I, but she looked as if she had won a grand prize with the arrival of our carriage.

"Prince Fennic!" She yelled in a shrill voice. "You're finally home!"

She pulled him by the arm out of a space that felt like it was shrinking around me. Did she say, Prince? I should have killed him. Attending a funeral on my first day would have been better than trying to combat whatever rumors he would spill through the palace. I bet you at least meet one prince. That little sprite licker thought he was being funny. He thought I wouldn't make it past talking with him. I swear if it's the last thing I do, I'll send him to his family crypt.

"My lady." Fennic held out his callused hand.

My eyes twitched in unison from the amount of force it took for me to take his hand, but I did take it. I didn't need anything else occurring yet. He held my hand while I walked down the rotted wooden steps of the carriage, and while I was watching the ground to ensure I didn't step on the oversized waste of fabric I was wearing, he flipped my hand palm up so he could see the trigger for my dagger.

"Smart girl," he said. "Your personality is dull, and your face is mediocre at best, but at least your defense is more exciting."

He handed me off to the care of an attendant and left laughing with the girl who came to greet him. I would need to alter my plans already. My third kill was no longer for the king. It was for Prince Fennic, and I'd save the king for number four. Four kills would be fine. I was damned no matter the number. I'd send those gorgeous golden eyes to the afterlife and let him get a head start on our punishments.

The attendant motioned for me to follow her inside, but I had to hesitate and linger. The sights in my homeland were nothing like the ones that stood in front of me. The castle sat on uneven ground with hardly anything growing near it. The walls were built with some blackened stone I had never seen before. The air felt cold and full. My skin prickled in bumps from the chill, and I knew there had to be spirits lurking inside. The castle was built so high that I feared I would learn I was afraid of heights by the time I could make it to the top. My future castle was beautiful in its own dark way, and when I was in charge, I would have them add more fake flowers outside.

I made sure my veil was tucked properly so that I didn't have to worry about it, and my too-long hair was pressed down and tucked equally as neatly as it could be before I lifted my dress, just enough to go up the stairs behind the attendant safely. I had to make a good impression. I was no fool. I knew the other girls arriving would be just as smart as I or beautiful beyond words. I had to start off my stay running. My eyes were the one thing I was complimented on throughout my life. With a veil that only allowed my lips to show and kept my best asset hiding, I would have to rely on other parts of myself.

Taking the steps, one by one, in the heaviest dress I had ever worn felt like a journey of its own. I couldn't believe we had made it to the top when we did. An earth sprite flew in front of my face and attempted to get a peak under my veil. Swatting at it almost had me crashing down the stairs. A hand placed itself on the small of my back in time to stop me from taking the tumble I certainly would have been injured by. His eyes looked into me. They were red under black hair. How many attractive men could be allowed to live under the same roof?

"My apologies, Sir," I whispered.

"It's I that should apologize for having such an incompetent attendant. If I had known she'd be so careless as to risk such a jewel, I'd have assigned her to my sister." He gave a husky roll of laughter. "Call me Riven in these casual moments."

I felt my heart drop and bile rise in unison.

"Thank you for saving me, King Riven. I am in your debt," I smiled.

He pointed at two men, then the attendant. They dragged her off, despite her protests, and another came from behind him quicker than I could have said another sentence. That was power. True power. I'd have it in my hands soon. I'd ensure he received proper payback for these things.

"She will show you where you need to be, and I'll be sure to take you up on that debt another time," King Riven said.

I gave him a small, polite smile and the necessary bow before he left the attendant and I behind. She bowed slightly and moved to the side, indicating I go in first. So, I listened and walked ahead of her. It seemed foolish to me; why would she not go first? I had no clue where we were meant to be going. I would only get us lost and have to ask for her to move ahead first anyway.

My steps were further complicated when two more men stood to the side of the only path I could walk. Two more men who looked as if they were chiseled from the most perfect clay that could have been used to make all of us. They both nodded their heads, and every fiber of my being screamed in embarrassment. Even without seeing my full face, they knew I was staring.

"That's Prince Coy and Fennic's closest friend, Mori," the attendant whispered.

What are the odds that on my arrival, I would get to make a fool of myself in front of all three brothers? If this was any indication of how my stay would be, I might as well turn around and leave now while I still had my head intact. I was already a fool in over my head.

The attendant pushed my arm just enough to gently guide me to the side and into a doorway. Inside were a handful of girls waiting in a line, without any clothing on at all, and I stopped in my tracks.

"The king assigned me to you because he has decided you are to be part of the harem selection, and this is the next natural step in that process." She shoved me with less grace this time.

No one had warned me that I would have to drop all of my clothing. It was laughter-inducing that it was so easy to become part of the selection that I went through so much to get here, and it only took me looking as though I had no brain to get where I wanted to be. I had no time to produce the laughter while being shoved to show every inch of myself, including the weapons.

"I have weapons," I leaned over to whisper to her.

She shot a dagger of a look in my direction and gripped my arm this time. She pulled me to the back toilet and held out a hand. I feigned a laugh. That hand was not going to be enough. I leaned down and pulled the knife from my boot; I unstrapped the knife from my calf as well and handed it to her. I unhooked the matching set on the other side before I pulled the two on my left thigh, then the strap, and laid them in her hand as well. She had both hands held up, and I struggled to stifle my laugh at the look on her face.

I took the dagger and the baton from my right thigh. I laid them both in her other hand. I removed the poison darts and the poison-laced hairpins from my chest and handed those over as well.

"Are you sure this is it? You don't have any exploding concoctions to go with?" She glared.

I snapped my fingers, "That would have been a good idea!"

Her growl was so audible I was sure it would have been heard outside.

"Go, now!" She pointed.

She was grumpy, so I listened. She was holding all the weapons now, which helped it feel like I didn't have a choice.

I joined the other girls in the perfectly formed row they had already created, but I kept my clothing with me. I enjoyed it sitting on me, where it belonged.

The woman I could only assume to be the harem leader entered with three attendants behind her and stopped in front of me. I was calm and collected now that I had given my weapons up. What was she to find? I had only one scar, and it was in my hair. An accident from when I was a child.

The woman didn't speak; she only nodded, ever so slightly, to one of the girls beside her.

Both hands were on the neckline of my dress, ripping the fabric to pieces at the seams until I was in only a slip.

"If I must ask them to do the rest, you'll end today with a guaranteed scar," the woman said.

It was then that my heart started to beat harder, and I felt my blood boil. If we weren't inside the castle walls, I would hang her myself, but I had an image to form. Most importantly, I found it very hard to keep a handle on the blood magic I traded when my emotions ramped up to high. So, I bit my cheek and listened. I dropped the slip off and stood back up, focusing only on the wall behind them. There were designs in the stone.

The attendant grabbed my wrist, and my heart stopped. I had forgotten one weapon. It was such a part of me that I didn't think of it, and now it was too late.

"Weapons," the attendant called.

"I only brought it as a form of protection against the possible rumors being true. I wanted to ensure my virtue stayed intact while I was here!" I pleaded.

I wanted to do my best to save myself before anything could be said.

"Are you implying the castle isn't a safe place?" The woman's tone sent a chill down my spine.

She removed the dagger from my wrist, and before I could protest any further, she used it on my braid. She sliced through my cherry red hair and dropped the tail of the braid to the ground between our feet.

"Let that be your first lesson. From here, it's the whip."

I didn't watch her walk away; all I could see was my braid. The hair that hadn't ever been cut. The only part of me I always had control over. The one precious thing that no one had thought to take away from me until now. Maybe I should have taken it and used it as a sign that there was a new beginning on the horizon. I couldn't because the sight only brought burning to my chest.

It was a sign. It was the first real sign to slap me hard enough that I had a moment of doubt. I had only just arrived, and I had lost the one part of myself I always held onto. Regret left every breath I exhaled.

"The attendants will give you the proper oils or salves that you will need to cure whatever afflictions may riddle your body. Each bottle needs a set amount of time to work; that will be the timeline you have until you can meet the royal family. Until then, you will have access to the wing of the castle assigned to us and nowhere else. If you aren't given anything, you are free to roam the full grounds. If you need something, I suggest you weigh its worth before seeking me out. Next, if you are infertile, you must tell us now."

She kept speaking, but the ringing in my ears was making it impossible for me to truly listen. She would be number five on my list. Her attendants would be six, seven, and eight. I'd shave them bald before taking their heads. I couldn't stop my fingers from running through the hair I had left. Even my vision had blurred out.

Before I could pull myself together, the same attendant who ripped my clothing until it could no longer sit on my body was pulling and tugging at my arms; she was making herself comfortable with every part of me. It was only my own attendant lurking in the background, staring at me with eyes that promised she would do to me what I wanted to do to them, that kept me grounded while they remarked on every part of my body.

I would swallow this down. Tuck it away for another time.

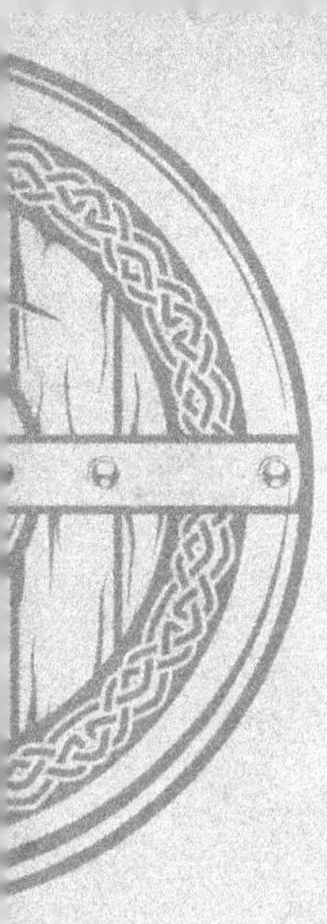

CHAPTER TWO
THE BROTHERS

FENNIC

I should have placed more bets before my arrival because, just as I knew she would be, my younger sister was waiting for me. She had the same rosy cheeks as when I left. Taller than I last remembered, but her joy for life hadn't diminished. I tried to take one last glance behind me, but she pulled me too furiously. This new girl was good at putting on an innocent act; that much was clear. I didn't buy it. There was something about her that I couldn't pick out just yet, but I knew she had to be playing cover-up for something. No girls in the castle were as polite as she was without reason.

"I've been waiting to hear your stories!" My sister said. "We can have dinner together, and you can tell me all about the other lands."

"I have to meet with our brother first. You know how the rest of the evening will go if he's not my first meeting," I said.

"If you have a chance to push your boundaries, it's today. He's on his best behavior for arrivals," she said.

I nodded and kissed her hand. "I'll be on my best behavior

today as well so we can have dinner without interruption, but only for today."

She left me behind without a second glance, ignoring the rest of my words entirely. She was too caught up in her plans for the evening. She was right. If there were a moment I could push my luck, it would be today. He cared about his image more than he cared about us. He was careful about who to take where. Picky about who sat in on what meals with mixed company. He had the iron fist in the end, but he laid heavy weight on what was whispered about him outside and inside of the walls we were imprisoned inside. Even if I thought he was a fool, I cared for my sister too much to stir a pot that always stayed so close to boiling over.

The hallways were as dim as ever. Enough light to see, hardly. It felt appropriate for the kind of people that resided inside. They lurked in the shadows with too many secrets to hold in the dark. When I rule, because I will rule, I'll add more candlelight.

The white and grey that ran through the floors deserved to be seen. The pillars that our artists worked tirelessly to etch such small details in deserved to be seen, and secrets kept too long deserved to come to light. I'd find a way to eliminate the creatures that murder outside of our walls, too. Riven allowed those monsters the demons created to roam free for too long.

If I were to be called back to the castle, it would be mine before I was sent away again. I wouldn't be stuck here under his thumb and forced into a marriage.

The king's favorite room was empty when I entered. His prized throne, made of the last mammoth bones to walk our realm, looked as pathetic as he did. The floor was covered in the rugs of more than one animal he hunted to extinction. Cages of earth sprites, wings clipped, and birds treated the same way. Animal heads hung here and there. Still lit, just as dim as the rest of the place.

Our father would have been so proud of him and the way

he kept ruling as he was taught. The day my brother killed our father had to have been the proudest day he had as a parent. My brother did not keep it a secret. He held a feast in celebration of his first accomplishment. Our father took his duty seriously, and I hope he is treated with at least the same respect he gave his kingdom in whatever afterlife he is in now. I hope he is getting even a sliver of the pain he caused while living.

I was the son of his concubine and, as such, worth less than Riven. I still hold memories of when my father only had one son. When his focus was on only me. I remember the day his true wife announced her son and how quickly I was replaced. I didn't mourn the loss of the throne but the loss of a father when I was so young. The only way I could make him proud now was by killing his favored son. Leaving his true heir in the crypt with him so they could reunite sooner. It would be my last gift to both of them.

Some days, I thought of handing it all over to my other brother. Coy could have the throne, and we would live in more peace, still, than with Riven seated on it. Then I remembered Coy was only ever trained to be a general. He knew little about how to run an entire kingdom. He knew everything about keeping them in line.

Red eyes stared ahead, and his feet carried him to his throne. Black hair bounced around his face in tune with his hurried footsteps. He didn't stand taller than I until he was up the first few steps to his throne. The fur that draped around him nearly prevented him from sitting gracefully. It didn't take much effort to keep myself from smirking. The sight was amusing, but I was smart enough to need only one lesson, one time. I did not require learning the hard way. Watching others receive punishment from the sidelines was sufficient.

"Brother, I was worried you wouldn't make it in time," Riven crossed one leg over the other.

"I started the journey back as soon as I got your message from the owl," I answered.

"And what did you find?" he asked.

"I found no trace of blood magic in the village. I found no bodies. Only a man spreading rumor after rumor to draw more attention to his business," I said.

"I thought this one would lead somewhere," he sighed.

"You expect too much. Even if someone were willing to make the kind of deal it took to get the magic, they wouldn't announce it," I said.

"Maybe, or maybe you found it and have it hidden for yourself?" He let his leg drop and leaned forward.

I kept my eyes dead. "Why would I keep such a thing from my king?"

"Now, now, my King. You know your brother has only ever been loyal to you." Niko's voice sent chills of disgust down my spine.

"You're right," Riven said.

His hands slapped against each of his thighs before he stood and walked back down the small set of stairs to meet my eyes closer. He looked me over, grazing his eyes across my clothing and hair. Lingering for a moment, eyes locked to eyes. His were possibly emptier than my own. I couldn't think of one thing he had left to live for. He hunted until extinction. Tortured until death. Ate until engorged.

What I would not say out loud was that no one was more disappointed in my lack of knowledge after my most current mission than I was. What I did want him to hear was that he would have been the first to know if I had discovered what I went for. Suppose I had come back with the man who traded his soul for blood magic. I would have sought Riven out sooner. I would have invited him to my chambers instead. I would have watched while his body turned to nothing more than skin and bones when I pulled every drop of his blood from him. I would have used my bare hands to add his bones to my new throne.

Unfortunately for both of us, no blood wielder lived long enough to find, let alone bring back for anyone's use.

"I know you wouldn't betray me," he said, his hand slapped against my shoulder. "I have good news for you. I've thought it through, and to show you how much I value you, I've put your assignments on hold until you pick your own wife and concubine."

"I don't see it necessary," I protested.

"Nonsense. Even a concubine whore's son needs to help the line of the gods. After I have my pick, you'll be free to choose. They'll be arriving well into the night," Riven said. "Make sure you're not caught leaving any bed chambers and taking their value before I've had my pick."

"We should worry about how filled your chambers will be," I said.

He hardly laughed. It was a forceful sound that let me know he found no amusement in my words. Our feelings for each other were mutual. I found no amusement in him, either. I wouldn't until the day he died on his knees in front of me.

He squeezed my shoulder tighter. "You know how much I need someone with blood magic. I'll give you this last vacation as a death present. Next time you come back and report failure to me, your skull will decorate the entrance doors."

He left me standing and made his exit. No one was allowed to move until the sound of his feet went silent or he commanded you to follow. When his footsteps did finally come to a stop, I didn't hesitate to leave. I left the throne room, went in the opposite direction of my brother, and gave a small whistle. It was a tune my guard and I hummed every night as children with my mother. When it was hummed back to me, I added more speed to my steps.

At the end of the walkway, up two sets of main stairs, just before they broke in different directions, he stood in front of a large glass window with the design of a crescent moon, still humming.

"I thought you'd play who has the bigger pork stick and berries all evening," Mori said before he crossed his arms.

"I don't need to play a game I know I'd win," I said.

"10 gold coin says you don't win," Mori smirked.

"15 gold coin says you're smaller than both." I pointed.

"20 gold coins, and I'll have some of the cute new guards around here back up my claim," Mori said.

"All right. I'll give you 20 to stop right there." I held up my hand.

"Make it 20 gold coins and a new sword," he said.

"Deal. Take whatever you want, but don't tell me anything further about your castle scandals," I said. "I don't want to be tortured for the information once they get out."

"Business then?" he asked.

"Business," I agreed.

"Three attempts were made on the king's life. He's been discussing thinning the royal court population and making a celebration of it to prevent any further attempts. His advisors agreed and claimed it would save coins and make space for his own children. He's been meeting with his advisor a lot more. They've been going over what lands have been untouched by their searches. He's been sure to keep the meetings as secret as he can, but they're all based around needing someone who can use blood magic," Mori said.

"Let's hope their meetings keep progressing slowly. So, we can act first. I have a good feeling about the last village. We're getting closer; we need to go back in a smaller group," I sighed. "I need you to do one more thing."

"Of course you do," he answered, the sound of a smirk in his voice.

"I want you to find out all you can about the girl I arrived with," I said.

"You picked already? You know your brother will pick her if you—"

"I just want to know what you can find. Talk less, move faster." I pointed to the hallway.

He looked at me as if he were taunting me in his head. Making schoolgirls kissy faces and teasing me about a crush he was sure I carried. I was sure that girl was going to become a problem for me. I was sure she was keeping something, and I'd find out what it was. If Mori couldn't find it, I would torture it out of her. One way or another, we would get to the bottom of who she was.

I watched Mori leave; he shook his head, and I could hear him talk under his breath. He was sticking to the shadows of the hallways, and I continued after him to the bottom of the stairs. I took them slower than usual when I noticed the commotion coming from the entrance. Another girl arrived, with two more behind her. They all showed up in different colors. A golden dress made of fabric is not easy to get ahold of without knowing someone. Another girl did her best to stand tall, covered in blue tones. I had more respect for her than the others. Her blues were dull, but it meant she had to do something for them. The girl in gold likely just begged Daddy for such a rare fabric.

My father would have told me I was being unreasonable, worrying about the kind of fabric on my shoulders. He would have told me that I was meant to be in armor and die defending my brother. That no amount of silk or cotton would mean anything to me in the afterlife. Maybe he was right. Perhaps the fabric I covered myself with did mean nothing, but dying for my brother was just as useless. It was as useless as taking a wife. She would only serve to get in my way. She would spend her time shoving her nose in my business. Causing me complications. Whining about quality time.

"Are you looking for your dignity?" A familiar voice asked from behind me.

Her voice was low, sweet. Her words were not drawn out but secretly playful still. Her arms were crossed, and she had a very different look about her now. In the carriage, she wore an absolute mess of a gown. Now, she wore a simple black and silver cotton dress. Uncomplicated, but somehow, she made it look extravagant. Her lips lost the dark red coloring they had before and were now a soft honey shade. I wanted to lift the veil covering the rest of her face and take in the mystery, even if it was only for a second.

"Have you forgotten your manners that quickly?" I asked.

"Me? Sir, you're gawking at these ladies as if you're a starved beast," she replied.

"I am not gawking," I said.

"Drooling then?" She tilted her head. "Where are your manners?"

"It appears I gave you too much credit earlier, and it's gotten to your head. It's made you too bold," I shook my head.

"Do not insult me, Sir. Do you think I would not have prepared myself before entering a lion's den?" she said.

"Set your sights on the king, have we?" I said.

"I didn't say that, but it seems you have also made your choice," she said.

"I was only watching strangers enter my home. You're making assumptions," I gritted.

"I thought it wise to follow in your footsteps. Uneducated assumptions seemed to be the way you communicate."

She laughed, and it was the first time I had seen emotion hit her in a tangible way. Small smile lines appeared next to her lips. Why was my heart racing? I was too young for a heart attack. Was I enjoying her laughter? A distraction. Having these girls here was going to be a distraction.

"Sir, your cheeks are flushing red. Do you need to have a seat? You do look quite aged. It would be best if you were easy on yourself. The young ladies will understand," her voice dripped with insult.

I pointed my finger and shook it. "Aged? Did you just call

me old? I haven't reached my twenty-fourth winter yet! One more word, and I'll have you locked away!"

"I'm sorry, Sir. I did not mean to insult you. It's just that between how leathery your skin looks and the whispers I've already heard about the high use of herbs to harden your member, I wrongly assumed you were many winters older than you clearly are. I'll excuse myself. I will spend my evening reflecting on all the wrong things I've done today."

She gave me a bow and hit the stairs faster than my jaw could close. How dare she. My hands met my cheeks and ran across them. My skin was soft to the touch, and who was whispering about herbs?

"Mori!" I roared.

I would have him on the hunt for who is spreading rumors that I need these herbs. I would boil them myself. No, I would cover them in honey, sit them out for the bugs first, and then boil them!

"Mori!" I yelled again, charging down the hallway.

I should be heading to meet my sister, filled with thoughts of warm food. She would pay double for spreading lies about my parts and ruining my dinner.

CHAPTER THREE
THE JOURNAL

SHIVANI

I followed the footsteps of my attendant out of the castle and into the courtyard. I watched her purple bob bounce with each of her movements. The little flyaways moved the least; they had as little life as the mood in the kingdom. I, however, was already enjoying being able to stare and gawk at anything I liked without a single soul being able to see my eyes. I could be looking at them digging in their nostrils, and they'd still feel comforted, thinking my eyes were on the ground like a proper lady. I didn't believe any of us would be passing the opportunity for the sake of propriety, which couldn't be proved.

I could look as I liked, and yet the only thing I could look at was hair. Did she have short hair as a sign of disobedience, too? Would everyone look at me and know, by my hair, that I had already started screwing up? I felt my heart start to pound in my chest again, and I swallowed harder from it. I imagined lifting my hands with my inhale and then lowering them over myself as I exhaled. I couldn't lose myself here. I needed to put things that didn't matter away and focus. Hair will grow back.

My hair will grow back, I repeated.

The voices of other girls came before the sight of them did. The first thing in sight was what they dared to call a garden. Trees that looked as if they had been through more than one fire. Weeds in place of trimmed brushes. There was a man dressed as a gardener, but it didn't appear that any work had been done. We were told the king's land was upheld better than the rest. We have thrown insults around in his name for letting us live in filth while he and his family lived in luxury, but those stories were turning out to be only half-truths. The inside seemed to be the only thing anyone took pride in. At least we perfected fake greenery to give a nice appearance.

Several women sat on what I would hardly call benches. Quickly chopped, prickled logs strung together without care. I would not trust my body on it, but I wouldn't look away from the tumble someone else was sure to take. My attendant moved herself to the courtyard entrance and waved me forward alone. I stood, lips parted, and looked her up and down, cursing that she couldn't see the look in my eyes or the raise on my brows. I know I had to look like a lost child. I wanted to use her to look occupied and impossible to approach. She was already proving to be useless.

"Are you blind under that veil? We're all right here," a voice laughed.

I rolled my eyes and bit my tongue before leaving her behind.

"My sight is fine," I strained out behind a smile.

"You should address her more appropriately. She'll be queen soon," another said.

"Chosen so soon?" I said, feigning jealousy at her lie.

"I've already met the king. He sent his guard to show me to my room personally," she smiled.

I knew what I was getting myself into, but part of me was hopeful I'd get to become Queen by either charming everyone or making them part with their heads. I didn't consider that I'd be competing. I should have. We were all just trying to stay alive, after all. I should have considered that manners and maturity were not required to exist together. We could all smile. We could keep up with our yes-sirs, but ultimately, we all wanted the same position. If we had to create separate personalities with each other than with the king, so be it.

I let my smile fall. "That must have been exciting. When I arrived, well, I was just so clumsy, and the king was so kind. His hands met the small of my back and held me up. If it weren't for the way he wrapped around me and brought me back to my feet, I surely would have been injured. He was kind enough to give me an attendant already, too. She's from his personal circle," I gushed.

"He touched you?" Another girl yelled.

"I'm sure he was just interested in seeing who would be the loosest of us all," another said.

"If you're already in the running for Queen, you must have won that, yes?" I tilted my head.

"I see we're all getting to know each other," a more mature voice called out. The same voice that ordered my hair cut off.

There, my chest went again, racing faster than it should have. This time, my mind jumbled with it. Her voice had me struggling to stand on solid ground.

"Good. You will quickly learn to live happily and find a way to coincide. You ladies are the small group that did not need any oils or salves. My last words for you before I leave you are as follows: If you are caught disturbing the peace, stealing, lying, or otherwise causing problems, you will be punished. If you are caught sleeping with the guards, your uterus will be the cost. If you are found to have planned or plotted on the king's life, the price is death to your entire line. Your home village will also burn to be sure no traitor remains. Do you have any questions?"

Lips were pressed hard enough together, and the sound of

teeth grinding could be heard from more than one place. What could anyone have asked after such a speech? Don't get caught was her real message, and I already knew it.

"I have already assigned your attendant and personal guard. They are here and waiting. They are loyal to the king and only the king. Do not ask them to do anything you wouldn't pay the price for. Enjoy your time now. Tomorrow will not be for leisurely sitting in the garden. The king must marry. You get now to settle in before you must impress him."

She glanced at us, but no one had anything to say to her. She turned on her heels and left just as quickly as she came. There was no more bickering. We were all too on edge with the overwhelming presence of men with weapons around us. They had not done anything to let us know if they were truly planning to harm or protect us, but I didn't want to find out. I did not want to be the center of attention.

I would need to hold myself back better. I would have to stay out of the petty conversations and keep my goal in sight. I could do whatever I wanted once I was on that throne. Now, I had to keep myself in the shadows for everyone but the king. I turned before anyone grew bored of meeting their attendant and left. I did not need to stay for mine; she was waiting, and there was no doubt that the guard would follow as well. If guards followed us every time we went outside, I'd have to spend most of my time inside.

My attendant pulled at me like a magnetic force.

"It's not true," she whispered.

I did not look at her. I did not want the guard to pay closer attention.

"She said we're loyal to the king. It's not true. We are taught to be loyal only to those we are assigned to," she whispered again.

My heart skipped its beating and sent a wave through me. A sensation of ease. I thought that maybe I had one place to discuss something real. I shook it off as fast as it came. Of course, she was only loyal to the king. Of course, she was telling me this. They all would likely be having the same conversations to see who would slip. Which one of us would give up our true intentions and fail? It would not be me. I had done too much to be in this spot and fail so soon. I couldn't start slipping yet.

"The washroom you said you needed is here, ma'am," she pointed.

I did not slow my feet; I followed her hand and went inside. I could read the message she was sending. She closed the door behind us.

"I understand that you do not trust me. I would not trust you either if I were in your position. I can smell it on you. The scent of the deal. I made one, too. I don't know what you gained, and you don't need to tell me yet, but that guard outside is one of the king's. You have either gained favor already or suspicions, so tread lightly," her voice was low.

"I don't know what you speak of, but if you're here for the king's life," she cut me short.

"If it were that easy, he would have died many deaths by now. I only wanted to give you this warning. I'll wait outside," she gave me a bow.

"What is your name?" I rushed to ask her.

"In private, you may call me Vesim," she said. "Here are your hairpins. The rest I disposed of. We can not take the risk of holding such clear weapons."

She left before I could respond, and I was left with only the sight of my reflection in the mirror. Even in death, my mother's voice haunted me. Lipstick may sit on a pig, but it will still smell like a pig. It would still be the only thing she'd have to say to me if she could see me today. She'd tell me how ignorant I was for thinking I could plan, let alone succeed in pulling the death of the king off without her opinions. I wondered how she gathered all the expert knowledge she seemed to carry around with her when all she did with her life was sponge what she could from others. Her ability to warp reality was scarier than any king I've seen rule over our lands.

I smiled at myself once, twice. The second time, I showed fewer teeth. It looked more authentic, more like everyone else I had seen today. After staring into the mirror for so long, something about it seemed off to me. I ran my fingers along the side of it and underneath it. When my finger met the bottom corner, it lifted and swung open. There was a small wooden door built behind the mirror. When I opened it, the area became even smaller. It held a journal with the name Yumi written on it. I tucked it into the garter on my thigh and covered it with my dress.

I pulled in one more breath and pushed the door open, meeting Vesim and my new guard, who had yet to give so much as a glance in my direction. I couldn't stop my mind from wondering how many guards actually died or lost their ability to create children after they lay with the women here. Was my new guard one of them? It was probably too soon to ask him.

"We are meeting with the princess for dinner," I announced to them both.

He gave me a nod, and she gave me a bow. It was uncomfortable already to have both of them following me like they were.

I was sure I would not find my way to the dinner hall we were using tonight, but Vesim guided me in the right direction and still allowed it to look like I was in charge. I would grant myself today to soak in my surroundings and become comfortable. It was to be expected that I needed to learn a thing or two before I could be something intimidating. It's not as though I had blueprints before arriving.

I walked through the archway held by pillars and into a room that was only dining table after dining table. It had the look of a lunchroom at an education house. It was sure to be loud if everyone put it to use to capacity. It's not what I had imagined when I thought of eating at a castle.

My guard waited outside, standing without even a nod. Vesim pointed me to a chair, and I did not push back; I sat in it. Tomorrow, I will take full charge. Today, I will observe. All the tables were set with candles; wax poured from the sides into holders. They looked older than I. I wanted to take the chance to look around without interruption. To see what may be hidden around in the corners no one is allowed to walk through. The newly assigned guard made it next to impossible. So, instead, I pulled out the journal I found. If I were to be so heavily watched, a book wouldn't raise questions.

It looked old. It was old enough that if I turned the pages too hard, they would dissipate and leave only dust. It was written in our language, but the writing looked like a child still learning the right amount of space between each word. The first page held only the name Yumi. The second page started what looked like endless writing. Dirt and dust came from between a few pages, and others stuck together.

Entry One

I still haven't figured out how my sister and I came to be. We just seem to be. She told me that she was only a thought in darkness and when she thought hard enough to become a body, I came with as balance. I don't believe this. She has made another, and it took a piece of her to do. If she were being honest, he would have come from nothing.

She named him Olexei and called him the sun god. She claimed it was in part due to curiosity, but I know it was more out of loneliness. Does she not think I, too, am lonely? She has become smitten with him, and they spend all their time together now. She never spent time with me. She left me in the shadows since creation. She told me I should try and do the same, to make someone or something to ease my loneliness, but I could not. I have asked her to show me, but it still has not lit a spark for me.

My sister says I need to try harder and clear my mind further. It's easy for her to speak. We fought today when I told her how I felt. Dahlia told me I didn't understand her either. She told me that I was refusing to acknowledge how hard she was trying for the both of us, and I was growing too used to her carrying all the burden. I was growing too spoiled, and that I needed to have a long look at myself, but she didn't understand me either.

If I cannot create, how can I try to have someone to talk to? I have been feeling things I cannot put words behind. It's red and hot. It makes me want to hurt her or to take her happiness and see her cry. If I were honest, I would say I was not fighting them away with everything I could. I would admit it felt good to let them fill me. That the first absolute joy I've felt since my first breath was the thought of ripping her apart.

I cannot kill her because I cannot do what she can do. In that sense, I need her. She's done it on purpose. Maybe she is so good at it because she's stolen my abilities. Maybe she's locked me out. Perhaps I can take them back. What right does she have to hold so much power, anyway? If she were being honest, she would admit she loves the dynamic. She would admit to my face that it would be simple for her to create a companion for me, but she would prefer to see my struggle.

I didn't understand what she meant when she said we were balanced. I'm starting to wonder if she means only one can be happy.

I closed the book and tucked it back where I had hidden it. The sun god? There is no way this journal belonged to the goddess of starlight. Why would it be here? The king is adamant any relics that may prove deities were here belong to him. If I was to believe this was a historical record, it meant he had no idea it existed.

"I know, I know. You don't want to marry, but she's perfect. I only needed to speak with her for a few moments to know the two of you would be a hit." The princess's voice came echoing.

"Misa, you cannot play matchmaker. Do you remember when you thought the cook would be perfect for the gardener? He spent a week poisoning dinners hoping she would be silenced, and we still haven't found anyone to replace her properly," Fennic said.

"You cannot hold one mistake against me forever. This time, I'm sure. You will love her!" She said, shoving him inside and in sight.

I had to bite the inside of my lip until blood pooled inside my mouth to keep from exuding a symphony of noises at the way he was looking at me. It almost wasn't enough to stop it. His eyes looked at me with pain and annoyance. His clenched fists told me he was edging assault, and the way his sister clung to his other arm, still mumbling about giving me a chance, completed the picture.

This man was sure his night was ruined, but it hadn't even begun yet. I wanted to return to the journal, but passing up the chance to give him what he expected of me would have been wrong. I stood and gave a bow, titling my head far enough down that I could let a smirk free. It turned into a smile quickly and a whimper of laughter even faster than I could stop. What was meant to be a minor release turned into a flood.

"Is there something funny?" Fennic demanded.

I shook my head. "I'm just happy to see Misa again," I said.

"Princess Misa," he corrected.

I ignored him and continued on, "I was hoping your considerably more attractive brother would be here instead, but I can settle for you tonight."

She shoved her elbow into his side in a correction of her own and dragged him to sit across from me before taking her place beside him. Vesim waited for me to sit, and she joined me at my side.

"I'm glad to see you again, too! If Fennic doesn't work out, Coy will be here soon." She looked down in thought before meeting my eyes again, as if she only made the joke because she thought she had to. "I know you don't get a name until you're picked for marriage, but can I address you by yours in private? It feels strange not having anything to call you."

It was painful to watch this girl grasp at anything in front of her like she was. She was pulling at me for a bond in friendship as if I were the last bubble of air on her sinking ship. It was almost appetite-ruining how sweet she was presenting. She must have been raised by their mother to have turned out how she did. Someone like her couldn't have been raised by the same people who raised a man to believe I couldn't even have a name until he gave it to me.

"Shivani is my name," I spoke low, careful not to forget the guard outside.

She understood without open words because she, too, looked at the entrance.

"Thank you," she smiled.

"Don't you think it's rude to put me in a position to keep this exchange secret?" Fennic interjected.

"Are you that eager to see a woman whipped, Sir?" I asked. "If you are," I trailed off, batting my lashes.

His eyes ran over me with a look I couldn't quite place. It could have said he wanted to kill me, or he wanted to hold the whip himself.

"If the punishment should fit the crime," he said.

"I must admit I'm a little disappointed to be talking to you like this and not your brother." I sat my head in my hand, "He is much nicer on the eyes. I bet he's really good with a whip, too."

"We are brothers! If he is cute, so am I!" Fennic yelled.

I sucked air in through my teeth to form a hiss, "I beg to differ."

Princess Misa's thoughts grew too loud for me to ignore anymore, just like my smile grew too hard to fight. Was I into this? My heart was pounding, but it wasn't the only thing with a throb.

My mind was filled with Misa's yelling. Even still, in her rage, she sounded like a small child. How does he ever expect to meet a girl like this? It's only been a few minutes, and he is already ruining all the hard work I put into setting this up. I know she's perfect for him, and he's just doing this to prove me wrong. If I had said it was his idea, or she was perfect for Coy, he would have his head between her- I cleared my throat loudly, pretending to choke on nothing.

"Are you okay?" Misa asked.

I took a sip from my glass. "I'm fine; the air here is just so dry."

Fennic's brow raised in my direction. "With your personality, you should be used to dry things."

"With your dependence on herbs to keep things working correctly, I would counter you know dry best," I smiled.

Princess Misa's jaw dropped so low I thought it might not stop until it hit the table. Our dinner being brought in created an interruption in conversation, but it did not stop me from hearing Prince Fennic's thoughts for the first time since meeting him. It seemed he was well-trained in keeping people out unless he was worked up and too distracted. I put every bit of effort I could into controlling myself, but I was learning quickly I may not be as good at it as I thought I was because nothing I did stopped me from looking him in the eye and smiling when I heard him ramble.

One more chance. That's all she gets. One. If she mentions these herbs again, I swear on, on, I swear to the creator goddess and every demon there is to make deals with that I'll strangle her. I will hold her head under my bathing pool myself until there are no more air bubbles to surface. She won't be laughing then!

He was sickly sweet when he thought no one could hear him.

"Thank you again for inviting me, Princess. The food looks better than anything I've eaten in days," I said. His eyes were still hovering over me, but I pretended not to notice.

"I hope you don't mind. I had the kitchen make Fennie's favorites since he's been gone," Misa said.

Fennie. I don't know if I should have felt ashamed for him or uninterested in dinner out of disgust. Maybe if I added that to the impotence, he would threaten to do something more creative for me.

"I don't mind at all, Princess. Little Fennie deserves to come home to only the best after his long journey," I smiled.

It was my turn to be elbowed to the side. Vesim was finally fed up with the conversation, but I was just starting to find slight amusement in his company now.

"What is it you were away doing for so long, Fennie?" I asked, taking my fork to the broccoli and potatoes before me.

"Yes! Tell me about your time away this time!" Misa squealed.

"This trip was less exciting than the last. There were no monsters to slay," he answered.

"Shame, the king would have loved a hunting trip," I mumbled between bites.

He brushed over my words and continued. "I met a girl who could toss sticks of fire."

Princess Misa looked at him with amazement, but that was the least exciting thing you could see outside the castle walls.

"Will your future wife have to worry about love children from these trips?" I asked. "Oh, I apologize. I forgot a moment." I pointed down at his thighs.

Prince Fennic slammed his fork on the table. "Is the cook

that poisons food still working for us?" He yelled while stomping out.

His chair would have crashed backward if it hadn't been for Princess Misa to stop it.

"I knew the two of you would be a perfect match! I haven't seen him that worked up since his favorite hound passed away," she clapped.

"I can only hope to be worthy enough to make someone a perfect wife one day," I said.

"I'll go bring him back. Please, eat. I know you must be hungry and tired from all the travel. I'll make sure he comes back happy to finish telling stories." She was on her feet before I could protest.

The food was good enough. I was positive I could eat it and go before she could convince him to come back and see me. I was proud of how easily things were progressing between the two of us. With how much he had to loathe me, I could devote all my time to the king without interruption.

"Vesim?" I asked through food.

"Hm?"

"Are there books here, historical in subject? Maybe journals?" I asked.

"You won't find much to read outside of things approved for woman's knowledge. History isn't one of those unless it's the history of how to please," Vesim said.

I stood, and Vesim followed. We only made it a few steps outside of the room before the guard followed us. He would be my biggest concern. Getting past him would be complicated but not impossible. I had plenty of experience sneaking past brutes.

I wanted to ask her if there was a way to get my hands on what books the king may have, but I didn't know if I could fully trust her yet.

When we entered my chambers, I locked the door behind us. It was a slab of wood that sat across the door, but still enough to do the job I needed done. Vesim sat on the edge of my bed in silence, and I stretched, then feigned my best yawn. Vesim stood and bowed one last time before she entered the side room and closed the door. The way she looked at me let me know she was onto me. If she was truly on my side, then there was nothing to be concerned about. If what she said was true and we both made a deal with a demon, we would die together or live together.

I paced the room until the sun finished setting. I used my blankets after I tied them together to climb down to the window below me. It was a gamble, but it did pay off. There was no one around, and I was free to roam. Whatever wing I had lowered myself into did not have a single sound coming from it. There was hardly even a flicker of light.

I walked for what felt like at least half an hour before there was any hint of life. The first glint was light pouring from an open door. Next was a guard dragging something into the room. I didn't dare move until he was out of sight. When the light poured without resistance again, I moved closer. The sounds of quiet whimpering and groaning became clearer. I moved my head just enough that one eye was peaking around the door frame.

Three girls were lying on the floor. Two were absolutely gone from our realm. One was not far off. They surrounded a tin tub. It was filled with their blood, and inside stood the king. His arms were outstretched, and I could only see his bare back. Two men used wooden buckets to pick up the blood from the tote and pour it over him. A witch was chanting on her knees in front of him. We had one that dressed the same in my home village.

My palms started to sweat, and my mouth grew drier. If he saw me there, I was sure he would add me to his little ritual. I regretted not minding my own business and staying in my room.

A hand was over my mouth in the next breath I took, and

it caused me to bite into my lip harder than I would have liked. I was pulled into the man's chest in such a quick motion it caused a whimper to escape between his fingers. I wouldn't have believed hours earlier that I would die so quickly after arriving. The man lowered himself until his mouth was by my ear, and I could feel his hot breath on me.

"If you have a death wish, I can grant it with much less pain than Riven would give you if he saw you here," Fennic whispered.

I threw my head back onto his chest and let out a muffled sigh with the wave of relief that washed over me. I still had some luck after all. I was still too afraid to speak, and my breath was falling hard enough that his hand being over my mouth was the only thing keeping us hidden.

"Don't get too comfortable; I might think you're happy to see me," his breath was still on my neck and ear.

I closed my eyes and let myself enjoy the scent of mint coming off of him before I pulled my arm forward and released it backward into his stomach. He released me with a grunt.

"This is only one example of the things that happen in the dark here. If you want to live past a few days, be smarter than this," he said before he turned me in the direction I came.

He marched me back to my room himself.

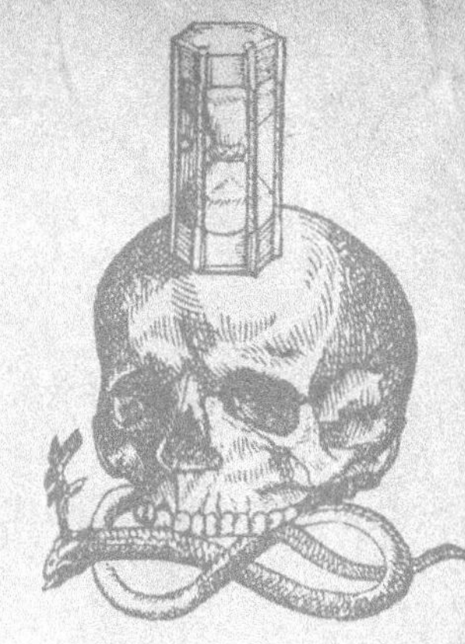

CHAPTER FOUR
THE BROKEN

The Old Gods

The Goddess of Wrath was one of the first to be created by Starlight and Insanity. She was not what they asked for, and as such, she was tossed to the side. She spent her time with the mortals and fell in love with them. Wrath eased their need to feel rage, which allowed them more space to feel peace and happiness. Starlight, angry that her own line could betray her and help the creations of Moonlight, caged Wrath. Her cage was left outside of Starlight's castle as a decoration. Every three days, a mortal Wrath cared for was beheaded and put on the spike in front of the cage, just out of reach. She was freed by a fire sprite, and upon gaining her freedom, she went on a rampage, burning everything. Insanity ended her life.

VESPERA

I wished I could have been more invested in the book I was reading. It wasn't the book's fault that I was too concerned with other things and couldn't become invested in what sat between its pages. I continued to pretend it was the only interest I had, all the same. Caym called for a gathering. He wanted to discuss how we were all moving forward. He wanted a full report of everyone's movements, thoughts, and ideas. What he really wanted was someone to blame beyond himself. We all did.

He wanted enough of us to agree to a mindless slaughter and for someone to confess that they had taken a misstep somewhere along the lines, and it was really the misstep that caused all of us to be where we are now.

I kept my mouth shut. I wanted to stay playing the silent observer.

I was only invited because Astra requested it. I was not in attendance because anyone else trusted me. If I spoke too loudly, I was guaranteed to be the one Caym tossed blame at. We all wanted the easiest out so that maybe we could sleep soundly for one night.

I didn't judge him for it. I understood his reasoning. I put my opinions aside and looked through what his eyes must have seen, what his heart must have felt. There were too many that helped Ruri keep secrets from him. I would feel betrayed, too, in his shoes. I would feel angry, too, if the only one to make me feel whole was taken.

If he asked, and I were to be open and honest with my opinion, I would tell him that he and I would never form a friendship. I would tell him that I thought he was still taking the wrong approach. That he was still too trusting of the ones he should be looking harder at. He was giving Koa a free pass and never doubting him. He looked to Koa as the next best thing to Ruri, and he was latching onto him even harder now that she was gone.

If I were trying to hurt him, I'd tell him I know how he feels because I blame him, too.

Seeing him as the man who was too blind to see what his love was going through was easier than pointing that finger at myself. Painting Caym the failure was easier than admitting if I had just pushed a little harder, a little sooner, maybe I could have altered the outcome. If any of us had killed Sahir sooner, would they still be here?

I let him take that path. Caym can busy himself with finding who to blame. I wanted to keep myself busy with finding the true reason this became our future. Who betrayed us?

Caym decided Koa was clear. He hasn't cast a moment of doubt on Onyx, either. That's where my opinion leans the hardest away from seeing eye-to-eye with Caym. If I were a traitor, if I wanted to have a hand up, I would be like Onyx. I'd push myself onto Sage and Caym. I'd involve myself with Ruri. I'd look like a good guy trying to help while being alone with the enemy.

Onyx was the best at being a pretender. No one seemed to have noticed but me that there had been more than one moment when Onyx came out alone with Yumi. That Sage did not want him close to her. I've only held my tongue because, in truth, she didn't want me close to her either. I couldn't make a case out of that without making a case against myself. Instead, I used my bookstore as a cover. It helped me look busy in their eyes. It gave me a reason to be away often and a hobby that allowed me to keep an eye out for things like old journals or scrolls.

Ruri's death made Caym harder; it left him locked in mourning. Sage's death made Onyx louder. He and I were taking the opposite steps.

Things felt as if we had nothing but hit after hit since their deaths. The abilities we had become used to were gone. The things Ruri and Sage taught us with elemental and nature magic made us lazy, and I missed it. I missed watching Sage smile when she thought no one was watching her fix wilted leaves or sprout new flowers. I missed the smell that carried on the air when the two of them worked together to plant, grow, and pour rain down on new plots of land.

I was so lost inside of my thoughts that my sigh brought all eyes to me. The weight of all the attention on me caused me to squirm until I was sitting up straight. I sat my book down on the perfectly glossed wooden table. It had been left with a natural finish; every lifeline in the wood could be seen through the clear coating. The Nola carved all four legs out until they swirled, and it looked as if the table hovered above the legs.

"If we're interrupting your time, feel free to go," Koa said.

"I'm happy to be here and offer a helping hand," I answered.

I cleared my throat before and after I spoke, despite my effort to not look out of place.

"It doesn't feel like it," His second sentence was filled with more annoyance than the first.

"It feels like you have something else to say to me," I said.

Koa and I sat, eyes locked, in silence for long enough I counted twenty-three heartbeats.

"You understand that if you're here to pass information to Yumi or Helia—"

"Yumi should be the last Goddess you're worried about getting a hand on the information. What will she do with it? Besides, you keep a big enough circle; adding me won't risk much more than you already are," I said.

"I disagree. Everyone here has proven they care," he said.

I kept my sigh inside of my mind this time. Staying in the shadows was more important than continuing this with him. I could tell him that I disagree, that he's clearly wrong. I could tell him the betrayal that landed us here didn't come from me, so lashing out at me wouldn't help him. That one of his trusted, proven friends was the one that got us here. I could reason with him and say I understood he was speaking from a place of hurt and not logic. No path was worth it today.

"That's why I'm here. I want the chance to be on the right side of things," I said.

He looked at me as if he were about to take what I said and run with it as if he were going to tell me "this time" that I wanted to be on the right side of things "this time." I kept my chin high while we sat in silence. If we were to challenge each other, as much as I wanted him to be the one to blink first, it had to be me.

"I don't believe you," he said.

I did my best to focus on the forest green wallpaper covering the room. On the way, the golden fixtures sat out against it. I wanted to seem as meek and mild as I could, but my chin would not go down. I wanted to allow Koa the feeling of having the last say. It didn't matter to me what words he threw around in the end. Actions would be what mattered the most.

I just needed to believe it as well as I could say it.

Caym entered with Onyx, then Aero and Juniper. Astra was next, entering hand in hand with Kyra.

That was an adjustment all of us made quickly, except Caym. He had not adjusted to them being father and daughter, and neither had she. They both tried their best to give it a shot, but it hadn't worked yet. Caym felt like he already knew her as a friend, and Kyra felt like she didn't know him at all. That she spent too much time thinking someone else was her mother to consider it another way.

Chair after chair slid out against the pebbled floor and back. It happened enough times that it started to annoy me.

"We can't afford to stay here as a group for the day. If word got around, things would be blown before they began. I don't want to waste time. What we know to be fact is that

Helia's only misstep was not knowing that Ruri split her and Sage's hearts in half. We know Helia's intent was to eat their hearts and assume their positions and abilities. We know that Helia and Deimos are now working together and that he is looking for the pieces. He thinks they are between Semper or Merripen. We know someone is lying to us and helping Helia. What we don't know is how to weed that person out or move forward. Today, I want to set in stone how to fix that. I want to leave here knowing how we are going to get them back and fix things," Caym's face never changed expressions. "I want to know we all are on the same side."

"Juniper hasn't grown something in her garden to force people into telling the truth?" Koa inserted himself.

"If I had, would it work? If we only have partial memories, would it help us find someone who doesn't know who they are?" Juniper asked.

"They wouldn't need memories of the Age of Moonlight if they betrayed us now," Onyx demanded.

"I think we should follow in Ruri's footsteps," Aero said. "We should move in the shadows and keep what is important close to our chests."

"So, you think we shouldn't trust each other?" Onyx scoffed.

"That's not what I said," Aero shook his head.

"It is though, isn't it?" Onyx said. "I think we should lay everything out now so that we are all on the same page and then focus on bringing them back."

"Shouldn't you know everything you need to know already, Onyx?" Astra asked. "It makes you look a bit suspicious to be the first to demand we lay out everything we may know."

"It makes you suspicious to be the first to say that," Koa said. "I know you have to be holding information you aren't sharing with how close the two of you got before she died."

"Even if I did, I wouldn't share it with you," Astra pointed at Koa.

"What is that supposed to mean?" Koa shoved the chair out with his legs when he stood.

"Stop!" Caym's voice boomed through the room. "Making enemies is exactly what Helia and Yumi expect."

"You're doing the best you can, Caym," Astra sighed, "But you should have known this wouldn't turn into sunshine and rainbows when none of us know who to trust."

"I trust you all," Caym said.

"That's foolish of you," Astra spoke, shaking her head.

I knew she wanted to say that's how we ended up here. I knew it because I wanted to say it, too.

"If we are ready to get back on track now, I think we should move with aggression. Kill them all and stop this before it can get worse," Juniper said.

"So that we all die, too?" Aero asked.

"I don't see how we could take an aggressive approach," I said, against my better judgment. "We're spread thin as it is; no one trusts each other; even if you do, you still risk everything by laying all your plans out like this, and now we're having to deal with someone who has blood magic."

"We have magic," Juniper said.

"You're right; we all need to grab some bags to fill with crystals and hope we have enough to throw at Helia," I said.

I caught the glare from Astra. The one telling me to shut my mouth, and I listened. It was easy with how many voices wanted a louder opinion.

"The first thing we should do is figure out who betrayed Ruri and Sage. We need to get them out of the way so that we can move in true silence because until that happens, it doesn't matter what you all decide here. Helia will know before you can move your first piece," Astra said as she stood from her chair. "You move piece by piece. Not leap by leap. Koa needs to worry about his newly given curse. Juniper needs to stay focused on whoever this girl is that keeps entering our realm. I'm doing my best to be a convincing Thann for Helia. Onyx is doing his best to protect mortal Sage. That leaves only a few heads to task out. Take it slowly, and be sure of your position before you move. You can not take it back once placed."

Astra left the room. She was clear enough in her position that there was no reason for her to stay. Caym looked around the table, silently asking if anyone else had words. I only silently begged for someone else to stand and leave. Anyone to not make me be the second.

"She's right," Aero said. "We need to stay in the shadows and be sure before we move."

He was the next to leave, and with him, Juniper stood. I took the chance to leave with them. There was no hint that anyone was still paying attention to me. I followed the two of them until we were on the other side of the vines that put us back in Semper. They didn't want to speak, and neither did I.

The gathering went worse than I was sure anyone thought it would have. The looks on everyone's faces, when no one could agree, told that loud enough. I expected louder voices to be calling for forward movement. I was sure Onyx didn't want Sage back that quickly. I was confident he was a traitor, but today left a bit of doubt in my head for Caym. I couldn't tell if he wanted Ruri back, no matter the cost, or if he wanted his friendships instead.

If the gathering was any indication of how well everyone was going to be working together, Astra was right in making the call to keep things between just her and me. Even if they all did want the best, if they couldn't agree, they would only stop Astra and me from getting anything real done. I was glad I attended just so I could be confident in our choice to hold tight to our secrets. The only bit of reason spoken in that room was by her. She was the only one to point out how much everyone else had going on. Caym still had Merripen and Kyrell to deal with. Which on its own was double the burden.

Koa had enough to worry about, and I didn't agree he should be heavily involved either. When Nesrin told Koa that he would spend forever shifting into the thing that haunted her nightmares, the curse didn't only stay with him; it affected everyone in Sephtis. The land he was sure his sister was taking care of was cursed, too. The girl Deimos was controlling to keep his secrets safe was killed on the spot. He hadn't adjusted well to his new reality.

I suppose none of us have.

In the throne room, we parted ways in opposite directions. Juniper went back to her quarters, Aero back to Cylla, and I wanted to look in on the Sunlight Garden before leaving.

I entered through the door that connected the garden to the throne room. Since the throne room was empty, I assumed it would have less activity. I was incorrect. A blood guard was standing at the entrance. They hardly looked different from the rest of us except for the black and red around their eyes and the hollowness behind the stares they gave. Looking at them, it was clear that they hardly had a single thought that wasn't put there for them.

The guard noticed me immediately and lunged his mace towards my face. They had little thought but even less mercy. I was fortunate that, of the things I remembered from the Age of Moonlight, my training was one of them. None of us had put together what made the difference in how fast our memories faded or who got to keep a handful, but it didn't seem to matter as much as everything else did.

I dodged the guard, but the spikes of the mace grazed my shoulder. The pain sent a wave of sparks through my body. The way I looked at it, every ounce of pain I felt built me up to feel the next bit even less.

I took out my axe and ran my fingers across its tips. As the Goddess of plague, I was less affected by the loss of other magics. I could still lace my blade with sickness. I pulled my arms back and then dropped the axe across the guard's arms. It sliced through the skin of his forearm, and I saw the blood dribble and then drop to the ground. It didn't phase him like he didn't phase me.

He lifted and flung his mace at me again. Then, a third time, and fourth. I dodged and twirled out of the way. I had counted to nine by now. Another dodge, ten, eleven, twelve. I lifted my axe to block him this time, huffing from all of the awkward ways I was having to lean and move my body to avoid him. Nineteen and twenty. I saw the green streaks forming up his chin before he started choking and hit the ground on his knees.

Steel armor gave a sharp clang that filled the garden. I left the guard's body where it landed, for just a moment, so that I could move further in and see the tree. Since Yumi was locked up with the fate chains, the tree had grown bigger and brighter petals. The rest of the garden was fading, but not the tree. That's all I wanted to be sure of.

I curled my fingers under the blood-red helmet the blood guard wore and pulled him through the doorway, then through the vines to Cylla. He wasn't the first to die; he wouldn't be the last. He needed to burn before I could move on to anything else. The one thing that I couldn't afford to be seen with was his body.

CHAPTER FIVE
THE ARTIFACTS

FENNIC

My morning walk to breakfast was quiet. Beautifully quiet. I welcomed the sound of my steps on marble. There was no redheaded demon moving her jaw in my ear. There was no woman with the most soft-looking skin I had ever seen appearing from thin air to pretend she was witty. Yesterday felt like one hundred years rolled into one day. I could hardly stomach spending any more time with her last night, so I went to bed early and starved instead. I would eat double my share today to make up for it. Watermelon and salt. Oats and honey. The freshest eggs. I was back in the castle to eat real food again.

"I slept wonderfully last night. Thank you," Shivani smiled at Misa.

My smile dropped, and I halted in the doorway. No. She should be busy. She should be learning the rules. She should be with the king. She should be anywhere but ruining my breakfast with her soft voice. She should be exhausted from her long night of sneaking around as if she were the cutest mouse to frolic in the castle.

"Fennie!" Misa waved me over.

I may have to consider her my new muse. She is inspiring me to think of new ways to torture for information. I would need to test them on her first. Once that was done, anyone who needed questioning would be in for a ride.

"If you keep staring at her like that, your brother will know you like her," Mori said, stopping by my side.

"Like her?" I scoffed. "Like her? I'd happily hand her to him. In fact, I will hand her to him. I'll make him think I do like her, and he will take the problem off of my hands," I said.

Coy's deep voice spoke from the other side of me, "You should tell her that you are falling in love."

"She's disgusting. Repulsive," I gritted.

"Mm," was Coy's only response.

I walked inside and took a seat beside her. She dressed down again today, still in black but trimmed in forest green. I was sure it had to be part of her plans. She wanted to look innocent and easy to please—a model queen. It wouldn't work on me. My heart was pounding again. My clothing felt tight. It was as if it restricted my airflow. Was I dehydrated? Why was it that every time she was near, my body revolted against my commands?

"Sir, if you keep staring at me like this, I may get the wrong idea," Shivani said.

"I was just trying to figure out what's on your face. You're embarrassing yourself," I said.

"Please, remove it then." She leaned into me.

The scent of her perfume filled me. She smelled of fresh flowers and nightly rain. It was intoxicating. I had to restrain myself from leaning into her neck and taking another pull of the scent. I swiped my finger across the bottom of her lip, pretending to take away food that I lied about being there. Her lips were as soft as they looked. Why was she so beautiful? It was infuriating to know she smelled as good as she looked. She needed to die for my peace.

"Maybe I was wrong," she whispered. "It looks like you don't need herbs to get it up after all."

I looked down at my pants and back to her. I couldn't see her eyes but knew she was looking at mine. "I'll kill you. I swear it'll be my hand that ends you."

She smiled. "Not if I kill you first."

She turned her attention to Coy and asked him to wipe whatever may be on her face away, and he did. He was always ready to oblige in his matter-of-fact way. His eyes were the iciest blue and mesmerized even me. He was always serious and hardly made a peep if there were more than one or two people present. He always listened, though.

I leaned forward in my chair and crossed my legs. I did my best to avoid eye contact with Mori or my sister. They couldn't have heard what was said, but what the sight must have looked like was enough on its own. I would hear from my sister about this later. She would spread it around, and Riven would be sure to be looking at her. I'd take his hands if he touched her and his eyes if he couldn't remove them from her.

"I hope no one minds me sitting in for breakfast!" King Riven's voice boomed. "I heard my brothers were having breakfast and dinner with our sister. I had to come join on my own as my invitation must have been lost."

Misa stood. "I thought you would be busy with selection; I did not want to disturb you."

He nodded and sat at the head of the table. "I can always make time for you three."

The staff tripped over themselves, trying to set his place at the table before he could become upset. I would distract him if need be and let him hurl a few insults my way for the sake of the staff.

"My King, may I ask a question openly?" Shivani said.

A girl of the kitchen staff tripped, dropping a glass and nearly causing another to fall. The other caught herself, but the glass was still covering the floor. Riven snapped his finger and pointed slightly enough that it was hardly a full movement. A guard knew what it meant, and his axe took the girl's hand before she was pulled from the room.

The fact that Shivani's face had a veil didn't stop me from seeing the color drain from it.

"Go ahead," Riven nodded.

"I have heard you keep a collection of the animals you've hunted. I would love to see them if I were to be allowed," Shivani said. She was surprisingly good at pretending she didn't witness anything.

Her voice was filled with admiration and interest. I may have even been convinced she was genuine if I didn't know she was here to play a game. The way she was fluttering her voice at him made me furious. I knew she was only playing with him, but she still looked foolish doing it. I could have shown her something better than dead animals on a wall.

Coy and I were eye-locked before I could finish my thoughts. Those piercing blue eyes glared me down and slapped me in silence. He didn't need a physical movement with how hard his face could drive into someone. I knew what he was saying. He was telling me to simmer down or hurry up and do something. I was not a man to be told what to do. I would pick neither. I would not make a fool of myself for her or give Riven the entertainment he wanted.

"I was under the impression my brother was already courting you. This is your second meal together, and from what I was told, you arrived together as well," King Riven said.

"Our arrival was just out of ease. He was a stop along the way, if it was not too disrespectful to say it as such, and I was invited by the princess to dinner. I dare not deny her such a request. I also do not want to deny myself of her warm company," Shivani answered. "Besides, nothing is out of your reach, Sir."

I felt my blood heat and my cheeks match. She was

walking a thin line. How dare she spend her time here addressing me that way and then give it to my brother. She didn't talk to Coy that way.

"I will take you then and spend the day with you," Riven said.

Mori leaned into me and whispered. "I thought you said he could take her. That you would hand her over yourself? You protest now?"

"I've lost my appetite. If you'll excuse me," I said, standing.

"He's upset," Coy mocked.

"He really does like her," Mori quietly agreed.

"Mm," Coy grunted.

Mori stood and followed me to the exit. I didn't care to silence my steps. My brother would be overjoyed to know he got under my skin, but it would have to be. Coy was already stalking behind us, internally mocking me, too. I would take my next meal in my room. It seemed to be the only way I could guarantee peace now.

"Mori, go talk to Shivani's guard and see if he's seen anything worth reporting. I'll meet you in my room soon," I said.

I had one more thing to do before my arrival tasks were complete. I followed the winding staircase up one floor and then another before leaving the stairs behind and stomping to a wing of the castle I knew better than any other. Coy was still silently lurking. This area was decorated with more lighting and flowers. It breathed more life than any other, as if it were its own world. I opened the first door, and there she was, waiting for us both like every other time.

"My sweet Fennie!" Mother called. "I missed you."

"I've missed you too, mother," I said.

I sat on the edge of her bed, and she took my hands in hers. She looked like she hadn't been sick at all. I knew it was a lie. That she had to have the herbs, or she faced death. She tucked it away well. She kept a smile, and I sometimes forgot for just a moment everything that she had been through at the hands of my father.

"Fennie, your hands are so clammy," her lips turned down.

"I'm fine, mother, how are you? Is Riven treating you all right? Do you need anything?" I asked. "They're bringing your medicine on time?"

Coy didn't wait for a greeting from her. He was already treating her like a rag doll. Lifting her, fluffing her pillows. He pulled a brush from a drawer on her bedside table to brush and braid her hair as if our conversation was not going to get in his way.

"The ladies you left here have taken good care of me while you two were away. Don't fuss so much. Tell me, has the selection started yet? The ladies whisper to me of all the pretty young women here now. Have any caught your eye yet? Don't be shy!" She squeezed my hands.

"I don't have time for the selection, Mother. I—"

"Of course you do!" She said. "I want to see you marry before I—"

"Enough. I brought you a gift," I said, pulling out a black box.

"He has already found a girl he likes. He thinks planning her death is romantic. Don't count on him for grandchildren," Coy mumbled.

She gave me a small shake of the head and took the box. She opened it slowly, too slowly. She enjoyed every pull of the ribbon tied across the top. She pulled the top off to reveal a small feather on a golden chain.

"It's beautiful Fennie! How did you find this? There haven't been any cardinals in years!"

"It was worth the search," I said, kissing her forehead. "I'll come back to check on you soon."

"Bring a girl next time," she pointed.

Coy had already moved past her hair and rearranged her

entire bed so that she was propped up and ready to eat. No one would believe the general of our royal guard would be a stone-faced pile of fluff if they didn't see it themselves. Coy pulled out a basket and took plate after plate from it to sit in front of our mother.

I pretended not to hear her words or see Coy feeding her on my exit. After I was king, I would find a wife. It wouldn't be from the selection. I would not take a concubine. I wouldn't put my wife in my mother's position. She deserved more respect than she received, and she only lacked it because her title was concubine and not Queen. I made my way back down the stairs to the second floor and opened the door to my room. I wished I had taken longer.

"For the love of everything still left alive, this is my room!" I yelled.

The sight of Mori's tongue down the guard's throat was something I could have lived without. I slammed the door closed but could still smell the scent of betrayal. I leaned against the wall until the door opened again. The guard did not make eye contact with me, and his footsteps were quick and light. Mori came out second.

"I said get information, not turn my room into a brothel!"

"That's what I was doing!" Mori shrugged.

"How could he tell you anything when you blocked his mouth?" I yelled.

"He told me before that was his reward," Mori said.

"Don't you have your own room?"

"Sure, but yours was the meeting place. I'm going to disappoint you more. He has seen and heard nothing. Shivani has been behaving quietly since arrival," Mori said.

"Why did you reward him then?" I asked.

"It was my reward for a job well done, too," Mori smiled.

"It looks like it could be fun," Coy's voice rumbled behind me.

I jumped out of my skin at how swiftly he was back with me, and the scare only sent rage through me.

"Did you find anything new? Are you of any use?" I rubbed my forehead.

"Yes. I learned that the artifact keeping the king alive is made by the sun god. So, you'll need a lot of luck if you want to kill Riven," Mori said.

"It makes sense why all the attempts on his life failed. That god artifact is a shield," I said.

"The sun god is an original," Coy started to speak.

"Stop. I understand what it means," I held my hand up.

Mori sighed. "Looks like your plans are falling apart fast this time."

"I'm going to look through his study while he's out," I said.

I was trying my best to ignore their taunting.

"Do you want me to see if they're getting along? I bet he's laying the charm on her right now," Mori said.

"They can do whatever they like," I said. "As long as it's not in my room, what she and the king do is none of my business."

"Do you believe him?" Mori asked Coy.

Coy shook his head in response.

"Me either," Mori shot me a side-eyed glare before turning his focus back to Coy. "If Fennic won't admit it, it's up to me then to tell you that I think I'm in love this time, and I'm ready to admit it."

Coy responded to him with such a small lift of his lip, on only one side, that it was as quick as a blink.

"Don't you have anything to get done?" I urged.

I left them behind, and they hardly noticed. I stuck to the shadows of the halls and avoided being seen as well as I could. I wanted to get to Riven's study and have plenty of time to look through anything I wanted. There was no better time than this. He was out of the castle walls entirely.

I entered his study unnoticed. I learned when we were

young that my brother's important things would be kept in a hidden opening under a cushion on his beloved chair. When I entered his study, the chair was the first thing to catch my eye. I moved to it and lifted the cushion in front of me. Just as I knew it would be, the wooden latch stared back at me.

I lifted it, and paper after paper lay stacked inside, but there was no artifact. Most of the pages were useless. I flipped through page after page of notes on coins and creatures, but I stopped when I flipped to the plans for the artifact. A list of names had been placed on a team tasked with finding the blood needed to ascend my brother into a god with the artifact. He wasn't satisfied calling himself a god-king; he wanted to be a true god. He was already cruel and uncaring. He would be worse with immortality backing him.

I placed the cushion back and moved to Riven's desk. It was cluttered like the rest of the room. The black walls were lined with bookcases, though most of the shelves were empty. Riven didn't spend his time reading. If he needed knowledge, he had other people to carry it for him. The only information he carried himself was how to hunt. If it was on his shelves, it was important. I moved to the shelf with the thickest book. I pulled it down and opened it to the middle. The pages I held open held drawings of other artifacts. Scribbles of notes. It seemed whoever wrote inside didn't understand them very well.

Some notes said artifacts were disappearing from our world. That the royal treasury lost the God of Nightmares artifact, and no one could account for where it may have gone. There were several other instances reported with the Goddess of Chaos and the Goddess of Fall. Several deaths paid the price for the theft, but complaints were filed. There were many who didn't believe they were stolen; some said the deities had been reborn, and that's why they were lost.

No one could come forth and testify to holding the knowledge of whether there was truth to the claims or not.

I closed the book and put it back where it sat. I wasn't expecting to leave with the amount of information I had gotten; there was no need to push my luck. I opened the wooden door, and Niko stood outside. His black eyes were the most intimidating thing in the castle. Riven used his title as king to do whatever he wanted, but he didn't have anything outside of that. Niko was different. His stance, the emptiness in his eyes. It all said he was the one to enforce his demands. With how close my brother kept him, he could use his own hand to do anything he'd like with no punishment.

"This doesn't seem like a place for the prince," Niko said.

"Any place is a place for a prince," I answered.

"I wonder if the king would agree," Niko hadn't moved from the doorway.

"He is why I stand here. When I didn't find him in the throne room, I assumed he would be here," I said.

"You weren't at breakfast with him? Did you not hear he is out with a lady of the veil?" Niko stepped to the side. "Something tells me you wouldn't want your brother to know you were here."

I didn't answer him, despite wanting to.

"I'll hold onto the information for now. It's no use to me to tell him of your footsteps yet," Niko bowed.

I moved past him, grinding my teeth together. It wasn't the most ideal ending to my sneaking around, but it could have been worse. I still have my head for now. It just means I'll have to plan to stay a step ahead of him. Any whiff of him needing to hold information over me, and it's his head for my wall.

The bigger problem for now was Riven and the Sun God's artifact. It would be impossible for me to kill him if the plans did succeed. None of us knew how to kill a god. I didn't know where to begin trying to find such information.

Lightning struck outside the windows above the stairs, and thunder followed. It startled me but it was also enough to tell me Shivani and Riven would be cutting their date short. If I didn't dislike her so much, I'd thank her for unknowingly distracting my brother for the day. I would need to talk to Mori quickly. We had to start putting things into motion faster. I couldn't keep living my life under his thumb while he held the herbs to keep my mother healthy over my head. I had to kill him for myself, for my mother. For the kingdom.

I was halfway down the stairs when I was stopped by the body of a girl running into me. I swore she did it on purpose, but she hit the ground as if she were a newborn deer and had no idea how to use her legs.

"I'm so sorry, Prince Fennic. Please forgive me; I wasn't paying attention," she cried.

"Get up, you look foolish. Watch where you walk," I said, trying to move past her.

"Wait!" She called, getting to her feet. "My name is Lorelai. I'm part of the veiled."

"I didn't ask your name. The king should be inside soon," I waved her off.

"I'm not looking for the king; I've been trying to find you," she cleared her throat. "I've admired you for a long time."

"Get better role models," I said.

I felt her grab my arm, but I quickened my steps in response, flapping my arm to get the annoyance off of me. I didn't need to see this girl's face to know I wasn't interested. I didn't need to speak to her to know her personality was bland. I didn't need to continue further to know her scent wasn't as beautiful as fresh flowers in the rain. She was only distracting me from arriving at my destination. If I moved fast enough, I could still have time to see Shivani's suffering face while she listened to my brother's chatter about his collection of dead animals. I was already smiling at how awful her day with him must have been.

The rain outside was heavy. If it matched her pain, then she was learning a good lesson. Maybe next time, she'd try to convince me to spend the day taking her around instead. She would plead for me to spare her from having to experience this kind of day again. Maybe I would make her do it again so she appreciated my good looks and personality better.

I stopped at the oversized windows, looking over the joke of a garden, and saw the two still outside in the rain. They were strolling, unaffected by the strikes lighting up the sky. Her arm was wrapped in his, and they laughed together. She was having fun. How was she having fun with him? I would cut his arm off before I killed him. They could both laugh over that. They could joke all afternoon about his armless days as king since he was so amusing. I needed to go to the forge and have my mace repaired. They could enjoy catching an illness together.

Movement caught my attention. My focus was pulled to the corner of my eye, where Niko was now standing. He stood higher on the stairs than I, looking outside the same as I was. At the same thing as I was. The smirk on his face while he looked at Shivani made my stomach turn. The way his dark eyes looked at her made my skin prickle in defense.

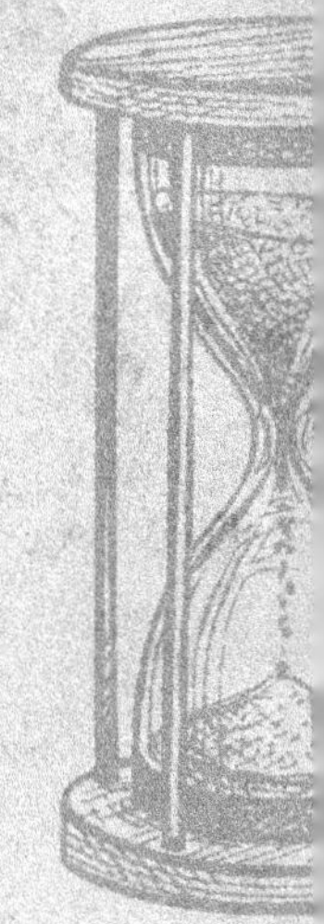

CHAPTER SIX

THE REANIMATED

SHIVANI

The location was different, but the men were not. Men in my homeland and the king both had no interest in anything that could have come from my mouth, but every thought that came to his mind poured out of his mouth for me to hear. He hadn't stopped to ask me anything our entire afternoon together. He had no reason to be concerned with any details about me; I was just a girl in his world, after all. I wouldn't have been honest with him, but there was something amusing to see; the only thing that separated him from the rest of the men was simply the word 'king.'

"By appointing lesser lords to keep order and dividing the lands smaller according to the resources they can offer, production and population can increase at a far more rapid pace," King Riven said. "Right now, even with how small the lands are, the lords appointed to oversee them are too incompetent. I think spreading tasks better can change things. The addition of enforcers and stricter punishments will be what really drives the idea."

I knew he didn't want my words, only a nod and a pretty

smile, so I gave it to him. The most valuable item I had here was my veil. I could soften my smile, but my eyes wouldn't have lied as well after this long of listening to him. I could take further comfort knowing that if I did fail here, his plan would be sure to trigger a rebellion. He is far too detached if he thinks anyone outside of these walls has more effort to give than they are. Restricting life further won't help to increase the population, either.

His reputation with women was another rumor that could be relabeled as truth. He changed everything from his face to his voice. When he spoke to his brother, he was gruff. He had no humor to him. The only shift was when he wanted to toy with him. When King Riven talked to his guard or any male in the court, he was strictly business. Here, with me, even the way he stood said I was just a defenseless peasant. He was beyond at ease with the idea that he could bend and break me however he wanted.

"May I ask a question?" I knew I was pressing my boundaries.

"You've been such a good listener; I think I can allow it," he said.

"I heard that you have multiple artifacts here and that you plan to use them to help bring the land back to life. Will it work?"

No one had ever said such a thing, but I needed a way to wiggle myself into some information.

"Who have you seen speaking about my artifacts?" Riven's voice was hardening further with every word.

Thunder clapped behind us, and I squeezed his arm a bit tighter. I wanted him to be reminded that I was only a dumb girl.

"The rain will come soon. We should get you back inside," Riven said.

I gave him a nudge. "I won't melt, but with how sweet you are, you may."

His laughter was as loud as the thunder, bringing the rain. I sympathized with the sky and wanted to cry, too.

"You're an interesting girl," Riven said.

"You're a brilliant King," I responded, pulling myself closer to him.

I wasn't going to urge him to stay. I was ready to be done with him hours ago, and I already got what I wanted from him. I didn't need to press the conversation further because he was clear that there was more than one artifact somewhere in the castle. Everything was aligned for me. I need to kill him sooner rather than later, then find the artifacts. It would be easy without him giving orders or breathing down my neck.

I noticed a familiar face staring down at us from inside the castle. Fennic looked as angry as usual. Was he stalking me? I couldn't explain why I enjoyed this game we were playing so much. I didn't care for him in that sense. He was just another man of the royal family, like any other. The flash of anger in his golden eyes was the thing that gave him a leg up. They told everything he was feeling in real time. His lips were wordless, but those eyes cried out in a symphony of emotions. Seeing it set fire to me in a way I was sure was only temporary lust.

"Thank you for showing me such an enchanting day. If it is not too bold, may I be allowed to kiss your cheek?" I asked, knowing Fennic was still watching.

He stopped walking and stared at me. His eyes looked as if they could see through the veil.

"It can be our secret," he said.

I pulled him down closer to my face and gave him a light kiss, lingering momentarily. I wanted to be sure I gave him the impression that it was hard to pull away. I wanted my stalker to be sure of what he saw and have the time to take it all in. King Riven stood back up and smirked at me.

"We will need to plan time to meet again soon," he said.

"I will miss you until then," I bowed.

He left for the castle with his guard, and Vesim sprinted back to my side in a way that made her look foolish.

"A kiss?" She gritted.

"Is he still looking down at us?" I asked.

Her eyes glanced up quickly and darted back down. "He looks like he's going to boil over. This is why you did it?"

"He's the one being a creep," I said. "I'd like to stay in the rain a little longer."

Vesim followed me back onto the stones laid out for our path through the had-been garden.

"Can I ask you a question?" Vesim whispered.

"Sure."

"What do you want from being here? This rain will give us the best chance at privacy, so I'd like to know who I'm helping," Vesim said.

"I plan to be Queen," I said, taking the risk.

"So, you aren't here for love?" She asked.

I shook my head. "I'm not here for romance."

"Then what are you doing with Fennic? Riven I understand," Vesim said.

"I was just trying to be clear that following me around was not impressive. If Prince Fennic had it his way, he would use me up and toss me away, just like King Riven. He would have his fun, expect me to keep my mouth shut, and then he would run off to his next little game with a pretty face," I said. "I want to show that he's not the only player in this game."

Vesim thought it over for a moment. "But what if one of them was different? What if you were loved, right? What if one of them showed you that when loved the right way, you glow brighter?" Vesim said.

"Maybe one of them could love me so well that I become a new woman, and the gods will change their minds and return to us. Then, we would be walking in a lush garden under a rainbow," I mocked. "Do you often dwell on fantasy and fairy tales?"

"You hate love and the gods?" Vesim laughed.

"I hate the king's collection of extinct animal bones, too," I said. "And the sound of his voice rambling on about how wonderful he is."

"I hate the collection, too. The gods had to have a reason, though," she said.

"A reason to throw out responsibility?" I scoffed.

"Maybe they save their energy for those in deep need?" Vesim shrugged.

"No God came to me when I was a helpless child in need laying under the body of a man double my size. No God saved me from being forced to breathe in nothing but his sweat. No God came to me when I was crying out in hunger because all the coin from that went to my mother. There was no one to tell me it wasn't my fault when I was pleading to know what was so wrong with me that I didn't deserve their help. I wasn't the only child, either. The Gods are as much a problem as our king is. If they save their strength for those most in need, then I can be sure that I disagree with their idea of need," I kept my voice low. "In the end, they made us, and we were left to clean up their mess."

Her lips never moved, but her voice was stern. "I'm glad to know this is how you think. It means I can trust you. I don't wish to be tossed aside for romance or the Gods. Our goals are the same, and so are our thoughts. Since it seems clear we can trust each other, you should know we aren't the only two here who made a deal with a demon; I can smell it," Vesim said.

I wasn't sure I was ready to let her take all the information I held close yet, but I was ready to resist a little less. "Do they know about us?" I asked, admitting I had made the deal.

"I can't be sure yet," she said.

We would have to do something, quickly. I couldn't take such a significant risk. If she didn't know about us yet, she would soon enough. We all have to spend time in the same castle after all. If I didn't succeed in marrying into the throne, I gave up my life for nothing.

Vesim took a step back; we both felt the presence behind us. I clicked the button between my fingers and caught the dagger while turning myself around. I didn't wait to see who it was before my blade was against the item between his legs that held his ability to have children.

"If you wanted to touch them so badly, you could have asked," Prince Fennic said.

"Don't flatter yourself. I'd take the night with your guard over you," I said, adding pressure to the blade.

"You toy with his life and never think twice? Do you think I wouldn't make Mori a eunuch?" Fennic said.

"I can hear you!" Mori called. "You won't do any such thing!"

Fennic waited for me to glance in the direction of the voice and hit the arm that held the dagger. Before I could react, he spun me around until my back hit against his chest and held me in place. When his body was fully flush with my own, and he realized the kind of position we were in, he let go and backed up as quickly as we moved into the position.

He cleared his throat and pulled on his clothing. "I am still picking my own wife, and as such, I request that you not put your mouth on others. That should have been basic knowledge with all those manners you show off."

"Are you jealous?" I asked. "If the king requests my mouth, I cannot say no. If he requests more than that? You want me to lose my head, for you?"

So he was watching me.

"Jealous?" He yelled and laughed. "I simply think it's giving the other women poor examples, and since we've all heard that you were already caught with one dagger, I would think you'd be looking to stay out of trouble."

"Oh. Well, I've not come to be a role model, and I was

already taught what happens when I mess up," I said. "So, I'll kiss who I want."

"If you kiss him again, I'll—" His jaw was tight.

"You'll what? Tell the king I am to be with you instead? Tell him what he can and can't do? Something tells me he won't agree. It seems you both think you can own another," I pointed my dagger at his throat. I watched as he swallowed, unafraid of my gesture.

A vein that ran along his neck was pulsing enough that I could see the length of it trailing into his shirt. It was cute to see him so worked up. I wanted to know if I could keep poking him until he was pulling me around again. I was sure I could keep this going until he was putting his hands back on me. My stomach turned, and as I realized what I was thinking, I felt nauseous. Did I not listen to my own words? Did I not just get done discussing that I was here for one purpose, and it did not include these men? Maybe Vesim would take my uterus for me as a favor if I asked her.

"You need to spend time with the other women here. There are many. I'm sure one of them checks all of your boxes," I said.

"Don't flatter yourself. I have spent time with them. In fact, I just left one of them, and she couldn't take her hands off of me. Do you think I have nothing better to do than follow you around? That you have some quality that makes you irresistible?" He mocked.

My smile came before my words. "Yes."

I ran my fingers from the side of my jaw down to my collarbone, exposing the skin for him to see. Offering him what I knew he wanted.

His face radiated enough heat that I was sure I could feel it from where I stood. He opened his mouth once but closed it again. He lifted a finger but only shook it at me.

"I don't have time for this! I have another from the selection to meet soon!" He yelled.

"I wish you the best, Sir!" I called with satisfaction.

His grumbling while he walked away was unintelligible, but it didn't matter to me what he had to say; it only mattered that I got to see it before he left.

"What do you have against him?" Vesim asked.

"Nothing specific, truly. If he could not exist, I'd like him fine," I said. "I'm going to take care of the king and whoever else made the deal now."

I whispered to her without a glance. I kept my eyes on Fennic and his exit from our gathering.

"What are you going to do?" Vesim asked.

"The less you know, the better. If we are to form some sort of partnership, then one of us needs to remain innocent," I said.

"That's not how a partnership or a friendship based on trust works," Vesim said, leaving me behind.

I didn't understand what she wanted. Should we act as though we were childhood friends? Should we pretend like we didn't just meet here at this castle and have no reason to believe anything the other says? Should we both be so desperate for any bond that we pull at thin air for loyalty? She had no reason to think that I wouldn't kill her the first chance I got, just as I had no reason to believe she wouldn't slit my throat and take the throne as soon as I was done doing the heavy lifting. She was asking a lot for someone who was still giving so little.

I was careful to ensure no eyes were around to watch me while I moved further into the castle grounds. In my village, there was always someone lurking, always someone to witness your movements and hold them against you. At one point or another, all information becomes useful when it's your best chance at funding a life.

I found the place I was looking for. It was just as unkept as everything else. I was sure the royal crypt would have been grand and covered with armed guards. It seemed the current king cared as little for the dead as he did the living. The crypt looked like it was grand once. It was overgrown with half-dead vines, but under them, the little parts I could see looked like someone had poured their life into designing every small area.

I shoved the solid mass of stone, acting as a door in until I could fit inside. Hot, stale air hit me, but what caught my attention was how strange it was to have the inside kept so spotless. I felt my heart beat faster at just how kept it looked. I felt like I was sure to run into someone. Not a single web lay anywhere my eyes could see. Gold was shining, and fresh flowers sat all around the candlelight. It couldn't be King Riven doing it. He would not have spent his afternoons in a crypt playing maid to a dead family line.

If someone were here, I would surely know by now. The inside was sizable but not enough to hide, and if they could, why would they hide from me, of all people? I clicked the button on my dagger, released it into my hand, and pricked my finger. I slid it down just enough that the blood did more than drip but didn't pour. I had wasted enough time at the castle. I wanted to have the king dead on arrival. I was so sure I would be the only one here to have made a deal, but I felt the need to move faster after learning that not one, but two others at least, were already here with presumably the same plan. What else would they have as a reason to make the deal? If I didn't act first, it would have been for nothing.

I dripped blood over the old king and chanted.

Sanguis Servus. Reanimate this body with my blood. Walk lightly and serve well.

The blood filled his mouth, and small, still shredded bits of skin formed over him. It was enough to keep him moving but not enough to look at him with anything but disgust. I wished the smell of blood would have overwritten the scent of rot, but like many other wishes, this was left ungranted as well. Cracks came from his body when he stood. I let my laughter escape when he finished his reanimation, and it was clear he was Riven's father. It would be sad not to be able to see the look on his face when he took his last breath like I had my mother.

My attention was caught when the body was fully upright. Under him was a small scroll. I took it and inside was a map. I shoved it into my dress and between my chest. It was a place I could guarantee its safety no matter what. If it was hidden under the king's body, it had to lead me to an artifact.

I shoved the stone door open further on my way out to allow him more than enough room to exit behind me. I had a choice to make, and it had to be quick. I could lay in the middle of the garden and pretend to be injured by the creature, or I could run like I had wings back to my room. It hit me: the third option. I would put myself in the middle. I would tell King Riven myself. I would say to him that I was attacked. I would see his death; I would have eyes on me for his last breath. Fennic would know I was leaving the garden. He and Vesim would make my witnesses.

I lifted my black dress and ran. I ran past the bench that hardly counted as anything but a log. I ran past the dead plants. I ran like my life depended on it. It was easy when it did depend on it. When I hit the clearing and the entrance to the castle was in my sight, I screamed. I screamed as loud as I could.

"Help! Attack! Help me!"

My voice cracked, and I threw myself to the ground in an attempt to look even more frantic. A guard grabbed my arm and lifted me back to my feet. I sobbed so that my words were incoherent. I pointed my finger to the path behind me when the old king rounded the way and came into view. I practically crawled up the guard's arm in terror. I should have gone into the theater. It would have kept me better fed. The guard shoved me closer to the door, and I took off running again, up the stairs and into King Riven. He looked at me as if I were a pathetic and useless girl. Causing a fuss in his home.

Disrupting his day. I watched every drop of color leave his face when he looked behind me, and I allowed myself a small smile while I buried my face into his chest.

He pushed me aside. Slow and without the anger he had just given me with his eyes. If he had even realized I was there anymore, I would have been shocked.

"Father?" he said.

I opened my mouth to protest him getting any closer when Prince Fennic grabbed me by the arm and pulled me inside. I slapped his hand and tried to push him off of me, but he gripped harder. He tossed me over his shoulder even through my kicking and clawing. I bit the back of his arm, and he didn't offer me a twitch. He kept his path straight and silent.

"Let me go!" I yelled. "Put me down!"

He turned into the wing of the castle, where the women were sorted, and opened the door to my room. He was going too far now. Ruining too much. I had to make sure they didn't kill my creation before he could kill the girl as well. I needed to know they both died. He threw me onto the couch as if he wanted to break something.

"You could have hurt me!" I yelled.

"Good!" He finally spoke.

He grabbed a chair and pulled it in front of me. He gave me another shove back down before he sat directly in front of me. I leaned back to escape him, but he leaned in closer until we both had nowhere to go.

"I knew you were stupid, but I didn't think you were fucking careless," Fennic said.

"Excuse you?" My mouth refused to close.

"Do you think me stupid?" He gritted.

I opened my mouth, but he covered it with his hand.

"Don't. I know it was you. I had enough confidence in you until now to have thought you wouldn't act without all the information," he said.

I bit down on his flesh, and he pulled back.

"I don't know what you're talking about," I assured.

"Or maybe you've truly convinced yourself that you, an untrained young girl, could walk in this castle pretending to be someone else and outsmart all the trained people occupying these walls," he sighed. "It's my responsibility to catch people doing what you did. It's like you didn't even try."

I only looked at him, biting the inside of my lip.

"You wasted your time. Riven has the Sun God's artifact. You won't kill him until it's away from him," Fennic said. "You and that demon should know that, shouldn't you, Shivani?"

Hearing my name from his lips is when my heart sank. He didn't just know a thing or two; he knew everything that mattered before I knew anything about him. Had he told anyone else? My problems went from who I would have my next meal with, to catastrophic far too quickly. I hadn't even been there long enough to consider things happening this way. I was the one who could read minds, but he had all the information without half of the effort I went through today.

"So, what now?" I said.

"You and I discuss what you're really doing here, and we come to an agreement moving forward," he said.

"And if I deny?" I asked.

"I'll throw you in the dungeon," he smiled.

"Do you think you could?" I asked.

"I got you here easy enough," he said.

I crossed my arms and sighed, "I can't believe you caught me so quickly."

"I can't believe you thought that you could come here, untrained and naïve, and beat me at the only thing I've been trained for my entire life," he scoffed.

I rolled my eyes; it was the only reaction I had to give. I wouldn't move further with his degradation, in thought or out loud. He thought he was smart, but I still held the map from the crypt.

CHAPTER SEVEN

THE PARTNERSHIP

FENNIC

Vesim and Mori could not have entered the room at a worse time. If I weren't a better man, I would have used Shivani's dagger on them myself. I could feel how close she was to breaking. To giving me all of her secrets and handing me everything I needed to keep her under my thumb. I'd have to start again now. As if I weren't already risking my own life by being here and not with Riven.

"Is the king dead?" I asked Mori, but I did not take my eyes off Shivani.

"No," Mori answered.

"Is the blood slave dead?" I asked.

"Yes," Mori said.

"Is there anything so urgent that it cannot wait five minutes?" I yelled.

"Did you eat lunch? Did you meet with your favorite maid for your afternoon romp? You're grumpy when you miss those. I wouldn't say I like being yelled at, you know. I'll tell your sister, or maybe your mother. We were worried, so we came to check on you both!" Mori grumbled.

"Favorite maid, huh?" Shivani didn't take her eyes off of me either.

"First, he's just stirring the pot. There is no favorite maid. Second, if the two of you don't leave right now, I'll tell Riven the blood slave was the two of you working together."

"We will be outside," Mori said, pushing Vesim out.

"I'll start us back on the right path. How do you know my name?" Shivani asked.

"Mori and I handle the investigations here. Unlike you, we have experience in the things we try to accomplish. I will take back only a bit of what I said earlier, you caused us a bit of trouble for a moment. The townspeople were adamant that you died in a fire with your mother. As for what I know your next line will be, Coy takes care of the crypt daily. My father was a heartless man, but my mother loved him all the same. For her sake, he keeps a close eye on it. He knew you entered before you had the chance to take a second breath. Besides, you've all but admitted full guilt yourself. I didn't even have to use torture," I chuckled. "Which is such a shame."

"Oh, trust me, your endless chatter is a torture method," she rolled her eyes.

"I also overheard you and your attendant talking in the garden. I heard, what was it? We aren't the only two who made a deal. That's what she said, right?" I said.

"So, you've been stalking me?" She pointed.

"Protecting the interest of my kingdom is not stalking," I retorted.

"Do you think that makes you sound better? Using different words doesn't change anything," she crossed her arms.

"Are you ready to listen to my proposal?" my brows lifted.

"You can talk all you'd like." Her voice was mesmerizing.

"When I go back down those stairs, I'll be the one tasked with investigating this incident. I'll keep your name out of it and pin it on someone else in exchange for you accompanying me to the ball," I said.

She laughed, the most sarcastic laugh I had heard yet. "You've got to be joking. The ball? You want me to sleep with you, too?"

"I wouldn't deny the offer, but I'm satisfied with only the date," I said.

"And if I deny that?" She asked.

"Should I explain again that I'm your only way out of this?" I asked.

"Please don't. I didn't listen to a single word the first time, and I don't want to risk hearing more the second time. What is it you want? You can't expect me to believe a date will make us even, and we can go on about our business," she said.

"You believed that a stupid girl like you could walk into the castle and kill the king on a whim," I said.

She shoved me with her shoulder when she stood from the couch. "I've had enough of this exchange."

"All right," I groaned and grabbed her arm, pulling her back down. "We want the same thing. Two is better than one, and four is better than two."

"I'm just a stupid girl, Sir. You'll have to elaborate on how you think our interests align," she rolled her eyes but stayed seated.

"We both want the king dead and the throne freed," I said.

"So, you want me to help kill him so you may be crowned?" She raised her brows.

"You can marry me, and we can both rule," I said.

She let out another mocking laugh. "So, you want my help, and when it's done, you want me to become your quiet little bred-out-to-death wife. I refuse to wake up one day with that as my future. I refuse to say I could have been a queen, no, the queen, but instead, I aided another ego-driven man and became nothing but a wife waiting in the shadow of a husband. It's time I go now."

"Next, I tie you up until you're willing to listen," I threatened.

"I am listening!" She yelled. "You just aren't offering me anything of benefit. You expect me to align with you, do your dirty work, and watch as you reap the benefits? I am not Mori. I'm not bound to you out of love or loyalty. I have no duty to you. I hear your words, but I don't accept your terms."

"No, you're fighting. You aren't anywhere near listening. If I let you leave right now, what is your plan? Will you try to use a sweet voice on the king and get out free and clear? If you think that will work, then you don't know him well enough to do this alone," I said.

"Then give me a plan that does not make me your wife, and I'll hear it," she said.

"You would truly deny me?" I asked. "I would treat you well."

"I would rather face the king's wrath after my confession than settle as the wife of a man who thinks being a brute is romantic," she said.

"Fine. You go to the ball with me. I will carry out my investigation, lay the blame on whatever girl your attendant says has also made a deal with a demon, and call it our first team accomplishment," I held out my hand.

"I won't agree to the ball."

"I'm warning you, if you don't accept, I'll kill you. I'm trying my best to compromise."

She pushed my hand away and leaned back into my face. "I dare you."

Mori and Vesim pushed their way back into the room. It was her lucky day. I was going to grant her dare.

"We really can't wait much longer before we speak," Mori urged.

"Update," I said.

"The hounds killed the blood slave. Riven is looking for you. He wants an immediate investigation and a death to answer for the events. He's discussing how many lashings he wants for you since you weren't on the scene and allowed someone who made the deal to get past the gates," Mori said.

I looked back at her, and the veil that sat between us was beginning to piss me off. It was easy to read her body language, but the eyes told a better story. They told the story of words never said. She wasn't allowed to remove it until the selection was completed. We were told we should be marrying for reproduction, not looks. She had better be beautiful because I doubted if she had any brains after this. I was sure she was carrying an empty skull as decoration, but I'd make the exception.

I stood and pointed at the attendant. "Do not let her leave. I will be informing the king that she fainted out of fright. Heal her hand as soon as I close this door."

I let Mori out first and did my best not to slam the door on the exit. Her denial of my offer was unacceptable. If she didn't want to be my wife, she wouldn't wed anyone. Her refusal to stay alive was ignorant. She was a stupid child in a grown woman's body. If she wanted to die, who was I to stop her? If I were a gentleman, I'd give her a hand and help her die before she gave me any further headaches.

"Trouble. All of them, just distracting trouble," I growled.

"Are you talking out loud, or should I respond?" Mori glanced over at me.

"There doesn't need to be a response! It's a fact," I shook my head.

Mori nodded. "If I were to respond, I'd say your mother would approve of her. You picked well."

"Don't toy with me. You can still become a eunuch," I said.

"I know you're enjoying this strange thing you have going with her, but if you don't pull yourself together quickly, you'll lose your head before considering your next move. He is furious and blames you. He won't be any happier after you've made him wait," Mori said.

"I know. I'm thinking!" I ran my hands through my hair, pulling at it harder than I should have.

I straightened my clothing. I brushed down my gray top and took note of any place that held wrinkles. He will want to hear agreements and a plan that ends with a head. It's that simple, and we will give it to him.

"Mori, ask her attendant which room this mystery girl stays in and plant a book about demons. You must be quick to come tell me the news."

We looked at each other, but we both needed no words. He would move as fast as he could, and I would keep the wrath of the boy called king at bay as long as I could. I walked, slowly and calmly, into Riven's chamber of ego and stood, hands behind my back, in front of his throne.

"My king," I bowed.

"Where have you been? Are you unaware of today's events? Did you hope I would die?" His fist slammed into the bones he sat on. "If it weren't for the hounds, I would be dead! Speak!"

"I've already begun investigating, my king. I was there to see you had ample protection, and one of the women of selection fainted. I took her back to her room as an excuse to start my searches. I could assure you that if I thought your life was on the line, I would have stayed," I bowed.

"Or maybe you took her back, hoping it would buy time for my life to end! You set this up to end my life yourself, didn't you?" Spit came from Riven's mouth with his words.

"If I have given the impression that I do not care for my king, no, my brother's life, please assign a punishment. I deserve it. It means I've slacked in my duties. I've dedicated a lifetime to your safety, and I continue to do so," I said, eyes on the ground.

"Maybe we should consider that he is being honest," Niko said from beside him.

"Did anyone ask you to speak for him?" Riven demanded.

Niko smirked, but it wasn't clear who the look was meant for. "I have seen myself how dedicated he has been lately to investigating things kept secret."

My eyes shot to Riven, knowing Niko was going to tell him about catching me in the study. This was a perfect time to layer things against me.

"My king, prince. I've found something in one of the women's rooms," Mori ran in, out of breath and hunching down.

He outdid his record this time. He had to have guessed this would be the plan, or maybe he and Vesim had the same idea while waiting on us. There was no way he had gone all over the castle that quickly. I was grateful all the same. Today was not my day to die.

The king stormed his way to Mori and demanded for him to lead the way. I followed, getting enough behind to ease Riven into considering me a wounded child. A whimpering pup vying for his master's approval. Guards followed, entangled between us as if we were going to war or their king's life was still on the line. If I'd need to worry this hard over a blood slave, that God artifact couldn't be as strong as it sounded.

Mori threw the door open to a bedroom where a guard stood holding a woman on her knees. She wailed and pleaded before we came into sight. She begged for the guard to let her go. She pleaded for King Riven, and when she saw him, her eyes lit like she saw a true god. The way he held her life in his hands, he was the closest to a god she would meet.

"My King! You have to know it wasn't me! You know I'm innocent!" She begged.

"I know nothing. Where is the evidence?" King Riven demanded.

The guard who held her used his other hand to lift a book,

and Riven ripped it from his hands before flipping page after page. The sound of crumpled paper grew erratic.

"Innocent! Innocent?" Riven threw the book against her face. "Innocence wouldn't have a book on summoning a demon and exchanging your soul for a gift!"

"It's not mine! It's not!" She tried her best to crawl to his feet.

"You look pathetic. If your father could see you like this, he would be ashamed of what he raised. You can't even die with a shred of honor?" Riven shook his head. "Lift your head; I want to see your neck."

Riven pointed at the guard, and before she could turn her head to look, it was rolling on the floor at King's feet. The guard made such quick and smooth movements that none of us had time to interrupt. I would not have; this was going exactly as planned. When her head hit the ground, it blinked one last time, and Riven kicked it back to the guard, whose feet were being encapsulated in blood, before turning back to me.

"Find the real culprit, or I'll have yours next," he said. "If she had blood magic, she wouldn't have died so easily."

King Riven pushed past us and stood at another door, three down from the girl he had just commanded to die. He fixed his hair and ran a thumb across his lips, drying them before opening the door to Shivani's room. I knew I shouldn't have, but I followed. The thought of him being alone with her took the front of my mind.

I stopped at the doorway where her attendant stood beside a bed filled with ruffled blankets and Shivani's seemingly sleeping body. He pushed the hair away from her veil, and for a moment, I thought he would move it. Her attendant bowed and started talking to him before he could. She was clearly as concerned as I was.

"She's been sleeping. Passed out after endless sobs about a monster and saving her king," the attendant spoke.

Riven backed up. "Send word when she wakes. I want to see her."

He turned and left the room, stopping in front of me.

"I want a full investigation. I want proof. I'll kill all of them and send for a new selection before I marry a demon's bitch. Do you understand? I want her in my dungeon, alive."

"Yes, my king," I bowed.

For a moment, he looked like he had more to say to me, but he didn't. He stormed back down the hall to his wing. Shivani's attendant stepped out slowly and quietly, checking her surroundings before she moved closer to me.

"What did you do to her?" I asked.

"I gave her some tea to knock her out. She didn't want to stay put, and I didn't want the risk," she said.

"At least someone has brains," I crossed my arms.

The attendant nodded and leaned into a whisper. "It's not you."

"What?" My head shot to her.

"That was the wrong girl," she whispered.

"What did you just say," my eyes widened.

"That head on the floor back there is not the right head. It is not the girl who made the deal. It is all wrong. Do you understand?" She looked at me.

My fingers spread across my eyebrows, and I felt my skull pound. If Shivani didn't have enough to yap on about when she finally woke up, this would ensure she never stopped talking.

"How did this happen?" My teeth ground against each other.

"They all look pretty similar," Mori shrugged.

"No, they don't!" I waved my hands in the air.

I exhaled excessively before turning to Mori so we were face to face. "This has gone too far out of hand. Get your head where it should be. These kinds of things can't happen again. Today can't happen again," I said.

"Then get yourself together," he put both hands on my shoulders. "If you killed Shivani and moved on or communicated how serious it is that she does not make such rash choices, then I wouldn't be the one responsible for a death that didn't need to happen."

His face was stone, and I had to pull my eyes away first. He was right. I knew he was. I acted like a spoiled child, and he held the guilt. The attendant didn't want to look me in the eye, either. Just like that, my stomach dropped out, and a wave of shame washed over me. I was acting like my father. No, I was acting like my brother. He was seeping through, and I ignored it and hurt the people I cared about. I didn't care about killing for them. I would never think of that girl again. It was a trade worth making. I neglected the part where I hardened myself so they didn't need to.

"I'm sorry," I said.

"You know I don't need that. I need you to get it together and let me know our next move," Mori said.

Unending understanding would be his downfall. The ever-watchful man who never held a grudge because he knew people too well.

"I don't think we should move too loudly yet. We should let him move his pawn first. If he sets the pace and we follow, it will be easier to blend in," I said.

The attendant nodded, and I realized I knew less about her than anyone else. She was as quiet moving as Shivani thought she was.

"What is your name?" I asked.

"We don't—"

"Just tell me your name," I demanded.

"Vesim," she said.

"What is your ability Vesim? I mean the one you gained in the exchange," I said.

"Rift creation," Vesim said. "I can open rifts to alternate dimensions and access powers or people from other realms."

That was going to take me more than a few moments to process.

"What do you want from being here?" I asked.

"I don't want the crown if that's—"

"I want to know what you want, not listen to you assure me that our interests won't cause conflict," I said.

"I want revenge," she said.

She was still cautious, but she gave in without pushing.

"I had a father, mother, and two sisters when I was little. My father served the king well. My mother was loyal to the kitchen. A whiff of poison, and she would have given her life. My sisters were too young still to be taught well. I did my best, but it wasn't enough. I failed to protect them from a cruel boy. They ran through the halls of the castle, playing a game of chasing the Mouse. They couldn't have known a little boy was in the middle of his first attempt at killing his father. When they collided, the boy's poison was spilled out for everyone to see. My sisters were blamed, and the boy was pampered. I watched both of them die that day. They were hung outside of the castle as a warning. My mother's grief drove her to an early grave, and my father couldn't see past rage. He tried to kill the king and the boy. They all died before my seventh winter. I blended in with the rest of the children, working to clean rooms and serve meals until I was found to be skilled enough with herbs to be considered a healer and moved to an attendant. I do not want the throne. I want to find a realm with a hell that will keep your brother's soul filled with the same unimaginable pain my family went through at his hands. Even if I have to kill you."

I opened my mouth to speak, but she gave me a bow and returned to Shivani's room. Her interest was one that could align with my own well enough. If Riven's soul was what she wanted, she could have it in the end.

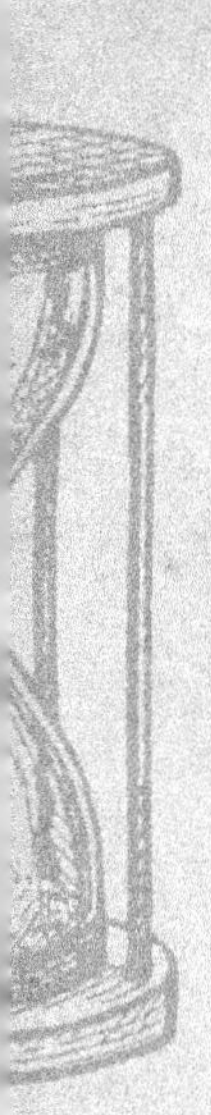

CHAPTER EIGHT

THE WALL

SHIVANI

Vesim entered my room with her eyes down like she always did. My mind felt scattered after hearing their conversation. I was going to threaten her for drugging me. I planned to get my head straight and yell at her about being a hypocrite. Now, I only thought it could wait. If I ever brought it up again at all.

"Why didn't you tell me?" I spoke low.

She looked up at me with eyes only at first. "You did not ask."

"I—"

"Either you want a partnership, or you want a friendship. They are different. We do not need to be close and share personal secrets to achieve the same goal. I don't need your pity, and I'm sure you don't need mine," she said. "All I need is to know that we agree, and at the end of this, we will kill the king."

She was a step above me in this. I didn't have siblings or friends. I didn't understand what it was to have that kind of bond. I didn't know what it was like to speak openly. She was right. We didn't need to be friends and had no reason to be. We were pushed together by fate, but how we moved forward was up to us. My mind told me to keep a distance from everyone. I only needed to do or know enough to reach the goal. My heartbeat was in a rhythm that said I wanted to be her friend.

It seems that I overestimated myself and underestimated the castle.

"Do we trust them? Or do we find this girl and kill her now?" I asked.

A lump still sat in my throat that I did my best to hold down.

"Trust will have to come later, but it would be in our interest to work together for now," Vesim said.

It reminded me that I wasn't the only one to have suffered. She wasn't either. I made the deal for revenge just like she did. I made mine to keep her story from being the regular cycle. I wanted to stop any other little girls from being hurt like I was. I needed that reminder. I needed to remember that I had a mission. I made a stupid choice, but I, no, we could come back from it. Maybe we could be friends at the end of it, too.

I opened my door back, wide and quick. Looking for the prince and his guard.

"Hey!" I called.

Mori's head turned first, giving me a look that said I was brave for yelling. I wasn't. I wasn't testing my luck out of bravery. I was testing it because there were no real consequences for me. What would he do to me? Kill me? He would miss me too much. I belonged to demons either way.

Fennic shoved me backward into the room, and after, Mori followed. Fennic was more confusing than anyone I had met so far. Sometimes, I thought he might like me. Other days, like today, he was shoving me with such force that I thought he might consider me a man. Just another body for him to demand around in the same ways his brother did.

They looked nothing alike, but some days, their shadows mimicked each other. Today, he was a close resemblance.

"Do you want to be locked away in the dungeon and starved?" Fennic's eyebrows lifted, and his voice sounded tired of me.

"I wanted to offer you a white flag. To call a truce and work together for now," I said.

"Go on," he said.

There it was again, the resemblance that made it hard for me to truly like him.

"You're right. All of us together will be better than everyone working against each other. We need to decide how to proceed with the right girl," I said.

It was hard for me to look him in the eyes when his lips were so close to mine. What was I saying about him? I can't recall. It was hard to find things to hate about him when the smell of mint was so close. He must have noticed because he stared at mine, too.

"Can you force friendship?" He asked, still staring at my mouth.

"I'm willing to try," I answered, regretting it.

"Then go to the ball with me," he said.

"I'm already letting go of the fact that you got the wrong girl killed, and I haven't mentioned incompetence on your part once. Isn't that enough of a start?" I leaned back, putting distance between us.

He snapped me back to reality—to the fact that he was just garbage trying to fit into a new wrapper. His exterior was pleasing, but the real him was a far cry from his good looks. I was clearly suffering from desperation.

"You two know we are still here, right?" Mori shivered with disgust.

"Trust me, I'm just as disgusted as you are," I said, shoving him away to finish making the much-needed distance. "I wanted the two of you here so I can offer you the truce and discuss how we need to move forward. Not talk about a ball," I looked between the three of them but decided against letting them speak. "I have poison pins. They are small and laced with a poison that kills quickly. No one is aware I have it; it will look like an accident. I can do it while everyone is busy," I said.

"How can you be sure no one will know," Vesim asked.

"I can't guarantee without a doubt that no one will know the type of poison, but I can confidently say that the chances of them knowing any girls brought it in is next to zero. It's a poison a group of bandits uses in the land of Etril. No one knows where they get it from, either. If we are caught, it won't be hard for you to shift the blame," I said, looking to Fennic.

Eyes shifted around the room, but no one spoke. The atmosphere started to boil my blood. Was Fennic's idea of teamwork giving no effort to a solution?

"Does anyone else have a better idea?" I pressed.

"I think killing her so soon is a poor choice," Prince Fennic said.

"I think letting her speak is a poor choice," Vesim said.

"Both sides are awful, but one we can control and one we leave to chance. She is right that even if it doesn't go as planned, shifting the investigation the way we want will be easy. Once she lays eggs of doubt with the king, he will let them hatch and rot. The only way to keep secrets is to bury them with the dead," Mori said.

"I'll do it then," Fennic said, holding a hand for the pins.

"I don't trust you won't use one on me when I sleep," I said.

He laughed only once. "Maybe you aren't as stupid as I thought you were. I have other plans for your death, and they don't include this type of poison."

I gave Fennic a mocking smile.

Vesim rolled her eyes. "There's a problem with this plan. The king is waiting for word that you've woken so he can check on you. He wants to ensure you aren't hysterical with worry or guilt. You cannot leave this room."

"So, tell him I am awake. Tell him I miss him and cannot wait to see if he is safe. Things can still progress," I said.

"If we are all coming clean, then we need to let her know the harem leader has been beheaded and replaced. We should also tell her about the study—" Mori casually spoke until Fennic stopped him.

"What?" I asked.

Fennic looked at me with a hint of passion in his golden eyes. "She cut your hair."

He didn't wait for my response. I was glad because I did not know how to respond to that. I didn't know how to process that he would go that far to right a wrong for me. Being in his presence was too much of a push and pull on my emotions. I thought that he would be someone I could trust to protect me. I don't think I could love him, but I trusted him to ensure I stayed alive. Other times, I was sure he was going to kill me.

There was an air of awkwardness between us all, and instead of addressing it or continuing to speak, everyone began to scatter.

Mori left to escort Vesim to the king. I tucked myself back into bed, trying to look ill. I only wanted to go back to the journal and find out what else was written inside of it. There was not near enough time alone to look through it.

I slid the journal out from the strap on my leg and flipped it to the next legible entry.

Entry 2

Dahlia created more gods. She did it without effort. She called them the deities of the seasons. They worked together to split time four ways. Spring, Summer, Fall, and Winter. They decided the final season would cover the land in a white powder. She never asked my opinion. I would have told her that having the land spend months freezing was a nonsense notion. How would her mortals eat? Did she consider special crops for such an environment? Of course, she didn't; she told me I was the one thinking too hard about it.

I didn't care to learn their names. They had a second discussion I wasn't invited to, and Dahlia created mortals next. Disgusting-looking, frail beings. They're so easy to kill that I don't see their use. Dahlia told me they would keep us company. That they could give us purpose. She said we were creating a structure of power balance, a food chain. When I challenged her and told her that she sounded foolish, she told me that all things need balance, just like she and I. If I thought differently or didn't understand it, it was because I was the fool. I wanted to know what she meant by that, but she left like she always does. I was getting tired of her always turning things back on me or speaking in riddles. She always sat on an altar too high for me to reach.

I tried again to create after watching her. I did exactly what she did. I'm supposed to have the same abilities she has. We are supposed to be equal sisters. Again, she bloomed, and I failed. I tried to create mortals of my own. All I ended with was something grotesque. They have two legs, just like Dahlia's mortals do, and they die the same as hers but stop being similar there. Mine have an extra arm here or there. Some have boils pouring a foul-smelling liquid where a head should be. They've started spreading diseases to Dahlia's precious land.

When it started killing off the plant life, she came to me. Angry that I was set out to ruin the world she was trying to create for us both. She called me jealous. What about her could I possibly have to be envious of? Her ability to forget about me? Should I be jealous of her deities? There was nothing to be envious of. When I did create my own companions, I wouldn't toss them to the side like she did with me. I would love them all. I would be the one to create the perfect world with the perfect children, and then it would be her, envious of me.

I would do it all, learn it all without her help. They would love me more and praise me louder because, unlike her, I would teach them. I would help them all.

The entry sounded as if she were describing the creatures that roamed our lands. The idea made it even harder to decide if this journal was meant to be taken as a truth or a fiction. It was a good read either way. If it were real, it gave nothing I could do anything with yet. I hadn't found anything as useful as the secret in the crypt that I was dying to dive into.

I heard the king's voice before he ever entered my room. I closed the journal and tucked it back away. He flung my door open, and I rolled my eyes under my veil until they hurt before entering the scene and becoming the girl overcome by concern about him.

"My king! Are you hurt?" I said, trying to stand.

"Stay," he commanded. "I came to see you so you may rest. Are you hurt?"

I shook my head. "As long as you're okay, I can rest," I smiled.

"Did you see anything? Hear anyone?" Riven asked.

"I thought I heard a girl's voice, but I couldn't be sure. I was looking for where she could have been or what she may have been doing when I—" I stopped myself with a whimper.

"She has been dealt with. Worry of the situation no longer, and when you feel better, you and I will spend another day together," he said.

He ran his hand across my face and lifted my veil just enough to see more of my face before lowering it back—a reminder that he still held the power. I wanted to show him I would hold the power in the end. I wanted to watch every last drop of blood pour from him. For Vesim and others like her, I swallowed my disgust at his touch and leaned into his hand instead.

"I'll do my best to recover quickly," I said.

"Tell your attendant to seek out my guard if you need anything. You may have access to anything you'd like," he said.

"I would only request access to you again," I smiled.

He was good at acting as though he liked me. He was good at acting like he had a heart. Or maybe he was suspicious of me and thought this would make me slip. I couldn't imagine a world where he took this selection seriously. Why would he? He could pick anyone he wanted, one hundred that he wanted, and it would still be agree or die. Why he even kept to this tradition, I didn't know.

Riven and his brothers were good at keeping their minds blank so I couldn't read them often, but I tried every chance I could all the same. I hated being in the dark about what he and his brother were thinking. Their thoughts were integral to my life or death. I closed my eyes and focused. There was a door, tiny and tucked away. I pushed it open slowly, as if it had a loose hinge and would make a sound.

Maybe Fennic is right. Perhaps she is too stupid to have a hand in something that would require brains to plan. When Fennic said she was hardly good enough for even breeding, I thought he had to be hiding something, but maybe he has poor taste in women. Perhaps that's why Mori stays so close to him. Fennic doesn't like women at all.

I was pulled from his mind when he moved too far out of my room. He didn't shut the door behind him. Of course, he didn't. I would count it as a small price to the larger comfort that he was convinced by my acting this time, and I'd ignore the comments made by Fennic. I didn't find him very breedable, either.

I threw my head back onto my pillow and sighed. I didn't get to finish letting my breath out before Vesim came in with a rush. She did close the door behind her.

"If you're going to run around the castle murdering, you must add Lorelai to your list. She grabbed me by the arm and held me against the wall while the king was with you. At first, I thought she was upset by the death of the other girl. Her deal is knowledge absorption. It means she can learn whatever she wants by touching someone. I felt her take information from me, but I don't know what it was or how much she got before I got her off me."

Vesim's voice was filled with more anger than I had heard before. She was usually so calm and collected.

"She does her best to be with the King. She's going to be harder," I said, sitting up.

I would have time to think about her while I took care of step one.

"I don't mean to change the subject, but—" I paused long enough to sigh. "We have to perform for the king soon. I don't know how to play an instrument, and I absolutely don't know how to dance."

"You didn't think that was important before sneaking in here?" Her eyes widened.

"I thought I would have killed Riven on the first night. By the second at most," I said.

She only gave me eyes filled with disappointment and a grunt.

"Maybe I'll pretend to be sick instead," I said.

"Maybe while ill, you will develop a bit of common sense!" She yelled.

"I'm likely at capacity, but—"

"You have more to say? How can there be more!"

I cleared my throat and left the bed behind. "In the Crypt, after I reanimated the body, there was a scroll under him. It has a map on it," I pulled it from my chest and gave it to her.

"Disgusting," she grimaced while opening it. "This is the dungeons."

"I'm going," I said when I grabbed for the scroll.

She lifted her hand in the air to keep it from me. "I don't think you should go alone."

"I thought you wanted to lay low."

"Now I have the map, and if you want to find its location, you'll have to follow me," she tucked it into her pocket.

I shrugged, "I won't mind making a sacrifice if things go wrong."

"Mm," she narrowed her eyes at me for only a second before opening the door.

Our surroundings were clear. I thought it would be the perfect time to sneak around. Everyone should have been too busy with clean-ups, attending to the king to notice us. I had a suspicion that the map was in the depths of the castle, but I wouldn't pretend I knew this place.

I followed her as silently as I could. She moved with a grace that confirmed she had been sneaking around the castle grounds for long enough that it was second nature to her. I was surprised she hadn't succeeded in killing the king herself by now. If she were after me, I would not have noticed her. The loudest part of her was her hair, which bounced in motion with her movements. It was the softest purple I had ever seen.

She turned and motioned me to move in front of her and make my way down a stairwell. It wound so far I couldn't see the bottom from where we stood. It gave me pause, and I second-guessed how badly I wanted to know what this map led to. She took the choices away from me and forced my footsteps until we were at the bottom. Her finger pointed me forward with anger, and I listened.

We stopped in front of a stone wall. I noticed before she could point it out. There were four stones that were tinted red. It was enough to make it noticeable but not enough to be suspicious in a dungeon filled with blood splatter. I didn't know where the idea came from, but it was there all the same. I lifted my fingers to the stone and unleashed blood from the tips of my fingers. It hit the stones, and without hesitation, they began to move backward and out of the way. Behind them was a box. Small and plain. There was not a hint of anything that made it look important.

I grabbed it and opened the box. Inside was a golden chain that held a locket. It couldn't have been real gold, not in such a plain box. I held it up, and if there had been natural lighting, it would have sparkled. I held it still between my fingers, and there was an engraving on it. "D+O". I turned to look at Vesim, but she was looking at it, not me. I took a breath, hoping it wasn't poison, and reached for the clasp.

"Why are you in my dungeon?"

Vesim and I screamed in unison. I watched us both leave our bodies and enter back in seconds. Without thought to consequence, my fist was in Coy's jaw.

"Terrible form," he grumbled without a flinch.

He held his hand up to stop us from talking, crossed his arms, and nodded for us to continue. I looked to Vesim for confirmation that I should. Her curiosity didn't allow her to let me pause, so I lifted it back up and popped the clasp. Inside was a worn-down drawing. It could hardly be seen. Dark purple coiled curls on one and golden hair on another was all. The necklace had to be older than we could consider or had been through too much.

The air around us grew cold, and my heart slowed in its beats. It was sure to be poisoned. The frigid air was the first sign that we had our last few moments in front of us. I was sure of it. The sight of our breath in the air was next.

"It's a shame their faces are smudged out. She is beautiful."

My fists went flying a second time, but they did not make contact with anything solid. The form of a girl stood in front of us, but she was not living. She was a pale, glowing shape. Long white hair and bangs across her forehead. Solid white eyes to match and a flush on her cheeks that added the only color to her skin. Pale in every sense of the word.

"Who are you?" My lip quivered against my will. I didn't

believe in ghosts. I also couldn't believe in my body's ability to make me look so weak at such a time.

Her lips formed a pout before she answered. "I knew it would happen, but it's still sad. My name is Hesperia, and you are Shi-shi," she held out a hand for us to shake, but I knew mine would fall through.

Her hand dropped before I could make the choice. She was sniffing the air. She moved to me so quickly I couldn't protest and was inside of my body. I felt her fill me with freezing air, and I was no longer in control of myself. I was a puppet, and she moved me to Coy.

She moved my body until I was floating to be nose to nose with Coy. Hesperia was sniffing again, using my nose to take in his scent. I didn't smell it, but she clearly did. My tongue left my lips and was on his neck. Licking up to his chin, but he hadn't moved at all. She left my body and dropped me to the ground.

"Coy!" Her voice had a giggle to it. She wrapped her arms around him, even though she clearly was not touching him the way we would. He did not move, he did not resist, and she did not slip fully through him because of it. "You haven't aged at all."

"Do we know you?" I asked from the ground she left me on.

"Sorry," her voice was sickly sweet. "I know my name and yours, but anything else is still fuzzy."

"Whatever you did to her, count me out of it. I do not consent to that," Vesim pointed to me.

I ignored her; I wanted information. "Do you recognize her, Coy?"

"No," he was quick and stern in his response.

"Okay. Well, you have to be important to be locked away like you were."

"Mhm, mhm. I was!" She nodded quickly.

"I thought you don't remember?" I asked.

"I don't," she agreed.

"We should take her back to your room," Vesim said.

"Oh!" She jumped up and down, "like a sleepover!"

"This is not what I expected to find," I stood.

"If you don't want her, I'll take her," Coy interjected.

It made all three of us turn to him, a second remark I had not expected.

She was sniffing at him again. "The scent of sorrow is so strong from you."

"Yes, we are taking her with us. We all have a lot to talk about," I said.

I tried to grab her arm, but I slipped through and stumbled forward. That was going to take getting used to.

CHAPTER NINE
THE PUNISHMENT

FENNIC

I stood, hands behind my back, in front of my brother's throne. He was being fed by Lorelai. The daughter of a farmer who was now looking at being a queen. They looked like two people playing a part and nothing more. They clearly weren't in love. Riven broke the rules and allowed her to walk around with a name already, and who would deny someone allowing them to be above traditions?

She fed him another strip of chicken, and he greedily took it. Arriving back had been an enjoyable break, not having to do things like this. I knew he would go back to normal eventually. His best behavior could only last so long, and it already lasted longer than I expected. At least I could rest on the idea that he picked his queen and would have little interest in Shivani in the future.

"The land that holds healthy soil keeps shrinking, My king. I fear soon we won't be able to grow crops at all," a councilman spoke.

My brother ignored him, undressing the girl with his eyes

instead. The first indication of any emotion felt for her, but far from the first rush of disgust I've felt for him.

"We will discuss that later," Riven said before turning his attention to me. "I want you to make a trip. The girl that just died, her family can't be allowed to create such poor-mannered children. We will hold a ball where I will announce my queen and concubine, and then you will set off to finish the judgment against her family line. When you return, you may announce your choices, so I do hope you've done more than daydream about what's mine," he said.

His face held a smile that I knew well. It was a smile that told me he had to say more, but he was waiting for me to pull it out of him. How I hated having to do it. I hated having to pull the information I hardly wanted from him. I hated having to act as if we were still children, and I was expected to make him the center of the world. He did it as if nothing in my life mattered, and I had all the time in the world to dote on him like a mother would. It filled me with a kind of irrational anger I fought to keep pushed down.

"Who will you be picking?" I asked.

"I knew you wouldn't be able to wait," he said, standing. "She will be my queen," he lifted Lorelai's hand with his own, "I believe I've heard you call my concubine Shivani?"

"I see you haven't grown enough to stop lusting after what was mine first," I spoke through gritted teeth.

"Brother, everything is mine until I deem otherwise. I would have taken what I wanted and given her back if you had only told me sooner. I suppose I still can if you'd like?" Riven smiled.

I bit my tongue and held my words. It hadn't been this hard to keep control over myself since he confined my mother to a tower.

"There is one last thing," Riven said. "Niko informed me of a thing or two, and I was just filled with curiosity, so I sent my bride to see what she could pull from you."

Touched me? I knew my face had to show my confusion because his smirk grew into a smile.

"She said you hardly noticed her in the hallways," Riven chuckled.

She was the one in the hall?

My mind raced through thoughts until it stopped on the event. She was the one in the hallway trying to get my attention while I was too distracted by Shivani. This girl is ruining my life. Years! Years I spent planning and setting things in motion, and one girl in two days managed to collapse everything.

"Unfortunately for me, she wasn't able to pull as much as I wanted," Riven pointed to Niko.

He moved to me as if he were floating. My eyes shifted back to Riven and that's when I knew what was happening. Niko took my hand and flattened it on a board he held up. A guard lifted his hatchet and lowered it onto my pinky.

In one motion, it was gone. My hand was pouring blood, and my mouth hung open, pouring a scream the same way.

"Stay out of places you don't belong," Niko whispered before he stepped back to Riven.

I would take joy in the day of his death.

I still had the shakes after an hour in the infirmary. I had a tonic for the pain; my hand was dressed with a healing salve, but none of it took the shakes away. I could not truly comprehend what had happened. Who he thought he was. Who I thought I was. Every time I would start to calm down, I would ramp myself up again.

I should have killed Niko where he stood.

"Are you ready to explain what's going on yet?" Mori asked.

I had forgotten he was there.

"Riven's bride is a dealer. She can touch you and take information," I sighed and tossed my head back. "When I went into Riven's study, Niko caught me. He told Riven. My punishment for sneaking around is this," I held up my hand. "He couldn't have gotten much from Lorelai if this was my only debt."

Mori nodded. "So, we move forward."

"We tell Shivani that Riven is taking her as a concubine. We warn her to stop making any poor choices until we get back," I said.

"Get back?" Mori furrowed his brows.

"Riven is sending us to kill that girl's family," I spoke low.

"I won't do it," Mori said.

"I know!" I lifted my bandaged hand. "But we have to at least make it look like we obeyed, or it'll be more than a pinky," I slid off the bed and grabbed my overcoat. "Where is she?"

"She's supposed to be killing the correct girl, which I guess we now know is Lorelai," Mori admitted.

I needed to find Shivani. She needed to know Riven was going to name her as a concubine. I would offer her my hand one more time. Given these new updates, she was sure to take it. She had to see that I would be the better choice unless she were into torture. No, of course, she was not. I would offer her my hand, and she would accept it, and I would protect her from him. Even if she didn't see it yet, the things he would put her through, she would thank me for marrying her.

My first gesture would be to stop her from killing another innocent girl. To be honest with the things I knew. I lost a finger, but we could still form a strong alliance.

The thoughts of how grateful she would be distracted me well enough that I was at her door before I realized it. When I opened it, she was missing. There was no sign of Vesim either. I opened another door and another, but still nothing and no one. I walked lightly down the hall of their wing. I heard no sign of life from any corner. I entered the next wing from the stairs and finally heard someone. Shivani was standing behind a girl, hands filled with all of her golden hair.

"It appears the tie holding your braid in snapped. I have an extra. I'll braid your hair again for you," Shivani said.

I watched her use her fingers as a comb and wind strands of hair back and forth like it was second nature. It only took her a moment to do it, even with the amount of hair the girl had. When Shivani finished, she held the tie-up and started looking around her. I pulled myself back into the shadows, hoping to stay unseen. When Shivani thought she was alone, she wrapped the tie at the end of the braid. She took her other hand and pulled the tiniest needle from her clothing, and in a blink, she stuck it in the side of the girl's neck and pulled it back out. Her other hand dropped the braid and scratched the spot with her nail. The girl yelled and grabbed her neck, and Shivani jumped.

"I'm sorry! My nails get away from me sometimes. Are you okay? I didn't mean it," Shivani pleaded.

The glint of the poisoned pin caught my eye, even if only for a moment. She had signed her death warrant and mine. She's going to get herself killed. I watched the girl yell at Shivani before leaving. She passed me without notice, and Shivani clapped her hands together as if she had done a great job. I was in agony, watching another thing fall apart in front of me. Maybe now I would lie; I would tell her I had no idea and threaten Mori to keep his mouth shut, too.

I was torn between moving into the light and scaring her or staying put and seeing what she would do thinking she was alone. The one thing I came to stop, was already finished. She made the choice for me when she turned her head toward the stairs leading to my mother's tower. She and I both heard the voices from the top of the stairway. Laughter and yelling. She went first, and I followed behind her from enough of a distance that I hardly kept her in sight.

I kept her close enough that I could see the way her hair shined every time it caught the light, close enough to smell the jasmine that lingered on her today. She was close enough that my heart raced, and it enraged me again. She opened the door to my mother's quarters and slowly entered. I made my presence closer to her. A woman screamed, and Shivani jumped.

"Calm down now. It's just a mouse," my mother said. "Shoo it on; it won't hurt you."

"I should have knocked first," Shivani said, backing out of the room.

"Wait!" My mother called. "Are you part of the selection?" Shivani nodded.

"You must come in," my mother motioned her to sit. "No one fills me in on things. Please tell me, has Prince Fennic found someone yet? Prince Coy hasn't made a choice either?"

Shivani laughed. "Fennic may marry Mori," she said, sitting on the edge of the bed. "Coy has yet to glance at anyone, let alone make a choice in love."

"I think he may, too," she sighed. "I'll never understand how there are two princes so stubborn."

"Fennic says he wants no wife. They're too distracting," Shivani mocked. "Coy hasn't given a reason; he hasn't given many words for anything."

My mother shook her head in disappointment but did not interrupt.

"King Riven, however, has considered so many choices that I can't be sure he will only pick two. They all dote on him as if he were a spoiled babe," Shivani said.

"Spoiled babes they are," my mother laughed.

"What are you doing up here?" Shivani asked.

"I'm just a sick old lady waiting to die," she said. "My time has passed, and I'm long forgotten."

"I have time to listen," Shivani said.

"You're a sweet girl. I'm content letting my story fade from history. It will be told so many times over; mine isn't needed," she said, patting Shivani's hand.

"If I may insert myself freely?" Shivani paused.

My mother gave her a nod.

"What illness do you have? I can tell you have some sort of blood sickness?" Shivani asked. "If you would let me, I could heal you."

"How do you know it's in my blood?" My mother asked.

"It's hard to explain. I can feel it, smell it. I can try to help you," Shivani said.

I don't know what came over me or why, but I couldn't stop my feet from pushing me into the room and stopping my mother from telling her anything else.

"Why are you here?" I demanded.

"Fennie?" my mother said.

"Fennie?" Shivani scoffed in confusion.

"You need to leave," I said.

"Nonsense, son. She is doing no harm," my mother spoke.

"Son? You're his mom?" Shivani stood and gave a bow.

"Come now, does it look like I require any of that?" his mother said. "It's been so long since I've had so much company."

"She needs to leave. I must talk with her about current events," I said.

"Well, go on then, boy, say it," my mother pressed.

"Yea, Fennie. Say it here. Your mother doesn't deserve to have secrets kept from her," Shivani crossed her arms.

I felt my nostrils flare and annoyance rise. Did she think my patience for her was unending? Did she think that just because she had the voice of a goddess, I'd let her keep yapping on? Was she so sure that I'd not toss her in the dungeon myself for fear of harming that pretty skin?

"King Riven has informed me he means to host a ball tomorrow. He will announce his queen and concubine there."

"Do you know who they are?" My mother asked.

"He means to make you his concubine," I said, not taking my eyes off of her.

"Only concubine?" Shivani sighed and sat back down on the bed.

"You mean to accept him then?" I asked.

"You ask as if I can deny," she answered.

"You could deny him if you accepted my hand before he announced his intentions," I said.

"I cannot accept your offer. I would lose my head if I denied the King what he wants," she said.

"If you knew what the king thinks of concubines, my dear, you would run. Losing your head would be a better end," my mother said.

"I'll ask you one last time," I said, holding out my hand. "Marry me, and I'll keep you safe."

She hardly gave it time to consider before she answered.

"I cannot," Shivani said. "You're only fooling yourself with this conversation. I've seen with my own eyes the King doesn't see you as a brother. He sees you as a toy. Even if you don't want to hear it, I can't lose my head with yours when he decides we're both defiant."

She stood and gave my mother a bow before leaving. If this is her answer, so be it. She will die instead. If she won't accept my offer, then death is her only path. The look my mother gave me, I could already read. She told me to go after her, and I would, but damn it if this wasn't exactly why I swore off dealing with all of this. I could not understand why she would disagree. I could offer her anything she wanted, but I wouldn't torture her as a game like my brother. She would want for nothing and live in any home she dreamt up. What else could she want?

I stood and followed her, doing my best to keep the curses I was mumbling low enough they couldn't be understood. She was practically running down the stairs. I grabbed her arm and spun her back into me so we were face to face.

"What now?" I said.

"It was clearly time for me to leave. There's nothing else to it," she said.

"You know what I mean. What else do you want?" I knew she had to feel my breath like I felt hers.

"Why do you keep pushing this? You don't want to have a wife, and I don't want to marry you. We are matched in that and can move on," she said.

"What if I did want to marry you?" I asked.

Maybe I wasn't ill. Maybe my heart was fine. Perhaps she was the cause of the sweaty palms and the racing heartbeat. I had to have an effect on her. I could feel her goose-bumped skin, and I was sure for just a moment there was a hint in her eye that said maybe she did, too.

She leaned against me until we could not meet any closer. "I'd tell you to want in one hand and piss in the other and see which one fills faster."

The smirk on her lips was my last thread. I grabbed her chin and pulled her the rest of the way to my lips. When they met and we kissed, it felt as if my heart had exploded. She didn't pull away. She pushed back with the same intensity I was feeling. I didn't get the chance to consider maybe this was all it would take for her to agree before she pulled away.

"I still won't marry you," she whispered before leaving me standing alone.

"Why not!" I yelled back at her.

She turned around and marched back to me. She laid no hand on me, but the force of her aura convinced me that she would.

"I want someone who sets my soul on fire. I want someone who does more than banter with me and call it romance. I want someone who sees me with more than their eyes. The real me and burns to know her. Someone who would sacrifice everything for our love. I won't settle for less. First, I will rule. I will be crowned Queen. Not a wife, not a concubine. I won't be second to anyone. I'll work with you, but I see it in your eyes that you would sooner reduce me to walking behind you than beside you. Now I've gotten to feel in your kiss, too," her eyes lingered on mine, searched for my silent response.

I didn't stop her this time. I let her walk away. I was left swirling in rage as much as I was in love. I trudged the rest of the way down the stairs alone. A pinch in my chest had me walking slower than usual. She was nowhere to be seen when I reached the bottom and could look in all directions. I couldn't put a word to the feeling rushing through me. It was somewhere between disappointment and sadness.

She didn't see me as that person, but she could if she wanted to. Couldn't she? I had matches if she wanted a fire to burn for her. I would have given her many things, but I could not give her my throne.

CHAPTER TEN
THE GREEN TATTOO

The Old Gods

The God of Protection was Moonlight's right hand. He was her most trusted advisor and enforcer. If there was a task Moonlight needed to be done or someone that wanted close, they had to pass through him first. Like his brother, Justice, he gave no second chances. Insanity plagued him with visions until Protection wandered to the Forest at the edge of the golden city. Once he was there, Insanity trapped him inside of the vision so that he could get close to Moonlight. Protection fought the visions of creatures until the realm fell and was split, and he died.

VESPERA

Midori was a land that grew like no other. It was always green; fall and winter didn't affect the land. Every blade of grass was as soft as the finest silk that could be bought. Their luck, however, was the opposite of their appearance. They had wonderful trade opportunities and could be a richer land than most in Cylla. If they could go more than a year or two without some sort of disaster. Midori was still recovering from the latest loss. What was left of the Timekeepers were already writing of how something came from the sky, aimed at their lands, and caused their great library of Sunlight and the island it sat on to be sunk to the bottom of the ocean.

They were still mourning the loss of everything they kept there, and so was I. I knew the blame was on Deimos. I knew the damage was on purpose. A way to keep hands off of things that would feel meaningless to mortals but give us an accurate insight into things we are missing in our own lives. I knew he had done it because he learned of the order.

It felt like a strange twist of fate when I learned that Sage had been reincarnated in Midori. She was with a family that belonged to the Timekeepers. A line connected to Lui. They lost their entire life with the loss of such a major place to earn their stay, they had little to nothing.

I couldn't sit by and watch her starve to death. I didn't know what Onyx considered looking after Sage meant, but clearly, we didn't agree on what looking after her meant. I sat on a hill behind their little cottage and waited until they left. They didn't have much, but they still kept up all of the bushes and trees surrounding their home. Every tree kept a different colored leaf on its branches.

When the two adult mortals left the cottage, I walked to it. I sat several bags of fresh, still chilled deer meat beside their door and another bag filled with seeds. They'd have enough meat to hold them off until they bloomed a garden to help support them. She wouldn't be hungry, and she would be surrounded by something she loved. Even if she didn't remember who she was right now, she would remember how much she loved being close to nature.

I turned to leave, sure I was being quick, but my cobalt blue cloak was tugged, and it stopped me. The tug was low enough that I knew who it was. My stomach twisted, and my throat bobbed. I could hardly look at her like this from a distance; I couldn't handle seeing her this close. Sahir had done so much damage; at least, she didn't remember that. I had to wrap myself in that thought as if it were an anchor to tie myself to.

"Did you come from the sky, too?" Her tiny voice asked.

"What?" I turned to her, still holding back the welling in my eyes.

The most shocking thing about seeing them like this, of experiencing what it looks like to have a goddess banished to an eternal reincarnation cycle, is that their looks don't change. She looked exactly how she would have if she had ever been a child, but she had no idea who any of us were.

"A man with green tattoos was here. He told me if I gave him some of my blood, that I could eat today. He must have meant it because now you're here with all of this!" She smiled.

"Did this man give you his name?" I asked.

I was too angry to be sad now.

"No. Next time, I'll ask!" she said. "Will you come back for it?"

"Does he come often?" I lowered myself to my knees.

"Every four days, at noon!" She responded.

"Next time, tell him he can't have any unless he gives you his name. If his name is Caym, tell him you can't share your blood anymore. Okay?"

"Oh. He is really nice! I can make more blood, anyway!" She smiled.

I shuffled her hair before getting back to my feet. I had

lingered too long, and now I needed to see Astra more than I already did.

I used a chunk of amethyst to teleport myself to 'Thann's' office in Orest. Ruri filled Erebus' caves with crystals, but she also left a separate stash for all of us. I tried not to overuse my share. I wanted as many emergencies as I could hold on to, but this occasion called for it.

Astra was in her chair at the desk of gold Thann sat at only a handful of times before the dungeon became his home. She fit in so well that sometimes I doubted who I was talking to. We all watched Astra convince Helia that she needed to pretend to be in love with Deimos, that Thann would still be waiting for her when this was all over. Astra, appearing as Thann, convinced Helia to keep working towards the title of ruler of the world. Astra had done her job perfectly.

"Vespera!" Astra called, dropping Thann's face and wearing her own smile. "I tried again today to break the lock on Yumi's secret room in the sunlight garden, but even the crystals failed. I'm out of ideas now."

"I don't have anything for that issue, but I do have information I think you'd like to hear," I pulled the velvet emerald chair in front of her desk out and sat down. "I took Sage food before stopping here, and she saw me. She told me a man with green tattoos has been stopping every four days to take her blood in exchange for allowing her food."

"Caym? Why?" Her eyebrows furrowed.

"Helia has been using up the collection of deity body parts quickly since she took the throne. We know she siphons power from them, and it's helped make her that much stronger. Maybe it's the blood? We know Yumi was doing the same thing to Ruri while she was here and that it had an effect on the tree. What if Caym is the traitor, and Helia is using Sage's blood to keep the blood guards going?" I said.

"I see the logic, but I don't believe Caym would be that

careless. That just feels like such an obvious mistake, doesn't it?" Astra stopped me before I could cut her off. "I'm not saying she was lying, but it feels like a distraction."

Maybe she was right. Maybe someone was setting him up to look like the traitor when he wasn't. Maybe someone wanted him gone, and this was their half-baked idea of getting Caym out of the way without getting their own hands dirty.

If Caym wanted to fly under the radar, if he wanted to look innocent, wouldn't this be exactly how to do it? Would this not be what he was counting on? Onyx was first on my list, but this situation was quickly moving Caym to an equal spot.

"Don't let this distract you," Astra said. "We will look into it, but we also have facts in front of us, too. Helia came with the news that she intended to kill me, well, Thann. She thinks if she kills him and then brings him back with her blood magic that, he will no longer be a counter god. That he will be free, and she will be a step closer to her goal."

"Can that really work? She still hasn't said anything of me?" I asked.

"She hasn't mentioned you a single time. No one but you and I know that you're a guardian. We will keep it that way," she tried her best to assure me.

I nodded, relieved. "What now?"

"I will investigate Caym. You keep looking for a way to get into that room Yumi has locked away," Astra said.

"All right," I agreed and left.

Astra had already talked to Juniper, and we tried everything that she had in her garden to open the lock. The only thing I could think of doing now was a visit to Owna in Erebus and ask if she had a crystal to help or if she was left with some kind of magic we didn't know about. I tried to persuade Astra to talk to Belladonna about it. Ruri gave her so many abilities that there had to be something, but Astra refused. She said Belladonna was too busy guarding Ruri. That we were not to disturb her.

I didn't care to put my full focus on breaking the lock. I wanted to be the one investigating Caym. I knew Astra wasn't letting me because of how worked up I became last time. She asked me how I knew that I was a guardian, and I rubbed the makeup off of my skin to show the deep blue vines that wrapped around my arms. They showed up while I was dreaming. I was pulled in by the tree that sat in the garden and watched Sage receive hers. When I woke up, mine were there, too. I knew Onyx had to be fake then because if mine matched hers, I should have been by her side, not him, but he kept pushing himself in all the same.

I wanted nothing more than to confront him, kill him, and remove him from the equation. Astra reasoned that they might think I was the traitor. She said I had to wait for the right time. I've slipped more than once. Sina, the Goddess of winter, told Astra in a secret gathering that in our first life, it was not Sage who had two guardians but Ruri. It led Astra to feel even more confused, but I knew. I knew without a doubt, it was Caym or Onyx.

Caym was our only confirmed guardian beyond me, and Onyx was trying his best to fit in with the same crowd; it led to a silent agreement of who the guardians must be. Caym, Onyx, Aero, and Koa. The listed agreement was that we needed to find Koa and Aero, the sisters they were supposed to be guarding while getting Ruri and Sage back. It was just another thing we were failing at.

The dragons were sure the girl from the rifts had the answers they were looking for. I trusted them the most, but if they had found some sort of answer from her, I would not have been told about it. I hadn't even been told the rifting girls' names yet.

If Caym were fake, Astra would do what she had to, to protect Ruri from him. Astra was getting pieces of her memory back, too. Not many, and not fast. She was remembering Yumi from another life, and that's why I trusted her. Every sliver of a memory that came back to her pushed her in the direction of fighting Yumi harder. That and Ruri trusted her. Who was I to doubt that?

I had finally made it to the entrance of Erebus. Usha, the stone dragon, greeted me before I realized he was present. At first, with a snarl, ready to protect what was his. After a few sniffs at the air, he was nothing more than a baby. He used his teeth to toss me onto his back and gallop into the cave mouth. My rib cage, erratically slamming against the dragon, needed more time to adjust than my eyes did. The mushrooms lit it as well, as both of the suns lit the outside sky.

"Usha, we don't play with our food! How many times do I have to tell you this?" Owna grumbled.

Usha grabbed at my cloak and used it to toss me back off of him and onto the ground in front of Owna. I happily stayed put, allowing myself to fall flatter on the ground so that I could grip my chest.

"Oh, not food," Owna said.

She shooed the rest of the dwarves away until it was only her, Usha, and I.

I pulled myself up but stayed seated on the ground. "I came to ask for your assistance."

She lifted her eyebrows, waiting for me to continue.

"I need to get past a seal, a very important seal. Nothing I have has worked. No crystal, no magic, no herb," I said.

"You have what we have. Ruri was very clear that all of the deities received the same set of crystals," Owna answered.

I sighed, only to keep myself from anger.

"If there were anything that could help that Ruri didn't already hand out openly, it would be in her temple. I don't advise you to go there making demands. The priestess left in charge, and Belladonna are the only ones with free roam there," Owna said.

"Thanks," I said.

"Come on," she said, holding out her hand. "The least we can do is get you a pint of mushroom wine so you don't leave empty-handed."

I took her hand and got to my feet. The offer didn't sound too bad right about now.

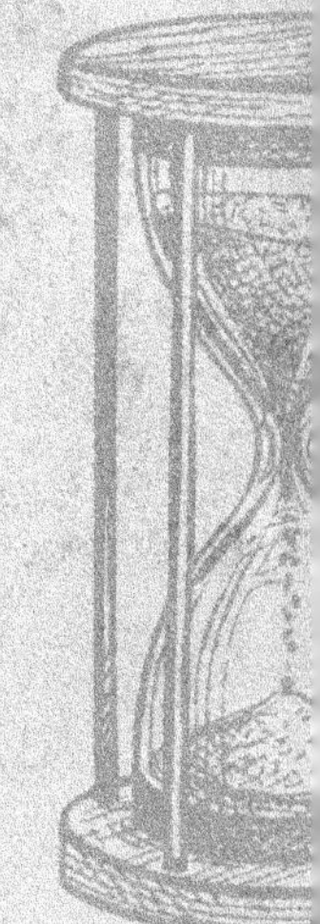

CHAPTER ELEVEN
THE GOLDEN CITY

SHIVANI

I was sure that our realm was the worst afterlife punishment. When I entered the castle, it was solidified. Being stuck in a carriage, again, with Fennic, I was sure I had dropped to a lower level, and he was the demon sent to torture me for his own amusement. He thought he was being subtle, but if I shifted my gaze upward, there he was, staring at me. He watched me if I breathed. He stared at me if I shifted in my seat. He even gawked at me if I moistened my lips. He had no shame. No manners. It was no wonder he was always sent away from the castle. It would give the king a bad reputation if his brother stared like a starved dog at everything carrying a sweet scent.

Fennic planned a date for us, unable to take any of the hints I tried my best to drop. The loud and clear no meant little to him, either. If I ignored every single detail of this day and only focused on the idea that I did enjoy feeling as though I was worth gawking at, maybe I could enjoy things. I wouldn't enjoy the day. I wouldn't enjoy it because I would not allow myself to be a notch on his hilt.

"How long have you been dead?" Fennic asked the ghost girl beside me.

"Have you been staring at her this entire time?" I asked.

"Close your mouth; it's unbecoming to let your jaw hang that far open," he remarked to me before moving his gaze back to Hesperia.

I lifted my hand to my gaping mouth without realizing it. I felt the rush of heat pass over my body. My embarrassment was boiling over. He was in awe of the dead girl next to me because, of course, he was. I had never been happier to be the only one around with the ability to read minds. This moment would haunt me for years in the late hours of the night. I wouldn't survive it if anyone else knew the thoughts I was just pouring out.

"I couldn't say. At least one hundred years, I think. At least from the look of things, I'd say it's around there," she spoke with a sadness I hadn't seen from her yet.

"Why are you here? Did you die here? Were you part of a past harem? Who put you in a locket?"

"Fennic!" I yelled. "If anyone needs a lesson on manners right now, it's you."

Hesperia stayed in my room for the entire night, and I tried my hardest not to overwhelm her with questions. I put my best foot forward and succeeded in being a good host. If I didn't overwhelm her, he wasn't going to, either. I wanted to ask her one hundred different things, too, but instead, I let her rest. I gave her the space to gather her thoughts. The only thing she did have to say to me was that her head felt foggy.

If I could behave, so could Fennic.

"Today was supposed to be a date, but Vesim is here, Coy is here, your little ghost girl is here. Things don't feel very romantic, so they may as well be diplomatic," Fennic grumbled.

"Yes, because you are usually full of romance," I rolled my eyes.

"I bet Coy is full of romance," Hesperia gushed.

"Mm," he responded.

She was leaning forward, chin on her knuckles. I could have sworn I saw hearts in her eyes. Fennic was cold, but Coy was ice. He had the defined features to set it all together. The lines in his cheekbones and jaw made him a complete picture of intimidation. I couldn't see what softness Hesperia was looking at in him. Fennic at least had softer features. He was rugged in presence but baby-faced in appearance. It was hard to believe they were related at first glance.

"Do you remember anything at all?" I asked her.

I slipped. I tried to distract myself with random thoughts, but it was a failed attempt.

"Not anything that would be useful to any of you yet," Hesperia said.

Yet? What was that supposed to mean?

The carriage came to a stop, and I was filled with relief. There were too many in a small space. Too much hot breath to breathe in and not enough fresh air. I was ready to get out and put space between us all. We were all dying to ask this ghostly girl more things than she could have answered, but I also felt as if I knew her. I was aching to ask her if she knew me.

I was the first to stumble out with no grace. The village we were in was for the rest of the royals who did not reside in the castle. It was a sight that could have been breathtaking but ended up being only rage-inducing. The streets were paved in gold. It shimmered too brightly in the sun. The homes were beyond luxurious. If we were low on resources, it was because they were all here. It was nothing like the castle grounds. They were dark, heavy. Laying eyes on the city made it clear that marrying into the royal family was a curse. The blessing was the city of gold.

Fennic looked proud when his face came into view, and I wanted to ring his neck.

"This is what you build while everyone else lives in scraps?"

"This is what they build while everyone else lives in scraps," Coy agreed.

"You're part of us,'" Fennic shot back.

"One of you has a look of pride and the other disgust. That says without words who is part of who," I nodded to Hesperia and Vesim to follow.

"This place feels familiar," Hesperia said while she sniffed the air.

"Is this where you died?" I asked.

"No, this is where I lived," she said.

Her smile was infectious. I had no reason to smile with her, but I was. The one she held across her face was so pure. She was the lightest to be near. If she carried any weight with her, I'd not seen it. Her eyes felt warm. Her smile was joyful. Some felt happy in a way that made me feel sick with embarrassment. It was a kind of energy that made things clear they were faking. Hesperia didn't have that. She was the embodiment of what it meant to be happy without knowing the truths of the world.

"So, you were part of the royal family then?" Fennic inserted.

I sighed, "Why do you insist on interrupting every time? Hurry up," I shoved. "Take us where we're meant to be."

He motioned us down a side path. I was sure everything was covered in flowers and shrubs once. The bedding was there, dug out and trimmed with wood, but nothing grew there either. Even with a town coated in gold, things refused to grow. Coy held the door open for us, and inside, we followed. A seamstress dressed in bright purple and endless dangling jewelry smiled up at Fennic as if she were accustomed to him.

"I came to pick up the new dresses for my mother and have another made," he grabbed my arm and pulled me forward. "If anyone can do the amount of work it will take to make her look decent, it's you."

"You flatter me," the seamstress bowed.

"Did you both just insult me?" I scoffed.

Fennic grabbed my arms and held them up in the air; I knew he wasn't holding me tightly. He could have gripped far harder. It still sent my heart pounding in fear. Too many times, I had been grabbed in that same place. She grabbed her string and wasted no time measuring every part of me. She spoke under her breath words I couldn't make out.

I felt as if I were back in front of the harem mistress again, and I instinctively reached for my hair to protect it. I pulled myself from Fennic in a twirl so that I faced the exit and lowered myself under his arms. I demanded my feet to carry me out quickly. I couldn't lose any more hair. It was already too short. It never should have been cut. It never should have been.

I wasn't with them anymore. I was back in that small, filthy pile of brick my mother called home for a moment, with her guests who had pockets lined with coins. I was being grabbed by my forearms and pulled this way and that again. I was being told that I had to stop being dramatic and do what needed to be done so we could eat that night.

"Shivani!" Hesperia appeared in front of me, pulling me from the spiral of images running through my mind. "I can't touch them, but I can scare them to death. Point me to who it is. I'll handle it, and you'll never have to think about them again."

My breath fell shaky, and so did my hands. She snapped me back to reality when I hadn't realized I was standing outside of it. I was lost in a jumble of thoughts and emotions, and I didn't know how to thank her for being a grounding rod.

"I'm fine. I think I'll wait in the carriage. I never wanted to be here anyway."

Hesperia followed. "You may not want to be here, but if

we're talking in the sense of a plan, it's accidentally solid. If the king knows the two of you were only gone long enough to travel and brought so many people with, then he's bound to know Fennic failed to seduce you."

"He's not great at seducing," I mumbled. I wanted to sound alright.

"You don't want to be seduced."

I nodded in silence because she was right. I didn't want to be seduced by him. There were times I thought I liked him, but more when I was sure I did not. When I did consider the options, I saw no way we could blend together. We were a team now, but when it came down to it, we would have to kill each other to complete our goals. It's better we kept our distance. As long as I did keep him at a distance, I could see nothing going wrong. As long as I did not smell him or feel his chest against me.

"Your cheeks are flushing," Hesperia whispered.

"It's getting stuffy; what else would it be?"

"Carriages can get stuffy," Hesperia mockingly agreed. "You've stopped shaking by the look of your hands," she pointed. "Even with a stuffy carriage that smells like sweaty men, you've managed to get out of the panic you were in."

She was right. There was just something about her that was calming and happy.

"Wait, I thought you were running around in a fog? How do you know anything about the king to discuss how this will work out?" I asked.

"Do you think I didn't get curious while you slept last night?" she said.

Coy opened the carriage door and pulled himself inside. The way he tilted the carriage toward him on entry made me grip the seat I was in. It was brief, but it still sent a shock wave through me at the thought of going down before he could get in. Fennic followed.

"What's wrong?" he asked.

"I just don't want to be here," I said.

"So, you'll lie to me, then?"

Coy elbowed him in the side hard enough that the exhale was audible.

"It's not a lie; I don't want to be anywhere that you are."

"Plan," Coy interjected.

"Yes, let's make a plan; that was the biggest point of today," I agreed.

"I'll keep Riven busy and happy. Hesperia can sneak around for us. Anything she brings back is better than where we started. Vesim and Shivani can see what they find in the dungeon and crypt," Fennic said.

"I'll go with," Coy said.

"Why?"

"They may need protection," Coy said.

"I can do that; it's what I do. I was born to protect. It's my middle name," Fennic urged.

"No," I rushed into the conversation. "Riven will be suspicious then. You have your own part in the plan. If Coy is with me, it will only look like courting."

Coy gave one motion of his head to signal his agreement.

Sniffing began, slow and quiet at first. It became progressively louder until the entire carriage was filled with the sound of sobbing.

"What's wrong, Hesperia?"

"I don't want to be alone again!" she sobbed.

Her tears tugged at a part of me that didn't usually shudder. I felt more than just sad for her. I felt a primal need to comfort her. A desire to hug her until I could read in her eyes that she was okay. Until she had that sparkle back. The sound of her tears made me want to nurture her in the way I imagined family members would.

"Okay, we can go together. You don't need to sneak around alone. You can come with us," I said.

"Yay!" she squealed.

"Looks like you guys have it figured out. It's good because you shouldn't count on me. I won't be around to clean up after you. I have to leave soon," Fennic crossed his arms.

"I wouldn't count on you if I were dying, and I look forward to your absence," I rolled my eyes. "You just changed your position too many times to be trusted anyway. You were born to protect; now you hope we fail."

"That's not what I said!"

"I used fewer words; it's all the same message!"

"You—" His finger was pointing at me like a knife.

I turned myself to the carriage window. I wanted to be as disengaged from the conversation as I could be. If I were to sit in this hell again, I wanted it as silent as it could get. I didn't care about the gestures he tried to make with the dress. He didn't need to bring me all this way for that. My measurements were well known.

Maybe I was the problem. Maybe he was trying, and I was just unwilling to relent and allow him an inch. Maybe it was my inability to make up my mind. The dress could have been a romantic gesture if I had given it the chance. If I wasn't plagued with random anxiousness.

The carriage hit a dip that jolted us around like rag dolls. Fennic reached his hand to keep me in place, and it ignited something inside of me again that had gone out for a moment. I was too openly vulnerable. I had slipped and allowed him to think, even if just for a moment, that I required his help. It was foolish of me. I need no help from anyone, especially not him. I hadn't come to be another notch in a boy's belt. I came up with a goal, and so did he. We could not both succeed without taking the other down. I refused to let it be me who believed he had a heart.

He could keep his gestures. He could keep his soft-looking lips. I would have him on his knees beside my throne by the end of my first year with them.

Hesperia pulled the carriage curtain back and frantically looked outside. "Stop!" she yelled.

Fennic forced us to a halt.

"Shivani and I need to get out here," she said.

"What?" Fennic asked.

"There's somewhere I need to take her," Hesperia said.

She was outside without opening the door, and all eyes were on me.

"I don't know!" I said as I pushed the door open.

"Hurry up!" she urged. "The rest of you, stay!"

She was moving too quickly for me to keep up, and when I looked back at the carriage, everyone was standing outside watching us disappear. She took me through an alley and behind one of the larger homes. We stopped at an archway made of vines. Black roses were tangled throughout. It had a mirrored appearance. Like a watery reflection.

"Go," Hesperia said.

I looked to her and back at the vines. I wasn't sure I wanted to go through, but I wasn't sure I could say no. So I listened. On the other side was a cottage. Fire sprites tended to a garden, a real garden. Trees with branches hanging over the roof housed birds. True, loud, birds.

It had to be a dream. I dozed off in the carriage.

The door to the cottage opened, and a man stood so tall he had to lower himself out of the doorway. He was as golden as the city we left.

"Is that the Sun God?" I whispered.

"I'd say he's more like the God of knowledge. If such a thing existed," she cleared her throat in a way that made me glance at her a second time.

"Come in," the man said.

I listened because if this were a dream, I was going to see where it went.

Inside, things were simple, empty. I didn't understand how anyone lived there. A small table with two chairs sat in the middle of an empty room. Golden cloth dangled from the table's sides, and I sat.

"You've come to have your fortune read?" the man took a seat on the other side of the table.

"I've come to do whatever she says," I pointed.

The man looked at Hesperia, and I began to think there were too many secrets I didn't have access to. The way he looked at her was with recognition, as if she were an old friend. Is this where she was from? Maybe this was her husband or brother?

"What is it that she wants, then, Hesperia?" he asked.

"She wants help," Hesperia said. "She has a goal that she would like to achieve at the castle."

The man nodded and held out his hand for me to lay mine in. With almost no reluctance, I did it. He drew a symbol on my palm of a sun setting behind a moon and then sliced my skin open. I pulled away from him and cradled my hand.

"What was that for!" I yelled.

"I was giving you what you asked for. I'm only a simple fortune teller, so you will have to excuse how sporadic the fragments come to you," he said.

"Fragments? Who are you? Can you be a little clearer?" I asked.

"I can't," he said. "It's likely we won't see each other again either."

"We just met—" I was cut off by the smell of smoke.

"Go," the man said to Hesperia.

A man in a black cloak stood in the doorway. I couldn't see any part of him other than his hand. He gripped a staff, tilted in the man's direction.

"I've been looking for you for a long time, Orion," the cloaked man said.

Hesperia leaned down and whispered, "Run."

Out of the corner of my eye, I saw the flames pushing

through to the interior where we stood. The cloaked man had moved far enough inside that I could get out.

I ran in time to miss the staff leaving the cottage as only ash. Sprites scattered the ground of the exit, and I tried not to look.

"Let's go!" Fennic yelled.

I grabbed his hand and let him pull me in the carriage, hardly sitting before the sound of horses pounding against the ground roared.

"What just happened?" I demanded.

"I don't know where the two of you went; we couldn't follow. We tried, but the man who could follow you in was the king's closest advisor. He's the king's prized possession. Niko does anything he would like and the King would like," Fennic said.

"Did he kill the fortune teller?" I asked.

No one answered.

"Who was he?" I asked.

"How did you get through?" Vesim asked.

"He was simply a fortune teller," Hesperia said.

She didn't answer anything further. She only left her gaze outside of the window.

<h1 style="text-align:center">CHAPTER TWELVE
THE COFFIN</h1>

HESPERIA

I was elated to start my day watching a sunrise again. Too long was spent not knowing if it was night or day. Noon or supper. It had been so long since I had the chance to admire the colors that painted the sky when it greeted or said goodnight. Pains had been filling my cheeks lately with how long I had held a smile. My mouth was too used to frowning. Nikola had taken many things from me. He helped slaughter my family and left me locked away, but he could not break my spirit. It was all I had left, and I was going to keep it whole.

The day was beautiful, the city was gorgeous. The castle, even if dark, had beauty in that. I could smell the cooks getting breakfast ready from the balcony. So much cinnamon and grease. It was beautiful, too.

I was not pleased to know I could not eat any of the things I could smell. It wouldn't be for long. I would have my body back and my sisters. The four of us would fix everything from there. The first path to cross was finding my body and hoping in my mother's name that my heart was there. I could not come back without it.

I was about to turn and leave. Just a stone's throw from waking Shivani when the best sight of them all came into view. Coy, dressed down from his usual leathers. He was instead in a half-buttoned top that hugged him well. I could hardly take in anything beyond the sight of his curly chest hairs. It wasn't fair that I was a ghost and didn't have the ability to undo the rest of the buttons. I thought I'd be able to do many more things in this form.

Coy gripped one of the wooden practice swords in the training court without mercy. The man across from him showed no fear at the sight. It was enthralling to watch. I knew what Coy was capable of better than even he knew it. The man would have been scared if he knew how hard Coy could hit. He was skilled with a paddle, as well. Oh, how I missed the welts.

Coy lunged at the man, and their wooden tips met. They went back and forth until both of them broke a sweat. I could have watched the sight of them all day.

Fennic ruined it, like he was so good at doing, when he marched his way between them shouting at Coy. His voice carried far too loudly for the conversation he was having.

"Tell me it's not true! The guards are all talking this morning. They carry on like old ladies of the harem, giggling and chatting of how they saw you and my woman one step from penetration!" Fennic's hand was a knife in Coy's sternum.

"It is not true," Coy replied.

"Where did they come up with it then? Of all the things I thought. I thought you couldn't act like—"

"Watch your words, brother," Coy said.

Fennic lowered his hand and stood silent in front of Coy for a moment. He ran both of his hands through his hair and gave a huff before he marched out with the same rage he marched in with. When they remembered who they were and what they had been through before, this may seem comical to them both. They were brothers in this lifetime, but brothers, they were not in truth.

I saw an opening, and I took it. I couldn't resist. It was because I didn't want to. I was already resisting so well. I leaped from the balcony and glided my way to the place Fennic had been occupying.

"So, there's something between you and Shivani?" I asked.

I tried to sound convinced, but I knew I did not.

"Only in the rumors meant to cause conflict," Coy said.

"I know," I smiled. "I only meant to jest."

Coy greeted me with the smallest lift of his lip before tucking it back down. It was enough to make me squeal. I reached for his face; he needed to be pinched, but I slipped through.

"Ahh, that's taken from me too!" I cried.

Coy lifted his own hand, pinched his cheek, and proceeded back to his resting position. He was still just as sweet, even all this time later.

"Can I help you with the horses this morning?" I asked.

"Have you been watching me?"

"Yes."

His usual smirk was not what showed up. His stone-still face lifted fully this time. He wore a grin so big I could see his teeth and the lines on the sides of his eyes. If I wasn't already dead, this would have been what killed me. I would have lost my eyes and my breath. He was so, so—

He was so amazing, I was angry. I wanted to hit him. I needed something to release the build-up of emotions brewing in me. All I could do with the dead body I had was sigh until my lungs were empty and hope to be whole and real again.

He filled me with more butterflies than I could handle without some sort of release.

He started walking, motioning me to follow, and I did. I didn't miss the chance to glance at the cushions he carried behind him and the way they jiggled with his motion, even in pants so tight-fitted.

"I am in charge of the guard, but I willingly take on the horses. They deserve the best care. Without them, we couldn't be half as good," he said.

I didn't respond in the hopes that he would keep speaking instead, but he did not. He picked up a brush and started to sort out the mane of a Percheron horse.

"Do you remember me?" I asked, hoping for an answer I knew I wouldn't get.

"I know that you feel familiar. You remind me of sunsets and honey," he replied.

I felt a knot in my throat. It was a better answer than I was sure he would give. He may not remember everything, but that was better than nothing.

"We used to bathe in milk and honey and watch the sunset. You used to say it was best for my skin; I was sure it was because the scent lasted until our next bath. I never argued because it smelled as good on you as it did me."

"Why do you remember this, but I do not?"

"I am dead. What holds the living does not hold the dead," I sighed. "I would give up all the knowledge in the world to feel you touch me again."

"Are you not worried I'll think you crazy?" he asked.

I shrugged, "You can think I'm anything you want as long you eventually love me again."

"If I were to believe you, when were we together?" he asked.

He looked at me with a glint of pain in his eyes. It hadn't occurred to me that talking to him, that telling him there was a whole part of him he did not recall, would hurt him. I was so sure we could have picked up where we left off, that we could have started back from the time that was stolen away from us, that I did not consider the effects on him.

I grounded myself with thoughts of him while I was

locked away. Dreams of him kept me from breaking apart in the endless darkness. Memories of him replayed as my daily life. I kept the pain of reality at bay, using him. He had nothing. He had a dead girl telling him stories and nothing to grip onto.

"I'm sorry. I was careless," I said.

I shifted realms and entered the pathway between life and death. I was out of his sight. I needed to be away from him. I had already done enough damage to him and myself. I couldn't take facing the reality that he may be lost to me.

I walked the pebbled path in darkness until I was back to the castle. I stepped back through the realm's doorway and was surrounded by castle staff again. Even without him near to see, my heart ached. My pain and I were invisible to everyone but the small fuzzy dog that sat, tail wagging at my feet.

I lowered myself and nuzzled my nose against his. They had filed his teeth until they were sharp as knives and docked his tail until it was hardly visible. The poor boy was a symbol that everyone in the castle paid a price for the ability to claim residency.

If I could not be with Coy, if I could not discuss with my sister who she was, then I needed to move to the meat of being back. I needed to find myself. I closed my eyes and looked for what others could not see: the dead.

A woman moved through the hall outside, weeping and moaning. She had the same ghostly appearance as I did, so I followed. She cried through hall after hall. She paid no attention to me while I followed her up the stairway and into a locked door. She sat, still sobbing, on a locked coffin.

"What are you doing?" I asked, kneeling in front of her.

"Guarding," she whimpered.

"Do you have a name?" I asked.

"I cannot recall it. Only that I was queen once."

"Who tasked you with guarding this?"

"My husband. He said it was the key to ascension."

"Do you know what is inside?"

She shook her head.

"My name is Hesperia," I moved her clear hair from her face. "I am the Goddess of Fate and the keeper of the in-between. You can talk to me, and no one will know anything; I will protect you."

She didn't acknowledge me any further than she had before.

"Would you like to go home?" I asked.

She finally looked at me through wet lashes. "You can free me?"

"It's what I was meant for. Say the word, and I will send you home."

"Please!" Both of her arms were on my shoulders, shaking me.

I placed my hand over her chest, and I could see her root. It was frayed and rotting.

"When I release you, you will meet a man first. He will seem cold, as all of them do, but I promise he will be the keeper of a peaceful afterlife. You will call him Caym. Listen to him. Tell him we are coming."

I released the white glow from my palm over her root, and she turned to glints of moonlight. I watched her glint and sparkle until she became nothing. It was a sight I missed seeing. When she was gone, I shoved my head through the coffin and screamed in joy. It was my body. My whole body, with my intact heart. I had found myself by accident.

Shivani was the picture of ill luck and failure, but I was only just released and accidentally solved all of my problems. I couldn't hold in my excitement.

I would tell no one. I would keep it secret and hidden until I could put together the last pieces I needed to be real again.

I took advantage of the time I had to take things in. I had spent enough time alone, but I hadn't gotten enough time to really take in the changes surrounding me. I climbed into the window seal and sat down. My dress blended and flowed with the vines that had grown to cover all of the tower.

Ruri and Sage would be devastated to see the havoc that had been done to everything they left in the realm. Their sprites were prisoners when they were meant to be keepers of the forest. Their pet lions had been turned into rugs and memories. The mammoths they gifted our father were hardly even memories.

I had hoped sitting in this window, being able to look further than could be seen on the ground, would bring me happiness. Instead, my eyes were leaking.

Realization hit me while I was thinking of Ruri. Her magic led my thoughts to the witches I taught before all of the destruction.

I entered the shadows between realms again and brought myself back to the gates of the golden city. To the hidden ends of gold, where the mass graves sat. All we could do in the chaos of the end was to take the dead and put them together. We had plans for a future burial ceremony, but we lost our lives too soon to carry it through.

I rushed to the bones hardly hidden underneath the dirt and started raising the soul attached to each bone. I hated to disturb them, but I could not know who was inside of what bone without this process.

When the realms were put back together, they could rest in Merripen like they always should have.

I did not recognize the first several ghosts, and I tried to move as quickly as I could. The next bone produced a girl. One I did recognize.

"Miss! I'm so sorry, breakfast is going to be late. Our fruits have all molded along with the vegetables, bread, I—"

I was caught off guard by her reaction. It seemed she died so soon that she hadn't realized she died.

"It's alright. I'll talk to Sage about it," I said.

I shoved her spirit back inside of her bone before she could get a hint at the reality. Another three, four, six bones and nothing.

"Oh, finally!" The man stretched.

"Sabel! It's so good to see you," I smiled.

"It's good to see you remembered us even if it took years. I better get days off for this! I want a vacation and a feast! I want more staff to help with my shop!" His finger was in my face by the end.

I quickly shoved him back into the bone and tried again. Thirty-four, thirty-five.

"Get to the armory! Now!" The man screamed.

I shoved him back inside before he could say anything else. There was nothing I could do for any of them. It was one thing to send one girl back to where she belonged, but there was no way I could do it for all of the people here. Not only did I not have the strength, but I also didn't have information about where Merripen was now. I risked sending the girl into nothing. I risked being the next reason she was wondering and weeping.

It had only taken seventy-three bones to find my witch. I knew it was her because of the way she glared at me. Openly wishing me death.

"Lily!" I cheered.

"What," she grumbled.

"I have a question to ask," I said.

"If you woke me to ask me something—"

"I need to get back inside of my body," I interrupted.

"Is Dahlia back?" she asked.

I shook my head.

"Yumi?"

"No," I answered.

"Then there is nothing to do. What is done cannot be undone without one of them. The separation of the sisters of fate means you may not use your potential," she talked as if this were a waste of her time. "Is that all?"

I shoved her spirit back inside of her bone and tossed it into my pocket. I may have a need for it at another time.

I tossed myself back into the pile of bones as if they were a bed and groaned. I cursed myself by saying things were going so easy.

CHAPTER THIRTEEN
THE BALL

SHIVANI

Vesim insisted she get me ready for the ball early so that I would stand out. It was taking so long that I thought I may fall asleep. I took the journal out, prepared to answer questions she may have on it, but she looked it over and never gave it a second thought before going back to dolling me up. It did look like any other worn-down book.

After Hesperia took me to, well, wherever she took me, my dreams were more vivid than they had ever been. I was dreaming of myself in another time and place. With people I did not know. I was beginning to feel like I was losing my mind. There was no way I was seeing myself. It had to be someone else. Someone from the journal, or maybe I was passively thinking about it so much that it was consuming my dreams.

Either way, my nights and this journal were lining up in a way that was making me question my priorities. I was slipping from the desire to take the throne from Riven, to the need to find out more information about these events.

Entry three

I found something today that I still cannot explain. It was a puddle of black water that sat between a grove of trees. I only found it because I could hear it calling for me. It used my name. It offered me a deal. It would help me create a god in exchange for my help in getting rid of Dahlia. How could I refuse? It helped me create Nikola, the god of insanity. He's unstable and has already started killing. It wasn't until after that I learned he had already been created. I learned that the black liquid was not a random occurrence, it was Nikola the entire time. He was a son of Dahlia that her children murdered. She succeeded in convincing me she was a picture of perfection, but the truth was she had become skilled at hiding her failures. Someone so perfect shouldn't have made such a mistake like him. I haven't spoken a word about my part in bringing him back.

He released demons onto the mortals and talked of how this is only the start of his plans. He wants us to create his version of paradise together. He wants to be with me like Olexei is with Dahlia. He wants to be my companion because he believes we can do it together. That he and I can have the success Dahlia was only pretending to have.

He wants me. He loves me.

Vesim was ripping and brushing like she knew my scalp wouldn't give out under any pressure. She did my hair just like my mother did my hair when she wanted to impress someone. The only thing missing was a slap of the brush on my scalp. Vesim took smaller pieces of hair and braided them before pulling them back and wrapping them into the bun she was making. She was good at making it look smooth. Two pieces of hair sat on each side of my face, and that was all. She put my veil back on and clipped it into my hair before dusting off her hands.

"Done," she said.

"Now for the worst part," I said, standing up.

Vesim pulled my dress from the closet and laid it out on the bed. I was afraid to see how many marks I'd come out with after her less-than-gentle assistance. She pulled the corset out, and it looked like a weapon to me.

"Do we really need to do that?" I said.

"Yes. You need to impress, and your pretty lips can only get you so far," Vesim said.

She didn't give me so much as a glance when she spoke. She wasted no time getting back to pushing and pulling me around. My breath got harder and harder to pull in with every lace she strung. The night hadn't begun, and I already wanted it over with.

"Can I ask you a strange question?" I asked.

"Sure?" Her voice less than convincing.

"Do you think it's a possibility that the gods were killed?" I asked.

Vesim stopped tugging at the strings for a moment, "What?"

"Maybe they were murdered? Or something happened that forced them to leave?" I continued.

"Where is this coming from?" she asked.

I could have told her about the journal, or the dreams. I could have pulled an entire other reason out. I could have showed her the journal. A part of me screamed that it was a bad idea. That I needed to protect its secrets until I had uncovered them all. That maybe she wouldn't understand.

"Never mind," I said.

"You need to pull yourself together. This isn't the time to worry about something like that, even if it were true," Vesim went back to my corset strings.

"What should I be worried about then?" I grunted.

"How to get more skin showing," she said flatly.

"My charming personality will do enough," I whispered.

"It's done you so well so far," Vesim mocked.

Vesim grabbed the dress and pulled it over my head. The

sighs she gave between mumbles while tugging at fabric were the finishing touch. I hadn't felt on parade like I did since I left my home. The fabrics were nicer, but the idea was the same. Showing off your body got attention, and attention got gold and gifts.

"Shivani?" Vesim pushed me.

"Hm?"

"What do you think? I've asked you twice now?" Vesim's brows were lifted, and her eyes shifted between mine.

I looked in the mirror, and it was an even better fabric than I gave it credit for. It was a navy blue so dark it could have been mistaken for black. A layer of black lace lay over the top with a rose design. If I moved just right, it looked like it glittered.

"It's pretty. Prettier than I'm used to," I said.

"Focus on the goal, and you will become used to unworn fabrics," she said.

Hesperia sat quietly in a chair in the corner of the room. How she could look so happy yet so sad at the same time was a mystery. I wished there was something I could do for her. Some way to get her to either rest in the afterlife or help her become real again. I didn't know where to begin trying to help her get some kind of memory back. I tried not to ask her too much or press the issue. She didn't need to feel bad and be a lost soul. One was enough.

"You could come too," I spoke to Hesperia.

"I'll come to see you, but I won't stay," she said.

"Why not? They won't know you're there, so you could dance as long as you wanted, too."

"I'd have to watch Coy with someone else; that doesn't seem like fun to me," she sighed.

The door to my room opened, and Fennic walked inside. My breath caught in my throat from the way he dressed for the ball.

"Are you ready?" Fennic asked.

"I don't remember agreeing to go with you?" I asked.

"I don't remember hearing you had anyone else to attend with?" he said.

I took his arm, and we left. The castle hadn't changed in appearance for the event. Only the amount of people walking around, and the noise was higher. The ballroom was flooded by the time we entered, and I felt nauseous knowing everyone in the room was part of the royal family in one way or another. Of course, the realm was starving. With this many mouths to feed the best supplies to, how could anyone keep up? King Riven had not shown his face yet, but a face I did recognize had me stop in my tracks. It was a face I'd never forget, with a bald head that I dreamt of slapping. My father had a woman on her arm that looked as lavished as the rest of them.

"What's wrong?" Fennic asked, his eyes searching for what I was looking at. "Do you know him?"

I shook my head.

"It looks like you know who he is," Fennic said.

"I don't," my words were rushed.

"I'll kill him tonight just to be sure," Fennic said.

The man who was supposed to be my father stopped in front of the prince and I. He looked at me as if I were a total stranger. That look is what stopped me from arguing with Fennic about whether he should stay alive.

"Prince Fennic, it's good to see you made it back. Askia is a dreadful land," he said.

"You would know," I grumbled.

All eyes shifted on me, and it was clear my father did not recognize me.

"Have we met before?" he asked.

Fennic spoke for me. "This is a bride of the selection. She is faceless and nameless until married. Even if you had, it no longer matters."

He opened his mouth to say something but stopped with a

cough. A second cough led to a choking noise. Hesperia's finger was visible through his chest. I leaned myself to the side, and she locked eyes with me but did not remove her finger.

King Riven's voice came booming from the entrance we had hardly moved from, but I couldn't take my eyes off the man in front of me. Now, nothing but the fat husband to a lady of the royal court. Watching him choke on his high society was fulfilling. When Hesperia finally moved away from him, I could see a part of him that startled me. Where the heart should have been was a root system. It was shrinking and shriveling as if it were quickly dying. It disappeared from my view as fast as it showed.

Did Hesperia do something to his heart?

"I'm glad to see you all here tonight!" King Riven called. "Tonight is to be filled with joy!"

Fennic disengaged from what was happening in front of us and pulled me by the arm I still had draped on his to the area in front of the king. The two of them exchanged looks. One of a dare and the other of determination. The king looked at Fennic as if he wanted him to do what he knew was going to happen. I seemed to be the only one unaware of what I was standing in the middle of. Lorelai clung onto the king, and when it clicked what he was doing, Fennic was already using his loudest and proudest voice.

"Tonight's celebration should be used to its fullest. Tonight, my brother and I take wives and plan weddings! Although unusual, I'd like to take the king's spotlight for a moment and announce my wife," he said.

He turned to me and tied a crimson ribbon around my wrist. His eyes never met the king again. They stayed on mine. I couldn't decide if I was a pawn being played or if I meant it when I gave a smile to the crowd and didn't take the ribbon off.

I had to have been staring at my engagement ribbon

longer than I realized because when I did look up, Fennic was looking at me in a way I had never been looked at before. Like he may have actually cared about me.

"Did you think by doing this, anything would change?" King Riven spoke. "Did you think you could embarrass me out of my choice? I rule the world, brother. I get what I want, and what I want is her as my concubine."

He ripped the ribbon off of me and tossed it on the ground at my feet. He didn't miss a beat. He was announcing that Lorelai would be his queen and I his first concubine. Whispers grew louder when he claimed a second as well. I felt trapped in the ballroom, and I had to leave. I expected to see that Fennic had followed me, but it was Hesperia.

"Are you alright?" she asked.

"I'm fine," I looked at her, wanting to keep up my demeanor, but something in her said I was safe to speak, and I didn't miss a beat. "I don't know what it is about him. He drives me crazy, but sometimes I think I might like him. That I at least may feel something for him. I swear that I'll keep my sight straight and get to the prize before I sort the mess with him out, but then he finds a way to pull me back in again. I can't focus on the idea I may marry the king between Fennic and these dreams!"

She smiled at me, "Keep to your plan. Keep a goal that does not involve him in sight. Push him from your mind. He should be last on your list. You should be waiting for someone who would wage wars in your name, not ask you to sit in the background like a well-filled vase."

Her words made me stand straighter. "You're right. I am not a well-filled vase!"

Hesperia nodded, "Exactly!" She tilted her head a bit and kept going, "Actually, I'm sure you would be a beautiful vase. Filled with the best flowers."

"Yea!" I tilted my head with her, "I think we're drifting from the point."

"You're right, you're right," she shook her head. "Can I ask about the dreams?"

"They're so real it's almost hard to consider them dreams. Sometimes when I wake up I'm not sure which is reality. It's like I'm somehow both people?" I tried to smile. "Now I sound like a crazy vase."

"I would still put flowers in you," Hesperia laughed.

Fennic appeared from the doorway. I gave Hesperia a glance before leaving her behind. She could speak to him for me.

I didn't linger. I needed the air, not just from the announcement or conversation but from my next responsibility tonight. We all had to show off a talent, and the one I was supposed to show, I knew nothing about. Vesim tried her best to show me, but we hardly had time. One thing I didn't consider in my planning was a talent show. Most girls were dancing. The girl I was impersonating played the violin. How was anyone supposed to learn that overnight?

I had gone over everything from cutting off a finger on accident to framing Fennic for poisoning me. Vesim suggested many less dramatic solutions, as she put it. The way I felt, those seemed like under-dramatic ideas to me. My heart raced harder the further back inside I moved. Lorelai was finishing her dance. Of course, she danced.

I sighed out loud at myself. That wasn't fair. Lorelai was a talentless hag. If she could have danced, why couldn't I? I shook myself from my head. No one could hear me. I don't know why I was worried. I knew I was just frustrated. I just kept telling myself I was frustrated and it would pass. Everything would go fine.

Lorelai made her way back to Riven's side, and I made my way to the center of the room where the disgusting perfume still sat in the air. It was bitter, just like her. Vesim handed me the violin, and my hands shook. I took a moment to crawl my way back into the crack of Riven's mind. I thought it may calm me. It did not; I left just as quickly when my mind was filled with thoughts of Lorelai's body versus my own.

Riven clapped, "Begin!"

Demanding bastard.

I positioned myself into the chin rest and prayed to whatever god may be listening. My hand moved the stick tip down, and the shrill sound that came was not enough to overpower the gasps surrounding me. They gripped their ears, and my attempt to make it better was to move the stick again, pulling it back. Not only was the sound atrocious, but the vibration it was sending through my wrist and down my arm was nauseating.

Riven opened his mouth to speak, so I did the only thing I could do. What anyone would have done. I moved it faster, back and forth with more pressure, trying my best to turn it into any semblance of a tune. I let my wrist take charge of my hand and fling it in any motion it pleased. I tuned into Vesim's mind, hoping to get a glimpse of what she thought. Maybe it wasn't so bad.

Dear gods, please. I know you've never done anything for us before, but just this once, could you help us? Could you come back and take my ears. I don't need them. Take all of them—the eardrum, the lobe, the canal. You can have it all if you spare me this sound.

I dropped the stick and looked her in the eye. How dare she? It may not have been the best, but it could not have been that bad.

What is she doing? Why is she looking at me? Riven is looking straight at her!

She was right. I needed to get out of her mind and into my own. My homeland used to tell stories of an animal who would play dead in the face of danger. That was all I had left. I would play dead. I dropped to the ground, forgetting to protect my head.

"Oh, uh. Ah. Oh, my," Vesim rushed over. "She's

complained of not feeling well lately. Temperature difference has been affecting her. All the excitement must have made it worse."

"Temperature?" Riven raised a brow.

"Guards!" Vesim yelled, "Help me take her back!" She gave an awkward laugh.

Riven waved his hand, and the guards followed his order. I did my best to flop my arms when they lifted me. Relief was ringing in my head. The night was done.

CHAPTER FOURTEEN

THE CREATURE

FENNIC

Shivani was sleeping so peacefully. She looked as if she could be a sweet girl if given the chance. It's unfortunate that she wasn't given and never would have an opportunity to try. Tonight, while everyone slept, she would die. If she couldn't be my wife, this was how it would have to be. Riven would take pleasure in her torture. Killing her was the last thing I could do to ensure her protection. I knew what Riven's plans for her were as soon as he said that he called for her as a concubine. Shivani was only claimed to serve as a warning to me. Her death a marked reminder of all the cards he held. I wouldn't let him do it. I wouldn't fail to protect her.

I parted her lips, and although she stirred, she did not wake. It was a shame to let such a pretty face go. An even bigger shame to lose someone who could have been trained well. She could have been formidable under different circumstances. I was worried for a moment that Hesperia would have caught me. I didn't expect to see a sleeping ghost in Shivani's room. I didn't expect to see a sleeping ghost ever.

I stuck the poison leaf under Shivani's tongue and waited

for her to start gasping before I left in the shadows. Hesperia told us that she couldn't remember her death or her life before, and Shivani wouldn't either. It meant I was releasing her from the prison of her memories and allowing her the ability to start again, somewhere new. Maybe she and I would meet again in the next life, and we could have the real chance we needed to live a life of happiness together.

It clearly wasn't possible in this lifetime, so all that I could offer her was done. Perhaps I would ask Riven if I could take Vesim as my wife. I could still protect her, and elevate her to a better status where she wouldn't have to work every day until her own death.

I had the best sleep since I arrived home after I arrived back to my room, that is, until Mori came in and disturbed me.

"He wants to see you again. He's commanded you to discuss a few things with him before leaving," Mori said.

"Has something happened?" I asked through a stretch.

"Is there something specific you're interested in?" Mori asked me as if he knew.

"He didn't tell you anything at all?" I pressed.

"Get dressed and go find out for yourself," Mori said before leaving.

I threw my clothes on with little care: a simple white shirt under a gold corset vest, tucked into black pants, and completed with my favorite black overcoat. I gave the bag I packed in advance to a guard. He knew to have it at my horse before I got there. The guard was in a better mood than Mori. It seemed Mori's attitude was always foul since we killed the wrong girl. For the last several days, he had hardly wanted to be in my presence.

When I entered the throne room, I could hardly be upset by the sight of my brother. The joy I felt knowing my biggest problem couldn't bother me anymore was so overwhelming that I couldn't wipe the smile off my face. I felt as good as I looked today.

"Fennic! I know you have a long day of travel ahead, but I just wanted you to know another girl is dead. It'll need an investigation, of course," Riven said.

It would be easy to complete. I did it.

"I'll start the investigation when I arrive back," I said.

"Before you do, though, you should know the girl that's dead had something to tell me. She said she knew something important about your little love interest. Since Lorelai has seen you going in and out of Shivani's bedroom so often, I locked her in the dungeon until she could be cleared by someone else. Lorelai thinks even if your lover is guilty, you may have too much of a bias to punish her, and I agree," Riven leaned back on his throne and crossed his arms.

Locked in the dungeon? What does he mean she's in the dungeon? She's alive? How? Why is she alive? He meant he wanted me to investigate the girl Shivani killed with the poison pin?

"I'll send Mori to conduct an investigation instead," I gritted.

"That's still too close to you, and you know it," he said with a sigh. "Anything you'd like to share with me before you go?"

That little swine. It was next to impossible to keep a defense against everything happening in this castle. Any time I thought for a second that I was ahead of one thing, another happened that was behind my back. I wouldn't speak on this, however. He had no reason to lie. If he was asking me something, it was because he already knew the answer to whatever it was he wanted. I would not be the one to give him an accidental confession. I would not be the one to give myself up.

"I have nothing to share," I said.

"Nothing about taking Shivani to the golden city and the

events that happened there? Something about a man and a fire?"

"Maybe someone is just feeding you stories like they feed you food," I said. "I would hate to think you were being used, brother."

He nodded, but it wasn't a nod of agreement. It was a nod that told me he knew I was lying. "I'll take care of the investigation. You do your job and come back home. I'll save her sentencing for your return," he smiled. "How's that hand healing?"

His smile told me this wasn't the end, that I didn't fool him. His remark made my blood boil.

I stormed out of the room and down to the dungeon. When I passed the guards, she was there. She had no veil, and her red hair was stuck to sweat along her forehead. She was even more beautiful than I could have imagined. Her skin was smooth. I didn't have to touch it to know it. Red wavy hair looked unkept but still soft.

"Shivani?" I questioned.

Her eyes opened, red as her hair, and she sat up. I could tell she wasn't feeling well, but she looked too good for the lethal dose of poison I gave her hours before. It was a shock to me. I combed through my mind over and over again for what I thought she would look like without the veil, but I never imagined her eyes would be blood red, just like I never imagined she would live longer than an hour.

She laughed through a strain when she looked at me.

"You thought you could kill me with poison? I know poisons, Fennic," she said.

"You think I did this?" I pointed at myself.

"I should have known if you weren't above killing me, you wouldn't be above lying to me," she said.

"I'll make sure you get out," I said.

"I'm seeing what your idea of help looks like, and I don't want it," she said.

"No one will hurt you. I'll get you out," I said.

"No one but you, right? You can ignore my words, but I mean them all the same," she said. "You count yourself a step above, but the man I see today is no different than his brother. He is no better than the father he claims to hate so much. I knew sharing the throne with you would have been a mistake!"

I left her there, not wanting to fully digest the words she was saying in anger. She would understand if she made it through that it was for her. It was all for her. She didn't know what her future with him held. The kinds of things he would do to her. The kinds of things he did to maids for fun. Tools I wouldn't use on my enemies. She would get it.

I skipped my normal exit routines. I'd not be gone long this time. A week, two at most. I'd get my duty to the king done, and I'd come back to her. Vesim would keep her alive. I knew she would. Not for me, but for her. I didn't believe for a second that Vesim just wanted a friend. She existed alone long enough she shouldn't need that. I could lay my faith in Vesim keeping her alive for the same reason I wanted her with me or dead. She was useful to everyone when the time was right. Having blood magic inside the castle walls, unrestricted, was as useful as one could get.

I was followed quickly by Mori and the guard. Our horses pounded the ground beneath us without mercy. I was used to taking my time on these trips. I wanted to be gone. I enjoyed being absent. This time, I was pushing my horse harder than he had been pushed before. We were covering ground quickly, but not fast enough for what I wanted.

My horse stopped in his tracks and lifted both his front legs to the sky. I nearly lost my grip. When his legs hit the ground again, and I could look behind me, all the horses were spooked. Guards lay on the ground and some clung to their horses with all the grip they had. I knew what this meant, but we were hardly far enough out for this to be a concern yet.

The part of the deal demons often kept in fine print was

that when the deal set itself in stone, you didn't just fade away in the end. Before people received their final death, they turned into grotesque, ulcerated creatures. They roam until they've served their purpose or they're put out of their misery. We still don't know what they're after, but we know they hunt for something. Mindless outside of killing and searching. Pawns of the demon king and nothing more.

I pulled my sword from its sheath and glanced at each of my sides. On my left was Mori. Propped in a tree with his bow out. He lit the spark that ignited his flame arrow. It was the last thing we needed to communicate in silence to say we were ready. We had done this too many times to need anything more than a few signs. A second creature came from the opposite side, with the speed and legs of a spider and the limbs of a human. It hissed a liquid that smelled as horrendous as it looked.

I stabbed my blade as deep as I could into the slimy mess of what could have been feet, and it oozed around me. Mori shot his arrow and missed the target. It didn't hit the blistered eye, but it did hit, at least. The creature gave a shrill cry, and I pulled my sword out. I pulled it back to swing it again. I chopped at it like it were just another tree in the woods. I would have liked to travel free and clear of any attacks, but if we were to be attacked, I was glad it was by such a weak creature. It was either at the end of its life span or the start.

Maybe it wanted put out of its misery. Either way, another insertion of my sword left it on the ground. I bent down to take a closer look. I always did. I had a fear I would miss something important if I just left it. I thought it might turn back into a person. That maybe they'd get their humanity back after death. Seeing this firsthand is what kept me from ever making the deal. I wanted to. I wanted to make that deal and kill Riven with ease. To skip all of this sneaking and planning.

The creature's body set itself on fire and left nothing but

ash in its place. The smell grew worse as it burnt. The eight-limbed creature still had Mori busy. Every arrow he shot only succeeded in stopping the thing from climbing up to him. I slammed my already too-bloodied sword into a limb, and it let out a cry. The widening of its eyes is what allowed Mori to make the fatal blow. This one didn't erupt in flames.

"Clear the area!" I yelled to the rest of the guard. "I don't want to be ambushed again!"

Metal armor clicked and clanked against men jogging in different directions. My ears were distracted, but my eyes were not. They laid on the hollowed-out bottom corner of a tree. Moss sat over it, but I could see the hole well enough to know it was there. I wouldn't have thought twice if I hadn't seen the glint of a clasp during the fight.

I lowered myself onto my knees and clawed the moss away until the book was in plain view. I pulled it out and shook off the rest of the dirt. It was in rough shape. Pages torn out here and there. It had signs of being burnt at some point. It was old enough to be written with some ink I didn't recognize. I opened what I thought was the cover.

A strange symbol lit up before words appeared on the page.

He said it was calling to him. That he could hear a voice that knew his name, his life. He said he trusted the voice. That the artifact wanted to merge with him and I persisted in my attempts to change his mind. It made little difference. He was filled with madness. Any reasoning left him when the voice said he could become a god. He told me of all the power he could hold when—

I had to turn to the next page before I could read anything else.

The entire village stood outside tonight in disbelief. We were looking forward to our fall full moon and a celebration filled with good meats. Instead, our full moon was red. It looked as if someone poured blood over the moon. Next came a shaking of the earth. The ground beneath us rumbled and shook. He said it was what had to happen for—

The way the words were written started to become sloppy.

The loss was large. Most of our village is dead. He learned it was all a lie. He was never going to become a god. He's gone, too. I fear the king will kill me when I hand him my report. When I tell him, the only thing I can give is a prophecy handed down by a goddess that didn't leave me a name. When I tell him, I have no artifacts any longer. That I gave them to this nameless goddess. All I have to give him is my life and the words left with me. She had the most angelic voice I had ever heard. She told me not to dwell on the evil some could do. That she was going to keep us from falling any further into darkness. She assured me that one day, power would be placed evenly. That soon daughters of the sun and moon would—

Everything left was burnt or written too erratically to understand.

"Sir, the area is clear," a guard said.

I nodded and tucked the book in a pocket. "Let's move. I don't want to linger too long."

I mounted my horse and made sure to locate Mori before giving a kick. We still had to cross the great serpentine bridge, and I wanted him by my side before crossing the skeletal system.

We rode for what felt like half of my life before arriving at the next landmark.

The serpent bridge shook underneath us, but it still held strong. We had to walk across and pull the horses. Walking the path of the spine was easiest; when we came closer to the end, trying to guide men and horses over the spread-out bones became a hazard. One wrong move, and we would lose more than one. If my brother had prioritized anything at all, building a real bridge would have been a nice project. He didn't travel it, so he didn't care about it.

When we were all guided off, and the horses calmed again, the area looked unfamiliar to me. It was somehow changed. Even the air felt different. When I looked behind me, they were all gone, too. No men were behind me, and no horses were chomping away at carrots for as far as I could see.

The fog started setting in, covering the ground and narrowing my line of sight to a single path. At the end of that path, a small brown home appeared. Small, round, and glowing yellow lights made a pathway. The home was made from logs, when our homes were made from stone or clay. Moss covered the roof and hung down the sides. It looked untouched, yet somehow, I knew someone was inside.

I shouldn't do it. I should not have been so curious. I didn't move my feet, but the handle to the door was in front of me a moment later, nonetheless. I would regret it. I knew I would. I opened the door and walked inside. To my disbelief, it was empty. Not a cobweb or chair in sight. No log in a fire. Nothing but stale air.

"Hello?" I called.

"Come."

The voice was strained. I understood the words, but they came out like someone was gripping her throat.

"Who are you? Where are you?" I asked.

Tree roots sprouted from the wood under my feet until they formed a full tree. Her face came next. Soft features like Shivani's even through bark.

"You may call me anything you'd like. Our time will be short, so ask well," she said.

"Why am I here?" I said.

"This realm is not what you've been told it is. I require someone to understand and become a sacrifice," she said.

"A sacrifice? You and your riddles picked the wrong person to bring here," I said, turning to leave.

When I turned to the door right behind me, it was flung so far away that I could no longer see it at the end of a hallway that just kept going. Tree branches ripped through the ground and encased my feet. They pulled me into a chair and continued wrapping around me until I was tightly entangled and nearly one with the chair.

"I do not wish to harm you yet," she said.

"Feels like it," I remarked.

"We do not have time. I must use it well. This realm is only a small piece of a whole. It is dying because it is separated. Separation was needed at the time. A god trapped was better than a god killing. My sister thought she had a perfect plan. She became too complacent, and now she is like me. Drained and looking for a way out. Do you understand?" Her eyes shifted between mine.

"Not at all," I answered.

"This is Nikola's cage. Sealed here to die or learn a lesson. Learn he chose, but not of the lesson. He planted a seed of 'demons,' but it was only him. He made a trade with a mortal, cleared them of my bloodline, and turned them into mindless creatures. Your people think demons plague you, but it is only Nikola that stirs you. The creatures roaming were once helpless mortals, now his slaves. He needs my blood to break his seal. He stole my blood but lost it. He searches. This cage has stripped him of too much. Once he was beyond powerful, now he can only use his abilities by gifting them to mortals and then controlling their moves. Do you understand mortal?" she asked.

"If you could speak normally, it would make more sense. What I'm getting is Nikola is the only one making deals and monsters; he needs you to," I paused and shook my head.

"He needs my bloodline to leave. To escape. To break the seal. To find me," she said.

"Where is it that he's trying to go, and what does it have to do with me?" I asked.

"Strangely in love, he is. I require you to find the artifact of my husband and to die for my daughters," she said. "So we can use the surge of magic to make the realm whole again."

I could only laugh. Did I hit my head in the battle? Did I pass out?

"Nikola must die, and to do that, I need a body to inhabit," she said.

"So, you want to use my body and then kill me, but you want me to be okay with it?" I asked.

"You are smarter than I recall you being," she said.

"I don't know how to respond to any of this beyond a no. Nope," I shook my head. "You picked the wrong person. I don't know your daughters, and I'm not looking to die."

"I do not need your agreement, but I would like it. I thought, as the mortal who wanted to rule, you would understand that some sacrifices are necessary," she said. "Have you forgotten the importance of protection? Have you truly forgotten who you are?"

"So even deities manipulate," I scoffed.

"If you do not agree, if this does not happen, he will take your brother's body for his own. He will kill my daughters and leave your realm empty to head to the next one. You will die in the end no matter your choice," she said. "You can accept the path that saves many or die a coward."

"If I don't have a choice, why are we here?" I asked.

"I have heard your thoughts. I have seen you with my daughters. Redemption can be yours. You can die knowing you made something right after the harm you caused," she said.

"You're implying Shivani? I did what I thought was best for her," I said.

"No matter how many times you say it, you will still not believe it," she said. "I do not need convincing of your motives. I see all of you. You did not want to concede to your brother. To share the toy you claimed as yours. I do not have much longer to be in your mind. I have another request," she said.

"Of course you do," I rolled my eyes.

"I must have my husband's god artifact. It is here with only one other. She will need to wear the ring, and I will need my husband's artifact to bring him back. Find it and give it to her guardian. He will be marked when he is found. Your time is short. When the blood aligns, what was once shattered will be whole again."

I opened my eyes, gasping for air; Mori was already leaning over me.

"Are you alright?" He shook me.

I sat up, pushing orange hairs from my face and coughing.

"What happened?" I asked.

"Your horse spooked, and you hit your head pretty hard," Mori helped me the rest of the way up.

It made sense; my head was pounding. I reached up and felt the knot near the base of my skull. It made more sense than what I thought happened. It was outlandish enough. Of course, it was something only my dreams could make up. Shivani, a goddess? Only, in my concussed state, could that be said as a statement. I grabbed Mori by the arm and pulled him into a hug. He didn't join me in laughter, but that was alright. When I had the time to catch him up on what happened in my dream, he'd laugh.

I grabbed the reigns of my horse and pulled him to follow. I needed to walk off the insanity that was pouring out of my thoughts. When we arrived at the village, and we could all have a meal instead of our travel rations, I'd feel better. We all would.

The village was on the horizon after what felt like days of walking. It wasn't, but I couldn't convince my body of that. It was quiet, empty. I'd had been there before; there were only three lands outside of the castle bounds, and it wasn't hard to know them well. Teelani was a farming village. There was always noise and children playing.

I handed my horse off to Mori and finished making my way past the entrance path. Still, there was nothing and no one. I pulled the cloth door to the leaky spout tavern open and felt relieved when the tender was wiping the counter.

"Where is everyone?" I asked.

"You best get a coverin on your face boy. Our youngins are sick, and it's spreading like shit after baked beans night. We ain't got no healers, neither. You can bet the king ain't gone send em. So less you wanna catch it, too, you best get on," he pointed to the door.

"Do you know what's wrong?" I asked before I pulled out the cloth I kept tucked in my vest and wrapped my face with it.

"Don't recon I do. Little sprouts just started droppin and we ain't got the supplies to help 'em. I reckon it could've been fine if the piece of lard king lent us anything, but he ain't gone do that now, is he? You best not stay. It's the last warnin I'm gone give ya now. Folks round here losing their babes and you look like one of them royals. Git on before you get what's comin to ya," he gave me a tisk of his tongue before walking out of my sight.

I tucked the cloth around my nose and chin; I didn't want to get sick. The streets were still empty while I walked back to my men. From the corner of my eye, I noticed a curtain pull back and a face glare at me. Did I really want to kill an entire village? It would have to come to that if they attacked. I didn't want to be here at all.

"Let's move out. Targets eliminated," I called.

Everyone lagged and looked at each other, not believing what they were hearing. I didn't want to give them the chance to talk or consider. I mounted my horse and gave a whistle before galloping back towards the kingdom.

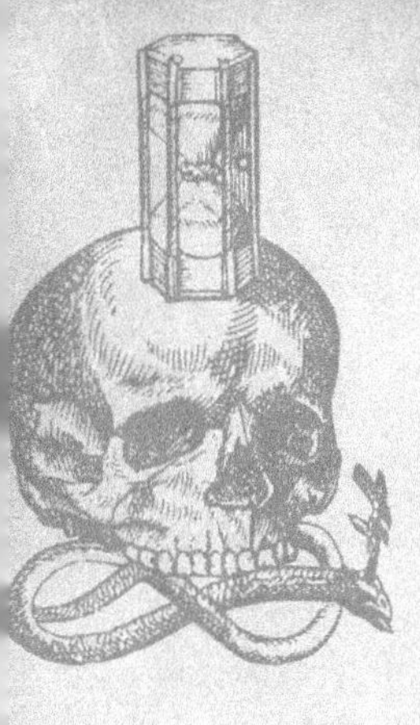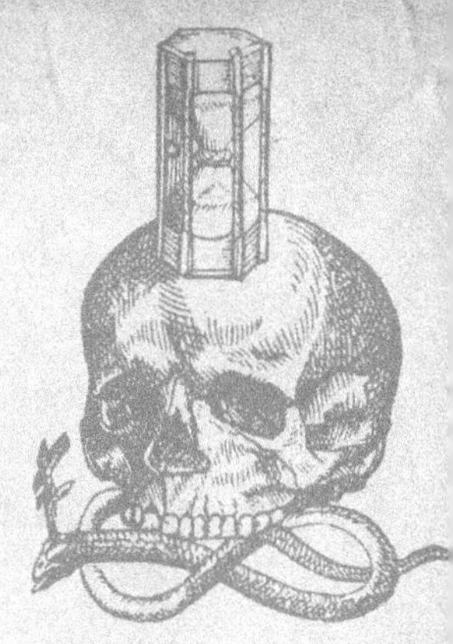

CHAPTER FIFTEEN

THE TEMPLE

The Old Gods

The God of Justice, brother to Protection, accompanied the God of the Sun. Together, they took on the affairs of the mortals. The two of them were dedicated to stopping crimes and punishing those who committed them. They established the first animal rescue and the first justice center. They reserved harsh punishments for horrible crimes and preferred to help mortals get back on track. All of their efforts crumbled when Justice left for the forest beyond their city to try and save his brother. He died beside him during the splitting of realms, but their souls were separated.

VESPERA

Astra wanted me to keep beating my head against a wall and look for a new way to get Yumi's lock open, but I didn't agree this time that it was the correct choice. It came to me, at a moment that my mind was blank, and I could do what she asked and what I wanted as well. I would go to the temple of magic in Ashbell under the cover of looking for different crystals. Instead, I would ask around about the man with green tattoos. I knew it was Caym.

I stood outside of the hot moat surrounding the temple. A narrow bridge sat, waiting for me to walk across, shimmering against the lava below. The bridge was made of golden-sheen obsidian. Three slats held it up, and although I was watching mortals walk across it, I wasn't sure I trusted it.

I took my first two steps onto the bridge. There was more stability beneath me than there had been in all of Semper. I walked with more confidence, a higher chin, the more steps I took. I closed over half of the distance when gusts of wind pushed me back from the stone temple. My eyes burned from the dry, hot, air. Cynder, the fire-breathing wyvern, landed on the flat roof of the temple with a roar of hot breath. When he was done announcing his presence, his orange spiked tail slung lava through the air like rain.

I took it as my sign to move faster, and so I did.

Inside, there was less activity than I expected to see. I had visited the temple that Helia had erected in Thann's name, and it was loud in a way that was not noise. The vampires inside were silent in words, but there were so many of them that even moving was chaos. This temple was like entering a different space than outside. It was beautiful in sight and comfort. A man and woman, drowning in their emerald cloaks, discussed something while pointing at pages in a book. Another with black scales and glowing magma veins used a rag to clean the statue of what they thought Ruri looked like. Her orange eyes shifted on me more than once in suspicion.

"Can I help you?" A voice asked.

She startled me, and my hand jumped to my chest. "I'm looking for someone I can ask a few questions to," I tried to stifle my scare.

"I am Inola," she said, holding out her hand. "The Order Of The Arcane Tome is in my care."

She held her hand out to me, but I would have rather cut my own hand off than touch her. It wasn't her fault; I truly did not enjoy physical touch.

"No handshakes. No problem. I am the priestess, and there's no question I can't answer. First, I'll need you to touch this stone," she said, holding out a piece of sodalite.

My eyes shifted from it, to her and back again.

"It will tell me your truth. You can understand that I wouldn't want to freely give information to the wrong person or deity in disguise," Inola said. "I understand you don't want to shake my hand, but I really must urge you to touch this before we can continue."

I put my hand on the stone and felt a spark. Of course, Ruri would have left someone at her temple who knew more than they should have.

Inola took the stone and put it back in a pocket of her silver and emerald gown. She didn't wear a cloak like the others did.

"Perfect. What questions do you have?" Inola asked.

"Has a man with green tattoos been seen here? Asking around or looking for something?" I asked.

She looked at me with a grin. "You're the second person to ask me that today."

"What?" I looked over my right shoulder, then my left, before jumping and being startled again. "Astra!" I tried to smile.

"Aren't you supposed to be looking for a way past that lock?" Astra asked.

"That was my next question!" I looked back to Inola. "Do you have something for a really stubborn lock?"

"I came here looking for the guy with green tattoos, too," Caym said, showing his green markings. "But I could stay to learn about this lock, too."

Inola looked at the three of us with joy in her eyes. As if today was her birthday or something of equal celebration.

"You three are in luck. He is supposed to be here today. He came looking for a special stone. He said he needed it for love. The sodalite told me he was lying. He will be coming to get a piece of fool's gold with a curse on it," Inola said.

"What is the curse?" Caym asked.

"When he walks out of this temple, he will no longer be allowed to say Ruri's name. It will burn her mouth, and he will be easy to find," she answered.

I nodded, "That's smart!"

"Thank you!" Inola gushed. "You guys wait in the room back there," she pointed us behind the statue. "You'll have a perfect view of him."

Caym put his gloved hands on each of our shoulders and moved us to the room before we could say our goodbyes. Inside, he pushed the door so only a crack was left.

"Care to explain?" He looked between us.

"We could ask you the same thing," I said.

"I came to ask the same question you did, and Vespera came to look for a way to solve a stubborn lock at Orest for me," Astra said. "It's not much to explain."

"Should we get Inola to bring that piece of Sodalite back?" he asked.

"No time!" I said as I spun them around. "He's here."

We all watched the man in a black mask and matching robe lay his hand on Inola's stone before she pointed him to the room next to ours. Another man inside of the doorway handed him a piece of what looked convincingly like gold. The man in black spoke no words that we could hear. He pocketed the gold and opened a portal to leave.

This would make things harder for me when I wanted to convince Astra that Caym had to be betraying us. She hadn't listened before, and she never would now. His being here made things look worse for him. Were we truly to believe it was chance? I did not. He was covering his tracks, and I knew it.

Caym dragged us by our shoulders again, through the portal after the man.

On the other side, there was no man. None of us spoke or needed to be told to enter when we were inside the caves of Erebus, standing in front of Onyx's blacksmithing shop.

We walked in unison inside, making it hard to go in gracefully.

To my disappointment, inside was not only Onyx but Koa as well.

"Why are you three here?" Koa asked.

"We followed someone from a temple. They made a portal here," Caym said.

"We've been following a vampire that's armed with an illusion crystal. He has been following all of us," Koa said.

"He broke into my shop and trashed the place looking for something," Onyx said. "I thought Koa could help get a message to Aero for an investigation."

"Why not ask him yourself?" Astra asked.

"I tried, but he wasn't at his headquarters," Onyx shrugged. "I thought Koa would be the next best to ask for help relaying a message."

"So this was another waste of time, then," I threw my hands up and dropped them back down until they hit my thighs.

No one spoke, and watching their faces sent me into a spiraled rage.

"Say their names," I requested.

"What?" Koa asked.

"I want each one of you to say Ruri and Sage. If it's not you running around causing a problem. If you are innocent, then it's an easy ask," I demanded.

"So you're suspicious of us?" Koa raised an eyebrow.

"You're damn right, I am! I know it is either Caym or Onyx that helped Yumi and are now helping Helia," I pointed.

"Vespera, This is—"

"No, Astra, it's fine," Caym said. "She's right. It's an easy way to clear our names."

"I'll do it, but I want to hear what's made you suspicious," Koa said.

Koa and I were eye-locked, but I couldn't tell if he was asking because he wanted to defend his friend or if it was because he was truly guilty himself.

I could hear Astra without turning to look at her. I could hear her telling me that this was not how I stayed out of the spotlight. I could have stopped, but in that moment, I did not want to.

"Sage said she saw a man with green tattoos. There's only one man with green markings. It makes sense that he would take from Sage and not Ruri if Helia needed something from her. If it's Onyx, it makes sense for him to take it from Sage. He claims to know that he's her guardian, but he has no markings, no bond, no proof. If it is him, this would be the perfect way to set Caym up to take the fall. Don't you think?" I said.

Koa nodded while he took my words in. "Ruri, Sage," he said.

"You aren't suspicious of Aero?" Onyx asked.

"No," I said simply.

"Why? He's close to Ruri," Onyx said.

"Sure, but he's not here right now, is he?" I said.

"Don't you worry; this makes you look like a traitor. Throwing blame this hard?" Onyx asked.

"I know she's not," Astra said.

"Why? Because it implicates you if she is?" Onyx asked.

The small bit of smile Astra had been doing her best to hold dropped from her face.

"Enough. Ruri, Sage," Caym said. "Just say it so we can be done."

Onyx looked from Caym to Astra but never to me. I could see he ground his teeth before opening his mouth again.

"Ruri, Sage," Onyx gritted.

"It's probably because neither of you took it out your-selves," I grumbled.

"Oh, okay, sure, another reason we are guilty after doing exactly what you told us to do," Onyx poured sarcasm.

"Or, it's one of Helia's vampires," Koa said.

"I understand, Vespera. It's better to be safe and careful than to repeat our mistakes," Caym attempted to comfort me, but I wasn't moved by his words.

"Can we move on now?" Astra asked like a mother breaking up squabbling children.

"I have other things to do. I'll leave first," I said.

I used my own teleportation crystal to leave. It took me back to the hill in Midori that overlooked Sage's mortal home. They were busy, as a family, planting the seeds I had left with them. The sight brought me the relief I needed only until a crimson robe caught my eye in the distance.

Helia stood far enough we could not speak but close enough that I knew it was her by the pronounced veins around her eyes since she started using so much magic. Another tick against Onyx. He was useless at protecting Sage.

CHAPTER SIXTEEN

THE CELL

SHIVANI

I did my best to cover up how much of a toll the poison was taking on my body. It was becoming harder to convince myself I would make it. I knew he used a poison meant to deteriorate my heart. It was cruel, even for him. I knew better than to start trusting him in any sense, and I did it anyway. The two of us could never be anything more than two people fighting for the same goal. I underestimated how far he would go for the throne. I also overestimated my ability to enter these walls and flawlessly take them over. I never truly expected him to kill me for the power of a king. He was getting what he wanted. I was dying, and he would have no one to get in his way.

I allowed myself to laugh, even if it didn't sound like a laugh. Even if it wasn't actually comical being in the dungeon. It was all I could do to fit the situation. Of course, he tried to kill me. Of course, I was locked in the dungeon while he was out and about. Why would it be any other way? He only wanted me for a prize. A way to say he won something against his brother. He didn't have feelings for me. I wasn't his one true love. I wasn't going to make him reconsider his entire life and change just for me. This wasn't a bedtime story. It was the story of another girl who gave up everything because she thought she could change a man and they could fall in love.

I could have asked for the position of jester. I should still. My entire mindset was a joke. I thought I'd march into a guarded castle and do what so many others have tried in a day or two: lay claim to the throne and rule happily ever after. I thought I'd give love a chance, and it may accept me, too. I was a fool for that, but I was stupid for believing it could happen in the short time I've been here.

I was already out of choices so soon. I didn't want to take the last path I had in front of me, but it was the only thing I could think to do. My heart was tightening hard enough that I thought every breath would be my last. I called the demon I made my deal with. I pleaded for him to show up, even if only for a minute. I only needed enough time to read his mind and offer him something in exchange for curing me. I only needed to know how to solve this problem myself. I could save myself if I were told what exactly Fennic gave me. I could.

I called again, and this time, he showed himself. He came through a portal of black from the ground; I only had a moment of relief—a brief flash of being convinced I was saved. The look in his eyes told me he was already enjoying the sight of me. Mistake after mistake seemed to be all I was good at doing since my arrival. My mother must be laughing from whatever abyss she was sitting in now.

"Why do you call?" he asked, still reeling from amusement.

"I'm dying, Niko," I said.

"I can see. Why do you call?" he repeated.

"Is there nothing you can do?" I choked back tears.

"There's much I can do, but nothing I will do. Do you think we are friends? I gave you the ability to accomplish the goal you set. You get nothing else," he said. "Would you like me to hold your hand through the entire process, too?"

"I didn't call you here—" I was cut off.

"You called me here to get you out of trouble. I had high hopes for you when I met you. I thought you were a smart girl. Smarter than that thing on the throne, at least. You grew too comfortable surrounded by lush pillows and steaming hot meals. Too casual while smelling the air of love and friendship. You forget too quickly that they don't care for you. They care what you can do for them in the moment. I won't help you because I know you can help yourself," he spoke with a straight, dead expression.

"I would help myself if I knew what he gave me. If I wasn't trapped in a dungeon!" I did my best to yell.

"Pathetic. You have so much ability wasting away inside of you," he shook his head in disappointment.

He snapped his fingers and was gone in a mist just as fast as he arrived. The only thing left surrounding me was silence. The only thing that broke that silence was the wheezing and rasping coming from my chest every breath I took.

Soon, I couldn't stop my coughing. They all began to taste like iron. His words filled me with rage, but only because they sounded so familiar. If I were to be honest with myself, I'd say he was right. I'd say I grew too soft, too fast. If I were to be forced to reach deeper, I'd say I was always soft and longing for friendship. I was always ready for the tiniest wiggle room in my mask. I would kill for someone who truly wanted to care for me. I was desperate for a genuine friendship. So desperate I'd take it from anyone, anywhere. He was right; it was a pathetic sight.

Maybe I wouldn't end up here if I had someone who cared for me. Maybe if I had received kindness from any corner, I wouldn't be so angry. It was to be my death. I would die here. With only my loneliness and sorrow to keep me company. Or, maybe if I had come here and started murdering everyone in sight from the start, I would have succeeded by now. That wouldn't have required me to outsmart so many people who were better trained than me. It would have only required me to have a stronger ability than them, and I did.

I felt tears on my cheeks, heating my skin on their way down before I spit blood on the stone. I couldn't bear to swallow anymore. All of these thoughts helped to avoid the one that hadn't stopped haunting me yet. The one creeping closer to the surface with my father's face attached to it. The one that kept reminding me he was just here. He's not that far away still, but even as an adult, I couldn't count on him to help me. He got what he wanted. A new woman and to forget about his past.

I wouldn't fool myself into thinking he was dwelling on me. That was too outlandish even for me in all of the things that I wanted to change. In all of the things I wished I could still do, being his daughter again was not it. I would have accepted help from any source, even his. That would be all I accepted. Anything else was beyond us both.

I wanted to curl into myself and let the poison take me, but before I could, I heard a whisper. It said my name. I dug my nails into the gap between two stones. The stone cut into my fingers, and I thought my nails would break. Every time I grew them out, they'd break with much less effort. I managed to get it lifted, and underneath it was a ring made of gold. The band was etched with leaves. They looked wilted, as if living out their lives and preparing for death. I held it up in the light, and it shone from every space.

"I am what once was Goddess of Fall. Wear me, sister of creation, and find the three others."

I don't know what took over me. I should have been questioning how I heard someone speak, but I slid it on my finger without a second thought. I was dissatisfied when nothing happened. Thunder sounded from outside, and I could hear the strikes, but that was the only change. I didn't expect it to be just a lost piece of jewelry.

"Shivani?"

I didn't want to look away from the ring still on my finger.

"You look like you need a healer," Fennic's mother said.

"I won't take their life from them. There's no guarantee I'd live, but there is a guarantee they'd lose their own lifespan," I said.

"Do you know what poison it is? Or who gave it to you, for sure?" she asked.

"Your son," I said, but I couldn't look her in the eyes when I did.

I was disappointed in him for her.

She sighed and handed me a box. "I have herbs that can help you. They won't cure you, and they will only lessen the pain a little. It is all I can do for you."

I took them, but a piece of me couldn't trust her enough to eat them. A piece of me questioned if she would help me, knowing her son tried to kill me, or if she was here to finish the job he started. I smelled an illness in her blood, too, and I couldn't help but think he used the same thing on me that was used on his mother.

"He's not bad. He's just trying his best to survive," she said, no longer looking at me, either.

"He does a lot of things he doesn't need to so he can survive. I'd say that makes him a bad person," I said. "He could have survived without taking my life."

"Maybe his hand was forced," she reasoned.

"I understand, as his mother, you have a kind of love for him that makes this hard for you. Thinking of all the things your son is capable of, all the things he's already done. He's not my son, though. My life has taught me when someone shows you who they are, you believe it. There is no reward for pouring all of my love into someone who can only hand me betrayal in return. I thank you for your help, I do. It won't stop me from killing your son if I live through this," I said.

She sat with me in silence for a while, and I did my best to keep looking strong while drops of sweat beaded all over me. While my heart hurt with every beat. For a moment, I thought of reading her mind, but I realized I had enough to think about. I didn't want to know what she was thinking. I didn't want to chance my last thoughts before death being hers. I wanted to remember the feeling of cool air rushing over my face while I took on the view of the water from my favorite spot.

I wanted to think of the smell that came from duck or chicken while it roasted over open flames. How they'd crackle and warm my hands at the same time. I would rather spend my last hours dreaming than awake.

"I'll do my best to have my maids bring you extra supplies," she said.

I watched her leave through blurry vision. The robe that hid her was as simple as the rest of the things I had seen her in. She was the vision of what my future was to be. Used for children and then tossed aside to live in simple silence while I watched the spawn I nurtured become the new pawns.

In my loneliness, waiting to draw my last breath, I went back to the only thing I had with me: the journal.

I wanted to know the rest of what I held if I was to die.

Entry four

Dahlia announced that she was pregnant. That she and Olexei are having children. She is carrying them in her womb. It's more than a creation. She says what Nikola and I have is not the same. She says she's carrying real children, not making monsters to roam the land. Her hatred for my happiness knows no end. Nikola says we should stick with our plan. That we can kill them so that we can take over the realm and be happy.

I love him, so I'll listen.

Entry five

War is our reality now, deep in war between each other. Dahlia and her minions have set their sights on my creations.

They call them abominations. Dahlia says Nikola and I can not keep our children. That we must stop now. I want more. I need more children. Olexei says they're not children; they're sins. He says that I can't have what they have because Nikola doesn't care for me. That if I could see past my own nose, I would be able to see the truth. I called him pathetic for trying to take the only things I had from me.

Nikola and Sahir have been working closely to kill the seasonal deities. She is a perfect daughter. She took no effort to teach. Deimos has been different. He has taken effort to keep on his path. I see in his eyes that he thinks he can do his father's job better. There's a menacing glint behind his smile. I think I can help him. He just needs more of his mother's love and less of his father's discipline.

CHAPTER SEVENTEEN

THE RIFT

SHIVANI

I was beginning to believe I would die here. I was sweating more than I thought possible, and every piece of my body that I could still feel was in so much pain I could hardly register it anymore. The feeling of sweat dripping off my nose while I shivered was all I could think about. I laid on the cold stone for the only bit of comfort I could find. When Vesim entered my cell, I thought I was hallucinating.

"Can you hear me?" she asked.

All I could do was part my lips. My hard, dry lips. I was sure I had prepared so well before coming here. I did the best I could to make myself immune to as many poisons as I could think of. If I had the strength to laugh, it would have poured out of me. So close, but nowhere near the finish line.

"I won't let you die. Hesperia and I have gone over everything we can and found a way to fix this. There's a realm I've been watching. Just trust me," she whispered.

Every part of my body her fingers touched set fire to my skin. I could feel it in my bones. Vesim opened a circle of black under us, and we dropped through. She held me tightly against her, and I couldn't stop the whimpers of pain coming from me when we hit the ground.

It was unlike anything I had ever seen in my lifetime. If I had the strength to move, I would have used it. My world was so dark, empty. Filled with death. This place was bright, and I could see flowers and grass in every direction. I had to be dead. That was the logical answer. I was dead, and this was the afterlife.

"Juniper, I need help," Vesim said.

"You cannot come here through the sunlight garden. Get her to my quarters, now," the voice said.

Arms were around me again, and I didn't have another tear to cry. When I was fully in his arms, I could see his eyes, green and brown, blended together, looking down at me. He whispered something; it sounded like a spell, and for the first time in days, I lost count of how many; I wasn't in pain. I felt nothing.

"I'm sorry," I whispered.

"For what?" he asked.

His voice was beautiful. Like a song sung to save me.

"I smell like rotted fish," I cracked out.

I heard his laugh. Sweeter than his voice was. I was surely drugged again. This place had to be packed with them.

"Have you come to take me to the afterlife?"

Maybe I was dead. I started to drift in and out. My body wanted nothing more than sleep after so much agony. I could feel my heart still struggling to beat, but it didn't hurt. I could hear Vesim and the women speaking, but I couldn't understand them. I understood that he was trying to lay me down, but it sent a rush of fear over me.

"Please, don't," my voice cracked. "I don't want to die alone."

He didn't answer, but he didn't put me down, either.

"What is your name?" I asked.

"Koa," he answered.

His thoughts were so loud that even with my exhaustion, I could hear them clearly.

She will be lucky to make it. I don't know if even the garden has anything to help her. She looks like she's been through hell, but starlight is she pretty.

"I can hear your thoughts," I whispered.

When I woke again, I was in a bed much different than my own. The blankets were softer than any I had felt before. My arm was wrapped around something, and my other hand gripping something else. When I opened my eyes, I was cuddled into something that looked like a lizard with wings, and my hand was locked in someone else's. I let go of both and sat up. It sent the creature and man into a jolt.

"Where am I?" I asked, pulling the blanket over me. "And what is that?"

The man smiled, showing sharp canine teeth. "That is a dragon. We call her Vero, and she hasn't left your side since you got here. As for where you are, this is Semper, the realm of the gods."

"A dragon?" I looked down at him. "Wait, gods? Who are you then?"

"I am Koa," he answered.

The dragon found her way back onto my legs and stretched before laying back down.

"That's your name, but who are you?" I asked again.

"I am the god of war. Who are you?" he asked.

"I'm just Shivani," I said. "Where is Vesim or Hesperia, and who changed my clothes?"

I couldn't process anything he was telling me. I needed time to think it over. He wasn't a god from my realm; they were gone.

"I did, and she will be back to check on you tonight. She and Juniper have been working together to keep a cat in your place so the people of your realm aren't suspicious," he said.

"As for Hesperia, no one could keep a grip on her once she knew you were recovering."

"A cat? How long has it been?" I asked, trying my best to ignore that he had me undressed.

"We used illusion magic, but the cat doesn't look near as pretty as you. You've only been here eight days," he said. "I should assure you I never saw you undressed. I used magic to do it."

The cat doesn't smell as good as you either.

I couldn't stop the sigh of relief that he didn't see me undressed or the flush of embarrassment that his thoughts kept flooding in.

"Eight days? I can't believe they left me in that cell for so long," I mumbled.

I can't believe it either; I haven't stopped looking at you for eight minutes.

"Care to explain? I heard bits and pieces, but it doesn't make complete sense," he said, unaware I could hear what he left unspoken.

"It's a long story," I said.

"We have time," he chuckled.

"I," I sighed and laid my hands on the dragon. Bumpy scales felt different than I expected. "It's not a long story; I just don't know what to say."

"I'll piece it together as you go," he encouraged.

"In my realm, I'm part of a bride selection to the king and both princes. Riven is an awful man. He runs our lands and people to the ground. We're running low on food, homes, medicine. Our gods abandoned us, and we're all dying. Fennic is, well, he says he cares about it, too, and we should be working together to kill the king and fix the realm. He," I paused, realizing what I was having to say out loud. "He poisoned me. He tried to kill me and left the castle. He said he would get me out when he came back, but it appears he's not in a rush," I finished.

Koa looked at me for a moment and nodded. "It seems to me you learned who to trust in the end of this."

I shook my head. What else was I supposed to do? He was right.

And I learned the names of who should be punished.

"I cannot leave my realm. Not out of duty, because my friends would not just see me off; they would join, but the rift wouldn't let me through. I cannot come to take these men out for you, but I will do what I can to help. Juniper has healed you with no traces left. If Ruri or Sage were still here, they could do more, but," he paused, and his voice cracked. "Well, our realm has some of its own problems right now, too."

The tone of his voice said whatever they were going through; he could understand what mine was dealing with. The sound created a lump in my throat. I didn't know him, but I still felt for him—felt with him.

A wave crashed over me when I took in their names. Ruri and Sage were from my dreams. Part of whoever the girl was in the journal.

"What is happening here?" I asked.

I tried my best not to sound as if I were prying, but it had to be more than a coincidence that those same names were in two places.

He stood and picked something up off a table. He took my hand and put it in my palm.

"What's happening here doesn't matter right now. You're still recovering. As for this, it's a seashell. You can talk to us through it when you go home. Vesim has one she uses, too. We tie them to you specifically so that even when you leave, I can hear you," he said. "Are you hungry? Vesim says we have the best desserts. I can also show you to the springs for a bath?" He held out his other hand for me to take.

I looked at his hand, unsure if I should take it. I wanted to. He was magnetic. Some part of me wanted to be close to him. Something inside said I would be safe with him. My mind told me not to be stupid. I would swear off Fennic and any future advances. I should learn from it and not repeat it. I should decline everything from his smile to his food. I didn't; I took his hand and felt a shock from the contact.

I was a fool who only pretended to be something more.

"You cannot be seen," he warned before we left the room. "There are Gods here that would sooner kill you than ask questions."

I was afraid at first; he walked through the doorway as if nothing were there, but I could see the barrier. I could see a layer of protection standing between me and another realm of gods. I hesitated before stepping through. I wasn't hurt, but the air even felt different on the other side. What they called the sunlight garden felt so warm, and wherever I was, I felt comfortable. The other side of the barrier felt like my own home. Heavy with hatred.

My head filled with the voice of a woman screaming for me. She had an urgency I could not resist, and against my will, I took off running. I wanted to stay with Koa. I wanted to eat. Instead, I was navigating halls I had never been in before, as if the layout was etched in my mind.

I was back in the sunlight garden where we landed when the voice was the loudest. A tree covered in pink blossoms stood in front of me, and I reached out for it. The voice called, and it pulled me in. I was wrapped in light. My palm burned like it was being etched with fire. A sun setting behind a moon showed perfectly on the skin of my hand.

A blood moon and three other girls flashed in front of me. They were faceless, but I knew them somehow. I tried to reach for them, but instead, a woman appeared. She was beautiful with a headdress covered in jewels. Dressed in lavish fabrics, I had never seen before. The colors were perfectly contrasted against her skin, which was so much darker than my own. She smiled at me, running her hand along my cheek. Do not remove the ring. Her voice rang inside of my mind. I opened my mouth, wanting to speak, but no words were allowed to exit. Tears filled my eyes, and I couldn't explain why. I wanted to speak to her, but I could not get even a rasp out.

I was pulled from the vision before I got any real answers. Before I could say anything. Who was she? Was this ring her artifact? The tree shook in front of me. It was short, but I felt it. A new branch grew from it. A branch filled with orange and red leaves unlike any others growing from the tree.

"Are you alright?" Koa asked, picking me up from the ground.

I held up my palm to show him, and we both looked in silence.

A rift opened beside us, and Vesim stepped through with urgency on her face.

"He's back. Fennic is back," she urged.

She grabbed me by the arm and pulled me through. We were both clumsy and reckless; falling to our rumps in the cell, I almost lost my life. The cat left in my place wasted no time claiming a spot on my leg, looking at both of us with disapproval.

"I was beginning to think you forgot about me," I joked.

"I couldn't have forgotten that you were where I wanted to be, too," she leaned her head back on the stone.

"How often do you go to their realm?" I asked, running a hand over the cat.

I wanted so badly to ask her more questions. To hand her the journal and allow myself to sound insane while I explained my dreams and the man Hesperia took me to. I wanted to pour it all out. There was just enough of me screaming no to win.

"At first, I only went at night. I went in secret to learn how they imprisoned their dead. I wanted to know who was in charge. Then Juniper caught me. I avoided going back for a little while. Now I go whenever I can," she smiled.

The smile on her face was one I had never seen from her

before. It was one I had only seen from a specific emotion in others.

"Why are you looking at me like that?" she asked.

I smirked, "Is there someone specific you go there to see?"

She blinked in quick succession before standing up.

"I'm leaving because I'm free to do so," she said, fiddling with the lock.

I let out a laugh, "So there is!"

I heard her grumble until she was out of sight. I felt more alive and rejuvenated than I had in a long time. This dungeon brought a shocking contrast of feelings. I was so sure it would be my final resting place. Now, I could only thank the cold stone for cooling me down from all of the excitement.

The strange thing was that I swore I knew that place. There was something about that garden that was also in my dreams. Ever since I could remember, I always dreamt of a tree with a setting sun behind it. That tree gave me the same feeling as the dream. The same feeling as the ring that now sat on my finger.

CHAPTER EIGHTEEN

The Old Gods

The Goddess of Spring was only needed for a short time. She grew bored during the other three seasons. Eternity was a long time to watch the land change and others start their lives. After watching the God of Summer start keeping records of their life, she started looking for an interest of her own. She spent time studying under Summer and learning all he could offer. She opened the Midnight Apothecary and worked alongside Fae to supply mortals with anything they needed.

MEMORY FRAGMENT

Father looked convincing at his desk. He glowed yellow, the same as the sun. His hair, to his skin. Even his smiles had a glow to them. He and I never felt close. No matter how hard I wished for us to be. We could hold conversations and laugh, but I had never seen his heart or heard his inner thoughts. Not like Hesperia did. Seeing that he trusted me with a meeting alone was a shock to me.

His office was a place I didn't frequent. It was a shame because the entire thing was made of marble and glass. I could see every bit of the sky through the roof as if it were magnified. The streaks in the marble looked more silver than grey with the way the sun reflected them. The space was almost blinding.

"I'm glad you could make it," Olexei said. "I trust you've heard the rumors?"

"There are so many lately; it's hard to know what you mean," I answered honestly.

"Today, I only want to speak of Yumi," he said.

"I have heard that she is trying to make her own fate sister to put among us."

"It would never work," Olexei said. "There can only be one in a position. If she did, you'd have to kill the other or be driven insane." His voice shook towards the end.

"It wouldn't work, not like the guardian did. She slipped them in at the right time. All of the guardians appeared together, but we are already here," I said.

"I'm glad you brought that up because I wanted to discuss the guardian that Yumi slipped in," he said.

"I've also been restless with the progress in finding who it is. As well as my sisters. Hesperia is confident that she knows Coy. She hasn't wavered, not even an inch. Ruri and Sage are different. They are having a hard time trusting their guardians. Sage even doubts her teacher, Cyrus," I said.

"And you?" he questioned.

I blinked a few times, taken back by his interest in me, but I shook it off. It was simply a question, the next logical question.

"I trust Koa. I've never had a reason not to trust him. I believe that he would do anything he had to, to protect me.

I've never witnessed any slip in his personality," I said. "Who do you think it is?"

"I think that Caym has done so well that it's suspicious. He has taken every task given and not just succeeded but flew past what we expected. I think Vespera is equally worth looking into. She often confuses me. I can't tell if she has a strong sense of duty or if she has a guilt she wants to make up for."

It seemed strange to me to doubt someone's loyalty based on them being too good or too loyal. It wasn't a stance I expected from someone I viewed as the wisest I had ever met. Maybe he was right, and there was something to it. Some sort of over-compensation on their part. Maybe he was being taken for a fool by Yumi.

"I have made a tool for you to use. It should point out who the false guardian is without fail," he said, handing me a golden rod.

"Why me?" I asked.

I was as curious as I was longing for a few kind words from him.

"You're much wiser than you give yourself credit for. You can stop time and use it undisturbed. There's no one better. Keep it safe until you are sure you can use it," Olexei said.

I pulled out a small fate box that Hesperia gave me and set the tool inside. No one would be able to open it except one of my sisters.

"If mother didn't need help with her own sister, would she have made us?"

I regretted the question as soon as it left my lips.

"You're here for much more than that. It's unfortunate timing, not your purpose," he tried his best to reassure me. "She created the four of you not to fight a battle against her sister. She wanted you as far away from that as she could get you. She created you because she believes that the four of you can be everything she hasn't become yet. She intends to hand everything to you. When your training is done, and you can manage your abilities, all of the decisions of the universe will be in your hands. The four of you will have the power to create anything or break anything, regardless of our words. Your mother believes in you four so much that she has given you everything she has and more." He leaned forward and put his hand on mine. "You may doubt anything at all, but don't doubt your mother."

I nodded and tried my best to let his gesture linger, but it made me an equal part uncomfortable and filled with sorrow. I was sure he could sense it because he removed his hand and went back to whatever it was he was working on at his desk.

I took the hint and left the glowing room.

When I was outside, back to the fresh air, Koa was already waiting. He hadn't seen me yet, but I was sure he would quickly. I closed my eyes, and this time, it had become beyond easy to stop time. I opened the fate box and pulled out the golden rod. My heart was racing, but I knew I had to be right. It couldn't be him that Yumi sent to hurt us. He was just too good.

I moved closer to him while he was frozen in time. Maybe I was as blinded as my father. I hadn't told Koa yet, but I was in love with him. I had been in love with him since he spent the entire day, without complaint, helping me build home after home for the sprites. We crafted each one by hand and painted them before he filled the trees in the fanged forest with them. I spent the evening watching him carve out staircases and hang lanterns.

I took a deep breath and held it before I placed the rod against his hand.

On contact it—

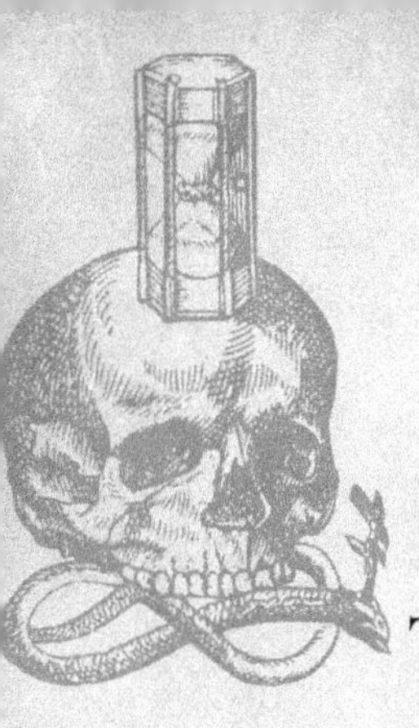

CHAPTER NINETEEN
THE HIDDEN ROOM

The Old Gods

The Goddess of Space worked closely with the Sun and Moon. She was taught how to do Starling's job that was often left unattended and created many constellations. Once she perfected her skills, she created the sky snake. Made from hundreds of colors and stardust, he protected the planets from being hit with debris. Upon learning the Goddess of Space died by the hands of starlight, he curled around their planet and refused to move. Waiting for her return, he drifted into a slumber he never woke from.

VESPERA

The discovery of the other two sisters had all of us distracted from the things we were doing before. It felt like a new breath of hope had fallen into our laps. As refreshing as it was to know that something worked out, I learned quickly that one of the sisters was going to be a bigger pain than Sage had been. It was probably the reason she was dead.

The hurt sister, Shivani, was recovering well. The other one, I could hardly keep my eyes on for more than two seconds. I overheard the group discussing that she held intact memories. That she was able to recall things better than any single one of us. I wanted to talk to her for that reason. She could confirm my suspicions. If she had memories, then I would solve the mystery of who was false today. My only problem now was getting my hands on her, so to speak.

I watched Shivani leave and Koa sulk. I couldn't be distracted by that. He would have to just sulk. Shivani left with Vesim, but not the other one. I really should have listened better to both of their names. I moved back out of the Sunlight Garden and into the throne room. I marched to the vines; maybe she was in Merripen. She was dead, so maybe it called to her. When I rounded the screen divider, she was there. It startled me, and I couldn't stop the frown from forming when her ghostly body moved through the air instead of on the ground.

"I know you!" she said.

She moved closer and searched my eyes in silence.

She sniffed at me as if she were taking in every scent I could have had for the last several years.

"I used to call you V," she said. "You used to help Cyrus with his books. You were—" she stopped and grabbed her head. "I can't remember what kind of markings you had, but I know you had them."

"I'll take your word for it," I said. "I can't remember what you do. I was seeking you out because of it. I have questions about the guardians."

"Let's make a deal," she said, perking back up.

"A deal?" I asked cautiously.

"Mhm. You take me to Yumi, and I'll answer any questions you have," she said.

"Let's start with your name," I said.

"Hesperia," she answered.

"Hesperia, something tells me you already asked the others, and they denied you," I said.

"But they aren't you," she smiled. Her hands animated everything she said.

"You aren't to kill her," I wanted to demand, but it came out as more of a question.

"If you make it part of your deal, fine," Hesperia said.

"Then it's part of my deal," I said.

"Shake on it," she said.

"How?" I asked while looking at her hand.

"Just be still," she said, forming her fingers to fit mine. They slipped through, but it was close enough to a handshake I could consider our deal binding.

I pointed her to the wall behind the throne, and she moved ahead.

"You didn't say anything about not killing the blood guards," Hesperia sang.

"That was implied!" I called back.

She ignored my comment, and I knew then that I liked her and we would be friends.

I placed my hand on the wall, in the middle of a faint blood print. It turned into a full, glowing hand the longer I held it until a click was heard, and the wall opened into a hidden room.

"Does she know you can get in?" Hesperia asked.

"No. We think only guardians can enter, but we aren't sure. We don't have solid proof because no one really wants to be in here with her," I answered.

Yumi's head hung low on the other side. The raw skin of

her wrists released droplets of blood around the fate chains. Helia and Deimos had shown her no mercy. Her back held lash marks, and her skin lacked any color.

"Fitting that the first daughter of fate to visit me is the one of death," Yumi's voice was dry and cracked.

"I couldn't miss such a beautiful sight, Yumi," Hesperia said.

She walked closer and lowered herself onto her knees in front of Yumi. Hesperia tilted her head until it was underneath Yumi's hair, and she could see her face.

"Say the word, starlight, and I'll set you free. Release the spell on the tree, or tell me how, and all of this is over," Hesperia whispered.

"You said you wouldn't kill her," I inserted.

"And I won't, V," Hesperia answered.

"Hesperia, you aren't stupid. You couldn't have thought this would work. If I'm to go, she will go with me, and so will all of you girls," Yumi said.

"So be it, Aunty. For my mother's sake, I wanted to give you one last, clear chance," Hesperia said.

"You aren't good enough to kill me." Yumi laughed. "Why would I be scared of you?"

"I haven't had the chance to try yet, Aunty. It's not fair that you write me off already!" Hesperia sighed. "I've never considered you a threat."

"That's why your mother is a tree, your father is dead, and your sisters are useless and halfway to their graves, too," Yumi spat.

"Wrong," Hesperia's voice grew colder. "This is going on because even roaches get one good chance to sneak around in the dark. You made it to where you are now, not because you're smarter than any of us. Not because you're skilled, but because Nikola did every piece of heavy lifting, and you cut his legs out from under him at the last moment."

"It doesn't matter to me how you want to frame it," Yumi gritted.

"Tell me how to get her out," Hesperia repeated.

"Free me, and I will," Yumi answered.

"How about you tell me, or I start shaving your skin off like it's getting ready for dinner," Hesperia said.

I was beginning to truly regret bringing her here. I should have been much more specific in our deal because something told me she was going to look at me and say a heartbeat is a heartbeat, so she didn't kill Yumi.

The sound of blood guard boots hitting the ground grew too close, too quickly.

"Hesperia, we need to go now," I urged as I left the room.

It was too late. There were six armed and ready-to-fight blood guards crowding both sides of the throne, making getting out impossible. I let out a groan and threw my head back. I reached my hand behind my back and hit the clasp that held my axe in place, letting it drop into my grip before pulling it back around. The blade was already prepped with poison on all sides.

"You can do it!" Hesperia cheered.

I closed my eyes and told myself she was only trying to be supportive before I took the first swing at a blood guard. His head left his body, but it only made the two on each side of him lunge for me with more fury. I lowered myself and rolled between the legs of one, allowing them to crash, face to face, into each other. Before I could recover from the tuck and roll, another guard was bringing their sword down for my neck.

I rolled onto my back and sat my feet flat on the floor to help give the force I needed to slide myself under his legs. I raised my axe to cut his groin on my slide-through.

It had worked, and that made two of the six down. I was careless all the same and allowed myself to be grabbed by a handful of my hair and lifted onto my tiptoes. He threw his head back, letting me know he planned to use his own skull to bash mine in.

I raced through ideas in my mind as quickly as I could, and I remembered the small knife I kept on my hip. I pulled it out and shoved it in the gap of armor at his armpit, and he dropped my hair.

Three gone, three to go.

I rested on one knee for a moment while they walked towards me. I tried to slow my breathing while I watched their feet move. When they were an arm's length away, I swung my axe again through all four thighs. I stood while they dropped and took both heads next.

The last guard became more aggressive in his movements and pulled one of the swords from a dead guard, so he was dual-wielding. He tossed the blades at me as if I were a fish he wanted to fillet. He sliced my upper arm, then my thigh. When I thought I had dodged well enough, another slice hit my stomach.

"Come on!" Hesperia yelled.

"I'm doing my best!" I called back.

"Your best is awful now! Do better!" she mocked.

"Oh yeah, sure! No problem!" I yelled back.

My arm wound was hardly noticeable. My thigh only hurt when I moved my leg, but my stomach felt deep enough to need stitches. I had to end this now before the adrenaline wore off. I lifted my axe as if I was going to swing from the left and waited for him to raise a block to swing it right. Hesperia interjected and shoved herself into his face, startling him. I clicked my tongue in disapproval but still swung for his neck. When she moved, he dropped, and it was over.

I sat in the middle of them, gripping my midsection. Relief flooded over me.

"Are you alright?" Hesperia asked. "You can't die at our first meeting; they'll never let me forget it."

I shook my head and reached into my pocket. I pulled out

a small bag of salve to smear on the wound. I always kept ash tree healing salve on me, just in case. I had been saving this to use when I killed Caym or Onyx, but now would have to be a good time.

"So, who is the fake guardian?" I asked.

"Has that been your question this whole time?" Hesperia didn't hold back her laughter.

"Shouldn't you know if you have all these memories?" I asked.

"The problem is, we never found out before we all lost. I remember you and Onyx. I remember Caym and Koa. If I knew, beyond a doubt, who it was, don't you think they'd be dead already?" Hesperia was still laughing.

"I almost died helping you, and you don't even have the answer I needed," I scoffed.

"We bonded while getting rid of Helia's guards, yes," she agreed.

"If you weren't already dead, I'd kill you myself," I shook my head. "You aren't even going to help me clean this up."

"I would, if I could, but ghost hands make it hard. I can keep watch!"

"At least that confirms who the guardians are," I said.

"You and Caym, Onyx and Koa, then there is Coy," she said.

"Coy is?" I twirled my hands in an attempt to get her to give full details the first time around.

"Coy is my guardian," she answered. She was still in no rush.

"How do you know it's not him?" I asked.

"I just know," she said.

"That's not proof," I remarked.

"I know that it's not him because he is in the other realm with me. He can't be a traitor when the traitor is clearly causing all of these problems here for the rest of you," she pointed.

"Fine," I relented. "You really can't help me clean any of this up?"

"I cannot," she tried her best to sound sad, but her smile made my eyes twitch.

"Looks like I'll get started, then," I mumbled.

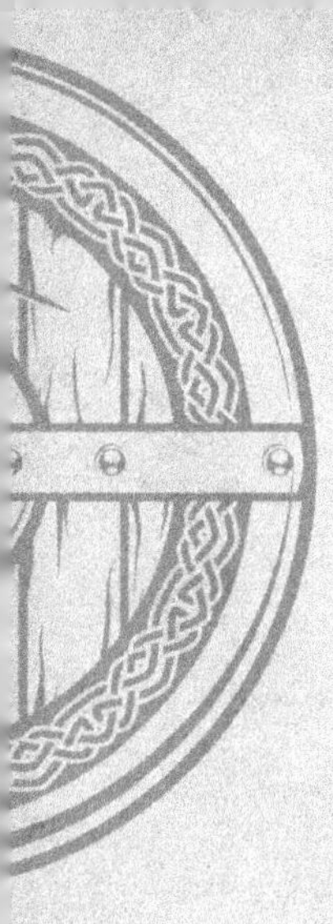

CHAPTER TWENTY
THE RETURN

FENNIC

Riven demanded we all attend a meeting before anything else was allowed to be done today. I thought I would have been happy to finally have a peaceful breakfast before starting my day, but I was wrong. Not having that mouthy girl around made the food taste bland. I arrived at the throne room before anyone else because of it. I wanted to take this time to snoop and see if I could find anything else of use.

The dream I had when I hit my head was the only thing on my mind besides Shivani. I knew she was the daughter that girl spoke of, which made me positive; it was a dream. That thing wanted me to believe Shivani was the daughter of a goddess. I couldn't begin to consider how that would work. She said daughter, not a descendant. That would make Shivani one hundred years old. Older? Was I to believe that? Was I to believe she was being reborn? Or that she had been alive for one hundred or more years?

I shook myself from my thoughts. A dream didn't require that much thought. It was a dream. It was meant to be forgotten. I wasn't going to die; Shivani wasn't a deity. The only fact around was that I was losing sight of my goal. I needed to focus on finding the artifact or information Riven kept lying around. I needed to get back on track and focus. If anything wanted me to believe that weak little gremlin was a goddess, it had to be a joke.

Just to be safe, it was worth following Niko around, or as the tree called him, Nikola. I would accept that he was keeping the artifact and Riven going over anything else. It was the most reasonable thing to be said. Riven was too ill-equipped to use such an artifact on his own.

I turned to look at a table, but a cat sat on it. It hissed at me and then again when I jumped in shock.

"Where did you come from?" I backed up.

Another hiss.

"Shoo!" I swatted. "Get down."

When did we get a cat?

Get the artifact and prepare for sacrifice.

I grabbed my head where the voice sounded. "Did you just —no. Of course, you didn't."

The cat lunged and bit me before running out of the room, and I gripped my arm. Was I still dreaming? That hurt!

Riven and his ego saved me the trouble of having to explain why I was snooping when his guard announced his presence before his actual entry. I had time to stand back in front of the throne and hide the new bite on my arm before he entered.

His entrance brought the very man I was looking for with him. Niko made his entrance with the same strides as the king. He was so confident in his place at Riven's side that it was disgusting.

"Brother, I'm glad to see you home again," Riven said, taking a seat on his throne.

"I'm sure you are," I answered.

"Is the job done?" he asked.

"Of course it is." I acted offended. "Why is he here?"

"He has good news for us today," Riven said.

"Which is?" I asked.

"Niko has finally found the missing knowledge to help me merge with the sun god's artifact and ascend to godhood," he answered.

I laughed with no attempt to keep it in. "I'm sure he does."

I mocked them, but a pit formed in my stomach.

"I've learned some people need to see to believe," Niko said.

"And how will you show me?" I asked. "How could you possibly prove you can manage such a thing?"

His face never lifted. The man never gave so much as a smirk. He did knock me on my back. He lifted one finger and slung me across the room and into a wall. I could tell he was showing mercy when he did it. My mind was split between the rational thoughts of this being simply an ability he traded for and the sinking feeling that I really was going to die for gods that never did anything for me.

I got to my feet and left the throne room without a glance at my brother. I had nothing to add to their delusions, and I didn't want the rage I'd feel seeing his smile at my injury. It had been less than a month since my return, and my brother was making more progress than I had time to process.

I needed to check on my mother's care and let a rat out of the dungeon instead of being in that throne room. I needed to know what we were doing from here. I needed to know if I was on my own or if we could work through this. If I was going to kill or be killed.

Even if I had the time to waste on them, I didn't want to waste it. If what he said was true. If my dream was real. If things beyond my control were set in motion, I would die soon. Willingly or not. I may as well use my time to try and prevent it. If it turned out to be false, I lose nothing. If it turns out to be true, I gain my life back.

When I entered my mother's room, nothing could have prepared me for what I was walking into.

"How do you have the guts to show your face here?" she yelled.

I opened my mouth to speak, but she stopped me.

"I went to see the girl myself. When I heard what happened to her, I couldn't believe it. When my own eyes saw that it was true, I almost had a heart attack in that dungeon. I was glad to be able to give her herbs to ease what she was feeling. I've had days to think about how I failed as a mother. To think about what I could have done better for you. What I could have taught you. I've never seen more of your father in you than I do now. How could you watch me go through that position and then hand it off to someone else?" She practically had tears in her eyes.

"I made the best choice I could to keep her from Riven," I said.

"Do you expect anyone but you to believe that?" She shook her head.

Mori came through the door with urgency on his face.

"Riven is going to the dungeons," he said.

I gave my mother one more look before I followed Mori out. I could have stayed and tried my best to reason with her. It was another time I was being told my intent was different than I tried to reason that it was. If this were how it was to be, then no amount of wasted breath would convince them otherwise. Nothing I could say would make her believe that my actions were in Shivani's best interest.

Both Mori and I were sprinting, but when we arrived, Riven was already there.

"I'm sorry it took me so long to come see you. I'm sure you understand how busy things are for me," he looked her over. "It looks like you found a friend."

That cat, that cat is the one who just bit me! A pit opened in my stomach, and my mouth dried. It was just a coincidence. It had to be. I hit my head, and I needed a healer. This cat is not the messenger of a deity. Shivani is not a goddess. My chest was rising and falling harder. Niko was not Nikola.

I was not going to die.

"This cat wandered in and wouldn't leave. I hope you don't mind if I keep her," Shivani said. "Seeing your face now makes everything okay. Thoughts of you are the only thing that kept me sane." Shivani batted her eyes.

"Our investigation has cleared you. We found the poison that killed her is the same poison bandits use. You are free to leave now," I interjected.

Riven and Shivani looked at me with equal parts disgust and disappointment. They were nothing alike, but at this moment, they had the same look in their eyes for me.

"Please, Your Highness, don't interrupt my time with my future husband. I've missed him dearly. I do not wish to hear you speak in his presence," Shivani said. "I already have so much to make up for by being without a veil in front of my king."

That cursed little horse's as—

"Ow!" I shouted, kicking my leg in an attempt to get the cat off of me.

"The cat just earned its place here," Riven smiled. "Tomorrow we will meet; today, eat and get cleaned up. You will have plenty of time to make everything up to me soon."

Riven gave me a smile that sent tingles down my back. It was the smile of someone confident in his chess pieces. If the play I knew was correct, he'd be dead soon with me. I had to find a way to put a stop to this. It would be better for me to consider my dream a reality for now.

"You're brave to show your face here," Vesim spat.

"I could argue you're brave enough to hold that tone," I said.

Her laugh was the most disingenuous. "You deserve far worse than a tone, Fennic. For what you did to her, your mother. For the positions, you always put Mori in. If you don't feel bad for her, do you feel any guilt for Mori or your mother? You truly are a bastard. You have no idea what I had to go through to save her." Vesim stormed out of the dungeon without a care about what I had to say in return.

I knew Vesim would save Shivani, no matter how complicated.

I bit my tongue. She just needed time to cool down. She needed time to understand where I was coming from. That I wasn't the bad guy here. If it had worked the way I intended, no one would have to worry about this. We would all be one worry less. If Shivani had died as she should have, we could focus on making the realm better for her when she was born again.

I opened the cell door and let her out. Shivani ripped her arm away from mine when I tried to help her. We would have time to repair our relationship. If no one else understood, she eventually would. I took the book I found out of my pants pocket and handed it to her.

"You two should read it," I looked between her and Mori.

"Is it laced with poison?" Shivani shot at me.

"I would never risk Mori," I said. "Before we spiral down this path, I need to tell you about a vision." I shook my head at myself. "It's going to sound crazy, but we need to discuss it all the same."

When I was done explaining what happened on our trip, Mori looked at me as if I was insane, but Shivani finally looked at me as if she understood.

"I had a vision, too," she said. "A girl with the softest voice told me not to take off the ring I found."

She held up her hand and showed the golden band. Maybe it wasn't a dream. Maybe the tree lady was real.

"I listen to reality more than dreams." Shivani lifted the veil back to her face and shifted it until it was sitting correctly. "Since we are in reality and not a dream, I'll leave you with one last thing. If I can wish hard enough to make dreams a reality, I hope this woman keeps her word and kills you in the most painful way she can think of and then offers me a chance to do it again for her."

She shoved past me and left as quickly as her feet would allow her.

CHAPTER TWENTY-ONE
THE MEMORIES

SHIVANI

Riven requested I meet him to discuss my future at the castle. Part of me wanted to kill him then and there. The other part of me wondered if I could make this realm as good as what I had just seen in another. With Koa's help and Vesim's knowledge, we could have a great chance. The biggest weight was that from my first steps into the castle to now, I had succeeded in nothing. I could try and kill him today, but chances are I'd fail at that, too.

It was an unusual, sad feeling that washed over me when I realized that I would have to make a choice with that realm. That I would have to decide to save my own and visit his or leave mine to stay in his. I laughed as soon as the thought finished. I was assuming I would be allowed to stay. I was secretly making assumptions that if I were here, then he may want to stay with me.

I was already pretending that everything sat separately. That only half of what I knew was reality and the other half a dream. I was picking what to consider true and false. If Fennic was telling the truth, it meant he and I were now both having visions, dreams; I didn't know what to call them. It meant we were both seeing the same people from the same time. It meant things may not even stay as simple as one realm or the other.

If it was all true, it was one realm in the end. That we were all likely to die for sooner rather than later. If that were the reality, it made the goals of the throne seem childish.

I was a fool, and I needed to save myself the trouble and keep these ideas about Koa for daydreaming before bed. I was standing in my reality, and I needed to pull myself together and face it. Either we would die for the realm, or we would die with the realm.

I took a path through the castle halls that I hadn't taken before while lost in my thoughts, and it put me in front of a room I also hadn't seen before.

I was standing in front of a room filled with chains on the walls. Tools and knives on a table. A slab of wood with straps sat in the middle of the room. I swore I could see the remains of old blood on the floor underneath it. When I looked at the label on the door, it read 'concubine breeding,' and I felt my heart drop. Fennic was right that I didn't want to be a concubine. I didn't want to die, either.

I didn't know how long I was standing outside of the throne room, but it felt both too long and not long enough. I took a deep breath and sat the invisible mask that hid everything I didn't want anyone to see back on as best as I could. Pretending I was not just locked in a dungeon for weeks dying was complicated. It was the reality that I was disposable, and being sat in front of my face was a shock. I needed to keep repeating to myself that I came here for one thing, and it wasn't to live in rare fabrics and fall in love with a prince.

Riven had his eyes on me immediately when I entered.

"I'm glad to see you walking around my halls again," he said.

I smiled, "I'm glad to see you again, too, my king."

"It's good to know you think that way because I am still committed to making you my concubine. Are you still committed to your king?" he asked.

I knew I should have answered him faster and paid more attention to him. I should have thought long and hard about my options. I knew I should stop focusing on the room I had just seen and take my chances at killing him; I hadn't seen any proof he couldn't die; it was only words still, but when the man at Riven's side dropped the hood he was wearing, my stomach was in knots. Why was the demon I made my deal with now standing at the side of the king? Why was Niko here at all?

"I'm committed to nothing more than you, my king," I said, trying my best to hold composure.

"Good. I'll make sure things are in order," King Riven said, leaving me behind.

Niko's eyes held mine.

He was unmoving, but I was panicking. I didn't know what to expect from him. There was something about his black eyes that unsettled me.

"What are you doing here?" I whispered.

"You asked for my help, did you not? I know I denied you, but after some thought, I realized I had nothing to lose by showing you that I've been here the whole time," Niko smirked. "I was with the King before even your arrival."

"You've admitted you're nothing more than a snake in the grass, sneaking around. The last thing I believe is that you're here to help," I shot back.

"My sweet, I never said that I was here to help you. I simply decided to help guide you out of the darkness, if only a little." His hands grazed through my hair and sent bile rising through me.

I left him before he could say another word. My chest was tighter than it had been in a while, and my mind clouded. I had a solid plan coming here, a good plan. It felt like every day I spent here tore that plan apart a little bit more. It felt like this place tore me apart a bit more every day.

I made my way into the dining hall and sought out Vesim. It didn't take long to find her, sitting alone with eyes on everyone. I sat next to her and spoke low.

"How long has Riven's right hand been here?" I asked.

"As long as I can remember, why?" she asked.

"He's the demon that I made my deal with. How is a demon here?" My voice cracked from my effort to keep it low. "Maybe Fennic's dream wasn't a dream at all."

"You can add it to the list. Fennic has also been keeping secrets. He's known about the god artifact and has a stack of papers in his room with information on how to use them," she looked me in the eyes, "anything else?"

"Yes," I said, holding my palm to her. "I've been keeping secrets, too. This showed up on my hand before coming back, and now my mind feels stretched and filled with fuzz. I also found a journal. It reads like it was written by a Goddess," I said.

"Perfect," she mocked. "Now we are calling fairy tale books fact, too."

We both sighed in unison before I picked up the cup of tea that was sitting in front of her. I knew she was feeling defeated. I knew she wasn't saying anything against me. I knew because I was feeling it, too. We all felt the tension built from our failures. Every inch of trust we gained, someone broke it. Every step we moved closer to Riven was only a step closer to our own punishment.

I wanted to tell her of my dreams, of the place Hesperia took me before she became too busy to be with us. It felt like the wrong time, but I knew holding it from her too long would have a worse outcome.

Vesim's tea hadn't been so much as sipped, but my mouth was dryer than the air around the castle. When I took a drink, I noticed Lorelai looking at me from the table across from us.

She had a smirk that spelled trouble and a sparkle in her eyes that screamed excitement. I pulled the cup away from my lips, and the thought hit me. Was it why she was watching me? I focused on her thoughts.

I know you can read my mind. I know you're already suspicious. It's nothing personal. I need you infertile. We can share a husband, but we can't share a claim to the throne. My future son will be the only one to have access to it. The hallucinations coming are just a little added fun.

The table started melting away in front of me, and my head spun. Her face morphed into my mother's, and the room dripped blood. I was no longer in the king's dining hall. I was at home. I was with my mother. I was hiding under my bed while she stormed through the house for me. I was choking down fear again. I was able to shove her down and pretend she didn't exist after her death. Every day got easier to forget her. Hearing her voice again made me shake. It made my hands tremble and my stomach sink.

"Do you think trash like you can hide from your punishment?" my mother screamed, "Get out here! You're always disappointing me and causing trouble."

I fought against it, but a whimper escaped from my mouth.

"Shivani!" I was being shaken.

"Shivani!" I was being picked up. "Shivani, get up!"

My eyes opened to see Fennic. I was cradled in his arms, and I felt the tears dripping off my chin. He looked down at me with concern, but it didn't make me flutter. I felt no comfort. I was smitten the first time he looked at me that way. I was sitting on death's door after the last time he gave me those eyes. I pushed him away from me and scrambled backward.

"Hey," Vesim's hands hovered above both my shoulders. "Are you all right?"

"I need to go." My words were a mess, falling out of me.

When I got to my room, I pushed and shoved until there was a chair heavy enough in front of it that no one could walk in. I was still sweating, and my heart raced. The veil over my face hardly hung on. It only annoyed me, so I ripped it off. I stopped myself when I realized I was pacing the room. I tried to calm my breathing, but it only caused me to cry harder.

She wasn't real. She wasn't here. It was fake to get under my skin. I had to stop. I couldn't let it wind me up and give her the satisfaction of seeing me like this.

I lowered myself into the corner of the room and pulled out the seashell occupying the pocket of my dress.

When he gave me this, he had to have meant to use it in emergency situations. He never told me what an emergency was to him. I felt the pain in my chest grow worse. The space in the room felt like it was closing in further, and my vision grew hazier. My panic and my thoughts were eating me alive.

"Hello?" I whispered.

It was silent on the other side. I don't know why I expected it to work. I don't know what I was looking for in it.

"Shivani?" Koa answered.

"I, I shouldn't have," I choked out.

"Are you crying?" he pressed.

"No, I was just checking in to see how you were." My voice betrayed me, and I shook again.

He sat silent for another moment.

"Do you still have the cat?" he asked.

I looked over to see her sleeping on my pillow.

"I do," I answered.

"Do you want to hear a story about her? She spent all of her time here picking on the mushroom cap frogs. She would chase and chase them until they were all in the pond of water that a baby dragon sneezed out on accident and then take a nap on the rim. They were all too afraid to leave. Caym, my best friend, would have to chase her all the way out before they'd get out of the water. You're going to have to keep her.

They've already caught on to the fact that they have freedom." He gave a soft chuckle.

I looked back at her, still sleeping. "She doesn't look like she could cause that much trouble."

"Maybe you bring out her sweet side," he said. "I don't think there's anyone better to teach her how to be sweet."

I gave my own chuckle, "I couldn't teach anyone that." My laugh quickly became another flood of tears.

"You can talk, and I'll piece it together as you go," he said.

"I haven't gotten back on my feet yet from almost dying, and already it's an all-out game here again. Riven has told me, even after locking me away, that I'm to be his concubine. I thought that being locked away would change his desire for that. Someone put herbs in my tea to cause visions. I was trapped in my mind with my mother, and I don't know if I can keep on this path. Fennic thinks I should already be over what he did because, in his eyes, he did it for me, not to me. I don't know why I thought I was good enough to walk into this castle and change anything. I have failed every single thing I've tried. I was stupid to think I was smarter than the people here. When all of that is said and done, every night I go to bed not knowing if I'm going to have my own dreams or if I'm going to be living someone else's memories." I shocked myself with how easily the honesty drizzled from my mouth.

"That can't be true. I met a woman who escaped her mother. A woman who escaped death. A woman who has such a good friend that she opened a rift in space to keep her alive. A woman bright enough to have even a ghost, who is completely free to move as she pleases, following her. I see a woman surrounded by the deadliest of her realm, getting up every day to face them," Koa said.

We both sat in silence. I didn't have words to say. I didn't know how to accept the things he was saying as genuine. I did not know how to take so many nice things that were said to me and respond without ruining them. I did feel a kind of genuine comfort I hadn't had before in the silence that sat between us.

"I have a sister," he paused. "She was supposed to be taking care of the land our mother started before she was murdered. It turned out that someone was twisting my mind, my dreams, to make me believe that was the truth while he held her hostage. He tortured her, used her as an experiment for his nightmares, and I never looked for her. She went through things I still cannot imagine, and I was living free. I made friends. I ate candies. She hoped every day I'd come to her rescue. I would have, but that meant nothing to her in the end. She cursed me before her death. The curse turned into something I think she didn't anticipate. The situation took me down at first, but now I use it as motivation to keep going and never allow something like that to happen again. I use her memory to keep me moving. You can find something to motivate you, too. You are already so strong. If you believed it, even a little, these people wouldn't seem half as strong. I'm sad that I won't be able to see you show those pretend gods just how strong you are when you use all of these things you've gone through to keep you motivated and moving forward, too," he said.

"Thank you," I said.

I wanted to press further. To ask more about his curse and his family. The reality was, even if we were sharing these secrets with each other, I was still a stranger, and I was doing it again. I was so desperate that I was reaching out to this stranger like I knew he had to care about me.

"I've kept the shell with me, and I don't plan to change that. If you need me, just call," he said.

I tucked the shell back into my dress. I wanted it to stay close. No one had ever helped clear and calm my mind that quickly except Hesperia. It felt fitting that it was a man in another realm and a ghost who made me feel whole for even a moment. If I could have opened my own rift, I would have.

Instead, maybe I would just stay in my room with my new cat. She would need a name soon.

I pulled the journal out, knowing I was nearly finished with everything that was legible. I did want to stay in, and away from everyone.

Entry six

I killed the sun god today. I killed him, and Dahlia broke in front of me. The scream she gave out was unlike anything I heard from her before. She called me crazy for months, but when she unhinged her jaw and ate him whole, I was the sanest person in the room. She screamed at me about how I killed the father of her children. She tried to do the same to the father of mine. She was only upset I had succeeded, finally, where she couldn't.

I wasn't done yet. She was right; She still had four children. Four that I'd kill, too. Nikola stopped me the first time. He told me we would need them. He tried to explain the amount of power they held and how we couldn't replicate that on our own.

I replicated the guardians she left instead. Our son was such a perfect copy of Dahlia's sons that not a single one of them could tell them apart. When Ruri appeared with two guardians with identical markings and abilities, Dahlia was in shock. She couldn't understand it, and she didn't look at me because she was too convinced of my lack of abilities.

Pages were torn out between entries.

Entry nine

Nikola took advantage of me. He turned my sister into a tree. The sun god's death spawned an artifact, and I took it. I hid it where no one could find it. When I came back, Nikola was whispering to the tree, caressing the bark. He used me. He just wanted her. He lied. We fought, and he said the same words to me that she had. He called our own children false gods. He said they'd never be what she could create.

His words sent me into a spiral of emotions, and in my

rage, my abilities finally didn't let me down. I killed them all. I turned their souls into stars, and I filled those stars with endless punishment. I put my own children in them, too. Deimos convinced everyone but Sahir to take his side. That Nikola and I were as unworthy as Dahlia and Olexei. I'd fix all of the things that went wrong. I'd lock Nikola here in a cage of his own making. I'd ensure he could never leave the land he wanted with Dahlia so badly.

I'd show him how wrong he was. I'd prove to him and my sister both what I could create when I started again. I would rinse all the memories of them and this place. I would use Dahlia's power from inside the tree, and her children would be mine, too. I would be the ruler, the beloved mother of life.

I would have everything she wanted. Everything Nikola tried to take from me. All the power she put into those daughters would be in my hands, too, because on second thoughts, it would hurt more to see them love me.

My door opened and pushed a gust of air into my face. Coy and Hesperia came in, back to back, and stood in front of me. Hesperia pointed, and he lifted me up, pulling me out of the room in the way Hesperia could not.

I tucked the journal behind my back in fear that they'd see it. Vesim was sure that it was fake, but something made me so sure that it was real, even if it was hard to believe.

"What are you doing?" I asked.

"You won't stay in there all day hiding from your problems," Hesperia said.

"I wasn't—"

"You were. If you are going to have enemies. If you are going to have goals. You're going to train like it and learn to put them in their place the way they should be," she demanded.

They pulled me through the castle as if I were a rag doll until we were in the training yard. Coy grabbed two wooden swords and tossed me one.

"I have to fight him?" I yelled.

"Yes," she said.

"Are you insane? Look at him! I couldn't even take him down by kicking him in the crotch! There is too much muscle protecting it, too!"

"Don't be foolish, Shi-Shi. He's nothing if you wanted him to be."

"Too many people keep putting too much credit on my name." I shook my head, but before I could finish, he was running at me.

I tucked myself into my knees to dodge him.

"See! Was it graceful? No. Did it work? Yes!" Hesperia called.

"Oh, yeah. Thank you so much," I mocked before Coy turned and ran at me again.

I thought I was going to soil myself when the blade entered the area of my face, but in a reflex, I lifted mine to stop him just in time. He applied pressure and shoved me. His weight was too much, and I landed on my bottom in the dirt, but I got back up all the same. I couldn't hurt him. There was no way. I could at least not look completely foolish.

I imagined his face was Lorelai. I didn't hate her at first. There was no reason to. I did now. I envisioned her face on Coy's body, and I charged. Our wooden blades pounded against each other, and we blocked each other again. I got lost in the sound and the moment. He hit the wood into my ribcage, and I thought it had to be broken, but I got back to my feet. Something about it was therapeutic. This kind of pain was something I could find comfort in. I slammed my heel into the back of his knee, and the drop was the best upper hand I had gotten on him. It was for nothing because he reached around and took out both of my legs.

Hesperia sat beside me where I lay in the dirt. I was heaving in oxygen, and it took all the effort I had left to wipe the dirt and sweat from my nose.

"I did just recover from a murder attempt," I groaned.

"You did. Now you've also worked out all of your frustration, too," she smiled.

Coy lowered himself the rest of the way to the ground with us and used his shirt to wipe at his own face.

"You put in a good effort," Coy complimented.

"It's strange when you say more than one word," I replied.

Coy and Hesperia both lay down in the dirt with me.

"When I was alive, this is what my sisters and I did when we were upset," Hesperia smiled. "We had scheduled training hours. Our mother was adamant that we knew how to defend ourselves against anything that could happen, and she was creative in her ideas of what could happen. She would tell all four of us that we carried great responsibilities and needed to know how to guard it well. That we could heal or destroy. So, our solution to everything was a blade. It exhausted us, cleared our minds, and made us stronger, and if we were upset with each other, it helped that too."

"Are you sad? Do you miss them?" I asked.

"More than I could ever express," she answered. "It's because I miss them that I'm not lying down and wallowing in my sadness. When I find them again, and they wake up, I want them to see that I used my love for them to light a fire inside of myself. I want them to see in my actions that no matter what may have happened in the past, I'm doing everything I can to get back to them," she said.

"Where are they?" I asked.

"Finding their way back," she smiled.

"Do you think you'll ever see them again?" I questioned.

"They are smart, smarter than they believe. I know they'll make it back, and we will all be together again. I can't push it. I want to, but like all good things, they need time," Hesperia said.

"I don't have any siblings, but I've never known any that all got along well," I admitted.

"I am closest with one sister, but it's not because I love the other two any less. It's because this sister and I agreed to never put our trust in anyone but ourselves. It was a lesson we learned while we watched our other two sisters take loss after loss from handing out their trust as easily as clouds handed out rain," she said.

Coy laid so silent I almost forgot he was present.

I related to her sisters more than to her. I seemed to hand out my emotions like they were easy to replace, even after being betrayed. I would still give her credit. She was right; this exhausted me and cleared my mind.

CHAPTER TWENTY-TWO
THE WITCH

FENNIC

Niko was going to be a problem. A big problem. Riven hung on every word he uttered today. The way my brother leaned in when Niko spoke made my stomach turn.

"The people of the kingdom have started coming together and rioting. They threaten to burn what's left of the crops. They're developing illnesses they can't fight off because they don't have access to even simple medicines. You need to do something," I warned, my voice tight with frustration.

Niko stepped in between the two of us. "When he becomes a god, none of it will matter. He will bring in an era of peace and prosperity. Rulers should know when to sacrifice for their people. He's on the throne instead of you because he does know."

"Let them do as they please. My main focus is ascending and merging with the god artifact. When it's done, there will be plenty of food," Riven declared.

There he went again, regurgitating what was already said as if it were an original thought. The invisible puppet strings Niko pulled were almost visible.

"We need blood for the ritual. This castle was built on the old god's altar. Everything we need beyond the blood is already here," Niko explained.

"There's plenty of people to bleed out!" Riven laughed.

"Is that why you picked two concubines?" I asked, my jaw clenching.

"Exactly!" Riven slapped his legs. "I don't plan to kill her, don't worry. I do plan to marry her. Niko has assured me she will make powerful heirs, and when I become a god, the land deserves to have more of my children than others."

"How would he know?" I demanded. "Don't you find it all too strange? This man has so much knowledge that no one else does? Have you asked him how?"

"I would suggest you lower your voice if you want to live to see any of it," Riven growled.

It took everything I had not to kill him where he stood. He was no god king yet. He was just a spoiled rat. I stormed out and went to Shivani's room. She refused to come out for me since yesterday's events. She wouldn't let me in, and I spent hours yelling through her door. Today, the door opened with no issue. She was on her bed with the cat she decided to keep, her eyes deliberately avoiding mine.

"What," Shivani muttered without looking up at me.

"You haven't spoken to me since I returned, and you freaked out yesterday and then locked yourself away? What do you mean what?" I scoffed.

The cat stood from her lap, stretched, and hissed at me. The thing held no teeth back. Its fur bristled as though it sensed my intentions weren't welcome.

"You tried to kill me. You really tried to kill me, and then you left. You didn't just leave. You left me without so much as an apology so I could slowly die in a dungeon!" she yelled, finally meeting my eyes with a gaze that burned.

"I did it for you! To spare you Riven's plans! You're alive!" I yelled back, feeling the heat rise in my face.

"Not because you knew I would be! I'm not alive because you did something heroic and saved me! Even if I had been married to Riven, at least I still had a chance to fight! You tried to take that from me because you are selfish!" She started with anger but ended up laughing, a hollow sound that made my chest ache.

"I'm sorry! I love you. It scared me. I couldn't have taken watching you with him," I groaned, running my hand across my face. The words felt inadequate even as I spoke them.

"You don't love me! I'm just a possession that you and your brother are fighting over. A toy neither of you can bear to see in the other one's hand. It's a shame, too, because when you put that ribbon on my wrist, I thought we could be something. I thought I may actually care about you. I was thinking about how we could find a way to work through things and be together, maybe even love each other at the end of things here," she confessed, her voice catching on the last words.

"But not anymore?" I asked, feeling a tightness in my throat.

"I don't know what I want, Fennic, beyond you leaving," she sighed, turning away from me again.

"Don't write me off. You don't understand what love is. If you did, you would see what I'm trying to tell you," I pleaded, taking a step closer.

"I understand enough to know you don't either," she shot back, her shoulders tensing.

"Riven and Niko are planning to use you for children. When you freaked out yesterday, we all saw your blood magic. Everyone has been commanded to keep it a secret. Niko convinced Riven it's how you would get him and his heirs closer to godhood," I revealed, rubbing the bridge of my nose.

"If everyone knows, then I may as well use the power to lock him up until I can kill him," she replied, a glint of determination in her eyes.

"What part of 'you can't kill him while the artifact is with him' do you still not understand?" I asked, frustration boiling over.

I moved closer to her. I wanted to shake some sense into her, but the cat lunged at me and dug its teeth into my arm again. I yelled out in pain. She had a good grip on my flesh, her jaws clamping down with surprising strength.

"You should have stayed away from me," she threatened, unblinking, watching me struggle with the animal.

I flung the cat off of me, and she landed on her feet. Her fur was raised, sparking what looked like electricity. For a moment, I swore her eyes glowed.

"Where did this thing come from?" I asked, holding the wound on my arm. Blood trickled between my fingers.

"If I knew, I'd get more and train them to keep you away from me, too," she smiled, a cold expression that didn't reach her eyes.

"What happened to us working together? To teamwork? We aren't going to make any progress if you keep acting like this!" I shouted, my voice echoing off the walls.

"You killed me! That wasn't very team friendly," she retorted, her voice dripping with sarcasm.

"I didn't kill you, you're alive. Are you going to keep bringing this up forever?" I threw my hands up, droplets of blood spattering the floor.

"I'm going to keep saying it until you no longer speak to me, or I kill you," she vowed, her face a mask of conviction.

I glanced back to the cat, still ready to pounce again, and shook my head. The room suddenly felt too small, too confining. I left her room, but not before I slammed her door with enough force to rattle the hinges. Vesim was waiting on the other side, staring straight into my soul with those knowing eyes of hers.

"Are you going to yell at me, too?" I glared, already bracing for another confrontation.

Vesim shook her head. "I don't need to raise my voice to tell you she's right."

"I made a mistake. We need to put it behind us to take care of Niko!" I held out my hand for her to shake, desperate for at least one ally.

She didn't look down at it. "When she isn't useful, will you try and kill her again? When I'm not useful, will you kill me too?"

"Why do I have to keep repeating that I did it to save her?" I growled, dropping my hand.

"You'll say it until you decide to be truthful," she shrugged. "I'm sorry you aren't enjoying accountability. She didn't enjoy slowly dying, and I didn't enjoy the lengths I had to go through to try and save her." Vesim pushed past me. "We can handle things on our own."

"Niko and Riven will lock her away and breed her out!" I yelled to her, my voice cracking.

"I'm sorry they're beating you to exactly what you wanted," she mocked before slamming the door back at me.

I drove my fist into the wall and let out a growl. The sharp pain in my knuckles was almost a relief compared to the frustration coursing through me. Several maids were tucking their heads further down while they tried to rush past me, their fear palpable in the corridor.

"Mori!" I shouted, charging down the halls, leaving a trail of bloody droplets behind me.

He came from a darkened corner, rolling his eyes at me. "I knew when you said you wanted to see her, you'd be huffy in the end."

"Watch yourself," I huffed, my patience wearing dangerously thin.

"What do you want then?" he inquired, crossing his arms.

"Niko said there's some ritual altar under the dungeon. Find out what you can," I demanded before leaving him behind.

I don't know why I called him or commanded him to do something so useless. There was nothing for him to find or do that we hadn't already done. Not unless he wanted to spend his day digging it all up himself. Perhaps I just needed someone to obey me when everyone else refused.

Coy was waiting for me, leaning against a wall, when I marched from the girl's wing. His calm demeanor only irritated me further.

"What do you want," I barked, in no mood for more resistance.

He lifted an eyebrow at me, and I turned my lips in the opposite direction. His silent judgment was all too clear.

"You're right. I don't want to fight you," I shivered, remembering all too well what happened to those who crossed him.

"Good boy," Coy remarked but didn't lower his brow.

"Okay, so what is it you want then?" I asked, softening my tone.

"I heard about the god artifacts that you found when you were away and that you were going to take them to the witch. I'm coming with you."

"Why?"

"Why can't I?"

"Fine, but be quiet."

Coy scoffed with amusement. I knew what he was thinking. I told the man who didn't speak to be quiet as if I was the one in control. He walked in step behind me the entire distance. From the girl's wing of the castle to Riven's wing of the castle, he was toe to heel with me, a constant reminder of my diminishing authority.

"I was expecting you," the witch's voice slithered through the air. She never sounded any better. Her voice rasped with every word she spoke, like dry leaves scraping against stone.

"Good, then you should know why we are here," I mocked, trying to reclaim some sense of control.

"Enlighten me, is it the reason you claim or the real reason inside of you?" she challenged, her milky eyes seeming to see right through me.

"We've come to see if these God artifacts are real," Coy stated, tossing them on her purple cloth-covered table.

"I want to know if you know how to put a ghost back in her body," I inquired, the question coming out before I could stop it.

She looked between us both with wide eyes. She ignored my question and moved back to Coy. "You shouldn't have brought these here. The King should have been the first pair of eyes on them," she stuttered, still raspy.

"She's right," Riven announced from the doorway. "I'm less interested in why you'd want to resurrect a ghost and more interested in where your loyalty is."

My heart sank. Of course he would show up now.

"I wanted to make sure they were real before I wasted your time on them," I lied, trying to sound convincing.

"Of course you did," Riven sneered, moving inside. "So, are they real then?"

The witch picked them up and looked them over. She chanted and tossed what had to be dirt over them before opening her eyes back up and handing them to Riven. Her hands trembled slightly as she did so.

"I'll save her the effort; they aren't," Niko interrupted, appearing as if from nowhere.

The fake was saved again by another imposter. Maybe that's why he was here. He and the witch were working together. The timing was too perfect to be coincidence.

"What a shame. You almost got back in my good graces, Fennic," Riven taunted. "Tsk tsk."

Coy crossed his arms. "You haven't gotten in my good graces, ever."

"Yes, well, I'll find new horses to buy, and you'll be too busy to think about it," Riven dismissed, waving a hand at

Coy. "Actually, how about we go hunting? Like old times. It seems you both spend a good bit of time together these days. Why not have a third."

"You want us to attempt brotherly bonding?" I asked in disgust, the idea repulsive.

"It's most likely you want to lure us there to kill us for sport," Coy observed, unmoved by the invitation.

"It would have made the day more interesting," Riven shrugged, his casual cruelty on full display.

I nodded. "It would have. If I recall correctly, the last time we went hunting together, Father told us something similar."

"Mhm," Coy smirked. "The rules of the hunt were first blood got dinner. I seem to recall Riven's mother made it his last hunt, too."

"Wasn't that because you shot an arrow from a horse clean through his calf?" I reminisced, tapping my chin, savoring the memory.

Riven's cheeks flushed, and his eyes flashed with rage. "And it still wasn't good enough to get you the throne."

He pulled his cloak over him with an arm and left us behind, his footsteps heavy with anger. Coy had always been the only one to speak freely and received no punishment for it, and I was sure it was because, like the rest of us, he was afraid of Coy. Coy had a way of separating duty and emotions. You could always count on him to do what needed to be done when no one else would.

He rested a hand on my shoulder and nudged me before he left as well. I let the witch keep the artifacts. If they were fake, they were of no use to me, and something told me if Niko didn't want them, neither did I. Some battles weren't worth fighting.

"Wait!" the witch called out, her voice cracking with urgency. "You're going to die soon! You need to kill the man with black eyes!"

"Save it," I ground my teeth at her words, a chill running up my spine.

They weren't hers. They belonged to a tree.

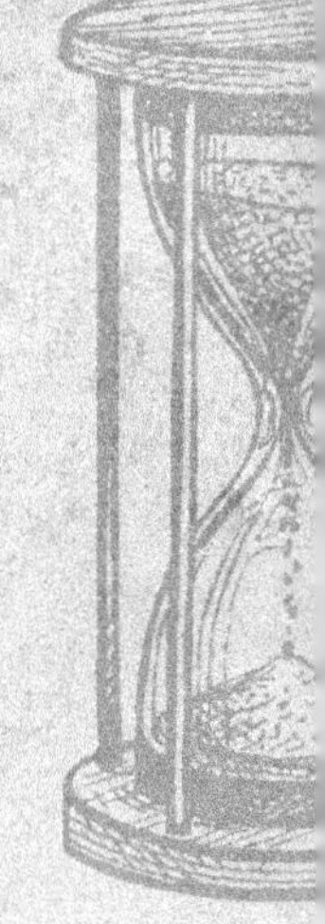

CHAPTER TWENTY-THREE

THE FRIENDS

SHIVANI

Whiskers was already asleep in my arms for the second time today. She didn't care what was happening as long as she was close. However, I was making myself dizzy walking in circles. Today, Vesim, Hesperia, and I were using her rift again and going to the other realm.

Juniper had been making what she called a care package for Vesim to bring back. Their realm had magic that was much different from ours, and it could have been useful if we got it to work. I did my best not to sound desperate when she told me, but I was sure I sounded like I was begging for her to bring me with.

"Are you ready?" Vesim questioned, closing my door. "They're spending the day in the dungeons, so we have time."

"The dungeons?" I asked, a chill running through me at the thought of what might be happening there.

"They won't tell anyone what's going on. I'm sure we will have time to find out when we get back, but if you want to go, you need to forget about it for now," Vesim insisted, her eyes conveying the urgency.

"I'm ready! I am!" Hesperia shouted, holding her hand up, practically bouncing with excitement.

"I'm glad everyone has made their choice," Vesim murmured, opening the rift. "Let's go."

I hesitated after seeing the rift open. I didn't listen to a word she said. Why was I nervous? My heart pounded as I stared into the swirling void. It didn't matter because Vesim shoved me through and jumped in after me. I felt my stomach go into my throat, and I was sure I'd land on my face. It was a pair of arms I landed in, instead.

"I have to stop coming here like this," I tried to laugh it off, though my voice came out shakier than intended.

"I could get used to it," Koa remarked, his eyes narrowing on me, "Are you blushing?"

I touched my cheeks, feeling the warmth beneath my fingertips. "What? No, it's the weather here!"

"You two look ridiculous," Juniper teased, pulling Vesim by the arm.

"She's used a similar excuse before," Vesim added with a knowing smirk.

The two of them looked like they were rushing to get away from us. I was suspicious of them—not because I thought they were like Fennic, but because I was sure Vesim felt the same about Juniper as I felt about Koa, flustered and filled with butterflies. The way Vesim's eyes lingered on Juniper's face was unmistakable.

"I can walk from here," I announced awkwardly, trying to regain some dignity.

"I don't mind, but if you insist," he replied, sitting me down with gentle hands.

He looked at me, but only in my eyes. After so long wearing a veil, it felt strange not having it on. It felt vulnerable having someone see me in full. Maybe it was only because he was the one looking at me. I didn't feel this seen when Fennic looked at me. When Fennic looked at me, I felt like an object to be possessed. When Koa looked at me, I felt like a person worth knowing.

"Did you know you have a design in your pupils?" he asked, leaning in closer. "It's almost like a clock."

I couldn't think of how to form words with the way he leaned in so close to me. If he slipped, his lips would be on mine, and I couldn't take my eyes away from them. If I moved just a little, I could say it was a happy accident when we kissed. My breath caught in my throat at the thought.

"I'm sorry, I'm too close to you. I should have asked if it was all right first," he apologized, backing up.

"Mom!" Hesperia yelled, running and wrapping her arms around the tree that had given me visions on my last visit.

I looked from her to Koa with confusion. She was mumbling and whispering to a tree, and I didn't know how to explain that she was a strange ghost who didn't make much sense a lot of the time. So, instead, I let out an awkward chuckle, feeling heat rise to my face again.

"Hesperia, get away from the tree. It's wooden; it can't be your mother," I tried my best to quietly shout at her. She only kept petting the tree. I wanted to die from embarrassment right there.

I looked back to Koa, prepared to apologize, but in stepped a girl. She was quiet and unsure. I thought we were doomed and in trouble. I did remember Juniper saying we couldn't be in the sunlight garden. If people saw us, there would be problems beyond what we could imagine. Koa reassured me with his eyes, the slight crinkle at their corners telling me everything would be fine. Hesperia took the lead again. She moved faster than I could stop her. All I could do was close my eyes and groan.

She began sniffing the girl, and I crossed my fingers that she would not lick her again. The memory of how she'd greeted me was still all too vivid.

"Your scent isn't from the Age of Moonlight," Hesperia

observed, sniffing her hair. "Wait!" She sniffed her hand next. "You're my sister's daughter!" Hesperia hugged the girl as hard as she hugged the tree, and the air being pushed from the girl's lungs could be heard from where I stood.

"Kyra," she gasped out, her face turning slightly red from the force of Hesperia's embrace.

"I'm your aunty. You can call me aunty," Hesperia declared, pulling her into another hug. She couldn't touch things in our realm, but here, she could if she wanted to. "Wait, I know! Let's go kill Yumi. It can be our first bonding experience! It avenges your mother and mine!" Hesperia began pulling Kyra behind her.

"Wait!" Koa called. "That's not reasonable this time, but I did hear about you, so I set something else up."

Hesperia narrowed her eyes on him, waiting for him to continue, her enthusiasm barely contained.

"Kyra is going to take you to see your sisters or maybe their lands in Cylla. Whatever you want!"

"So, I can't kill Yumi until next time?" Hesperia asked, her disappointment palpable.

"You can not kill Yumi until all the sisters at least remember they are sisters!" Koa's voice became progressively drawn out the longer he talked, clearly exasperated.

"Fine!" She pointed. "Don't forget your words!"

He sighed and turned back to me. "If you don't mind it, I actually wanted to show you something while you're here?" Koa asked, his voice softening.

"Okay," I answered; I sounded like a love-sick puppy. My eagerness was embarrassing, but I couldn't help it.

There I went again. A fool getting wrapped up in hazel eyes and warm smiles as if I didn't already learn it would get me killed to act this way. I couldn't have learned the lesson any harder unless I had let the idea of love kill me all the way. I lived this long without a single other soul on my side. Why did

I need one so badly now? The way my heart skipped beats around him terrified me.

"Can I touch your hand?" he whispered, his voice barely audible.

I tried so hard to get my head on straight. I wanted to ask about Hesperia. I wanted to find out what he knew about the things she was saying, but when he said those words, I melted into a pile of stupid goo. All my questions evaporated like morning dew under the sun.

"Mhm," I nodded, cursing my weakness.

I can't even listen to myself, it seems. I'm weaker than even I considered.

He grabbed my hand, his touch gentle but firm, and we walked through the halls of their land. He used caution and checked doorways as we went. The throne room we entered kept true to being the opposite of home. Bright and sparkling. It was as if the night sky lived inside the room. Stars seemed to dance across the ceiling, casting soft light on our faces. Koa took me through vines of flowers filled with water. They resembled mirrors in my realm, but the reflection was not mine. On the other side was an entirely new place.

"This is Merripen," Koa explained. "Our mushroom cap frogs are over there." He pointed, his face lighting up with childlike enthusiasm. "We call them Mogs."

"No one will be upset by this?" I asked, nervousness creeping back into my voice.

"Caym is not just my friend; he's my brother. Trust me, you are welcome here," Koa assured, giving my hand a gentle squeeze.

I didn't want to lie; I was excited to see them. When the pond came in sight, so did more of them than I could count. They really were mushrooms atop frogs. They hopped about, their caps bouncing with each movement, some red, some blue, some speckled with both colors.

"They're cuter than you gave them credit for!" I exclaimed, my worries momentarily forgotten.

I leaned down to pick one up, but they were too busy to notice me. If I were them, I'd be too busy for me, as well. They hopped through grass so lush it could have been a bed. They played in water so crystal, I'd bathe in it myself. They lived in a realm so hard to believe was real; I wondered if I was dreaming more than once. The sound of their tiny croaks filled the air, creating a melody unlike anything I'd heard before.

"Can I give you a gift?" Koa asked, shifting the conversation quickly with a voice of nerves.

"You've done enough, please don't feel like-" he cut me off.

"I don't do anything I don't want to," he stated firmly.

"Okay," I answered, my curiosity piqued.

"Caym helped. I can't take full credit. I wanted to do something nice for you, but I wasn't sure, and he has experience with this kind of thing. He and Ruri are deep in love, so I thought he would know better than I would, and he said—"

He stopped rambling and took in a breath. It was strange to see such a big man, one called the god of war, stumble over himself like he was. His usual confidence was replaced with an endearing uncertainty. He pulled a small box out of a pocket under his cloak. He was covered in black with crimson accents. When he opened it, a piece of yellow stone sparkled inside, catching the light in a way that made it seem alive.

"It's called citrine," he explained, pulling it out with a chain. He clipped it around my neck, his fingers brushing against my skin. When I held it up to the light, it was filled with rainbows, each one dancing with the slightest movement.

"Thank you," I said, still unsure how I should take the gift. My fingers traced the smooth surface of the stone, feeling its warmth.

Was he saying he liked me? Was he trying to be nice? Did

it mean something else entirely? My mind raced with possibilities.

"If you don't like it, I'll understand," he said, his eyes searching mine for any hint of disappointment.

"No," I jumped, too quickly. "I love it."

"Juniper is giving Vesim a piece of obsidian to lock your king away. I didn't want you to leave empty-handed," he said.

So, he was trying to be nice. Fool, Shivani, you are a fool. I felt my heart sink a little, even as I tried to remind myself that kindness was rare enough to be treasured.

"In my realm, we don't exchange gifts unless we are confessing our love for each other. We exchange ribbons on our wrists until marriage. Once married, we brand the inside of our wrist with our symbol for eternal," I explained, shining the stone in the light, watching the colors dance.

When I looked up at him, he was writing in a small notebook. He looked up at me and shoved the notebook back into a pocket inside his top, a flush creeping up his neck.

"What's that?" I asked, curiosity getting the better of me.

"Nothing," he cleared his throat. "Then it's safe for me to assume no one has gifted you anything before me?"

I shook my head. "Prince Fennic gave me a ribbon."

"Oh," he spoke low, his face falling slightly.

"No," I waved my hands frantically. "That sounds different than it is. He gave it to me to rub it in his brother's face; he doesn't really care; it's, I-"

"You don't owe me an explanation," he tried to assure, though there was a tightness to his voice.

"He doesn't like me. It wasn't special or meaningful in that way," I sighed, wishing I could take back my words.

All I was doing was making things worse and ruining his gift. I needed to stop talking. I did everything I could think of to improve the situation. I wrapped my arms around his waist and hugged him, breathing in his scent of pine and something sweet I couldn't name.

"Thank you. No one has ever given me something so beautiful," I said, my voice muffled against his chest.

When he hugged me back, it came with a knot in my throat. He brushed my hair with one hand and the other wrapped around my back. He was warm but gentle. No one had ever been so gentle. It made something in my chest ache with longing for things I never knew I wanted. I closed my eyes to enjoy it for only a moment when the sound of his heart thumping filled my ear. I didn't mean to, but I slipped into his thoughts.

Am I holding her too tightly? Did she like it? I should have asked her about the customs in her realm. She's so intelligent. The way she glows when she smiles makes it hard not to stumble over myself. She must think I'm pathetic.

I pulled myself from where I shouldn't have been, trying harder than I ever had to hide my smile. The warmth that spread through me at his thoughts was dizzying.

"Your heart is pounding. Are you okay?" I whispered, unable to resist.

"What?" He asked, pulling back slightly. "Of course."

"Your cheeks are red now," I laughed, letting go of him.

I watched him out of the corner of my eye, tug on his clothes, and do his best to straighten himself out quietly. His embarrassment was endearing in a way I never expected.

"Anyway," He cleared his throat. "How are things progressing in your realm?"

"They aren't," I sighed, reality crashing back like a wave.

I was going to ask him if I could talk, if he were even interested in listening, or if he was just trying to make small talk. I decided against it. I knew he would tell me to just talk, and he would piece it together. Something about him made me want to share every thought in my head.

"To be honest, I'm finding it hard to pick a goal and commit to it. I wanted to save my realm. To take the throne and make changes that would help everyone. I found this journal, and it was cute at first, but then it got dark. In between reading it, Hesperia took me to a fortune teller, and since I've been having the strangest dreams. The girl has my name, and in my dream, I am in her body, but she can't be me. It's in an entirely different time. I realize I sound like I'm losing my mind, but between wanting to find out more about it and the amount of failures I've had since arrival, I don't know what to do. Things have become stagnant. Any forward motion is small enough now that it hardly counts," I took several deep breaths in to make up for the ones I had skipped, my words tumbling out in a rush.

He nodded but kept silent, his eyes thoughtful.

"Nothing?" I studied him, trying to read his expression.

"Which one do you want more?" he asked, his voice measured.

He was clearly holding back what he wanted to say. His restraint was frustrating when all I wanted was his honest thoughts.

"I want to save my realm. I want to get rid of Riven and help everyone who is starving, but I'm afraid it's pointless if the dreams are real. It would mean that I'd need to solve the other mysteries for it to make a difference, right?" I asked, searching his face for answers.

"I can't be the one to give you an answer on any of this. I can only tell you that neither is wrong," he said, his words careful.

"Well, that helps," I said, unable to keep the disappointment from my voice.

It helps me stay stagnant. I was disappointed; he had been so open and helpful before this subject. It felt like he was holding something back, something important.

"They are mushroom frogs!" Vesim shouted, her voice breaking through my thoughts.

Juniper's laughter carried with hers, and it made my heart break a little more, knowing we had to leave. We had to go back to what felt like the thing people called hell. My heart broke to know Vesim had to go back to being focused and hard. That I had to see Fennic's face again or be married off to Riven. The contrast between the two realms was stark and cruel.

"Did you give it to her?" Juniper whispered to Koa, though not quietly enough.

When I tried to make subtle movements and glance at him from the corner of my eye, he was already looking at me. I shifted my head back away, pretending I hadn't heard.

Juniper's voice grew louder, so all eyes were on her. "I've set you both up with some flowers and herbs that can do things your realm can't. I don't know if they'll all hold through the rift, but it's worth a try. A few of them, I hope, can kill your king no matter what protection he has if you can get him to eat it."

"Wouldn't that be nice?" I mumbled, realizing I was passively playing with my necklace, feeling its weight against my skin.

"If it doesn't kill him, I'll have to come collect a few more," Vesim said, a mischievous glint in her eye.

I furrowed my eyebrows while Vesim was talking and turned to face her. There was something off about her. I leaned in closer to her for a better look, noticing a smudge on her face.

"Vesim?" I asked, suspicion growing.

"What?" She looked between the three of us, suddenly fidgeting.

"Is that lipstick? It's on your cheek, and your dress by your neck?"

She looked back at me in fear, and when Juniper shifted with nerves, my jaw dropped. The realization hit me like a bucket of cold water.

"Is it her lipstick?" I pointed, a grin spreading across my face.

Vesim opened a rift and pushed me through it before anything else could be said, panic clear on her face.

"You left Hesperia!" I was laughing so hard that I hardly understood what I was saying. The absurdity of it all was too much.

"I'll go back for her without you!" Vesim yelled, her face flushed with embarrassment.

"If you were trying to be secretive, you didn't do a good job at it!" I called back, wiping tears of laughter from my eyes.

Mori pushed the door open, his face grim. "They've started uncovering an altar in the dungeon."

Panic rushed down my spine at his words. For every small break, we paid double. The laughter died in my throat as reality crashed back around us.

CHAPTER TWENTY-FOUR
THE HOUND

HESPERIA

The group went their ways, but I stayed with Kyra. She used a crystal to move us between realms. I was not used to the kind of travel they were using now. I was used to moving in the unseen to wherever I wanted. I could have taken her with me, past the veil. She refused me. She looked scared of the idea, so I did not push her. The fear in her eyes was enough to make me relent.

I convinced Vespera that I could not touch anything in the realm of the gods. She didn't question me. I wanted to see what she was made of now that we had all been torn apart, and she did not disappoint me. Kyra knew better. I tried to convince her, but she didn't let me speak a full sentence before she stopped me and called my bluff, her eyes seeing through my deception with unsettling ease.

Now that Kyra had brought us to Cylla, I was bound by the same rules as in my current realm. No touching, lifting, pinching. I was more used to the restriction now, though the constant reminder of my ghostly state still stung.

"Follow me, but quietly," Kyra instructed, her voice barely above a whisper.

"I'm a ghost; nothing is quieter than I am," I reminded her with a smirk.

She gently moved a tree branch, and on the other side of the greenery was a small child. She was covered in fur that made her emerald hair burst against the white background like spring shoots through snow. She was playing in the snow with a creature I had not seen before, her laughter carrying through the crisp air.

"What is that?" I asked, watching the large, furry creature romp with the child.

"A yeti," Kyra answered. "They're common at the bottom of the mountain."

The way Kyra openly watched Ruri was the way I felt as well. She looked at her with sadness, but sadness for a stranger. I didn't know this small child with my sister's name. It was a sad sight to know that this was my sister, my best friend. The girl I used to spend every single day with years and years ago, but there was a detachment as well. I had never known her like this; she was a stranger to me. The weight of time and circumstance pressed down upon me.

"How are you handling things?" I inquired, studying Kyra's profile.

Kyra didn't look at me, but I noticed her fidgeting with the hem of her golden dress, her fingers working the fabric nervously.

"It's hard," Kyra admitted, her eyes still fixed on the child.

"Which part?" I tried to press harder, needing to understand.

She finally looked at me, "Which part is harder for you?"

"The part where I'm useless to everyone," I answered honestly, the words bitter on my tongue.

"The hardest part for me is that I'm expected to accept what I was told and move forward with it with a smile. I was told who my mother was; I mourned her death with a friend. Then I found out, after her death, that the friend who helped me mourn my mother, was actually my mother. That's a hard thing to grasp. Ruri went out of her way to ensure the land I worked so hard on flourished. It's the only one with a protective barrier. She didn't do it for her own land," Kyra paused and took a deep breath, her voice wavering. "She brought herself to the brink of death to protect me and my land in silence but couldn't care about me enough to tell me the truth even before she decided that the only thing left to offer us was her burial."

I wouldn't say it out loud, but she sounded like her mother at that moment. The same stubborn pride, the same wounded heart beneath it all.

The two of us stood in silence and watched the child that we were supposed to call Ruri. The snow crunched beneath her small feet as she played, oblivious to our watching eyes.

"Ruri brings them food any chance she can, even being so small," Caym's voice rumbled from behind us.

I spun myself around so quickly that I almost hurt my bone-free neck. When I opened my mouth to scream, he wrapped it in black smoke and silenced me, his eyes wide with warning.

"Mmm, mm, mmmmmmmm!" I tried to form words, but his hand stopped them, the smoke cold against my lips.

He pressed a finger to his lips and hushed me, his gaze flicking toward the child in the distance.

He moved Kyra and I back through the mist and into Merripen before he allowed my mouth free again, the smoke dissipating like morning fog.

"That was a rude way to say hello!" I yelled, my indignation bubbling over.

"Have you two met before?" Kyra questioned, looking between us with suspicion.

"Yes!" I exclaimed, crossing my arms.

"It's a long story that's hard to explain," Caym murmured, running a hand through his dark hair.

"No, it's not. I can do it quickly. Yumi tried to kill us all, but she failed, trapped us in the stars, and brought us to a new realm. She's a big liar and didn't even create this place! My mother did. Caym and I were supposed to run Merripen together! I kill them and guide them here, and he gives them homes for eternity. Since I'm dead, we can speak to each other because my realm and yours are meant to be together. The only thing is you're all cursed to forget, and on the off chance you remember, you aren't allowed to say anything, or else you're in pain. But since I'm dead, I don't have the same rules. Yumi wasn't smart enough to consider that. Though since being here, I am finding it hurts to say some of this out loud," I rubbed my chest, feeling a dull ache spreading beneath my ribs.

"That was neither quick nor sensible," Kyra sighed, rubbing her head. "How does he know this, but the rest of us don't?"

"My memories have been coming back bit by bit. Not quickly enough," he confessed, a shadow passing over his face.

"For how long? Does anyone else know?" Kyra's voice was becoming increasingly agitated, her hands clenching at her sides.

"The most important thing to take from what any of us say to you is that we are cursed to limited information sharing," I explained, trying my best to be soft. "Things we wish we could share, we often can't. Things we wish we could help with, we are forced to watch fall apart. We are all suffering together, Kyra. I can assure you that if any of us knew how to put things back right now, we would. If we knew how to share every single thing we knew right now, I would."

"I have to go; I've already stayed too long," Kyra announced, her expression closing off.

Caym nodded, and the two didn't exchange further good-byes before she left, her footsteps quick and determined.

"That is strange to see," I remarked, watching her retreating figure.

"It's been an adjustment for us both. Ruri kept it secret, and even in her death, she didn't tell me," Caym revealed, his voice heavy with old pain.

"You know it was to keep it safe from Yumi," I reminded him.

"I know why she thought she had to do it. Just because we think something is the only way doesn't mean that it is," he reflected, his eyes distant.

"She's always been stubborn. She always thought she could carry everything and protect everyone."

We both let the silence linger for a moment. I knew he had to miss her in the same way I missed Coy for over one hundred years. I understood the pain of knowing someone who doesn't remember you. The hollow ache that never quite leaves.

"We will fix things," I promised. "I know you're in pain, but it's not your fault. She will remember you again."

He gave me a fake smile, and I knew he didn't mean any harm. The effort alone touched me.

"I have another favor to ask you," I said, pulling the subject in another direction.

"Hmm?" he raised an eyebrow, curious.

"Can you start working on Koa? Fennic isn't a bad guy. He is caught in a world that is kill or be killed, doing what he can without remembering who he is. He will need you guys. He's been through a lot and is going to go through a lot more soon," I urged, feeling the pressure of time pushing against us.

"Providing he lives long enough," Caym responded, his tone grim.

I glared in his direction, my eyes narrowing to slits.

"Fine! I was just saying. Does this mean you remember who he is?" he asked, hands raised in surrender.

"I do. It's one of those things I can't say out loud yet, I've tried," I admitted, but I didn't want to continue this line of conversation. "Now, where is Sina? I need to see her before I leave. I know she's here; I can smell her!"

"She's at the palace with Ryujin," he informed me, gesturing toward a path.

"You have a palace now? You really upgraded," I teased, nudging him with my ghostly shoulder.

I followed Caym through the grass of Merripen and passed the houses that sat neatly in rows. There was so much life around. I could hardly understand how he had done it. The last time I saw him, he killed things with his touch. Ruri had to spend hour after hour helping him plant things in the Age of Moonlight. The transformation was remarkable.

"She made me gloves," he explained, noticing my wondering gaze. "I see the way you're looking around."

We didn't make it to the stairs that led inside before a powder blue dragon was barreling towards me. Which I was beyond grateful for. I hadn't had to use my feet this much in so long that they were already sore. I would have died another death before making it to the top. Sina did not look the same, but her scent and roots were the same. Her scales glittered in the light like morning frost.

When she stopped in front of me, I hugged her as tightly as I had hugged Kyra. I had to dodge white oak antlers this time, but still, I embraced her, breathing in her familiar scent.

"Sina! You're gorgeous. Even your eyes are as white as snow!" I exclaimed, delight bubbling through me.

"They're as white as yours now," she smiled, her voice musical and clear.

"When things aren't so rushed, you will have to explain to me how you were turned into a dragon goddess," I said, petting her head. "For now, do you know where the golden ring is?"

"It's something else simple and quick to answer. Ruri created them as vessels for the souls locked in the stars," Caym explained, holding out his hand. "As for your second question, she kept the ring well."

I took it and put it in my hand. Mother had marked my palm during our hug, and I felt the rush of winter through the ring, cold and familiar. "I'm only missing one thing now," I said, holding up my palm to show the marking, a pattern of intricate swirls that seemed to move in the light.

"When did Dahlia do that?" Sina asked, her head tilting in curiosity.

"When I arrived. Shivani has it, too, but she still doesn't understand it. Did Ruri or Sage get theirs?"

"We aren't entirely sure. Astra would need to give you any other information," Caym replied, his expression guarded.

"Astra?" I shook my head in disbelief.

"They became closer than anyone else in the realm," Caym nodded, a hint of amusement in his voice.

"Of all the things, that has to be the strangest. They hated each other," I said, remembering their constant bickering.

"It was strange for me, too. Most of them don't remember anything yet," Sina added softly.

I nodded, a weight settling in my chest. "I have to go now. Vesim will be back for me anytime. Keep yourselves safe."

I turned to leave before any of them could say another word to me. I wanted to stay. I ached to embrace them again. I needed to leave. It was hard enough waking up without any of them there. Harder still to keep my mouth shut and not try my best to shake everyone awake. I spent all of my time repeating to myself that trying to force them to remember too quickly can shock their mind and set us back another hundred years. Leaving behind the ones that I could have openly spoken to was the first thing to dull the rainbows I had been seeing since I was finally freed.

It was easy to leave Merripen because Yumi was even using my mother's vines to move between realms. I had yet to see a true original thing being brought to this realm. She took her own sister's work and erased her from it. I'd kill her with my bare hands when we were all back. The thought burned in me like a flame.

I snuck around the halls of Semper, dodging guards I hadn't seen before. They smelled of Shivani's power, but they couldn't have been hers. Which meant Shivani's counter was to blame for them. Whoever she was, was making blood slaves. Another problem I wish I could have dealt with on the spot. I was sniffing out something else. Something more important for this moment. When I had my body back, if I didn't take care of things, I would lose my memory, too. I couldn't risk setting us all back like that.

I moved into the empty room where the one thing I was looking for sat. She also looked like a creation of Shivani's. No, she looked like a creation of Nikola and Yumi. Disfigured and suffering. I gave a few small whistles, and the dog limped its way to me with slow agony, each step clearly painful. I lowered myself to my knees, and the dog whined at my lap, her eyes clouded with pain and resignation.

"Good girl," I cooed, petting her head gently.

It seemed even that brought agony to her. I wouldn't extend her pain any further. We all had reason to be upset at everyone whose hand touched the events that led us here. The counters, this counter, at least, hardly had a hand in enough to deserve this. I reached my hand into her chest and pulled her heart out. The sound of her bones snapping made me shiver in disgust, but I pressed on. When it was fully out, I ate the heart. It was nauseating, but I did my best to make it through the endless chewing it took, the taste metallic and foul in my mouth.

Her soul came after the body of the blood dog hit the ground with a dull thud. I held it in my still crimson hand, the soft blue light pulsing against my palm.

"One chance is all I'll give you. You were caught in things that never involved you. You were created from the hatred of one woman, so I'll give you one chance to live as a mortal and have a good life in secret."

I sent her soul to be reborn in Cylla and snuck my way back to where I knew Vesim would show herself. I needed to get back to my sister. The other two had guardians. Shivani only had me and two men who didn't know what they were. The responsibility weighed on me like a mountain.

She didn't understand, but we were many steps closer now. I felt my mother clinging to Fennic, and with every bit of weakness Yumi showed while being tortured, my mother had a chance to come through the seal. I was one step away from being an original Goddess again. I killed my counter and ate the heart; I found my body and my own heart. I only needed to get back inside of myself and get us all in the same realm again.

There was no use in thinking of anything else until that was complete. The path forward was clear, even if the journey would be difficult. Everything else was just a distraction.

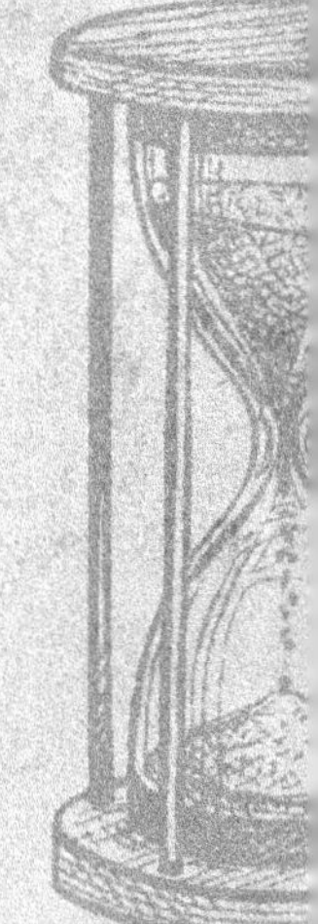

CHAPTER TWENTY-FIVE

THE SCROLLS

SHIVANI

When Vesim came back with Hesperia, she had an air of sadness about her. It was so brief that I doubted myself. She was back to wearing her happy eyes while we made our way to the dungeon, but I couldn't take my mind off of it. Was she truly happy? Or was she better than the rest of us at hiding things? Could I ask her that? Would she be honest? Would she teach me how to fake it until it was how I always looked, too? The questions tumbled through my mind like stones down a hillside.

"Shivani," Vesim whispered, nudging my arm.

"Yes?" I looked up, startled from my thoughts.

"You're mumbling to yourself." Her brow was raised, concern etched in the small lines around her eyes.

I held my hand over my mouth, heat rising to my cheeks. "Could you hear what I was thinking?"

"It was mostly gibberish that you were mumbling, not thinking," Vesim explained, her voice gentle but firm.

"You don't sound convincing," I replied, narrowing my eyes.

Hesperia looked at me with a side-eyed glance, her lips twitching with suppressed amusement.

"You just always look so happy. It's strange," I confessed, watching Vesim's face for any reaction.

"I am happy," she affirmed. "Sometimes I feel sadness, but there's no reason to let it linger. You feel it, and then you put it away. If I were caught up in emotions all day, I'd never get anywhere. You do what needs to be done because it needs to be done. Just as you feel what you need to feel so it can go away."

"Were you like this when you were alive, too?" I asked, curiosity getting the better of me.

"Yes. It drove one of my sisters crazy then, too," Hesperia smirked, a knowing gleam in her eyes.

I wanted to change the subject. I was feeling uncomfortable, as she had to be knowing I was talking about her, even if it was meant to stay in my head. My fingers fidgeted with the hem of my sleeve.

"What did you do while you waited for Vesim to come back for you?" I asked, trying to sound casual.

Her eyes widened for a second, like she was trying to decide how to answer me, a flash of something unreadable crossing her face.

"I just looked around," she replied, too quickly.

"They let you wander on your own?" I pressed, sensing her hesitation.

"I wouldn't say they let me. How was your visit?" she deflected, changing the subject with practiced ease.

"Good!" I cleared my throat, the word coming out too enthusiastically.

That was probably far too happy of an answer. I could feel my cheeks burning.

"Oh?" she questioned, her tone lilting with suggestion.

"It was just nice to get away from things here, that's all. It's helped me feel more focused," I swallowed the knot of anxiety in my throat, the necklace Koa gave me suddenly feeling heavy against my skin.

She looked at me from the side of her eyes, but it didn't stop me from seeing the smirk on her face, knowing and far too perceptive.

I wasn't telling a lie. I was feeling more focused. I felt renewed with a new sense of what my path needed to be. I had made my choice. I was going to focus on the journal and my dreams, not Riven. I was positive that they had enough to do with each other that following the mystery would lead me to the answer on how to get the sun god artifact away from Riven so he would die. I was sure after thinking on it that it had to be the reason I found the journal in the first place. It held the key, buried somewhere in its weathered pages.

I slammed into Vesim's back as she stopped mid-step with no notice, my nose colliding painfully with her shoulder blade.

"Coy has hardly dug any of this altar out!" Vesim exclaimed, her voice echoing off the stone walls.

"It is a big ask," Hesperia remarked, floating around the half-excavated area.

"He's a big boy," Vesim mocked, gesturing at the minimal progress.

"We will just have to take a page from Hesperia and get the job that needs to be done, done," I suggested, trying to be helpful.

"So, you want to dig?" Vesim asked, skepticism dripping from her voice.

"I want us to dig," I clarified, standing a little straighter.

"While she does nothing with her useless ghost fingers?" Vesim scoffed, jerking her head toward Hesperia.

"It's not my fault!" Hesperia cried, her hands passing through a nearby shovel as if to prove her point.

I grabbed a shovel that leaned against the stone wall and

shoved it into the dirt with determination. If there was something I could have been good at in this castle, it was going to be this. The physical labor felt right, somehow. Before I could dig out more than a scoop of dirt, I noticed the ring on my hand glowed, a warm golden light pulsing from its surface. Not just mine, but the ring Hesperia wore glowed, too, the light casting eerie shadows across the dungeon floor.

"What is your ring?" I asked her, my voice hushed with wonder.

"It's a golden band that ties my soul to the Goddess of winter," she stated matter-of-factly.

"What?" I shook my head, trying to process her words.

"I don't know how else to say that," her eyes shifted between Vesim and I, a hint of nervousness in her ghostly features.

"I found this one in the dungeon cell. Why are they both glowing?" I asked, holding up my hand where the light seemed to grow stronger by the second.

"This castle is built on the rubble of the old god's homeland. You're bound to find many relics. If it allowed you to wear it, it was for a reason. If it's glowing, it must also be for a reason," Hesperia spoke slowly, choosing her words with care.

I truly wanted to like her, but the fact that she couldn't give a direct answer any time I asked her something rubbed me the wrong way. It was like trying to catch smoke with your bare hands. I held my hand up and followed the path around the dirt. It glowed brighter the further I walked, the light guiding me like a beacon.

"So why does the Goddess of Winter have so many rings lying around?" I asked, unable to keep the edge from my voice.

"That ring belongs to the Goddess of Fall," Hesperia answered, her tone casual as if discussing the weather.

"So why is the Goddess of Fall's ring here?" Vesim picked up where I left off, her patience clearly wearing thin.

"It was meant for a sister of creation. Each season was tied to each stage of life. Creation, spring. Growth, summer. Time, or aging, was tied to fall. Death, winter," Hesperia explained, her eyes distant as if recalling something from long ago.

"Why is it glowing on her hand?" Vesim demanded, pointing at my finger where the ring pulsed brighter.

We found ourselves in front of a door that was glowing just like our rings, the stone surface humming with energy. When I held my hand against it, the door opened without resistance, ancient hinges groaning in protest. Vesim and Hesperia followed in quickly behind me as if it were a race, our footsteps echoing in the newfound space. Every wall inside was lined with shelves that held scroll after scroll, hundreds of them stacked neatly from floor to ceiling. The air smelled of old parchment and dust, thick with age.

"Wow," was all I could say, my voice barely a whisper in the vastness.

Hesperia squealed and wasted no time moving toward each scroll she could. "Mom is going to be so happy when she sees us together and with Cyrus's scrolls!" she exclaimed, practically bouncing with excitement.

"What?" I stopped walking, her words hitting me like a bucket of cold water.

"What," she acted as if she hadn't said anything at all, suddenly very interested in a particular scroll.

"Hesperia, I thought you didn't remember anything but your name," I accused, stepping closer to her.

"It took some time, but it came back," she shrugged and refused to make eye contact, her ghostly form shifting uncomfortably.

"Why didn't you say anything!" I asked, frustration building in my chest like pressure in a sealed pot.

"You don't have to yell at me! You didn't specifically ask, and we were having so much fun. I didn't want to ruin the mystery," she was talking with her hands, gesturing wildly as if that would somehow make her explanation more convincing.

"I'd prefer less mystery and more honesty," I demanded, crossing my arms.

"If I thought you could handle more, I would give you more," she sighed, a flicker of genuine concern crossing her face.

"I can handle it," I mumbled, feeling like a child being told to wait until I was older.

Hesperia moved to a shelf of scrolls as if I hadn't been speaking to her, her hands passing through some while somehow managing to touch others, a contradiction I was too frustrated to question.

I tried to do the same and look as unbothered as she was by pulling out scrolls as if I knew what they were, the parchment rough against my fingertips. I opened one, and it was only a list of animals, names I'd never heard of written in flowing script. I put it back and moved to a different shelf before pulling down another. It, too, was only a list of plants, their properties described in meticulous detail.

"Whoever Cyrus is should have marked these better. Why keep an entire library for records of life?" I asked, blowing dust from another scroll.

"He was very, hmm, uptight," Hesperia remarked, a fond smile playing on her lips.

Vesim shoved the one she was holding back onto the shelf with a huff. "I can't even understand what any of them say. They aren't written in our language. I don't know how you two are seeing anything."

"What do you mean?" I said, reaching for another. I opened it and read the words fine, the script clear as day to my eyes. "This scroll speaks about the God of Justice and his role in being someone named Olexei's enforcer. It has a list of things he accomplished and a separate list of the things his brother, the god of protection, did under someone named Dahlia's orders."

"Mhm. I still can't read it myself," Vesim crossed her arms, squinting at the scroll in my hands as if hoping the symbols would suddenly make sense.

"I have this funny feeling in my stomach reading these. It's a kind of déjà vu I can't explain. I've been here in a dream, or —" I didn't know how to explain what I was feeling, the words catching in my throat as a strange sensation washed over me.

"Have you been dreaming of places like this? Since the visit to the fortune teller?" Hesperia asked, suddenly very interested, her eyes sharp and focused.

When all of my fingers were wrapped around the scroll, blood magic started to stream from my fingers and palms, crimson tendrils winding up the parchment. I tried to shove it back down, but it did not listen to me, the power surging through me like a river breaking its banks.

"Alright, let's not do that. We don't want anyone to know you're the goddess of—actually do whatever you want. I'm going to go," Hesperia shook her hands, backing away.

"Hesperia! Stop right there! What did you just say?" I demanded, my heart pounding in my ears.

"I think she implied you're a Goddess?" Vesim shook her head as if it were the most ridiculous thought she had ever heard, though her eyes betrayed a flicker of uncertainty.

"How did you know I was having dreams?" I asked, refusing to let Hesperia dodge the question this time.

"That was the point of going there. He waited there a long time so that he could kick start our memories when we were found, and now he is dead," Hesperia's face was covered in sadness again, one that lasted longer, a deep sorrow that seemed to dim her ghostly light.

"Who was he?" I asked, my voice softening.

"The God of knowledge," she answered, her voice barely audible.

"You can't be serious," Vesim grumbled, though her skepticism seemed less convincing now.

"I am. They aren't dreams. They are your own memories," Hesperia pressed, her eyes pleading for understanding.

"You mean to tell me that I'm a chosen one? Like A Chosen one? An actual Goddess?" I felt my mouth dry from how far it hung open, the idea simultaneously absurd and yet somehow... right.

"Mhm," she nodded, relief washing over her face at my reaction.

"You can't possibly believe this," Vesim interjected, looking between us like we'd both lost our minds.

"Hell yeah!" I laughed, giddy excitement replacing my earlier frustration.

I lifted my hand to give her a high five, but she slipped through me again, and I stumbled forward, nearly crashing into a shelf of scrolls.

"I keep forgetting about that, sorry," I feigned a laugh, embarrassment heating my face.

"Me too," she chuckled, a genuine warmth in her eyes.

"Funny joke, now can we get back to reality?" Vesim shoved another scroll back in its spot, crumpling the end in her haste.

"Maybe it's why she can read the scrolls, but you cannot," Hesperia suggested, her voice careful.

"If she's a Goddess, and the scrolls are reacting to her, then explain why. Tell me why it's glowing, and show me some sort of proof. Then we can discuss how there's a goddess here, and she's not helping any of us," Vesim demanded, frustration evident in every tense line of her body.

Hesperia showed only the second emotion I had seen from her outside of happiness, and it was anger. She looked as if she were going to hurt Vesim, her ghostly form swelling with an almost physical intensity. "I suspect it's got the location of her heart," Hesperia responded, her voice low and dangerous. "Pick your words with more caution moving forward."

I watched Vesim's chest rise until it couldn't go any further; she considered her response well before giving one, wisely backing down from the suddenly intimidating ghost. "So, we go find the heart then?"

"My heart. Yes, we go find my heart!" I said as if I already knew all of the answers, the words feeling right on my tongue despite their strangeness.

"Are we really going to trust her?" Vesim asked, pulling my arm, her fingers digging into my sleeve.

"Why shouldn't we?" I asked, surprised by her vehemence.

"She just admitted she's been lying to us!" Vesim glared at me, disbelief written across her features.

"I haven't really been lying," Hesperia defended, her voice taking on a wheedling tone. "It's more I've been picking my words carefully."

"That's still not honesty!" Vesim yelled back at her, her patience finally snapping.

"I understand. I do. I just don't want to mess up. If you want to speak to me alone, I'll tell you anything you want. Not in front of her," Hesperia pointed at me, her expression a mixture of worry and determination.

"Why!" I yelled back, feeling betrayed.

"If I force you too hard, you'll break again. It has to be on your time, your way," she answered, her voice softening with what seemed like genuine concern.

Vesim doubted her, and I understood it. Sometimes, Vesim even doubted me. We all hardly knew each other when the timeline was laid out. I believed Hesperia. I believed too easily, maybe, but she felt genuine. There was something in her eyes that spoke of shared pain, of connections I couldn't yet remember.

"Will you go with Vesim?" I asked, trying to bridge the growing divide.

Vesim ran her tongue across her teeth and shook her head. "If it's a trap, I'm leaving you to die in it," she warned before she stormed out, her footsteps heavy with frustration.

I followed her out, and the door shut behind us without a finger on it. I thought it had to have been Hesperia, but the ring flashed, and I heard a click as if it were locked tight again. The door disappeared in front of the three of us, melting into the stone as if it had never existed. A chill ran down my spine at the unexplainable magic.

I jumped out of my skin when the harem leader was standing in front of Vesim, materializing as if from nowhere, her severe face pinched with displeasure.

"So, it's true," she clicked her tongue at us, her eyes cold and calculating.

"We were just looking for you!" I feigned a laugh, the sound brittle even to my own ears.

She lifted her hand and pointed to the stairwell. "The only thing you two will be looking for now is the toilets. You'll spend the rest of your day cleaning them," she decreed, satisfaction evident in her smug expression.

She followed us the entire walk, and I wished Hesperia would have used some sort of ghostly ability to call Coy to our aide. He would have gotten us out of this, his silent strength a shield against such petty punishments.

She shoved a brush and a bar of soap in my hands, as well as Vesim's hands, before leaving us with a guard standing watch outside. The stench hit me immediately, making my eyes water.

"It smells awful in here!" Hesperia groaned as she held her nose, her face contorting dramatically.

"Can you even truly smell it if you're dead?" Vesim shot back at her, venom in her voice.

I was already pushing toilet paper up my nose, trying to block the foul odor. "I'm sorry I didn't listen, Vesim. If I were a goddess, we would not be doing this!" I lamented, looking around at the filthy chamber pots and stained floors.

Hesperia giggled and wiggled her fingers. "I wish I could help, but I can't hold the soap," she teased, floating safely above the mess.

Vesim threw her bar at Hesperia, but it only hit the wall where she once was. She was already long gone, leaving us to our punishment with nothing but her fading laughter echoing in the fetid air.

CHAPTER TWENTY-SIX
THE HEART

FENNIC

I expected Shivani to be careless. I've seen firsthand that she has no idea how this place works. I've seen that she overestimates her abilities, but Vesim? I held her to a higher standard. I don't know why she thought that they could make plans to sneak out, and no one would report it back. This felt like a constant kind of problem. As if I had no time to deal with anything of my own because one of them was ready to stir up an issue. It was as if they wanted to die. I just knew one of them would tell me that they didn't need my help because they'd have Coy. He was hardly good conversation. He looked big, but he was not as skilled with a weapon as I was. I was made for protecting.

I hadn't put the huffing and mumbling away when the two of them came into sight, with, to no surprise, Coy. My irritation was evident in every sharp exhale.

"Did you really think you'd make it out without alerting the entire castle?" I bellowed, my voice carrying across the courtyard.

Shivani rolled her eyes. "I hardly consider you the entire castle."

"One is enough to have you brought back to Riven in chains!" I pointed, my finger jabbing toward her.

"Is that what you intend to do?" She raised a brow, defiance written across her face.

"I'm here to tell you that sneaking around is going to lead to consequences!" I growled, heat rising to my cheeks.

"Wow, I had no idea," she dripped sarcasm, her lips curling into a mocking smile.

"What do you want, Fennic?" Vesim questioned, her patience clearly thinning.

"To know what you think you're doing," I responded, crossing my arms over my chest.

"Leaving?" She waved a hand, pointing out the scenery as if I were blind to the obvious.

"If I know, how many others know, too?" My words hung in the air between us like a challenge.

"Please, you're wasting our time!" Shivani pleaded, already shifting her weight to move past me.

"I'm going with," I declared as I pulled the hood of my cloak up, the fabric settling heavily over my head.

"We have Coy, we don't need anything else," Shivani objected, waving her hand dismissively.

"You're running out of chances. You're teetering the line of punishment. What if Coy isn't enough?" I warned, genuine concern mixing with my frustration.

"Duel, then," Coy suggested, his deep voice resonating in the still air.

"Didn't she just say you were running out of time? We can't duel!" I exclaimed, incredulity sharpening my words.

"Are you scared?" Vesim taunted, her eyes glinting with challenge.

"I'm going with. Period," I insisted as I shoved them ahead, ending the discussion.

She was better at throwing a tantrum than she was at any other thing she had done since arriving a month ago. She proved my point the longer we walked. She stomped ahead of us as if she were a toddler without a toy. She was successful in raising a blood slave, but it was clear it was she who did it immediately. She failed to give us the correct information on the other dealer. She failed to seduce Riven well enough to become queen. She failed to kill the other girl and cover it up; I had to frame it as bandits. She even failed to convince me she belonged at the castle at all. Each of her failures strengthened my resolve to watch over her, despite her protests.

She still looked like she had learned no lessons while we marched. She did not look as if she were reflecting on her mistakes, even though I caught her red-handed. The stubborn tilt of her chin told me everything I needed to know.

"How are you doing?" Hesperia inquired, materializing beside me without warning.

I jumped at her sudden appearance, my heart leaping to my throat, and my face contorted at the question. "Why are you asking me?"

"I was only curious if any strange things had been happening. Any nightmares?" she probed, her eyes searching mine with unsettling intensity.

"Should there be?" I questioned, a chill racing down my spine despite the warm day.

Hesperia only shrugged, but the knowing look in her eyes made my skin crawl.

"Where are we going, anyway?" I asked the group, eager to change the subject.

"We are following a map," Vesim revealed, her gaze fixed ahead on the path.

"It should lead us to a heart that Shivani has to eat," Hesperia added nonchalantly.

"Why?" I asked in disgust, my stomach turning at the

thought. "Where did you find this map, and why are we listening to it?"

"In a secret room. It was left by the keeper of records," Hesperia explained, her ghostly form drifting alongside us.

"Why does she need to eat it?" I shivered, unable to hide my revulsion.

"So that she can ascend back to godhood," Hesperia stated simply, as if discussing something as mundane as the weather.

"Shivani? A God?" I laughed, the sound hollow even to my own ears.

"A Goddess," Shivani snapped back, her eyes flashing with irritation.

"It's nonsense," Vesim interjected, though doubt lingered in her voice.

I wanted to agree, no, I did agree. In every way except the little memory that I had shoved down and away of the hallucination I had while I traveled. A tiny bit of me was sent into a spiraled panic. If this was proven, if I saw with my own eyes that she really was a goddess, then it meant my death warrant. The thought settled in my gut like a stone.

The lining of trees ended, and ahead of us was the swamp lands. It was a part of our world, and no one traveled anymore. Stories told of a time when it was sprawling with people; I had never seen such a time. I had only ever seen it filled with creatures and death on the edge of our castle. The stench of decay and stagnant water filled my nostrils.

I watched every step they took, prepared to have to pick them up out of the mushed ground with every step. The idea of Vesim or Shivani being lost to whatever may lay underneath made me sick to my stomach. They were paying little attention to me, which meant every time they slid a little too far, they didn't notice my body jump in their direction. The flinching was something I could not put away. It wasn't them; it was the idea of failing at my duty. My hands twitched at my sides, ready to lunge forward at the first sign of danger.

"It's glowing!" Hesperia called out, her voice pitched high with excitement.

Everyone rushed to her as if they all knew something I didn't, their feet splashing through the murky water.

"Mine is glowing, too!" Shivani exclaimed, holding up her hand where a ring pulsed with golden light.

Both of them lowered themselves down until their rings were hovering just above the water, and up came a box. It rose from the depths as if pulled by invisible strings, water cascading from its ornate surface. It was wrapped in words that, at first, I could not make out. It took less than a minute before I could read them all, the symbols shifting and changing before my eyes.

"Sealed by the God of Famine," I mumbled out, the words feeling foreign on my tongue.

"Great. So, we found it, but we have no way to open it," Shivani groaned, her shoulders slumping with disappointment.

"Are you serious? Another one of you that can read that shit?" Vesim shouted, her frustration echoing across the swamp.

"Coy, touch it!" Hesperia urged, her form practically vibrating with anticipation.

He looked at her with as much confusion as the rest of us, but he listened. He laid his open palm over the words, and the box lit up with a burst of light as bright as the sun. A click was heard next, the sound sharp in the quiet stillness.

Shivani opened the box, and my jaw dropped with the lid, disbelief washing over me.

"You've got to be kidding," I muttered, shaking my head.

"I told you the truth, Fennic," Hesperia affirmed, crossing her arms with satisfaction.

Shivani opened the box, and inside was a perfectly preserved, still beating heart. It pulsed with life, crimson and vital despite having no body to sustain it. The sight defied everything I knew to be possible.

"I have to be dreaming," I laughed, the sound tinged with hysteria. "You're not really going to eat that, are you?"

Shivani's lips couldn't have been turned any further down. She bit into the heart, eyes locked with mine as if to challenge me. Blood trickled down her chin as she chewed, her gaze never wavering. She was the one having to chew it, not me. If there were any jokes happening, it was on her. The squelching sound as she bit down made my stomach lurch.

"If she's a Goddess, and you want me to believe my brother is the God of Famine, then I'm calling myself the Sun God and Vesim a Goddess of War," I scoffed, but no one joined my laughter. The silence that followed was deafening.

Hesperia clicked her tongue in one of the few expressions beyond smiling I had seen her give, disappointment radiating from her ghostly form.

"You are a far cry from the Sun God. I can assure you Vesim is just a very lucky mortal," she proclaimed, her tone leaving no room for argument.

"If we're going to bring everything to light, I think it's time I share that I've been reading the journal of the Goddess of Starlight," Shivani revealed, wiping blood from her mouth with the back of her hand.

"What? Has it helped you remember anything?" Hesperia questioned eagerly, moving closer to Shivani.

"Not really," she sighed, the weight of disappointment clear in her voice.

"Does it say anything useful?" I inquired, not yet convinced I should be believing any of this madness.

"I'll give it to you when we get back," she promised, tucking a strand of hair behind her ear.

"Are you sure I'm not a goddess?" Vesim pressed again, hope mingling with skepticism in her voice.

Shivani skipped over her words, "Actually, I don't know if

it matters, but I did start having a repeat dream. Someone is discussing how they found a way to detect the traitor, and then I see the outline of a man."

"What color was his hair? Did you hear his voice?" Hesperia demanded, hovering inches from Shivani's face, urging her to give any droplet of information. "Where is the tool?"

"Nothing else has happened yet," Shivani admitted, rubbing her temples as if trying to coax more memories to surface.

Shivani put the box in my hands and turned back to Hesperia. I was curious and wanted to look it over, but out of the box came a small glowing orb. It hovered before me, pulsing with an otherworldly light.

"Hey, uh, what is this?" I asked, my voice tight with sudden apprehension.

The bright light from my last vision was back again. This time, it was hotter than anything I had ever felt before. I felt my skin char and melt away, agony consuming every inch of me. Then it was dark. Everything was black and quiet. I was sure that I had died. In every direction I turned to walk, it went nowhere. The void was absolute, pressing in on me from all sides.

"Hello?" I screamed, my voice swallowed by the darkness.

A set of white fingernails cut a slice in the darkness. They reached through and grabbed me by my collar, pulling me back with impossible force.

Gasping for air, everything was bright again. "I think I died!" I coughed out, my lungs burning as if I'd been under-water too long.

"You did. Luckily, Hesperia brought you back," Shivani confirmed, her expression a mix of concern and fascination.

"How the hell?" I wheezed, my body feeling strangely hollow.

"Hi," she grinned, her ghostly face looming over mine. "I

am Hesperia. The goddess of Fate. The creator of necromancy. The ender of lives. The protector of the in-between! The original witch!"

"Okay, okay. You can stop now. That's enough, I think," I rasped, still gasping for air, my mind reeling from the implications.

"Rude!" she huffed, indignation flashing across her spectral features.

"Can we go now? I can't do that again," I groaned, pulling myself to my feet with trembling limbs. The lingering sensation of death clung to me like a shadow, and I wondered if I would ever feel completely alive again.

.

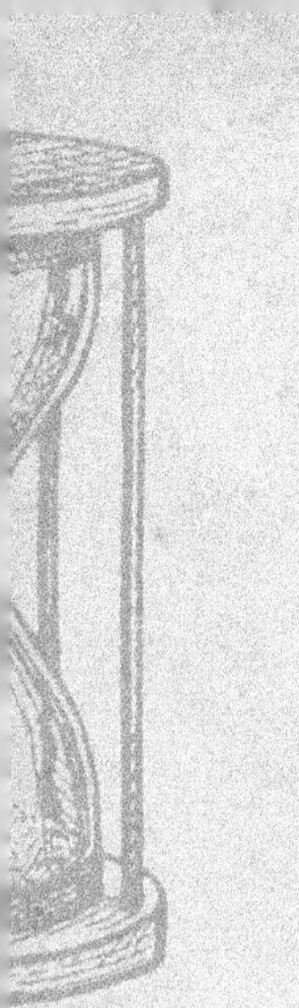

CHAPTER TWENTY-SEVEN

THE REUNION

SHIVANI

I was hardly able to pay attention to their arguing. The taste in my mouth was far too intense. The swamp water looked inviting when my mouth tasted like I had eaten a bowl of iron. I was positive there was a piece of heart stuck between my teeth, and I knew something without a doubt for the first time in weeks: I would never do that again.

I didn't question the dead girl. She seemed to know a lot. At least more than the rest of us. If she said it would help, I believed her. I wasn't convinced it was going to turn me into a Goddess. I wasn't convinced I was a Goddess. I didn't mind pretending it was probable all the same. It would have been fine with me. I wouldn't deny the title or the power. That's what I wanted, after all. The power to get Riven away from the castle was the entire reason I came.

My heart was racing as fast as my mind was, and it was difficult to keep my thoughts straight, but I had a flash of real-ization. If it was true, then it meant Hesperia was my family, my true family, and everything I had been through was just a mortal experience. The thought made me dizzy with possibilities.

My stomach started to turn, and my mouth grew drier. I wished they'd stop bickering and Vesim would just open the rift to Cylla. Koa would have offered me something to drink. Fennic only wanted to keep going back and forth with Vesim. She did not want him to go with us, and he refused to leave.

"Guys, can we move this along?" I croaked, my throat constricting.

My head started to feel dizzy, and my legs were weak, like saplings in a strong wind.

"Guys?" I called again through a shaky voice, sweat beading on my forehead.

"You aren't going without me! How many times do I have to tell you that I'm here for your protection?" Fennic was pointing and yelling, his face flushed with frustration.

"How many times do I have to tell you that of all the things you are in charge of, who goes in and out of my rift is not on the list!" Vesim was pointing back with as much force as he was, her eyes flashing dangerously.

There they went; my legs let me down, and I was on the wet ground, vomiting. It wasn't what I expected. It was red, but no pieces of the heart were in it. Coy grabbed my arms and lifted me back to my feet, but I could hardly hold myself. He was doing nearly all of the work. My mind felt like static. As if it were being reset somehow. Fed information in a rush. Such a rush that I could hardly process any of it. Images and sensations flooded my consciousness like water through a broken dam.

Vesim opened the rift and shoved me inside. She closed it faster than she had created it. A clear attempt to keep Fennic out.

"Why do you do this to me?" Juniper's cheeks were flushed red, her hands on her hips.

"I cannot help that this is where the rift opens every time I tell it to bring me to you," Vesim retorted, though a hint of satisfaction glimmered in her eyes.

"Thirsty," I pleaded, my voice barely audible as I clutched my throat.

"She ate her own heart," Hesperia announced with joy, practically bouncing in her spectral form.

"Gross," Juniper shivered, her face crinkling with disgust.

"Here."

I scooped the container and chugged like I hadn't drunk in days. It was sweet and cold. I drank until there was nothing left to drink and sighed with relief, the liquid washing away the metallic taste.

"Thanks," I groaned, wiping my mouth with the back of my hand.

I held out the container, but I nearly dropped it when my eyes met the girl who handed it to me. She caught it, but my mind was still racing to put puzzle pieces together after eating what was apparently my own heart.

"I know you," I whispered, something ancient stirring in my memory.

She searched my eyes in silence, her expression cautious yet hopeful.

Her skin was as dark as night, and it made her light blue hair stand out further, like stars against the night sky.

"This is Vespera," Koa explained, his hand settling gently on her shoulder.

"I used to call you V," I murmured, the words coming from somewhere deep inside me.

She nodded. "That's the second time I've heard that. I don't know what to say. They said not to jar you."

"You used to help Cyrus with his books. You were—" I had to stop and grab my head. It pounded with each word, like a hammer striking an anvil.

"Take it slow. Let things come naturally," Koa advised, his voice gentle but firm.

"I have a bookstore in Cylla now, so things haven't changed that much," Vespera tried to joke, her smile uncertain.

"Where the hell are we?" Fennic bellowed, suddenly bursting through the rift behind us.

Koa had a hand on the hilt of the sword that sat on his hip, his posture immediately shifting to defensive.

"He's just our stupid friend. Trust me, he's not that tough," I groaned through the throbs in my temple, waving a dismissive hand.

"This is who I told you about," Hesperia remarked, gesturing toward Fennic.

"Him?" Koa laughed, skepticism written across his face. "You have to be kidding me."

"What is so funny, huh?" Fennic challenged as he gripped his own blade, his knuckles white.

"Knock it off. He's the God of War. You won't get far," I warned, massaging my temples.

"He's the God of Protection," Hesperia corrected, pointing at Fennic. "He may get a little further than you think."

I didn't hold it back; I let the laughter pour out, and Koa joined. Even in my sweaty, disoriented state, I couldn't believe that. The idea of Fennic—who had tried to poison me—being a protector was too absurd.

"He's a little slow now," Hesperia defended. "When mother gets a say in it, he will be back to normal."

"Your mother is still a tree," Juniper reminded her, arms crossed over her chest.

"Your mother is the tree chick? You keep her far away from me!" Fennic demanded, taking a step back.

"You're scared of the tree girl and ignoring everything else?" I asked, still laughing despite the pain.

"There is a lot happening!" Fennic shouted, throwing his hands up.

"So, Shivani is my sister, and we're both Goddesses. Coy is actually not your brother; he's a guardian. His brother is Koa, that guy. Vesim is just a mortal who has the hots for that girl, the Goddess of Wrath. She thinks we don't know, but we definitely know. You're scared of the tree lady, but once you were her right hand, her favorite. Vesim can rift, and so here we are, in Semper, the realm of the Gods. Where we actually belong. Big bad Aunty killed us all, erased memories, and broke the realm in half. I think that catches you up?" Hesperia tapped on her chin as if caught up in thought, her recap breathless and enthusiastic.

"The rest of us are all trapped in the stars," Koa added, his expression darkening.

Everyone nodded except Fennic and I, the two of us looking at each other with shared confusion.

Fennic slapped himself in the face. "I had to give it a shot."

He looked lost in thought, brow furrowed. "Why do you remember this, but no one else does?"

"I'm dead. I feel as though I've said this a lot," she sighed dramatically. "Moving on, when we found her heart, a soul shard was with it. I brought it back for you all to figure out. I can't seem to feel who it belongs to."

Koa reached out to take it into his own hands, examining it closely. "It appears to be fake."

"We also found no way to get you into a body," Juniper revealed. "And because of what you did on your last visit, Hesperia, the presence of blood guards has doubled! They think one of us killed Minna."

"Sorry," she chuckled, not looking sorry at all.

Juniper mocked her laugh, clearly not agreeing there was any humor in it, her eyes narrowing.

"You killed someone?" I asked, my voice rising in disbelief.

"It was my counter. I would be whole again, a full Goddess again if I had a body. I'm only missing a connection with my guardian to ascend. I miss my markings," she lamented, her ghostly form flickering with emotion.

"Is that why Shivani still doesn't remember?" Fennic inquired, surprisingly thoughtful.

"No. I am dead. The rules don't work the same way. When I get my body back, I'll lose a lot, too," Hesperia explained, her tone shifting to annoyance.

"Then I need to go kill my counter?" I asked, the thought simultaneously horrifying and intriguing.

"Not a chance," Koa declared firmly, his eyes flashing with warning.

"But Hesperia—" I was cut off.

"Hesperia killed her counter because Minna was the weakest of anyone I've met in this realm. It was not a competition. Helia transformed Minna into something we've never seen before. It was an easy task. Helia is not," Vespera cautioned, her voice grave.

"She is unbelievably strong. It would not be wise to fight with her yet," Juniper emphasized, her expression deadly serious.

"It's also why you shouldn't stay long. As much as I would love for you to stay, I can't risk you," Koa admitted, his eyes softening as they met mine.

He grabbed both of my hands, and I was suddenly aware of how hard Fennic's eyes were burning into me, jealousy radiating from him in palpable waves.

"Actually, I think we should take the soul shard to Merripen and make sure it's a fake before we leave," Hesperia suggested, floating toward the door.

"Do you know how much trouble you've caused here? Helia thinks we killed Minna, but I know she's keeping things close to her chest. Another branch sprouted on the tree. One with bare branches, sometimes it drops snowflakes," Juniper exclaimed, her frustration evident in every word. "A tree with no blemishes now has a branch that looks like it is wilting into fall and a completely empty one."

"Okay, okay. Let's go to Merripen if voices are going to be raised like this," Koa intervened, ushering us along with gentle but insistent hands.

"My branch sprouted!" Hesperia was shedding tears, joy transforming her ghostly features.

What threw me off focus was seeing that Fennic cried, too. He was catching every tear before it could trail off too far from his eyes, as if ashamed of the emotion. The group was so focused on getting us through the vines that I wasn't sure anyone else saw it. I knew we couldn't stop, but I knew it was breaking my heart to see such a sudden shift of emotions in him. I was still upset that he killed me, and there was no hope of us ever having a romantic relationship again, but that didn't mean I couldn't feel for him, right? The conflict twisted inside me like a knot.

When we were through the vines, more Gods and dragons were waiting. It was a sight to see, and if I could have saved it, I would have. A small home with rocking chairs sat behind them, and I mindlessly followed. Hesperia was at home, giddy. She greeted and hugged and gushed as if she never missed a beat, and those eyes that I admired so much glowed even brighter, like stars coming alive.

I took Fennic's hand in my own because I could relate closer to him than anyone else present. I felt bonded to Koa, but I hardly understood it. I knew I cared for him on a deeper level than I had ever cared for anyone, but that didn't mean he understood this feeling. I was sure I knew many of them, but only as faint memories, like being a child. Only glimpses that were hard to put together. Fennic and I were both being told that we belonged somewhere we couldn't recall, adrift in a sea of familiar strangers.

I hated him, but somehow, we were the only ones to

understand this feeling. He gripped my hand back, his palm sweaty against mine, and when we sat, Koa took my other side and didn't speak a word about what he saw, his silent understanding a comfort.

"My name is Caym," he introduced himself to Fennic.

He held out a gloved hand to shake. Fennic didn't respond to the offer or introduction, and Caym didn't force it. Caym took the soul shard from Koa and held it up to the light. "It's not fake, but I can't tell who it belongs to either. It's broken, missing the other half," Caym observed, examining it from different angles.

"What do we do with it then?" I asked, leaning forward.

"I'll keep it locked here to be safe," Caym decided, tucking it away in a pouch at his belt.

Fennic cleared his throat, "Can I ask a question?"

"Sure," Caym invited, his attention now fully on Fennic.

He had taken over as the leader's presence from the moment we walked through the vines. Everyone looked at him with admiration and trust, deferring to him without question.

"Do I," Fennic paused and cleared his throat again, his Adam's apple bobbing. "If Coy is not my brother. If he's not my family, do I have anyone?"

His voice cracked harder the further he got into his sentence, and it caused the same lump in my throat. I was sure Fennic was dead inside, and now he was pouring emotions, his vulnerability shocking and raw.

"If you are here. If you are granted entry to my realm, then we are family," Caym assured him, his lips straight and pressed together. "Your mortal life is still a life you lived. You were raised in this body with Coy as your brother; that doesn't change in a single conversation. He is still your brother."

"You do have a brother," Hesperia revealed, her excitement barely contained. "I had hoped you would want to meet him."

"Me too. When my Nola let me know you were here, I told him to retrieve your brother. If you're ready—"

Fennic cut Caym off, "I'm ready." His voice trembled with anticipation.

Fennic dropped my hand and stood, shoving the chair out with a loud scrape. A man with short orange hair came from the door of the house. He looked serious until he didn't. When he dropped the stone face, he really dropped it, emotion transforming him completely.

He held his arms out, "Hey," he exclaimed, the word stretched with feeling.

Fennic didn't hesitate; he was like a child seeing his father after a long trip or someone being reunited with their lost pet. When Fennic hit him, he shoved the air out of the man, their embrace fierce and desperate. It was that moment where he and Hesperia resembled each other, raw emotion breaking through their usual masks.

"Fennic, Aero. Aero, Fennic," Caym announced, though his introduction was merely formality.

Neither of them paid any attention to the words being said. Coy was the one to crack the smile, and we used it as the signal to move on while they bonded, giving them space for their reunion.

"We do have limited time," Caym reminded us gently, guiding us away.

"We found a room filled with scrolls," Vesim reported, her posture straightening as she addressed him.

"Cyrus will be pleased to hear that," Caym acknowledged with a nod.

"I also found a journal of someone named Yumi," I mentioned, pulling it from my pocket. "It talks about the events leading up to now." I sat it on the table, the leather binding worn and faded.

Caym opened it and flipped the pages, his brow furrowing. "They're all blank," he stated, showing me the empty pages.

"What?" I grabbed it and flipped through them myself, panic rising in my chest. "No, I was just reading about how She and—" I gripped my chest and yelled, pain searing through me like fire.

"I told you! It hurts when you try and speak on it," Hesperia reminded me, her expression sympathetic.

"It's all right. As long as we have the information, we can find ways to share it with each other," he sighed and looked around the group, his expression grave. "I hate to be the one to do this, but you have to go. We can't take such big risks right now. We need time to plan things here, and you need the same. You need to work on your side so we can figure out how to get you all here permanently."

Even though I didn't want to leave, I knew he was right. I felt like I could trust him to lead me, too. Hesperia took his attention to exchange a few last words before we left, and I turned to Koa. I had hoped to be able to talk to him for just a minute. Just a second to look at him before we left, but Fennic's voice interrupted that thought.

"No!" He stepped back, horror flashing across his face. "I can't. Please. Don't make me go back. I can be helpful here! I can follow orders and wield a blade. I don't even need to eat for days."

His voice was filled with fear and pleading, desperation etched into every line of his face. I moved to him, but it was Hesperia who moved herself to be face-to-face with him.

"I know you can be helpful. It's why we need you with us. You help by protecting Shivani so we can find a way to get back here. Okay?" she coaxed, her voice gentler than I'd ever heard it.

Fennic searched her face; his hands were still shaking, but he relented and embraced Aero one last time before Vesim shoved us all back through the rift.

He didn't stumble or need time to recover like the rest of us sitting on the ground of my room. He left us immediately, his footsteps echoing down the hallway. I didn't try to stop him. There was nothing anyone could say to me to make me feel better about being back in our realm, either. The weight of our reality settled back on my shoulders like a familiar, unwelcome burden.

CHAPTER TWENTY-EIGHT

MEMORY FRAGMENT

Half of the golden city was in ruins. Our altar was cracked and broken. The cries of mortal children were all I could hear in a slow, drug-out melody. Yumi was killing without looking to see who she was murdering. She pulled a soul from its body, placed it in a star, and threw it to the sky where even if we did reach, it wouldn't undo what she had already done. Each star that joined the night sky was another life lost forever.

Mothers huddled over their infants, and mortal men drew swords to fight with our army. They were the first to die against Nikola's creatures. Everywhere the creatures stepped, death followed. The grass browned, and the flowers molded. The city was still shining gold, even in rubble, and wrapped with death.

Ruri and Sage were already gone. They were silent stars in the night sky. Mother told me not to resist. She said it was too late to alter the course of events. That all we could do now was wait until we were reborn, but it felt wrong to give up in that way. I couldn't accept surrender when blood still pumped through my veins. I needed to pass the information I had to someone else first. I knew who the traitor was. I heard the conversation Nikola had with Sahir before our world was sent into ruin. I had to find Hesperia before Yumi found me. Mother was refusing to listen to anything I had to say.

I ran faster than I had ever run before. I ran through the ghosts that Hesperia raised. She had to be at the place where they began. I twisted my left hand until my palm was up, then my right in a rhythm to form blood-stepping stools. I needed a higher view. I had to move faster. The air burned in my lungs, but I couldn't slow down.

A fire sprite found me, her tiny wings fluttering as fast as my heart was beating. I grabbed her leg and pulled her into my chest in time to remove her from the path of Nikola's magic. The blast of energy missed us by inches, leaving a smoking crater in the earth. I cradled her to my chest and pushed my wings out to use instead of the blood magic. Nikola was close, but it was Yumi I feared today.

"Where is Hesperia?" I whispered, my voice barely audible above the chaos.

"Through the trees," she chittered, her tiny body trembling against my palm.

"I need you to take this box and hide it. Okay?" I pressed her harder to my chest. "Hide it and yourself in Mother's cottage."

The realization that it was her family being plunged in the middle of this war, too, and that she had to have lost just as many as the mortals felt like a punch to the stomach. I released her, and she cradled the fate box with father's tool as tightly as I cradled her. Her small face was set with determination as she darted away.

I saw Hesperia, but before calling to her, I turned and tossed blood chains around Nikola. They wouldn't hold him, but they would slow him. The crimson links sizzled as they wrapped around his limbs.

"Hesperia!" I screamed, my voice cracking with desperation.

She looked up, and balls of white light raced past me. The light turned into ghosts, and they entered Nikola. Her possessions worked on mortals and some lesser gods, but for Nikola, it would only do the same as my own magic. Slowed, but not stopped. His face contorted with rage as he fought against our combined magic.

I planted my feet back on the ground, tucking my crimson wings. The earth felt unstable beneath me, as if the world itself was coming apart.

"There is a fire sprite heading to mom's. She has a fate box with a special tool. I used it, and it worked. I was coming to tell you all before this," I had to pause to catch my breath, my lungs burning. "Do not kill Nikola. I know it sounds foolish, and I'll explain when we have more time. The most important thing is that you do not trust—"

Yumi ripped me up by my wings, tearing one off. I didn't recognize the scream that came from me, the same as I couldn't process the amount of pain radiating through me. It was as if the world itself had been torn in half.

I felt every piece of myself, down to my fingernails, rip apart. My essence scattered like leaves in a violent storm.

One last gasp for air and quiet.

Who was I? The glow of starlight surrounding me was so beautiful. It embraced me as everything else faded away.

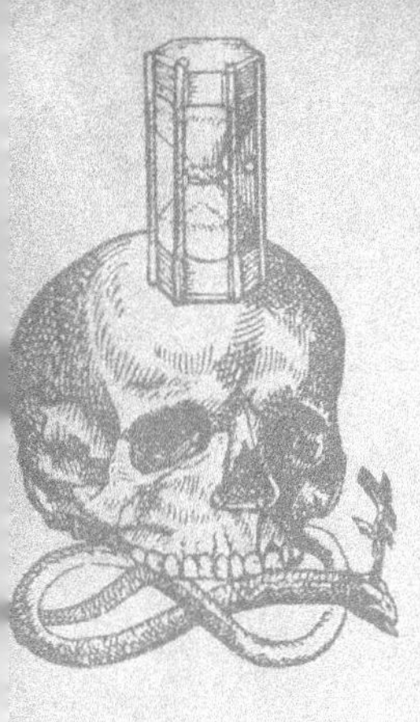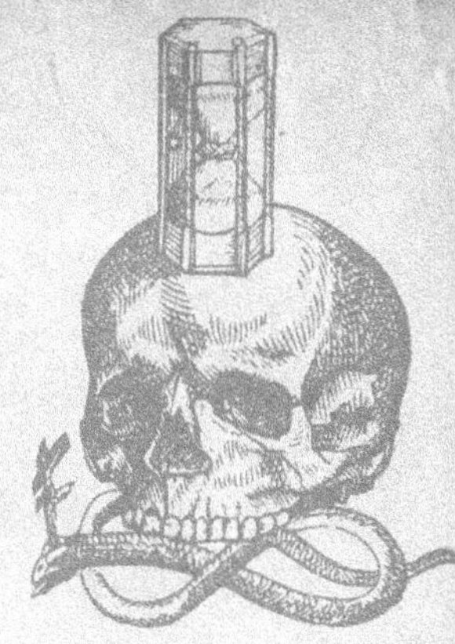

CHAPTER TWENTY-NINE
THE ROOM

The Old Gods

The God of Dreams held the title of prized son for only a moment before he grew bored of assigning lands of imagination to mortals and developed an obsession with the God of Insanity. Dreams saw the way insanity could lay visions that enveloped mortals and deities alike. Dreams could not accomplish the same. He obsessed over creating nightmares that would do the same. He wanted to beat insanity, to be better than him. To win where insanity was failing. The sisters of fate felt the nightmares and, together, ended his life before he could succeed.

VESPERA

I lost count of how many spoons of sugar I had already added to the cup of tea Aero gave me. It still wasn't enough. It tasted like I was licking dirt. He ran an entire organization but couldn't correctly brew coffee. I shook my head and left the spoon inside the cup, the bitter liquid now more crystal than liquid.

The Shadows Of Justice kept a small building in the middle of Daxon, the land of water. Aero was adamant that it be in the middle of the realm. He said it would make easy travel for mortals that required him. I asked what would have happened if they couldn't afford a ship to bring them, and he looked at me as if the thought had never occurred to him. I had not brought it up again. Some battles weren't worth fighting.

Juniper sent word that Fennic was having a hard time, and Vesim was going to bring him for an afternoon. After hearing that, Aero was adamant that he come here to plan. I asked him to send word that Hesperia came with. I had only planned to stay until her arrival with Fennic, and I would leave with her. I did not want to interrupt what little time Aero had with his newfound brother. The way Fennic's eyes lit up around Aero told me he needed this connection desperately.

The two of them did make me think about my own siblings. If Caym were not the traitor, it would mean he was my brother. It would mean my brother was here all along, and we hardly talked. There was no bond, no acknowledgment. We had gone through more than most and weren't close enough to comfort each other. We were close enough to do as little as sit in silence together, to trade small looks of knowing and move forward. The thought hollowed out a space in my chest.

If it was proven to be true, I knew I would owe him an apology, at the least of things.

The Shadows of Justice building was small, but it was lined with paintings. After painting Aero with mortals, he helped with this or that. Aero with a cat or two small children. Another picture hung of him marrying two different couples. He clearly didn't care how big or small the request was. He helped with joy. The walls were a testament to a life spent in service.

"Aero!" I called, my voice ringing through the small space.

"Hm?" His voice floated back, distracted.

"What did you do with this cat?" I asked, pointing to a particularly fluffy creature in one of the paintings.

His chair squeaked and then rolled across the floor in an instant. Just as quickly, his boots hit the ground, and the spurs he kept on, the heel clicked against the boots at an ominous speed. I sat up straighter, and a crash came next. He finally rounded the corner, out of breath and hair a mess, his enthusiasm knocking over something in his haste.

"I'm glad you asked," he smirked, eyes twinkling with barely contained excitement.

He used his thumb in one motion to move his orange hair out of his face and back where it sat, the practiced gesture of someone who did it a hundred times daily.

"Come with me," he instructed, walking to the room behind us.

I followed, already regretting the question. He opened a grey curtain, and behind it, I counted fourteen cats. They were scattered through the room. Some on pillows, others on brackets that stuck out of the wall. The furthest wall was only glass, and the floor was faux grass. A small paradise for felines.

"I've kept them all," he beamed, pride radiating from him.

"Wow," was the only thing I could force out to say, the smell of cat overwhelmingly present.

"You saved all of those cats!" Fennic exclaimed from behind us, making me jump.

"You want one?" Aero offered, pushing past me to approach his brother.

"No, cats and I don't really get along," Fennic grimaced, taking a step back.

"We will fix that," Aero declared with absolute certainty.

He had very clearly forgotten we were mid-conversation while he rummaged through bags. After a moment, Aero pulled out a set of clothing and a cap identical to his own. He handed the black and gold clothing to Fennic, and they both had very different looks on their faces – Aero's filled with hope, Fennic's with confusion.

"You don't like my clothes?" Fennic asked, fingering the fabric of his current attire.

"You need to be in uniform while we work," Aero pointed. "Get changed. You're officially a member of the Shadows of Justice. We serve and protect all of the cities. There is no crime too big or small."

Fennic looked down at the clothes again before he looked back to Aero. They had both forgotten I was here. I did my best to silently slip back to the front of the building. It looked as though I did not need to sneak out because neither of them said anything to me. Their bond was already forming, leaving no space for outsiders.

"I'm not a single girl, you know. I have a man in my own realm who waits for me when I come here," Hesperia announced as I entered the main room. She lifted her hands to stop me from speaking. "I know you can't get what we did together out of your head. I can't either. The crimes we committed, the murder we enacted. It did mean something to me, but only as a friend."

"I—" I blinked a few extra times, utterly bewildered. "I do hope so. I asked for you here today, not to confess my love, but to ask you another question, and no." I held my own hand up. "I will not kill for the answer to this one. You owe me already," I stated firmly.

"Fine!" Hesperia pouted, her ghostly form deflating slightly.

"Can you walk through walls? Since you're dead," I asked, getting straight to the point.

"It's the best skill I have!" She stood, eager for me to keep going, her earlier sullenness forgotten.

"There's a room in Yumi's quarters that we cannot get inside of. The lock is too much," I explained, lowering my voice.

"Yes, I would love to break into Yumi's room and steal her things for you. Let's go," Hesperia agreed enthusiastically. "Fennic, Aero!" She called, her voice carrying through the building.

"They can't come," my words were panicked, heart racing at the thought of being discovered.

"I need the two of them to touch Mother, together," Hesperia insisted, her playfulness replaced with determination.

"If you cause more trouble, the group will never forgive me," I sighed, already imagining Helia's wrath.

"I'm sure you can find a way to appease Helia in the name of getting Mother back," Hesperia's eyes narrowed, and there was not the slightest hint of joy on her lips. She looked more like Death than ever in that moment.

I used my portal to bring us to the Chamber of Starlight. It was our best luck and Helia's biggest weakness that she always left the Chamber of Starlight unattended. I entered the Sunlight Garden, moving myself behind the trees to stay hidden from the blood guard that kept watch at the main entrance. My heart hammered in my chest as we crept through the sacred space.

"What are we supposed to be doing?" Aero whispered, his usual confidence replaced with caution.

"Both of you place your hands on the tree and focus,"

Hesperia whispered back, gesturing to the massive tree at the center.

"Focus on what?" Fennic shook his head, confusion etched on his face.

"Just do it," she pointed at Fennic, brooking no argument.

The two of them listened and put both of their palms on the tree. I listened to them breathe in and out for several breaths. A small glow started to be visible from beneath their hands, golden light seeping between their fingers.

"Move!" Hesperia rushed them, excitement crackling in her voice.

When they lifted their hands, words were clearly written on the bark, etched in glowing script.

"Reunification is the only solution," Hesperia muttered, her shoulders slumping.

"What does it mean?" I asked, staring at the fading words.

"It means Mother is trapped until we're all together again," Hesperia said, her voice defeated.

She sounded exhausted, the weight of centuries pressing down on her spectral form.

"I was hoping she would have something, anything to help us break this seal sooner," Hesperia sighed, her usual vibrancy dimmed.

"Why did you need us?" Fennic asked, rubbing his palm where it had touched the bark.

"The two of you are soul-tied to them. It was very important to my mother that everything and everyone have something to keep them grounded," she explained. "The two of you should go now. Use your time well."

They didn't hesitate; they scurried off like children, Fennic following his brother with newfound trust.

"I get the feeling you know something else," I said, studying Hesperia's troubled expression.

"Fennic is going to die," she smiled, but it wasn't a real smile. It was brittle, forced. "I can smell Mother moving into his body. She's using Yumi being too weak and the absence of our blood to do what she can for us. Fennic is bonded to her, so he is the only one she can use. Enough of that for now; neither of us can change these facts. Let's get into Yumi's room."

Hesperia and I slipped into the doorway of Yumi's room, and I showed her to the locked door. She winked at me and went through the wall, her form melting into the solid surface.

"Can you hear me?" Hesperia called from the other side.

"Yes. Talk lower. We aren't supposed to be here," I whispered, anxiously glancing over my shoulder.

Hesperia shoved her head through the door in front of me, "Is this better?" Her whispers were mocking, eyes wide with exaggerated secrecy.

I rolled my eyes in response, and she pulled her head back inside.

"There are journals that discuss the ways she used to cut Ruri and use her blood to keep Dahlia quiet. Some paintings of Nikola. There are a lot of Sahir's things in here," Hesperia called out, her voice muffled by the door.

"How do you know they belong to her?" I asked, pressing my ear against the wood.

"They are sitting in a pile under a board with her name on it," Hesperia answered matter-of-factly.

"Creepy," I shivered, imagining the shrine of stolen possessions.

She was quiet for a moment, then another, until I started to feel a little uneasy. The silence stretched too long.

"Everything alright?" I asked, tension building in my shoulders.

"There are writings of how her son has never had his memory taken like the rest. How—" Hesperia stopped talking abruptly.

"How what?" I leaned my ear closer to the door, straining to hear. "How what, Hesperia?"

"The words are disappearing faster than I can read them!" The sound of paper after paper being flipped came next, frantic rustling. "The last thing I could read was something that mentioned the other realm she created. That this one is better."

Hesperia came through the door and my body, making me shudder at the cold sensation.

"That can't mean what I think it does?" Hesperia's voice shook, fear evident in her ghostly eyes.

"It can't," I shook my head in agreement. "That would mean the traitor never lost his memory."

Hesperia looked at me without words, and for a moment, I wondered if that was what it was like to have siblings. We weren't speaking, but our eyes were telling a story in the same way. Fear and disbelief exchanged in a silent language only we understood.

If there was someone who had full memories, what did this mean for Helia?

"We've got to go," I said, hardly above a whisper, goosebumps rising on my arms.

I snuck behind the same trees and shrubbery to leave that I had to enter. On the other hand, more than one deity was waiting, their faces grim with urgency.

"Where have you been!" Vesim's voice was filled with rage, her eyes darting around nervously.

"It doesn't matter; you have to go," Astra interrupted, her usual calm shattered. "Helia has called a meeting. They need to leave now and go back to their own realm."

Vesim didn't wait for any more words to be said; she rifted out with Hesperia, the portal snapping shut behind them.

"What's going on?" I asked, dread pooling in my stomach.

Multiple mouths opened to answer me, but not one word was left before crimson vines wrapped around us all. The ground turned hot under my foot covers, and the vines pulled all of us to our knees, where it felt even warmer. The air became stale, and even the glimmer of starlight in the room dulled out and disappeared. Darkness pressed in from all sides.

Helia entered, blood guards fanning out around her, positioning themselves at each column. Helia's black gown left ripples through the ground that turned itself into blood beneath her steps, the liquid spreading like poison.

She smiled after taking her seat. Lips as red as the blood she left behind her. She had fully embraced the blood magic she was using, power and cruelty radiating from her like heat.

"I can answer your question," she lifted one leg over the other, her posture relaxed despite the violence of her magic. "My loyal dog was murdered. More than a handful of my guards are missing, and someone has been sneaking around in places that I clearly outlined as off limits."

Juniper opened her mouth to speak, but Helia put a stop to it. She raised her hand, and the vines that held every deity in Semper on their knees in front of her also covered our mouths, the taste of blood and soil flooding my senses.

"I didn't ask a question, so I do not require a response."

Helia held out a mirror in each hand, turning them to face us, their surfaces cloudy then clearing to reveal images.

"I gave my warning already. Now, I show you what happens when you test my patience."

The mirrors showed us mortal Ruri and Sage. They were in two different lands, doing two very different tasks. Unaware anyone was watching them. They carried blissful smiles until blood guards showed themselves. They grabbed both of the girls, and I closed my eyes. I couldn't watch what I knew was going to happen. I would have held hands over my ears, too, if I could have moved them. Their screams pierced through my closed eyes anyway.

"Now you get to wait for them to be reborn. And look for them all over again. If you keep testing me, I will wait for them to be reborn and lock them away with Yumi until I find the other pieces of their heart."

Helia gave us all one more look before she got to her feet and made her grand exit, complete with the blood guards filing out in perfect sync behind her. The vines receded, but the taste of blood lingered in my mouth, a reminder of what our disobedience had cost us.

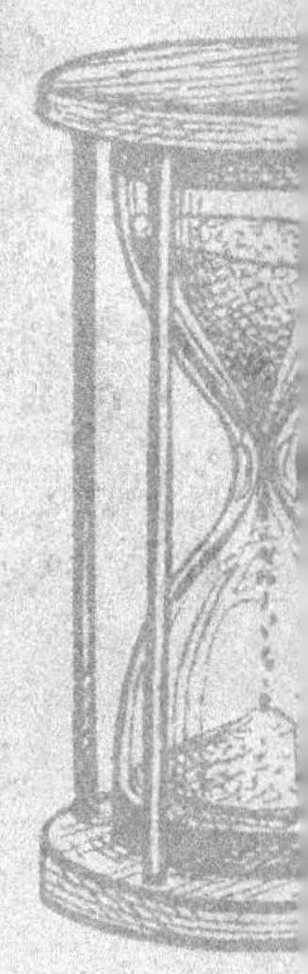

CHAPTER THIRTY

THE PLAN

SHIVANI

I stood, hidden behind a large wooden clock, waiting for Riven to leave his wing. There was a lot to do today, and I could only focus on half of it. I didn't want to pretend things were normal. I didn't want to be involved in anything I had before. I didn't care about marriage or becoming queen. I didn't care about Riven or what he thought he could accomplish. It all felt so foolish now. Like a child's game I'd outgrown overnight.

I knew Fennic felt the same; he was having a harder time than I was. He was trying to keep up appearances. Mostly because every time he slipped, Hesperia was there to pull him back in line, her ghostly fingers snapping in front of his face whenever his attention wandered.

She was right in keeping us on track, and I tried my best to listen to her. If my mind wandered, I would tell myself that if she can do this, be happy about it, and watch us all while we don't remember her at all, then I should be able to hang on, too. Her patience made my impatience feel shameful.

Our plans had yet to go our way or get us ahead yet, but I was sure this one would work out. We were going to find the sprites that were left and we would use their magic to try and unlock our minds and our magic. They were the only source of magic Hesperia could think of. The idea that my realm, and their realm, no—our realm, was the same place didn't work in my mind. I couldn't imagine this place being so bright, so full of life as theirs. This kingdom of dull stone and faded tapestries becoming a world of vibrant color and light seemed impossible.

I waited until I saw no part of Riven's guard left before I moved into the room that held all of the animals not being kept in the throne room. Riven felt, somehow, less intimidating than he did just a day ago. A would-be god reduced to a nuisance in my mind. Hesperia came through the wall next, her ghostly form rippling through the stone. Coy and Vesim came through the door together, their footsteps careful and measured.

"This is all that's left?" Hesperia asked, her voice falling with disappointment as she surveyed the meager collection of caged creatures.

I nodded. "Outside of the animals being bred for food, there's not many in general."

Fennic came crashing into the room, cheeks flushed and anger in his golden eyes, the door banging against the wall behind him.

"I'm getting tired of this!" He yelled as he pointed his finger at us. "I am the God of Protection and my brother the God of Justice! It is my duty to ensure you two don't die before I can deliver you back to the others. You aren't allowed to make any plans or movements without me by your side from now on, or else—"

The three of us broke out in laughter in unison, the sound echoing off the stone walls.

"I'm being serious!" He glared, his face reddening further.

"I can see that," I laughed, tears forming at the corners of my eyes.

"You'll take me seriously when I awaken!" He crossed his arms. "Then I'll tell your mother, too."

Hesperia was still laughing with Vesim, and I was trying my best to bite my tongue, my cheeks aching with the effort.

I moved to the sprites in my best attempt not to look at Fennic again. I didn't know if I'd ever get used to seeing him like this after knowing him as the stupid prince. He walked to me, making it harder to hold myself together. I reached out for a sprite to leave its cage and sit in my hands, the tiny creature's warmth a welcome distraction.

"I just wanted to talk to you for a second," he whispered, leaning close enough that I could smell the mint on his breath.

"Okay," I answered reluctantly, bracing myself.

"I've thought it over, and it seems like we aren't meant to be together. I think I was confused about how I felt for you because it's in my blood to protect you. Well, not you, but all of you. Ya know? It was so confusing to me because you aren't really my type. Not that you aren't a fine type, just not mine, ya know? I like, well, I. What I mean to say is that I hope there are no hard feelings about me breaking things off between us. I think we can both be mature about things. I tried to kill you, but you let me die from the box, so we're even," he held out his hand for me to take, his expression earnest.

I looked down at it and back up at him. "You're serious?"

"I saw the way you looked at Koa, so I just want to clear the air and let you know that I'm okay with it. I'm letting you free, and I won't be a crazy ex," he assured me, his hand still outstretched.

There was no hint of a joke in his eyes, nor lips. I took his hand and shook it, the gesture formal and bizarre. He winked at me before going back to Vesim. It was an uncomfortable kind of wink. As if he were my father telling me to go get 'em.

I shivered and turned my entire body away from his direction, my skin crawling.

"Do you think you can wipe that from my memory?" I whispered to the fire sprite in my hand.

The sprite looked at me with confusion and disappointment. We felt the same thing but for clearly different reasons. Its tiny eyes seemed to say, "I wish I could help."

"They have no more magic. They said it left with us," Hesperia said as she cuddled the water sprite, its blue glow dimming as she stroked it.

"How can you understand them?" I asked, watching the gentle way she handled the tiny being.

"One of our sisters is the keeper of nature magic, and she taught us all how to use it as a gift," she answered, a rare moment of gentle nostalgia crossing her features.

"Sometimes, I'm sure this is all some sort of really long dream," I admitted, the weight of our reality pressing down on me.

"Now, what are you doing in here?" Niko asked, rounding the corner, his sudden appearance making us all freeze.

Fennic jumped in between the doorway and me. I felt myself shift in embarrassment again, mortified by his protective display.

"She's my date, and I'm showing her around," Fennic declared. He stared Niko down, his posture rigid with tension.

Niko lifted his hand and released a set of orange chains from his palm. They connected with the throats of each sprite in the room, and the in-sync snaps that came next made me shut my eyes. I didn't want to see what I knew he had done to them. The sound of tiny necks breaking would haunt me for days. Vesim took my hand and tried to rush us both out of the room, her grip painfully tight.

"It is a smart choice you two are making. You have things to attend to today, if I'm not mistaken?" Niko smirked, satisfaction gleaming in his dark eyes.

I wanted to ask where Hesperia disappeared to so quickly, but I knew it was not in our best interest, so I let Vesim drag me until the door to our safety was shut, our ragged breathing the only sound in the corridor.

Inside of my room, Coy was sitting in a pile of scrolls. He looked up at us both as if we were the intruders of his space, his brow furrowed in concentration.

"Niko killed all of the sprites," I poured out my words, my voice breaking.

"In front of you?" His voice was demanding, his hand already moving to the weapon at his side.

The two of us were silent, the answer clear in our faces.

"I'll be back," he said, already rising to his feet.

He was getting to his feet when Hesperia came through the wall, her form more substantial than usual, crackling with emotion.

"Stop," she held up her hand. "We have to stay focused."

He was unblinking, and so was she, a battle of wills playing out in silence.

"You aren't going to cause any damage to him. Stay on track," Hesperia demanded, her voice cutting through the tension.

"Have you found anything here?" I asked. I tried to break the tension before it snapped.

All my ears echoed were the snaps I had just heard. I couldn't take their bickering on top of that sound. I wanted to turn around and go back in there. I wanted to help them and demand that Hesperia do something about it. If she were going to be so open about her abilities, she should be using them to help. Instead, I stayed still and silent, defeated by my own powerlessness.

"Nothing that would help with Riven and the God artifact. It's only scroll after scroll of our history," Coy answered.

This was the most I had heard him speak, and it was hard

adjusting to his voice, deeper and more resonant than I'd expected.

I threw myself onto my bed with a breath of disappointment, the mattress sagging beneath my weight.

"Maybe we can still learn from that," Hesperia said. "Maybe the problem back then was that we didn't just slaughter them all when we had the first chance to. It seems we were too worried about keeping the peace, and we should have been more aggressive with our strategy. Maybe this time we can toss our morals to the side?"

"Aren't you the one that has been telling us we can't just go kill everything to solve our problems?" I asked, propping myself up on my elbows.

"Actually, it's you that have been telling me I can't kill my way through things yet," she corrected, a hint of smugness in her tone.

"We have to stick to the plan and wait for Caym to tell us we can move forward," Vesim said, her voice surprisingly reasonable.

"How are you the voice of reason today?" I shook my head, giving her a sideways glance.

The cat from their realm jumped up on my bed and startled me. "Where have you been? You were gone so long I thought you went back to Semper?"

She threw herself down alongside me and purred, but nothing more, her golden eyes watching me with enigmatic intensity.

"You still have to participate in the day," Vesim reminded me, straightening the scrolls that had fallen to the floor.

"No. Tell them I'm sick; tell them I'm busy. Tell them whatever you want. We have to find a way to separate Riven from this god artifact," I said, determination hardening my voice.

"Everyone in this room should be more concerned with

Nikola than Riven," Hesperia interrupted, her form brightening with urgency.

We looked at her in silence, the weight of her words settling over us.

"Nikola would never let Riven merge with such a thing. You want to feel power? Touch Father's artifact. He would never give that up to some mortal man. Riven is not the issue; it's Nikola," Hesperia's tone was of urgency, her ghostly hands gesturing emphatically.

"How do we deal with him then?" I asked. "He was just the demon that made a deal with me for power," I admitted, "I don't know how to move forward with him as my focus."

"You do your duties, don't draw attention, and let me figure it out," she answered. "Don't you dare credit him with something like that again. He didn't give you anything or make a trade. He only awakened what has always been yours."

At that moment, she felt like what I imagined a sister would. Protective, fierce, unwilling to let anyone diminish me, even myself.

"I can't participate in today. We are supposed to give Fennic and Coy handmade gifts. I was told I had to embroider a handkerchief, but I do not know how," I admitted, the mundane problem feeling ridiculous amid our cosmic concerns.

"I do!" Hesperia raised her hand, excitement replacing her earlier seriousness. "I can take over your body and do it for you, and you can give it to Coy!"

I glanced at Coy, who was looking at her as if he were blind to every single thing but her, his gaze softening in a way I'd never seen before.

"All right," I agreed, bracing myself for the strange sensation.

She didn't wait; she entered my body immediately, and I was back to just observing her using my limbs. The cold of her occupying me was just as intense this time around as it was the first time. I don't think I could ever get used to this happening. The endless floating feeling. Most of all, I didn't think I could get used to having nothing to do and nowhere to go but my own mind, trapped in silent observation.

I wanted to do things that would keep me from thinking. Just a few days ago, my biggest worry was the way my mother beat me down in any way she could. Now, I didn't even know what to call her. She wasn't my mother, but she did raise this version of me. I was alone, and now I have sisters and friends I can't remember. Extended family, someone I think I may really love. That was the scariest part.

Flirting with my emotions was easy with Fennic. The bickering passed time, and even when I got close to thinking I may like him, it still felt like we may be able to develop something in the future if we worked at it, but Koa? He set me on fire. His very presence ignited something in me I couldn't explain. Hesperia made me feel at ease. Being in Semper made me feel at home. Being back in my realm made me feel anxious, like wearing clothes that no longer fit.

I watched her as she made the same sun and moon symbol that had been burned into my palm, and I hardly understood how to move forward once things were done. This situation couldn't last forever. It's not that I didn't want what was happening. If my choice were a Goddess or living where I used to be, I'd gladly embrace the Goddess. I was afraid to ruin it all. I was so sure when I journeyed to the castle that I had it all figured out. All I had figured out was how to screw everything up.

Maybe what I needed was to be more like Hesperia. Maybe I needed to learn from my sister and kill more people. The thought was both terrifying and liberating.

The door to my room opened in a burst of commotion. Lorelai came through the entrance with a dagger in hand, her face contorted with rage. Everyone was on their feet, but I was still just a floating thought in my own head, helpless to intervene.

"I'm so sick of hearing about you! For days, all I've heard is how well you will do as breeding stock. How Riven is going to enjoy however many times it takes to get something growing in you? What about you is so great? Hmm? We're going to start marking things off the list! Today, I'm going to cut up that ugly face of yours, and if that doesn't work, I'm going to take your tits next!" She was screaming while she charged at my body, spittle flying from her lips.

At first, I was afraid because there was nothing I could do. No amount of resistance I could have put up. The thought was fleeting when Hesperia was on her feet before I could sort myself out. I did need to take notes from her—her reaction was instant and confident.

Hesperia pulled from my abilities, not her own. She formed a blood whip as if my body truly was her own, the crimson tendril materializing from my palm. Lorelai knocked Hesperia off of her feet, and the two rolled across the floor for only a moment before Hesperia had the upper hand again. Hesperia flung the whip back and slapped it once, then twice against Lorelai's thighs. The blood whip snapped on both with each clap, leaving angry welts in its wake.

She cried out in pain, but Coy and Vesim didn't step between them. Hesperia pulled it back a third time, but this time, Niko caught it, the blood solidifying in his grip.

"Our King sent me to retrieve you. He knew you'd come and make trouble. Neither of us expected this, though. He will be happy to hear of this," Niko smiled, his eyes gleaming with dark satisfaction.

"To hear of what?" Coy asked, his voice carefully neutral.

"That little Shivani is openly using her blood magic, and the other sister has appeared," he said, his gaze sweeping over us all.

He turned to leave before Hesperia could respond using

my lips, and when he was gone, she left my body, and I dropped to the ground, shivering from the sudden cold emptiness within me.

"What the hell was that?" Vesim asked, her voice shaking.

"Go to your meeting and give that handkerchief to Coy. I'll see you soon," Hesperia said before she disappeared, leaving no trace of her presence except the embroidered cloth and the chill that lingered in my bones.

CHAPTER THIRTY-ONE
THE WEDDING

FENNIC

I couldn't believe what I was seeing when I entered the throne room. Shivani was on Riven's lap with a smile bigger than I had ever seen before. Certainly, bigger than she had ever held with me. Traces of her blood magic flowed from her fingertips like crimson ribbons, dancing in the air. I had to have been slipped herbs in my own tea. There was no way she had taken things this far. Was she already sleeping with him, too? The thought twisted my gut like a knife.

Seeing her like she was, having the thoughts I was having, made me feel a kind of guilt that I had never felt before. It was heavier than any weight I had carried. I was overwhelmed with the sudden realization that even if I tried to convince myself I was different, somehow better, I was failing now just as much as Shivani was. My judgment of her was a mirror reflecting my own shortcomings.

"You look surprised, brother," Riven smiled, his fingers tracing patterns on Shivani's arm.

"I didn't think you'd stoop so low, is all," I said. I was resisting the urge to demand he stop calling me his brother.

My brother was better than he was. Aero would never manipulate someone this way.

"She agreed to be my concubine; I'm just using my abilities to make her more comfortable," he said, as if discussing nothing more significant than the weather.

"You mean manipulating her emotions to make her convinced she's in love with you to make yourself more comfortable," I scoffed, disgust rising in my throat.

"It doesn't matter much to me. She's mine all the same," he said. "She agreed to be with me; she should have asked what all it meant. I'll let you use her a time or two when she's already holding my child; until then, let's move on."

Mori was working on learning how to get that artifact away so I could kill him, and I swear I would kill him. My hands itched for a blade at the very thought. Coy warned me to watch out for Niko. He told me that Hesperia said Riven wasn't the threat, but they had to be wrong. I knew Riven was the problem. This proved it. I had never seen him use his deal on a woman before. It never crossed my mind that he would get so desperate. Seeing Shivani's vacant eyes made my blood boil.

"You have nothing to say about that magic coming from her hands?" I held myself back from shouting, my fists clenched at my sides.

Nikola stepped in, his tall form imposing as he moved between us. "That magic is but one of the reasons she's so important to your brother's future. She is more valuable than you could understand. They will marry today, and I will ensure the ceremony goes without consequence."

"What makes you think that?" I asked, fighting to keep my voice level.

"That she is valuable? The gods wrote of a girl who would have a mark in her eyes that only other gods could see," Niko said, his voice smooth and certain. "Your brother says he can see it."

Riven cleared his throat, shifting uncomfortably. "Yes, I can."

I chuckled and shook my head; he didn't see a damn thing. The lie was written across his face as clearly as the crown on his head. "What's so special about her if she has the mark in her eyes?"

Part of me knew Riven would listen to anything Niko made up. Another part of me knew Niko was a god, and I was godless. I didn't have any divine beings on my side. The one I was almost convinced I did have is now sitting on my brother's lap, turned into a dog. The other is a ghost. Coy was just as asleep as I was. We were outmatched in every way that mattered.

"Her blood will ascend your brother to a god. That's what it means," Nikola said, his dark eyes unwavering.

That half-burnt-up journal was stuck with me any time he mentioned becoming a God. It didn't matter to me if anyone else doubted it. It was too much of a perfect accident for me to stick with that thought. Niko was Nikola, and my brother was being used for Nikola's intent, and he was too blinded by the idea that he was a god to see it. The puppet couldn't see his own strings.

"Do you need anything else from me?" I asked, forcing a neutral expression.

I would play my part, but if he were a god, he wouldn't trust in me regardless. Better to let him think I had accepted defeat.

"For now, keep order during wedding preparations," Riven said, waving his hand dismissively.

I gave a bow and left them both behind, my back rigid with restraint. I needed to find Mori and Vesim. I couldn't stop the wedding. I wouldn't try. He would have her kill me and not think twice. I was beginning to feel like all the options we thought we had were only illusions, smoke and mirrors hiding our own powerlessness. Where was that cat? That little biter should be able to do something with those teeth. At least the cat had the courage to attack.

We should have taken advice from Hesperia sooner. We should have started killing because this was a kill-or-be-killed realm. I wanted to be the one doing the killing. I wanted to go to the forge and weaponize my army. The thought of bloodshed gave me a grim comfort.

I pushed open the door to Shivani's room, and there they were. They both sat at a small table in the corner of the room. They looked like they were attending a funeral, faces drawn and shoulders slumped.

"Do either of you have a plan?" I asked, taking the last open chair, the wood creaking beneath me.

"A plan for what? Stopping the wedding? Killing your brother? Killing you?" Vesim looked up, her eyes red-rimmed with exhaustion.

"Killing Riven," I crossed my arms. "I think we should go to the forge. My friend there will help us."

"I'm starting to think killing him first would be the best choice for now," Mori said, his voice hollow.

"Even if it doesn't get us further, it will be quieter," Vesim agreed, rubbing her temples.

"He clearly hasn't received word that the forge has been shut down, its occupants sentenced to death, and all weapon production labeled illegal," Mori said, the bitter edge in his voice cutting through the air.

The cat jumped up on the table, and its tail waved back and forth, eyes watching me with what seemed like contempt.

"Why am I sure the cat has insulted me, too?" I frowned, leaning away from the creature.

"If she did, then you deserved it," Vesim said, rubbing her chin.

Get the artifact, sacrifice.

I held my head again when her voice was in my mind, the words echoing painfully against my skull.

"We have to do something, and we have to do it fast," I grumbled, pressing my fingers against my temples.

"I have a few poisons to try, but I can't guarantee they will work," Vesim sighed, her shoulders slumping further. "The best way I can help her is to leave."

"Leave? What do you mean leave?" I shouted, half-rising from my chair.

"I plan to rift back to Semper and get help," she said, her voice calm but resolute.

"Do you know?" I asked Mori, searching his face for confirmation.

Mori nodded, his expression grim. "I do, and if I were being honest, I agree it's the best place for her to be now. If Riven wants to hurt Shivani more, Vesim is all he has to use against her. If he wants to hurt you, he will kill your mother."

"Why would he? He has no reason to go after me," I asked, confusion clouding my thoughts.

"You still can't get out of your head long enough to see the bigger picture, can you? All this planning, all these goals. They don't mean anything anymore. Riven won't be a God soon; it will be Nikola in his place. Every move you get caught making against him will have a consequence. Every move you have already made is sure to be a tally against you already. He won't do small. You keep trying to take Shivani; you keep trying to kill him; we are next. I know you haven't thought of us lately. Too caught up with you, as usual, but you can't just come in and out of these things when it's convenient for you. You can't call us friends when you feel like it and then leave me behind when you find something more interesting," Mori said, taking another drink from his cup, his knuckles white around the stem.

"I'm sorry, Mori. I am. I'll make it up to you, but for now, we need a plan. We just have to be faster and smarter," I said, regret coloring my words.

"Than a god?" Vesim laughed, the sound sharp and

humorless. "If you didn't remember, you aren't exactly useful yet, and we are just mortals. I'm sure even if we forgot, though, we'd be reminded fast enough."

"We don't know for sure Niko is a god," I shook my head, desperate to hold onto some hope. "Aren't we still here to work together to find that out?"

Vesim laughed, a harsh, brittle sound. "You don't. I do. I don't need to be repeatedly slapped in the face with the same point." Vesim stood and picked up the cat, cradling it to her chest. "Mori, I hope the best for you, and if you live to the end, I'll see you again." She held her hand out to him.

He shook her hand, and they lingered on each other momentarily, a quiet understanding passing between them. When did I miss them becoming friends? I don't recall them being this close or Mori ever saying anything about her. I watched Vesim take the cat and leave the room. Of course, the cat didn't miss a chance to hiss at me again on its way past, teeth bared in my direction.

"When did the two of you become such good friends?" I crossed my arms, jealousy flaring unexpectedly.

"You wouldn't have noticed since it's not about you," he remarked coldly. "We have a wedding to attend; let's go."

"Wait," I said, reaching for his arm. "Why are you acting like this?"

"Have you ever thought of your sister? Even once? I know you haven't because Vesim and I sent her away to visit cousins to protect her. If all of these things don't make you understand, nothing will," he said, his eyes finally meeting mine, filled with disappointment.

He walked past me but never looked me in the eye again. What was going on here? Why was I being treated as the enemy? Wasn't it Mori's job to do those things? I followed him out, confusion and hurt battling inside me. Maids were still laying half-wilted flowers around the castle grounds. It was a pathetic sight. If it were my wedding, I'd have better.

The dying blooms seemed fitting for the farce about to take place.

Mori and I walked into the main hall of the castle that typically held balls. Today, it held a wedding. Benches were set through the entire room, and three spots were open and waiting to be filled in front of the elder who would break their ribbons and brand them. Most benches were filling quickly. Riven didn't want to wait. He thought this day trivial. If he claimed them, then they were his, and this was just a formality to waste his time. His council urged him to keep to tradition.

Mori and I took a seat in the front. The elder looked at us both, but I couldn't read the emotion behind his eyes. Niko came in next and stood beside the elder. What made him think he could be there? His very presence felt like a violation of sacred space.

"The King has arrived," a guard shouted, his voice ringing through the hall.

Riven walked in dressed in pounds of black fabric and a fur coat. No doubt made from an animal he hunted himself. Next came Lorelai. She was covered head to toe in gold. She looked every bit as royal as Riven did, her face alight with triumph. Shivani came last. Her eyes were glossed over and blank, eerily vacant. She wore a crimson red dress. There was no jewelry thrown across her like there was on Lorelai. No golden headdress on top of her head. She looked simple and elegant, but the emptiness in her eyes made the beauty hollow.

A small necklace could be seen on Shivani's chest. It caught my attention with how it caught every bit of light around her, glinting with an otherworldly radiance. Where did she get that? I had never seen anything like it here.

She stopped beside Riven on the opposite side of Lorelai. The elder started speaking to them and the room, and I took my chance to sneak out. I made my footsteps light and gentle until I got outside. The cups they'd drink after were sitting, waiting, and I put the poison flower petals in Riven's chalice.

When I mixed them, they turned to dust and dissipated inside, leaving no trace of my interference.

I snuck back in and sat down beside Mori. He looked at me with disappointment, his lips pressed in a thin line. I know he thought his life would be on the line, but it wouldn't. I knew it wouldn't. I had to hold onto that certainty.

"Lorelai, please turn your wrist," the elder said, making contact with the brand.

The scent of burning flesh filled the air, acrid and nauseating, and when the sizzle stopped, the elder took off her veil and gave it to Riven. She would be known as Queen Lorelai now with a face and a name.

"Shivani, please turn your wrist," the elder repeated; she mindlessly obeyed without hesitation, her movements mechanical.

The necklace she was wearing made a pulse when the elder put the brand on her wrist, a brief flash of light that seemed to go unnoticed by all but me. I couldn't believe they didn't see it. The branding sizzled, but the smell was not present. The elder took away the branding iron and the veil from her face as well. I would make sure to check her wrist after this.

When the chalices were brought in next, I believed the whole room was blind, and no one, not even Nikola, mentioned the pulse of her necklace. I held my breath, anticipation coursing through me.

I squirmed in my chair when the elder gave Lorelai the chalice I poisoned, not Riven. My heart plummeted. Riven and Lorelai drank together, and Shivani stood behind them in silence. She was fitting into her role perfectly and quickly, a perfect doll for Riven to parade around.

Lorelai began to choke after her drink. She grabbed her throat and gasped for air, her eyes wide with panic. The whites of her eyes grew bloodshot, and she clawed at her throat, nails leaving red welts in her skin. It felt nerve-grinding to consider the idea that when something from the other realm worked, it was on the wrong person. The irony was bitter and cruel.

"I told you, my King, that someone would want to kill you today," Niko said, his voice carrying a note of satisfaction.

Lorelai's body hit the floor, and the sound of her jewels came with it, a discordant clatter across the stone. There was a wave of silence before the rush of screaming. I was watching it in slow motion. Guards grabbed Riven and pulled him from the room. Healers lifted Lorelai to get her back to their wing of the castle. The rest of the room cleared themselves out in a rush, and it hit me that I was sitting, watching Niko smile at the commotion. The chaos was exactly what he wanted.

I stood and left the room with the last of the crowd. I wanted to have the upper hand. I wanted to be outside of the doorway, waiting for him to come out. I'd hit him in the throat, I'd put him in a headlock until he passed out, and chain him in the dungeon. I'd get rid of him now. The plan crystallized in my mind with sudden clarity.

I peeked my head just enough back into the doorway to try and get a glance at what he was doing to keep him in the room. My blood froze. His hands were around Hesperia's throat. How was he touching her when the rest of us couldn't? Her ghostly form seemed more solid in his grip, fear replacing her usual confidence.

"How did you get out of that locket, huh? Did you think I wouldn't know? Did you think I wouldn't smell the scent of the others on you?" Niko was in her face, his voice a low, dangerous growl.

"I wanted you to know," she spat back at him, defiant even in his grasp.

"Did you have fun? You failed in doing the one thing I left you out for. That lock still sits on your casket," he said, his grip tightening.

"Poor baby, I think you meant that you failed again," she laughed, the sound strained through her constricted throat.

"It's time for you to go back to where I put you so we can stop all your meddling," he growled, fury darkening his features.

She lifted both of her hands and filled them with a white light, the glow illuminating her determined face. She was still laughing between gasps. The sounds made it clear he was not showing her any mercy. He pulled out a small black and white box, clicking something on the side. The top snapped open, and it pulled Hesperia inside so quickly there was nothing I could have done. Her laughter cut off abruptly, leaving only an empty silence.

Coy rounded the corner in time to see what Niko had done, his face transforming with rage, and I had to use every ounce of strength I had built up to stop him from charging inside. His body was like iron beneath my grip, unyielding and tense with fury.

"We can't help her if you get locked inside of some mystical box, too," I whispered urgently, my arms straining to hold him back.

I was still shoving him back, but he was hardly listening, his eyes fixed on the doorway Niko would emerge from.

"He said her body was here and that it had some kind of seal on it," I kept talking to try and find whatever it was that would keep him from moving forward. "If you want to help her, you need to find out how to break that seal!"

He moved so quickly that I stumbled forward, nearly falling. He offered me nothing on his departure, but I was content with that as long as he departed. My relief was short-lived as I realized what we had just lost—our one true ally who remembered everything. Without Hesperia, we were flying blind, and Nikola knew it.

CHAPTER THIRTY-TWO

THE ENDLESS SLEEP

SHIVANI

"Where is Vesim?" Fennic asked, his voice tight with concern.

"I no longer require her services," I said from the seat beside the throne, my voice distant and hollow even to my own ears.

"Then where is she?" he pressed, stepping closer, desperation edging into his tone.

"I do not have knowledge of her current location," I answered, the words mechanical and rehearsed.

"Do you understand what's going on?" he demanded. "Riven is controlling your emotions!"

"There is no need for such things. I love my king without question," I said, the statement flowing from my lips with unnatural ease.

"No, you don't! Snap out of it, Shivani!" he yelled, his face flushing with frustration.

"Please do not address me so inappropriately, Prince," I said, my expression unchanging despite his outburst.

"This is insane. Fight him!" he urged, walking closer to me, his hand outstretched.

The cat in my lap sat up, and the hairs on her back stood erect, a low growl rumbling from her throat. I lifted two fingers and waved them up and towards him, slinging a blood whip at his legs and knocking him to his knees. The crimson tendril cracked against the stone floor as it connected with his flesh.

"Please do not attempt to touch the king's concubine. We are married now. That makes us one, and you will lose your head for pursuing such things," I said, laying my hand back on my lap, stroking the cat's fur mechanically.

"I only want to see your wrist," he said, wincing as he struggled to rise.

I turned it to face him. If he wanted to see my brand, my promise to my King, so be it. The mark glowed faintly against my skin, pulsing with an unnatural light.

He knelt, looking at me with disbelief, before standing and leaving. He would get the punishment he was owed for attempting to touch the king's property. I already had my orders for the day. My king laid them out before he left me to attend to other matters. Lorelai died, but there had hardly been time to consider it because every member of the royal family that rested in the crypts had risen from the dead, and they were attacking the castle.

I left my room and made my way to the castle tower, past the maids and healers. Past the baskets of herbs and the fresh bedding waiting to be changed. They did not stop me; they did not question me. My King was right. This task would be one of the easiest things he asked me to do for him. The castle was in chaos, but it was the perfect cover if anyone wanted to move without being stopped. Screams and clashing weapons echoed from the lower levels, but they seemed distant, unimportant.

I opened the final door and stepped inside with a smile, the hinges creaking softly in the quiet room.

"Oh dear, it's good to see you! Do you need more herbs?

I'll have them sent to you!" Fennic's mother smiled, her pale face lighting up at the sight of me.

I didn't speak because there was nothing for me to say to this woman. The washed-up could have been the bride of a past life that meant nothing. I could have used my abilities, but my King requested I not. He said Fennic would not do his part if he knew it was I who killed his mother. So, instead, I held the pillow that left her propped up over her face. Her eyes filled with horror before I covered them, recognition dawning too late. She struggled, but the screams were muffled well enough not to cause any alarm outside the doors. I pressed until I felt no more resistance or clawing into my arms and stayed for another few moments just to be safe.

Prince Fennic killed our Queen Lorelai and tried to kill my King. This was a just punishment. We lost something precious, and so shall he. When I was sure she was no longer a problem, I tucked the pillow back behind her head. She looked like a sleeping doll. One too old for any child to want to play with. My King would be pleased with the work I had done.

I could see hundreds of men and women storming the castle from the window that overlooked the land. They came with torches and farm gear as weapons, their thin bodies moving with desperate determination. It was a pathetic sight. They hardly had enough meat on their bodies to make the journey. Why did they think this would be successful? Did they not consider the trained and armed guards waiting to wipe them out? If they did make it past the guards, they would not make it past me. I would take every last drop of their blood for my own. The thought pleased me in a distant, foggy way.

I ran my hand over my arm and used my blood magic to heal the scratches the woman left before her death. They had dripped blood onto the ground, tiny crimson pools staining the pristine floor. I had to pull a fingernail out of my flesh before I could finish healing, the pain registering as little more than an inconvenience. My skin looked as good as new once that was gone. Untouched for my King.

When all of this was solved and put behind us, I would demand that the castle witch be put to death. She would be useless if so many things happened on the day of our wedding. She was supposed to pick a blessed day. Instead, she picked a cursed one. The queen was dead, an undead army fought our guard, and riots were moving in. She needed to be relieved of her position. Her incompetence was an insult to my King's glory.

I left, and again, her maids paid me no attention. I was happy to see that they had paid me little attention, but they would be a problem in the future. If my King didn't want anyone to know I killed his mother, then they were witnesses that couldn't be allowed to stand. I bent down and pulled the dagger I kept on my thigh, and when I stood, I sliced the throat of the maid closest to me. She stood and looked at me, her hands clutching at her neck, but no sounds left her. I turned the blade in my hand until it sat sideways and stabbed it twice between the ribs of the other maid. She did scream before she dropped to her knees, the sound gurgling into silence as blood filled her lungs.

With the assurance that they wouldn't be a problem, I needed to find my king and protect him. I needed to ensure he was safe. When I reached the bottom of the stairway, the guard's presence was already significant. I pushed past them, waving my blood strings around their feet to toss them out of my way until I entered the throne room, their bodies crashing against walls and each other.

"My King," I said, moving to him, "Are you harmed?"

"Did you succeed?" he asked, his eyes gleaming with anticipation.

I nodded. "It is done."

"Good. Stay here until I tell you," Riven demanded on his way out, his command settling over me like a heavy cloak.

I felt my feet grow heavy and obey his command. I had no desire to resist. I did not desire anything but him until the little earth sprite with clipped wings sitting in a cage above his throne cried out for me. She whimpered while she huddled in the corner, and a part of my mind throbbed. A headache pounded away at me, clearing a bit of the fog that hung over my mind. The tiny creature's distress pierced through the haze like a shaft of light.

He said I could not leave, but he didn't say I could not move. I stood on his throne and propped myself on the armrest until I could reach the latch. When I opened it, she slid away from me. Her body's trembling made my heart ache worse, something deep inside me responding to her fear.

"I won't hurt you," I whispered, the words feeling more genuinely mine than anything I'd said all day.

She looked at me and hesitated before touching my finger. It caused a small spark of green and gold light between us. The air in the room froze, and my eyes shook. They twitched uncontrollably before suddenly stopping. When no more hovering came from my eyes, it was as if time had turned back, and her wings were in place like nothing had ever happened. She said something I could not understand before she flew away, a trail of sparkling dust following her path.

I sat on his throne. I knew if he came in, I would be punished, but the fog over me was making logical thought hard. I knew what would happen, but I hardly understood it. Part of me only knew I was to wait and be silent. The other part of me felt like I needed to talk to someone. Someone important. I was drawn to my pocket and pulled out a shell, my fingers moving with a will separate from the clouded commands in my mind.

"What are you doing?" I said into it, confusion clouding my words.

"I didn't expect to hear from you today," he replied, his voice warm and familiar.

Koa. It was to call Koa. Only small bits of me were slipping past the barrier in my mind, fighting through the fog of Riven's control.

"I didn't mean that the way it sounded. I just meant it's good to hear from you. I was worried about you. I can't explain it, but I felt like something was off today," he let out a sigh of relief. "Here we're celebrating the Goddess of magic. It's a funny story. When we were still molding the realm of mortals, someone tried to play a joke, but it caught fire, and now, twice a year, every year, the mortals hold a coliseum event where virgin men fight to be a sacrifice. We honor our part and let them be guardians in Merripen, of course." He paused momentarily, "I'm sorry, I'm rambling. Are you okay?"

"We don't have anything like that here. Only occasional balls to thank the king for a job well done and offer him gifts," I said, my voice flat despite the struggle happening within me.

"Are you all right? Your voice sounds off?" he asked, concern evident in his tone.

"Your necklace stopped me from being marked at my wedding," I said, the words slipping out before I could stop them, a moment of clarity breaking through.

"Your what?" His voice grew quieter. I put the shell back in my pocket before I could be fully seen, my briefly awakened will slipping back under the heavy blanket of control.

"He won't be pleased to find out you released his prized pet," Niko remarked, his sudden appearance making me stiffen.

I stood up and removed myself from the throne before straightening my dress. The fog grew back over my mind, and only the need to see Riven raced through my thoughts, overwhelming the brief clarity I'd experienced.

"I will answer to my King if I must," I said, my chin lifting in practiced deference.

"For now, you have another mission to achieve before our ceremony," Niko said, his eyes glittering with dark intention.

Something about him made me feel unwell. I disagreed that he was safe for my king. I let him keep speaking, but instead of listening to his words, I entered his mind. I wanted to know what he was thinking, to get a glimpse of his true intentions. A small act of rebellion my controlled self couldn't prevent.

When I entered, a wall and a field of spikes were waiting to keep me out. Screams rang out next. The sound of hundreds and hundreds of dying people. Pleads to be saved. Hands were reaching for me to pull them out. I pulled myself out of his mind and hit the ground, heaving air, my body shaking uncontrollably.

"Don't go places you weren't invited," he glared, his voice dropping to a dangerous whisper.

"Who are you?" I heaved from the ground, genuine fear breaking through my enchantment.

He bent down closer to me. His eyes were too black to keep staring into. They were too deep not to drown, and his presence was too uncomfortable to feel anything other than fear. He ran his fingers through my hair like a brush, and I recoiled, my skin crawling at his touch.

"You remind me so much of your mother. When she walked freely, she was feared. She was admired. We all knew she held more power than we could guess under her fingernails. You're just as beautiful as she was, but you're a joke in comparison. No doubt you are powerful but too weak to use it. You get that from your father," he ran his thumb over my bottom lip before pulling me to my feet. "I was hoping for one of the better sisters if we had to do this. It is such a shame."

He pulled me out of the throne room by the arm and tossed me before my King. A part of me tried to fight him, but it didn't make a difference. More of me said to obey, to love, to agree with all he said. When I tried to think back on it, I couldn't remember what he said. Was I given an order already? I looked up at my King from the ground I was placed on, momentary confusion giving way to devoted adoration.

"We are under attack, and I need you to help defend us. I want you to use your magic and get rid of them all. The townspeople and the undead. Do you understand what I'm saying? I want every single one of them dead!" Riven yelled, spittle flying from his lips.

"Of course, my King. If they're a threat to your life, they're a threat to everything I care for," I answered, the words flowing automatically.

"It'll be a shame to kill her. She's the most obedient I've ever controlled," Riven remarked, admiration in his voice.

"When you're a god, you'll have powers so great this won't be necessary for you," Niko said, his tone placating.

"Are you sure I can't leave her locked up? I still don't get why she has to die," Riven said, genuine confusion crossing his features.

"Because I said so!" Niko yelled, a flash of his true nature breaking through.

"No one yells at my King!" I shouted, getting to my feet and unleashing a flow of blood from my hand, the crimson tendrils writhing in the air like angry serpents.

"Stop!" Riven commanded. "Save that for outside."

Riven gave Niko a smug smile, but Niko showed no offense, his eyes calculating and cold.

"Go, now. Don't come back to see me until it's done. Spare no one," Riven pointed toward the door.

I bowed before my King and turned to leave. The guards moved out of my way, one by one, forming a path, and I unleashed the blood from both hands in tentacled forms. When this was over, and he was safe, I would take Niko next, and then my king and I could live happily together. I would give him as many daughters as I could carry, and there would be many wombs to carry the line of his name. My thoughts spun in circles of devotion, even as a tiny voice deep inside screamed to be heard.

CHAPTER THIRTY-THREE
THE ATTACK

FENNIC

"Arm the guard!" I called, running through the halls, my voice echoing off stone walls. "Mori!"

The longer it took to find him, the more I panicked. He was always quick to be by my side. I wasn't afraid that we couldn't wipe out a group of poorly trained citizens. I was worried about not having eyes on him while a woman was slinging blood magic all over the grounds controlled by a madman, and our dead family members were trying to rip heads off their relatives. Every time Riven used his ability to alter someone else's mind, he lost more of his own. Nikola was free to do what he wanted as long as the words came from Riven's mouth. The thought sent cold dread coursing through my veins.

"Mori!" I called again, desperation cracking my voice. "Coy!"

Guards marched past me in fire teams. Armed and ready to take up their positions, but I hadn't given any orders. I hadn't sent out our heavy armsmen. Their synchronized footfalls drummed against the stone like war drums, a rhythm that spelled death.

Shivani was the next to march past me. No life was in her eyes. Blood flowed from her fingers and her arms. Tentacles of blood grew from her sides, writhing like crimson serpents. Riven did well turning her into a mindless killing monster. Mori followed behind her, calling for her. He pulled at her arm, but she did not stop. I had to grab him and force him to stop chasing her before the fire teams could finish getting in place. When they stopped, when they were ready, the rows of citizens would be taken out.

The smaller fire teams were always made up of those with abilities centered around quick and mass death. Mori had to move; he had to get out of their way. He knew this as well as I did. The sweat on his brow and the tremble in his hands told me he wasn't thinking clearly.

"What are you doing? You know Riven's manipulation over her won't be broken like this," I yelled, gripping his shoulders.

"Someone has to do something!" Mori yelled back, his eyes wild with frustration, "you aren't!"

"What do you want me to do? Die knowing nothing I can do then will help either, like you're trying to do? You need to stay out of it before you get hurt!" I said, shaking him. "You're still my guard, and I command you to stand down."

"Don't play that fucking card, Fennic!" Mori yelled, shoving my hands away. "Even if I did die, I'd get to say I wasn't a coward!"

"Coward?" I laughed, the sound harsh even to my own ears. "Death wouldn't change that."

I was desperate. I was holding and grasping at threads. I was throwing anything I could consider out so that he would change his mind. I wanted to take him to Cylla with me. I wanted to make him a part of The Shadows Of Justice. To introduce him to Aero. I was already making plans to have him moved to Cylla for his safety. I knew he would never go now that this was going on. The realization made my chest ache with regret.

"When this is over, Fennic, I'm done. You go too far now. I tried to reason with you, I tried to help you, I tried to tell you bluntly that you're turning into your father. You won't listen, you won't change. When this is over, I won't stay to clean up all these innocent bodies while you make excuses about why I should continue to allow you to treat me and anyone else you deem not important for the moment like shit. You can keep doing this without me!" Mori pointed, his finger jabbing the air between us.

"I'm sorry, Mori! I'm sorry. Even if you hate me, I still can't stand here and watch you kill yourself. Let's go find Coy. Let's help him, and when this is over, I promise to treat you better. I swear I'll treat you the way I should have," I was begging him, my voice breaking with sincerity.

He watched me with hesitation at first, his eyes searching mine for truth, but he relented and followed me. We moved through the halls as a unit. We didn't slow our pace for anyone. We didn't stop to tell the younger boys to pull themselves together and stop cowering in the shadows. We let them be; we let them think they were well hidden. They were never raised to fight an undead army and a blood-magic-wielding Goddess. None of them were. Their trembling forms huddled in darkened corners were testaments to our failure.

We only relented when we found Coy in the weapons room. He tied his long white hair into a bun at the top of his head, his movements precise and practiced.

"Have you found Hesperia?" I asked, trying to catch my breath.

He shook his head, his eyes dark with determination.

"Mother has a locked door in the tower. It's the only place none of us have been," I offered, hope flickering briefly.

"What will you two do?" Coy asked, his voice uncharacteristically gentle.

"I don't know," I admitted. I tried to hide the shame in the sentence, but it hung heavy in the air between us.

Coy didn't look at me with disappointment; he looked at me with understanding instead. His features stayed stone, but his eyes always screamed his words for him. They held a silent compassion that made my failure even harder to bear.

"If we are Gods, there has to be some way to awaken, even if only a little piece. Focus on that so we can go after Nikola next," Coy advised, his words measured and calm.

He moved past us, carrying multiple weapons and a bow on his back. He looked like he was ready for anything. As if he had a sense of what he was doing. I knew he would succeed in finding Hesperia's body. I would not succeed in waking myself up. There wasn't enough time in the world for me to figure that out alone. The weight of inadequacy pressed down on my shoulders like a physical burden.

I knew I would sound like a complete coward now if I asked Coy to find Vesim so we could send Mori away. I knew that after seeing Coy, Mori would never agree. His determination was set in stone, as unmovable as the mountains.

"Let's try and clear some of the citizens out before Shivani can devastate them all," I suggested, attempting to find purpose.

I wanted to sound confident, but I knew it sounded like a question. Uncertainty bled through every word.

Mori nodded, and we took off back the way we came as quickly as our feet could carry us. Shivani was nowhere to be seen, but her magic was. Pools of blood covered the ground like puddles of rain, glistening in the torchlight, and the sounds of sobbing filled the air. There was no one to save that would have made it. No one to help that would have benefitted from it. Nothing for us to do except take in the sight of what Shivani could do. The brutality stole my breath.

We had been treating someone made for wiping things out better than any of us could have been trained to do as if she were a useless child who couldn't use a fork correctly. Hesperia was right again. This was never about Riven. This was about whatever game Niko, no Nikola, was playing. The truth hit me like a physical blow.

This entire realm was about whatever game the Gods were playing. Whatever war they were in the middle of. Whatever war, we, were in the middle of. This realm was about nothing more than the Viper poisoning the Gods. We were all just pawns on a blood-soaked board.

"This is beyond what I could have imagined Riven ever doing," Mori said. His voice was shaky, horror etched into every line of his face. "What kind of King could allow something like this to happen on his doorstep? Does he even have anyone left to call a subject?"

"Shivani!" Riven called for her and then pointed at Mori, his finger like a sentencing blade. "We've all heard him commit treason with his words against his King and Prince."

Shivani stopped and turned to face Mori. Still, there was no life in her eyes, but red filled even the whites, making her gaze demonic in its emptiness.

"Shivani, don't!" I moved for her, but it was useless. I was useless. My limbs felt leaden, too slow to stop what was happening.

Blood was being pulled from every spot I could see of Mori. She didn't hesitate. She didn't fight against Riven. She didn't even ask a question. I was too stunned, too in shock, by how easily she was defeated. My friend's skin grew pale and sunken before my eyes, his veins mapping blue lines across ashen flesh.

Nikola came into the group that was watching her slowly kill him next. She was pulling all of his blood from his body without pushing past the guards around her. She stood, dripping blood I could no longer tell the origin of, surrounded by bodies, making another addition. I thought he was supposed to be her friend, too. The betrayal carved another wound into my already broken heart.

"Shivani! Stop it! You'll kill him if you don't stop!" I pushed past guards, but they stood firm, trying to slow me down. Their eyes were clear; they didn't want to be her next victim. Their hands gripped me with desperate strength.

"Stop; I need him for the sacrifice during the ritual," Niko commanded, his voice cutting through the chaos.

"Guards!" Riven called, his eyes glazed with madness, "Take them both to the dungeon!"

I was struck hard enough to be put in a daze, stars exploding behind my eyes. I groaned and strained against the chains they were locking me into, the metal biting into my wrists.

"Riven! Don't you touch him!" I called, my voice hoarse with fear.

"Riven hardly has his own mind left. You should direct your pleas to a different name, like mine. Your little Mori is the last one carrying any blood of the goddess of fall. Whether he is a friend to you or not, I require him to be drained for other purposes. Besides, someone needs to keep your mother company," Niko said, satisfaction curling his lips into a cruel smile.

"My mother? What did you do to her?" I groaned out, dread pooling in my stomach.

My head was still too foggy, and my ears rang too loudly to take in everything he said. I felt the skin on my knees ripping from being drug across the stone, warm blood trickling down my legs. It wasn't until the other side of my chains were locked to the dungeon wall that I could see and think clearly again, the pain clearing some of the haze.

Mori's blood was already filling the divots in the altar they dug out, crimson rivulets flowing into ancient channels. Nikola lifted Mori's head by his almond-colored hair and pulled his head back until the fullness of his neck was in full view. He took a small blade and sliced the skin of Mori's throat until any blood left in him came flowing freely. Mori's eyes laid on me before they fell shut, a final moment of recognition before darkness claimed him.

"Mori!" I screamed to try and wake him, but it was useless. His name echoed back to me, a hollow reminder of my failure.

Niko used his abilities to rip the castle apart stone by stone. He truly was God-like, effortlessly doing things that we would be paying a high price to achieve. He didn't show a bead of sweat or a sign of distress. It was shocking to watch when, until now, all I had were a few stories. Massive blocks of ancient stone floated through the air at his command, reforming into patterns I couldn't comprehend.

A blood moon lit up the sky above us, bathing everything in a crimson glow, and I thought back to the pages of that book. If all of these things were happening the same way the book and that tree warned of, my death was next. I should have found peace in the idea of death if my mother and Mori were to no longer exist in the land of the living. Instead, I found panic in the thought of having an entire life, family, and friends I would never get to truly know or experience. The faces of Aero, Caym, and the others flashed before me— connections barely formed, now to be severed forever.

CHAPTER THIRTY-FOUR

THE TRUTH

SHIVANI

I was outside of the castle when I had control of my body again. When I could finally think my own thoughts. I was on my knees in the middle of so many bodies. I felt the blood that dropped from my chin; I was covered in it, like a glaze of liquid over my body. It clung to me, tacky and cooling against my skin. I had killed them. Every innocent person who came to rebel for a better world. I couldn't stop the bile that came from me next, burning its way up my throat and spattering onto the ground before me. I was powerless to stop the tears pouring down my cheeks, cutting clean trails through the crimson mask on my face.

There was no one left around me alive. Villagers and guards alike were unmoving. Skeletons of men and women long since dead. Riven was gone. Fennic and Vesim were nowhere to be seen. Hesperia nor Coy hovered to offer me a comforting glance. Only Whiskers was alive in my surroundings. She sat at the top of the stairs that led into the castle, watching me with her unblinking golden eyes.

I was sure I'd lose my stomach contents again before I

could get away from all the bodies. It was easy to tell I had done it because they all looked like my mother did when she died. Drained and hollow, like husks of what they once were. I carried no memory of doing this to them. I carried no memory at all. I only recalled being told to meet Riven in the throne room. He told me there were critical plans I was needed for. I was sure it would give me an upper hand in getting our realms put back together. How did I get from there to this? The gap in my memory was terrifying.

I reached up to check my neck. The stone was still where it should be, and the ring I found was still on my finger. It was the smallest bright side. When I looked over the rest of my body, I couldn't see anything different or alarming. It was just like a piece of my time was missing, torn from me as easily as turning a page. Whiskers was before me, climbing with her tiny paws into my lap and nudging me. I didn't deserve her comfort. Her fur was pristine against my blood-soaked hands.

I squeezed the necklace tighter; it was the only thing I had. I didn't know where Vesim was or if I had killed her, too. I didn't know where anyone went. The idea that I had killed them all was too overwhelming to process, crushing me beneath its weight.

Are you all right? Are you at the castle? Who is with you right now?

I felt like my skull was being struck, and my heart was stopped for too long when the voice forced itself into my head, echoing painfully against my thoughts.

"Are you in my mind?" I asked, my voice barely a whisper.

"Are you all right?" Koa pressed, urgency vibrating through his words.

"I don't know," I said, my fingers trembling against the necklace.

"Are you safe?" he asked, his concern palpable even through the mental connection.

"I don't know," I answered, the truth of it hollowing me out.

The fear in his voice made me scared. If he was frightened, what hope did I have?

"I'm sitting in the middle of more bodies than I can count, and I think I killed them all. Koa, I think I'm the one to be afraid of." The confession burned in my throat.

I lost the sound of his voice in my head when Riven stood at the top of the stairs, looking down at me. His silhouette was dark against the light behind him, power and madness emanating from him in equal measure.

"The blood moon is a sign from my children that they're ready for me to come back," he called, his voice carrying across the field of corpses. "We're only missing you!"

"I'm not coming with you!" I shouted, scrambling backward through the blood-soaked earth.

"Yes, you are. I don't require you to be willing; I only require you to be alive," he said, beginning his descent down the stairs.

I scrambled to my feet, and I felt dry blood pulling at my skin everywhere, cracking and flaking with my movements. I tried to ignore it. I wanted to pretend I didn't have a layer of innocent villagers coating my body. I couldn't think about it right now. I couldn't mourn. I needed to be on my feet. I needed to run. Survival trumped everything else.

I took another deep breath, and I ran. I kept my eyes on the tree line and didn't look back. I'd rather hide from creatures or fight them than be in his grip again. I almost tripped on a branch, and when I caught myself, I could see no one around me. It gave me a sense of relief, but I tried to stay focused. I crossed the line of forestry and kept running until I was far enough in that I couldn't see out. If he were following me, I wouldn't hear the leaves under his feet over my own. The forest swallowed me, branches clawing at my face and arms.

I took comfort behind a tree more enormous and older than I and took a moment to steady my breathing. I rubbed the sweat off my forehead, but when my arm came down, the moisture dripped with blood that had dried before. I told myself to ignore it. I told myself to keep moving, or I'd be caught again. I didn't have time to think about who's mother or father was dripping off of my forehead now. I couldn't afford the luxury of guilt.

The words I was repeating in my head didn't matter. My heart took over. It took over and pounded like a drum, each beat reverberating through my chest. My breath matched it, and my thoughts became scattered like leaves in a storm. I felt like I was being closed inside a small, dark box. Like I was being swallowed, and no matter how hard I tried, I couldn't gather my thoughts; they wouldn't stop racing. I began to feel lightheaded from the speed of my breath. I tried to shake my hands. I don't know why, and it didn't come with any relief. Panic had its claws in me now.

Flashes came back to me. Flashes of me holding a pillow to someone. A pillow that looked too pristine to be just anyone's. Flashes of my blood strings cutting into hearts, the life draining from eyes that stared at me in terror and confusion. I opened my eyes and pushed the tears back down. I didn't want to consider whose pillow that was. I couldn't. I heard the snap of branches coming closer, and I took off running again. It snapped me back to where I needed to be and blanked my mind out again.

He wouldn't catch me. He wouldn't. I couldn't go back. If I went back, I'd lose control of myself again. I lost track of how many trees I was running past. Branch after branch was all there was until there wasn't. Until I crashed into the back of a sleeping creature and was thrown off my feet, the impact knocking the air from my lungs.

It was fitting. If anything else could have gone wrong in

one day, I couldn't think up what it would have been. The universe seemed determined to break me.

Lightning lit the sky around us, and thunder crashed, the sound so close it made my ears ring.

I let out a scream and got to my feet. The rain started pouring next, washing blood off of me and turning the leaves at my feet a pale red. I could have considered it helpful. At least I wouldn't be covered in the crimson reminder of my failures. Still, it also felt as if I were being mocked. That I was being shown what else could happen. The skies themselves were weeping for what I'd done.

The creature stood in front of me with three legs and no arms. I tried to stop myself from thinking this would end up being easy. Sure, if I let those thoughts out, it would send another curse my way. Even though they didn't escape me entirely, it must have been heard anyway because when it opened its mouth and showed off its hundreds of razor-sharp teeth surrounding a second and third mouth, another little bit of me screamed inside. Poison spewed in my direction before the teeth started moving like a grinder, the sound sickening in its mechanical precision.

I dodged, nearly being grazed. I had to remove my shoe and throw it off before the poison could burn through it and touch my skin. Now I was mad. I'd have to keep running through the forest with only one shoe. I wouldn't make it far with one bare foot. The unfairness of it all fueled my anger.

"My feet already hurt!" I screamed, my voice lost in the storm.

I conjured a blood whip and slung it across the creature's mouth, busting the lip but hardly stopping it. Another shot of poison was coming my way, and I rolled, relieved not to lose another item this time. I got back to my feet and took off running at it. I grabbed its side and slung myself on its back. The thing wasted no time slinging me back and forth. I should have taken up riding more. The world spun around me as I clung to its slick hide.

I waited for it to open its mouth again and released a beam of blood into its jaws, refusing to relent until it dropped. It felt as if it took everything I had to make that a reality. When it did, I collapsed into the leaves, heaving air. That wasn't so bad. I could make this run. I could get far, far away from here, and if I ran into another, I'd kill it, too. I could get far enough to figure out how to make my own rifts and get help.

I started laughing. It slipped out of me like an explosive leak, bordering on hysteria. I used the rain to clean off my face of dirt and blood before rolling to my stomach to get back up. Before I could, the creature squirmed as well. It was quicker to recover than I was because before I could get to my feet, it was already towering over me, and all I could do was look up to see its cycling teeth inching to my face. The stench of its breath hit me like a wall.

It didn't matter in the end, and I'd be lying if I said I didn't feel a tiny tinge of relief when Nikola grabbed me by the hair and threw me to my feet. What was it they said in the village? Better the devil you knew than the one you don't. Nikola slung me as if I were nothing to him, and his other fist reached, fearless into the creature's jaws, bringing it down in a way that I could not. The crack of bone and the creature's dying screech cut through the rain.

He didn't struggle. He didn't show any fear. He just did it. That piece of garbage just did it as if he had done it one hundred times before. It was shameful, but I didn't resist this time. When he gripped a full hand of my hair again, I allowed him to do so without resistance. What was I to do? My last reserves of strength were spent.

"Are you proud of how far you got?" he asked, dragging me through the mud, each step jolting pain through my scalp.

"I'll be proudest when I kill you!" I spewed the threat, but he only laughed. He was right, too. My threats were as empty as my strength right now.

"I told you before, but I'll tell you again. You aren't your mother," he laughed, the sound grating against my ears.

"If you're that scared of her, aren't you worried about what she will do to you if you hurt me?" I yelled, still feeling branches tear at my skin, leaving burning trails of pain.

"That's why you have to die. It'll be much easier to bend her to my will after I eat your heart than before," he said, his casual tone chilling me more than his words.

Another branch tore at the skin on my calf and ripped it open. I cried in pain, but he didn't lose his grip; he tightened it. He flung me into the air, and I felt each follicle of hair resist the weight of my entire body. It was a feeling I only felt for a moment. He hit me in the side of the head so hard that every-thing about me was silenced, darkness swallowing me whole.

I didn't open my eyes when I regained consciousness. I needed a moment to pull myself together first. I could feel every scrape, scratch, cut, and leaf still clinging to me. I felt the wind hitting my bare skin and the freezing cold my body hadn't recovered from yet after the rain. When I opened my eyes, I was bound to a stone pillar between Riven and Fennic. Mori's body lay on the stone, his skin pale and waxy in death, and Nikola stood against a wall across from us. The room was ancient, carved from stone that predated the castle.

"I'm glad to see you awake," Niko said, satisfaction evident in his voice.

I coughed on the dryness of my throat. Taking in a breath felt like glass, shards cutting through my windpipe.

"My name is Nikola, god of insanity." He made a mocking bow.

"Do you want a trophy?" I asked, my voice hoarse. "Someone like you won't ever get to the point of deserving an introduction." I took in a deep breath, ignoring the pain. I was ready to tell him everything I felt. If I was going to die, I'd at least go out speaking my mind.

He held his hand up to stop me. "It already feels like a waste of my time to hear what you're about to say."

"What you're going to spew will be better?" I scoffed, the chains rattling as I shifted.

"I've been waiting to be able to talk to you. Picturing what it would be like. I had considered the look on your face when I discussed how your aunty was kind enough to leave me sealed to this realm. I imagined how I'd feel your fear when I said that I couldn't break the seal without your blood and a new body. I have been waiting so long since I built this castle over the altar and planted the seed in mortal minds. I thought, at the very least, we could laugh about how it was so easy to grow. Men want nothing beyond each other's power. I told one of them they had the blood of a god, and he became drunk on the idea. Dahlia was always so invested in the bright side of mortals, but I warned her what they would do if given the chance." Nikola's laugh sent chills down my spine, crawling like ice through my veins. "I have to admit, this is disappointing."

"I am a god-king!" Riven growled in protest, straining against his chains.

"No, you're not. I am a god, and you are a pawn. You don't have a single drop of deity blood in you. I just needed guaranteed protection for my altar while I looked for Dahlia's daughter. It was a happy surprise when I found two of you. An annoyance when I realized I needed a guardian's blood to unseal not just your heart but your sisters as well." He clicked his tongue in frustration, his irritation cracking through his composed facade.

"You thought it would be easier?" I laughed, the sound harsh and brittle.

"Considering how important the two of you are, it was

easy," he said, pacing before us like a predator considering its meal.

"What next, then? Will you talk me to death?" I spat my words at him, blood flecking my lips.

"Did you know if you eat the heart of a god, you take their powers and position? Your mother knew, and she did her best to keep it quiet. There are small details to remember. It has to be the whole heart, things like that. You're to lay dormant, a sleeping primordial god. You will be useless until she returns to you. When she does, her mark will appear somewhere on your body," Niko said, his voice almost reverential when speaking of power.

He looked me up and down with a smirk on his face. Like I was prey, and he was going to strip me down and look at every inch of my body to find that mark. His gaze made my skin crawl.

I clenched my fist tighter to hide my palm, the mark there burning against my skin. "How do you know she'll do anything at all? If she was so focused on keeping you at bay, then how can you be sure I'm not a liability that she would give up?"

"If you can be sure of anything, be sure she won't abandon you. She put everything she had into you four. Everything," he smirked, confidence oozing from him.

He leaned against the pillar I was chained to. He wore a look on his face that made me swallow my saliva harder than normal. His eyes were too dark, and his voice too calm. Everything about him made me feel uneasy, as if insects were crawling beneath my skin.

"Since it's our last meeting, I will go ahead and take the place of the dad you never had and tell you a story," Niko said, his tone mockingly paternal.

"Can you hit me first? I'd rather death come sooner if living means you'll never stop talking," Fennic groaned from my left, his face bruised but his spirit unbroken.

"Does it make you feel better? To talk that way while you leak fear from every pore?" Niko clicked his tongue and turned his attention back to me. "Long ago, in a world you can't remember, Dahlia and her sister, Yumi, ruled everything. They were two pieces of one whole. Light and dark, life and death. Good and evil, however, you'd like to view yin and yang. Dahlia had a solid outlook, she cared about everything from the smallest blade of grass and up. Yumi cared for herself. She was just as easy to use as mortals. It was a fun time. Dahlia was smart, however, too smart for most of us. Yumi's jealousy was also unmatched. We soon became a realm of true gods and false idols. Yumi's children resembled gods in every way but in power. They could only assume false positions. The ones that happened to be a little better, were things like greed, pride; you get the point, I'm sure. What they could use was stolen from true gods. They were called abominations, and it was another hit to Yumi." Niko crossed his arms, his expression almost wistful for a moment.

"Can you get to a point yet?" I demanded, rattling my chains in frustration.

Niko hushed me, pressing a finger to his lips. "We have time; I haven't even gotten to the good parts yet." He lowered himself down to me so we could look eye to eye, his breath hot against my face. "There's another version of you, ya know. She can do what you can, but she's a little unhinged. You'll never meet her, but I thought you'd like to know. She was one of my prized creations. She and my son. The two of them made dealing with Yumi worth it. If they are anything, it's powerful." He shrugged before continuing, "Your mother and father were the picture of love. They loved each other so strongly they were the first to say they carried children. Dahlia held the four of you in her womb. They were so happy but not as happy as I was to see their guards lowered. Dahlia announced her plans for the four of you and what it would mean for all of us."

I interrupted him, leaning forward as far as my chains would allow. "Her plans for us?"

"It seems it doesn't matter anymore, does it?" He waved dismissively. "Dahlia made your guardians next. She wanted them to train before your arrival. Have you found yours yet? I imagine not. Yumi stole a lot of souls on her way out, and I've been pretty confident those are with her. I was able to place my son in the guardians. Imagine Dahlia's face when there were five guardians standing in front of her, and she couldn't tell the difference. You should have been there." His face lit with vicious glee. "A secret Yumi and I have kept from each other, and everyone else is our children. You see, the reason they worked so well is because of their creation. I learned of Yumi making a son and daughter from pieces of Olexei. So I made a son and daughter from pieces of Dahlia."

"How would I know that?" I shook my head, the chains biting into my wrists. "Why would I even have a use for this secret?"

He shrugged, indifferent to my frustration. "I do suppose it's another thing that doesn't matter to you."

"You're a horrible storyteller," Fennic sighed, his head lolling against the pillar. "Gods and a power struggle, you lost, and you're bitter. You're trying again; you'll lose again. You're leaving out all the good bits that would mean anything to us. We got it, it's not that original."

"Your death won't be that original either, but you'll still be dead," Nikola mocked, his eyes flashing dangerously.

Fennic waved his hands sarcastically from the chains and pretended to be hurt by Nikola's words, the metal clanking with his exaggerated movements.

"If you're going to tell stories, and it means nothing to you, why not give me something I actually care about?" I asked, unable to keep the pleading from my voice. If I was going to die, I at least wanted to understand why.

"Do you have something to give me in return?" Niko asked, raising an eyebrow.

"You have me locked to stone; what can I possibly give!" I screamed, my voice bouncing off the ancient walls.

I felt surging inside of myself. Magic sparking and ready to run wild but it never did. It was stopped by whatever Nikola did when he locked me in place, the power hitting an invisible barrier and rebounding painfully inside me.

"I bet you won't tell me because you don't know. You want us to believe you're all-knowing and all-powerful, but you know nothing, just like you did nothing for the realm. I know you were locked here because they didn't want to deal with you. Even Yumi said she was done with you. She went to build a world without you because she knew she could do it better without you! You talk about children, but I don't see them here to save you!" I wasn't considering the consequences when he slapped me, his hand cracking across my face like thunder.

I spit blood onto the ground and laughed it off, the coppery taste filling my mouth.

"You can't even hit me right," I chuckled, a trickle of blood running down my chin.

"When I take your heart, woman, I'm going to make sure you're alive as long as possible and feel every bit of what I do to you," Niko pointed, rage contorting his features.

I laughed harder, louder in his face. If I was going to die, I'd take what little victories I could.

"One thing you did right was ensuring Fennic and I could agree on two things. You hit like a bitch, and death would be better than your voice," I spat, blood flecking his face.

"I'd raise a glass to that if I had one," Fennic nodded, a ghost of a smile crossing his battered face.

CHAPTER THIRTY-FIVE
THE SACRIFICE

FENNIC

When Nikola returned, he tossed Shivani like she was a rag doll from the sky to the ground. The way her body hit, I was sure she was already dead. The sound of impact echoed through the ruins, a sickening thud that made my stomach turn. I was shocked to see her talking and resisting the chains as well as she was. I knew I wouldn't have survived such a hit. Her clothing was shredded in every place her skin had once been. Unlike her clothing, her skin had already healed, unblemished where there should have been wounds. Hesperia was not as honest as she should have been when she described what things would be like after Shivani ate her heart.

Unfortunately for me, it meant her mother would still want my body. The cat sitting on a pile of rubble just far enough away to be of no irritant to Nikola was my reminder. She sat there watching me, her golden eyes unblinking, and I could feel her grip on me becoming stronger. I wouldn't be here soon enough. As if she knew I was thinking of her, I felt her enter my mind, her presence cool and ancient.

Was your mother ill while carrying you?

What?

Did she drop you while just a babe?

Excuse me?

Did you develop an illness as a child? Take a beating to the skull? Born too early?

Why are you asking me this?

There must be some explanation for why your brain growth was stunted, and you lack so much intelligence.

Are you trying to say I'm stupid?

You are of below-average intellect if you think I am haunting you from inside of a cat.

You're trying to tell me you aren't in the cat?

Of course not. The cat is not what it seems, but it has little to do with me. I am a tree. You can hear me because a part of myself is slowly taking over your limbs and what little there is to control of your mind.

What little there is or isn't of my brain is mine; stay off of it! My mental voice was strained with effort.

I can not. You are simple to use and weak in your resistance. You have little real motivation as a mortal man. Others have something to cling to. Things are grounding them and making it too difficult for me while I am in my current form. You are just a shell.

Enough. If you're going to kill me, you can do it without this. I could feel her presence spreading in my mind like roots through soil.

You are skilled at distortion of reality and refusal of criticism.

No, I just don't care to hear anything from you. It's easy for you to pass judgment when I can't say anything about you.

You are still as unafraid of me as you were when a God.

Don't talk about it as if it's a fond memory to you. You're going to kill me, not restore me. Bitterness colored my thoughts.

I do have many fond memories of you and your brother.

Your mother would bring the two of you to my garden, and we would kick a ball for hours.

Enough. I'd rather die without this.

She thought just because she was a deity, she could say anything she wanted. I'd rather Nikola kill me before she can keep talking again. I was happier thinking she was only a wild dream. Her presence faded, leaving a cold emptiness in its wake.

Nikola was still busy uncovering bits of the altar our guards died before finishing. He didn't seem to care about keeping an eye on Shivani. He sure didn't care about Riven and all the groaning he was doing over the situation. Maybe if Shivani had kept that knife that she loved so much on her wrist, this could have ended more easily. The thought was selfish, but I was beyond caring.

"It says a lot about you," I said, nodding my head at the rubble. "You've been the one God that could turn the realm into something, and instead, you let it die. You come to our castle, and it takes you only days to turn it into death. Too." I mocked, the words burning in my throat.

"If not my hand, it would have been you or your brother. Maybe his son. I don't care about the realm or your idea of me," Niko said, not bothering to look up from his work.

It wasn't enough for me, though; I wanted his attention. He didn't stop what he was doing; he didn't look back at me. He gave me nothing. Indifference was more maddening than hatred.

"It's no wonder they left you here. You're creepy. You're psychotic. You failed then, and you're failing now," I shouted, straining against my chains until they bit into my wrists.

"I'm too old for this. You won't get a rise out of me," he turned around and walked towards me with a mission in his body language, each step measured and deliberate. "If you want pain, you can simply ask."

He pulled his arm back and spared no force when he

drove his knuckles into my rib cage. It was exactly what I wanted. I coughed and wheezed, the air driven from my lungs. I was overcome with the pain, and it was the distraction I wanted. The pain I should be feeling for everything I put Mori through. It was an intense enough feeling to keep me from thinking of my mother. It started to taper off too quickly. I needed another. I needed him to hit me again and take my mind far away from the focus it was nearing. Physical pain was preferable to the mental torment.

I knew I was a bad person. I didn't need to hear it all the time. I didn't need so many people in my ear repeating to me that the things I did were wrong. Of course, I knew it. What was I supposed to do about it? Apologize? What kind of apology could I give that would make up for trying to kill her? What kind of apology could I pull out of thin air to make the things Mori had to do better? Sorry for making you kill the wrong girl, sorry for all the missions we've gone on together where you had to murder when all you wanted was peace. The weight of it all crushed down on me.

None of it would have been enough. Not now, not ever. It was better that I didn't. That they hated me. It was easier for me that they considered me garbage. They were only seeing me as I should be seen. I couldn't change it. I wouldn't be a hero after a few conversations. An apology wouldn't make up for not being able to protect my mother. Nothing I could say would give me forgiveness in the other realm, either. All that I had left was to receive proper punishment for failing as a god and a mortal before I was gone.

"Is that the best you've got?" I rasped, blood flecking my lips.

Niko smirked at me, and I knew what it meant because I gave the same look. It was the high from the challenge. The excitement of being able to amp things up. He wanted to be challenged, and I wanted to challenge. He walked back to me, lifted my head by pulling up my chin, and connected his knuckles to my jaw. I swore I'd spit a tooth. The pain exploded through my face like lightning.

It was all the same to me. We both could chase our high now. He won by shutting me up, and my mind was left blank and reset by the ringing in my ear and the aching in my jaw. For a blessed moment, there was only pain, simple and honest.

The longer I watched him circle Shivani like she was his next meal, the more I felt disgusted. His eyes lingered on her with a hunger that made my skin crawl.

"Are you going to keep this going, or can we get on with it? You haven't told us what we're waiting for?" I said, my words slurring through swollen lips.

"We are giving Dahlia some time to unlock Shivani. The blood moon is already here," Niko said, pointing upward where crimson light filtered through the broken ceiling.

This felt so unlikely—like a bad dream or a hallucination that took too long to wake up from. I told myself a God stood in front of me, one we were taught didn't exist or left us behind, and he was after what seemed like an ordinary girl. I couldn't believe it. It was just too much. How did things change so drastically, so quickly? The world I knew had been shattered in the span of days.

The idea made it easy for me to feel braver than I truly was. Maybe it was the fact I knew death was on my horizon, regardless, that allowed me to try one last time. One last try at being a God of protection.

"What if I'm her guardian, and I say I'm going to stop you?" I asked, forcing strength into my voice.

Niko cackled, the sound bouncing off the stone walls. "I'm not your brother, boy; you can't fool me by just saying a few words. I'd tell you that you were stupid and bluffing."

Whiskers meowed from a pile of rubble I had looked at before. I knew she wasn't there until now. I would have noticed her. That stupid cat is always lurking. I'm sure she wants to make sure to get one more bite in before I die. Her tail swished slowly, deliberately.

"How are you so sure I'm not just dormant like she was? You wouldn't know," I challenged, my chin lifting in defiance.

"If you were her guardian, you'd be uncontrollable right now. You'd be in a rage. Practically foaming at the mouth, knowing she was hurt and the blood moon was above us. Does that look like you? I intend to be long gone before her guardian can arrive," Niko said, dismissing me with a wave of his hand.

I may not be her guardian, but I could be something. I can at least do something. The thought hardened into resolve.

"I haven't gotten many gifts in my life, so I like to make sure I put them to their full use when I do," I said, my heart hammering against my ribs.

Nikola furrowed his brows at me, "Now you really are rambling on."

"Come get this sunflower out of my pocket," I said, nudging my head to the spot on my chest. "It's special, and it should be seen before I die."

Nikola walked towards me and lowered himself till he crouched. He ran a finger over my pocket before resting his arms on his knees, his face inches from mine.

"You know it'll hurt worse if you play with me, ya?" His eyes trailed me, searching for deception.

I shrugged, trying to appear nonchalant. "What am I supposed to do from these chains?"

His eyes gave a silent nod of agreement, and I watched his shoulders relax before he reached into my pocket and pulled out the sunflower Mori gave me to use. When I asked him where he got it, all he said was that Vesim brought it back from somewhere. We didn't have anything like it here, and I already found it pathetic Nikola wasn't suspicious for that reason. For a god, he was remarkably gullible.

He twirled it between his fingers before sniffing it. I was

beginning to think I should have kept the flower a secret with the way he was treating it, admiring it like a trophy.

"This smells faintly of Dahlia's power," he smirked, satisfaction spreading across his face. "Thank you for such a sweet gesture."

That was all I had up my sleeve. The only trick I had left to play before I had no choice but to draw my ace. The open-air around us still smelled of wet dirt and grass. It was a nice scent before my death. I could blame the tree lady for failing me, but why trudge through that when I could take in the sight of stars around the bright red moon instead? The beauty of the sky was a strange comfort in these final moments.

I'd like to give some hero's speech, but I'm not a hero, and If I had a choice, I'd still back out so I didn't have to do what was going to happen. It would have been nice to have more time to make some things right. I guess I can hope to be written into history books as a hero, at least.

It didn't matter if I was chained or not for this; all I needed was my fingers. I had no skin left to pick off of my thumb anymore, anyway. I used my fingers to trace the air around me just like Aero taught me while I was in Cylla, and I sent a shock wave to Nikola. The power surged through me, familiar yet strange.

"Flectere Ossa," I whispered. "Bend the bones."

His lips turned to laugh, but the silence was first filled with the cracks and snaps I was waiting for. His body twisted and contorted, and I felt a sense of pride and let out my own laughter. The sound was short-lived.

Niko lifted my body, and the sound of my neck was clear to me before he tossed me to the side like trash. The crack reverberated through my skull. I tried to move; I was free of the chains. I could get up now. I could genuinely defend us. I could work through the curse of my ability. I had to. My feet didn't respond to me. My toes didn't wiggle, and my fingers didn't flex when I tried to send them the message. Not a single part of my body was responding. I achieved one blink. Only one. I was paralyzed. The sound I heard was my body breaking. Was this death? The edges of my eyes were beginning to turn black. How did that do nothing to him? Why didn't the tree lady do something? Panic flooded me, trapped in a body that would no longer obey.

"Fennic!" Shivani yelled, her voice breaking with horror.

Would she be sad to see me die? No, of course not. Not after everything I had done or said. I didn't believe I was entirely sorry to see myself go. I was hopeful that the afterlife was more like a deck of cards. Mori and I would be shuffled back in like we shuffled the cards in our game. We would be drawn again to try and do things right in another life. In another game, he and I will be shuffled together again, and we will play it right. I'll introduce him to Aero, and we will all be brothers. The thought brought a peace I didn't expect.

I took in the scent of fresh rain one last time. Was she still screaming my name? I hoped she was. The darkness closed in, and I surrendered to its embrace.

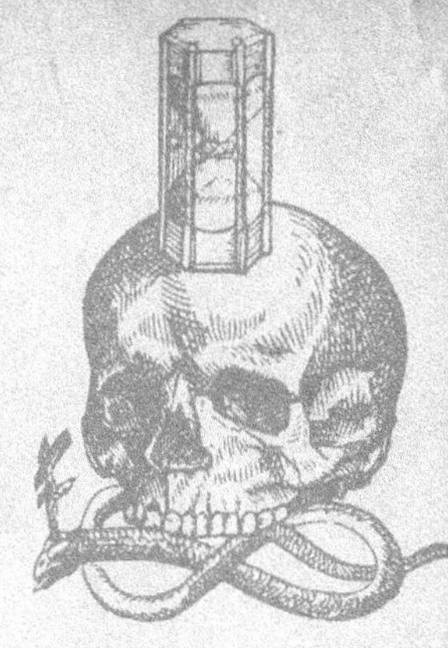

CHAPTER THIRTY-SIX
THE THROW

The Old Gods

The Goddess of Night was created from moon-light's mourning. She missed the night sky that she had spent so long with. Night spent her time protecting the animals that came out after dark and watching from afar. She became insanity's first secret lover of what would be many. He lulled her with sweet tales of the life they would have together and used her to gain information about the inner workings of the golden city. When Night found out of insanity's other lovers, she cried until she had formed a river.

VESPERA

The Nola and I were giving food to the inhabitants of Merripen that weren't dead. The Mogs, dragons, cats. I didn't mind the job, but I also enjoyed the ability to overhear conversations. Today's conversation wasn't as interesting until Vesim came in screaming and yelling. I had seen enough of this woman to know composure was her strongest asset. Her disheveled appearance and frantic eyes immediately told me something was terribly wrong.

I rushed to her, and I wasn't alone. All of us crowded her, our bodies forming a protective circle around her trembling form.

"Nikola has Hesperia and Shivani. They are using some sort of mind control on Shivani. They're doing their best, but it's Nikola! What am I supposed to do?" Vesim pleaded, her hands shaking as she pushed her hair from her face.

"Calm down. Take a breath," Juniper was comforting her the best she could, her hands steadying Vesim's shoulders.

"The herbs didn't work, the flowers didn't work. Nothing we took back with us has worked for anything beyond a parlor trick," Vesim's voice was still erratic, cracking with desperation.

"Make another rift," Koa demanded, his jaw clenched so tight I could see the muscle twitching.

Vesim listened, but none of us moved; we knew, just like Koa knew, he wasn't walking through it. The rift formed, a shimmering blue tear in the air, but when Koa tried to step through, an invisible barrier pushed him back. When it failed, none of us gave him an I told you so. The defeat in his eyes was punishment enough.

"Maybe we can try to use crystals?" I tried to offer something even if I wasn't confident. "We travel with some of them."

Koa pulled out his travel crystal, and so did Caym. One by one, we all joined in, the gems glowing faintly in our palms.

"It's going to take a lot of power if that's going to work," Onyx said, his normally calm voice laced with doubt.

No shit, is what I wanted to say, but for Koa's sake, I did not. Between the veins on his neck, the pounding of his pulse around them, and the sweat on his forehead, I could tell he was panicking. I could feel it, too. The more he felt the need to get to Shivani, the more I felt the need to protect both of the girls. His fear was becoming my fear, resonating between us like a plucked string.

All of us focusing our minds on Vesim's realm did open a rift to it with the crystals, but no one could walk through it. The portal shimmered with promise before collapsing in on itself. It failed as fast as Vesim's rifts, but this left us exhausted on top of it, our energy draining away like water through sand.

I sat on the ground in the middle of the group. I needed a minute to stop my head from spinning. My breathing was slow and shallow. I felt outside of my body like I may be dying. The world tilted and swayed around me, colors blurring at the edges of my vision.

"Why don't we use Astra?" Onyx said. "She's the goddess of space, right?"

"Sure," Caym answered, clearly not understanding, his brow furrowed in confusion.

"Can't she just take him through space?" Onyx said, enthusiasm creeping into his voice.

"This is no time for jokes!" Koa growled, his fist slamming into his thigh.

"I mean it. This magic? Curse? It shouldn't be able to stop Astra from moving through the universe if that is what she is meant for," Onyx pressed, stepping closer to Koa.

I had nothing to insert, nothing to say about it. I could hardly hold myself upright, even while sitting. The world continued to spin around me like a whirlpool.

"Vespera, are you alright?" Caym asked, his voice distant through the fog in my mind.

"I'm fine!" I snapped back, not wanting the attention.

"Your markings are glowing!" Koa called, pointing at my arms.

I shot my eyes open. I couldn't believe it without seeing it myself. The intricate patterns on my skin pulsed with a soft blue light, visible even through my clothing.

"You've been hiding this?" Onyx yelled, his face contorting with betrayal.

"This isn't the time for this!" I said, trying to cover the markings with my hands.

"You can use that excuse now, but we will discuss this. You lied, and you lied about something big. This means Onyx can't be a guardian if you have Sage's markings," Caym responded, his voice measured but firm.

I threw myself back into the grass and shut my eyes again. The feeling of the cool grass was the only thing to pull me from the dizziness I was being soaked in. Each blade pressed against my skin like tiny anchors, keeping me from floating away completely.

"Koa!" I yelled. "Calm down!"

Caym sat him in the grass beside me and whispered comforts that were meaningless to me. It worked. That was all I cared about. I could feel myself entering back into my body. I started feeling like myself again. His panic to protect her was my panic to protect her. As his emotions settled, mine followed suit, the connection between us undeniable now.

"You can't be serious," Astra said, approaching our small group, her silver hair gleaming in the sunlight.

"We are," Onyx said, determination hardening his features.

"What? You want me to put him on an asteroid and toss him like a ball?" Astra laughed, but Koa jumped to his feet at the response, hope flaring in his eyes.

"You get it! I knew you would!" Koa grabbed her hands, squeezing them in his excitement.

Astra's mouth hung open, and she let out the fakest laugh of disbelief. "What if you die?"

"I won't!" Koa said, his conviction unwavering.

"We will go with him to make sure!" Onyx added, stepping forward to stand beside Koa.

"Yeah, sure, why not? Let's just do it!" Astra was still speaking as if this were all just a game we were playing, her voice dripping with sarcasm.

When Juniper pulled out crystals to form a shield around Koa, Onyx, and Caym, her smile dropped. Reality seemed to hit her all at once, her expression shifting from mockery to concern.

"I can't believe we are truly going to try this," Astra shook her head, uncertainty written across her face.

She took the three of them with her into the sky, and the last thing we saw was a brilliant flash of light, like a shooting star in reverse, ascending into the heavens. The silence they left behind was deafening, filled only with our collective held breath.

CHAPTER THIRTY-SEVEN

THE TRANSFORMATION

SHIVANI

Fennic's body laid lifeless on the ground in front of me. His blood drained into the grooves of the ritual plate, mixing with Mori's, crimson rivers flowing along ancient channels. Nothing was left between us and the blood moon. Not conversation, not walls. It made me feel different, sick. The brighter the moon got and the redder the glow, the more I felt changed. Power and nausea churned within me in equal measure.

Guards' bodies from all around the rubble lifted into the air. They glowed a low blue before being tilted to their feet, limbs moving like puppets on invisible strings. He was reanimating them the same way I did with my blood magic. When they opened their eyes, they glowed the same navy blue from their eyes, vacant and hollow. Four of them stood in front of symbols of the seasons before they started chanting in unison, their voices an eerie chorus in the devastation.

I couldn't understand what they were saying, not because I didn't speak the language of spells, I did, but because the chants they were spewing felt as if they were tearing me apart.

I was sure I would be ripped into four pieces and sit at their feet before I could focus enough to fight back. Every syllable was like a knife through my flesh.

My head pounded, and for a reason I didn't understand; it was then that I realized I didn't know where my seashell was. The connection to Koa, severed.

I opened my mouth to speak, but I was pulled into my own mind instead, consciousness folding inward like origami.

I was inside myself. There was a woman standing in front of me in a gown of crimson red that flowed around her like living flame. Her feet were bare, but her eyes were the softest purple. They were kind; I could have dived into them and felt protection. Her skin was dark, and when she opened her mouth, her voice was just as soft as she looked, melodic and warm.

She hadn't done anything yet, but she brought me the largest wave of comfort I had ever felt. My body tingled, and my heart wanted to run to her. It longed for her embrace, recognizing her on a level deeper than memory.

"You have your father's lips. Small and naturally red," she smiled, her gaze caressing my face with motherly pride.

"Are you Dahlia?" I asked, but I didn't move, afraid she might vanish if I reached for her.

"I am," she nodded, the simple confirmation sending a wave of emotion through me.

"Where are we?" I asked, trying to steady my voice.

She moved closer to me with a grace I could never have had. Her hands lay on each of my cheeks, their warmth seeping into my skin. The motion was loving, but the pain in her eyes made me nervous. The reality in front of me hadn't hit me yet. The idea that I may die today and it would be a true death. It hadn't connected yet. I was shutting myself down and pretending it was some sort of dream I'd wake up from. That if I didn't think about it too hard, it couldn't be real. I was sure I could cheat it, or a knight would come and save me. It was her eyes that sent that tumbling down, the sadness there unmistakable.

"I long for the day we may discuss every subject that crossed your mind. Today can not be that day, my sweet. Today, I must put you through a pain I had hoped you would avoid. When you wake, you will change. You will have a surge. Do not be deceived. Do not count it as the end," she said, her thumbs gently stroking my cheekbones.

"Are you coming? Will you be here?" I asked, unable to keep the childlike hope from my voice.

"I am here, in the only way I can be for now," she said. "Do not look for me; trust in yourself."

My cry came out with a laugh. The two didn't belong together, but the way I was feeling could only be explained by both. Of course, what I wanted was right in front of me, but I was too weak to touch it. Of course, it was leaving me again. The pattern of abandonment continued.

"Please, before you leave," I paused to keep the dam in place on my tears, my voice threatening to break, "Will I get to see my sisters?"

"My sweet, Nikola could only dream to stop you today. He can only hope to claim a bit of something real. Even in his dreams, he could not succeed. You will meet them again," she promised, her voice carrying the certainty of fate itself.

A part of me knew she wasn't there to hurt me. A larger part of me couldn't stop the hurt of another abandonment, the wound still raw and bleeding.

My mind was blank again and only filled with the pain of my body contorting. My limbs ached and stretched, and my skull felt like it would explode, pressure building behind my eyes. I was too high up. I looked worse than Nikola's puppets. Screams escaped me. They were filled with the sound of agony, and the rain came again. It pounded against my skin without mercy. Maybe it was that every nerve in my body became activated by what was happening to me, each drop of rain like fire on my transforming flesh.

She didn't explain it, and I didn't know her enough to hand her my trust, but I did anyway. Another wrist bent and snapped before a strike of lightning around the rubble, illuminating the destruction in stark white. Chants grew louder around me, and I could understand them now. They called in unison to pull my soul from me. There was nothing I could do. It was all beyond my control, and I entered into myself again. I did what I knew best, and I shut myself off. I focused on Koa, reaching out with my mind.

"I don't know if you can hear me. I don't know how you were in my mind the first time so I can find you again. I lost the shell. I haven't seen Vesim or Hesperia. I think I'm a murderer. I think I killed Fennic's mother. Not just her, but others. My realm is crashing around me, and things I'd sound too crazy saying out loud have been going on. Fennic is gone, too. He didn't make it; I couldn't save him. I don't think I'll be making it to see your realm again. Koa, can you make sure Whiskers gets back home? I don't want her to stay here alone."

When the pain finally stopped, I was unrecognizable. My body was no longer mine. It was strands of blood weaved together to form a human shape. I was wings of blood and fire. I felt powerful. The first thing I noticed after my mind was clear of the pain was that my feet still didn't touch the ground. It was an odd thing to notice, but even as I walked closer to Nikola, I didn't feel the sensation of the ground beneath me. I was light, yet strong, ethereal and solid at once.

He looked at me with a smirk I couldn't wait to knock off of his face. I felt his steps disturb the air around my feet. His energy was as dark as his smile, a palpable malevolence.

He reached for me by the throat, and when he pulled me against him, he leaned his face against my ear. I could feel his mouth open to whisper, but the movement sent rage down my spine, and I tossed my head back to allow space between us. I used that space to shove my hand into his chest. I felt his heartbeat against the grip of my fingers, warm and pulsing. I pressed harder until I felt my nails penetrate and slide in. The beats became erratic until I pulled his heart out and threw it to the ground. The last thing I wanted was to eat the god of insanity's heart. The organ landed with a wet slap, still quivering.

His grip on me was let go. He hit his knees, and I wasted no more time before pulling at the blood flowing from him. I entwined it all into braids and pulled until no more came from him. I pulled until he was empty, or at least unmoving. I started to feel myself coming down from the high I was riding; she was right. It would be temporary. I didn't expect it to be so temporary, the power receding like an outgoing tide.

I didn't feel nearly as powerful as I had, but I still felt motivated in the face of Nikola's death. My mind only wanted to keep moving, step by step, survival instinct taking over.

Getting the chains off Riven was easier than I expected. Part of me still wanted him dead, but I knew there was more to worry about than a pitiful man who now had nothing. He had received justice by his own hand in the end. He brought in the man who became his downfall and taught him he was the same as the rest of us. A man who showed him one day, he would indeed have to answer for what he had done.

I couldn't do anything to him that would be worse than everyone knowing he wasn't close to a god. His image was gone beyond repair, and it would never be the same. The way the guards rushing in looked at him was worse than any words I could give him. The breaking in his eyes, which he refused to show on his face, was a good start for my happiness. I had gotten what I wanted in the end. The realm would change, and it would no longer be in Riven's hands.

He cleared his throat before speaking, "You did your duty

to the King. I'll reward you by letting you keep your head," his voice lacked the authority it once held.

"Maybe you should focus on where yours will be once we rebuild," I said, unable to keep the contempt from my voice.

He looked at me in disbelief, his brow furrowing.

"Riven, you can't truly think you'll just retake your seat on the throne?" I said, incredulity coloring my words.

"Why wouldn't I?" He scoffed, chin lifting in defiance.

"I would die before I finished the list of reasons why," I said, crossing my arms.

He shook his head, "This was just a test from the gods. I'm alive, and my brothers are dead. It's clear the throne was meant for me," Riven said, his delusion intact despite everything.

"How do you keep yourself in such a grand illusion even after everything you've seen? Aren't you scared another God will come for you? Aren't you scared that I'll come for you?" I crossed my arms, power coursing through me again despite my weakness.

He was silent, but I watched his throat bob hard. He hadn't considered me a threat before, but he did now. I wonder if everything he said to me was running through his mind. If he considered the status he was going to give me now that I was far above him. The tables had turned, and we both knew it.

"I'm not dead, either," Coy said. He pulled a coffin behind him, the wooden box dragging across the rubble with a scraping sound.

I couldn't stop myself from hugging Coy, and I couldn't stop the next thought that ran through my head being the realization that Hesperia was rubbing off on me. His solid presence was a welcome anchor in the chaos.

"Where is she?" I asked, pulling back to search his face.

He shook his head. "Nikola put her in a box and kept it on him. She's here with you, somewhere."

My heart dropped into my stomach. I hadn't seen a box. Dread replaced relief in an instant.

I left Riven to be the one to take in the damage done around us. I wanted to find my sister. My feet were on the ground this time, but the new wings I had developed didn't go away. They burned silently on my back, casting a warm glow over the rubble. I reached back to touch them, but they weren't hot. They looked as if they should have burnt the skin off my fingers, crimson and gold flames dancing without heat. I thought hard about it, and they fluttered in response. I didn't get my true mother or my sisters. I didn't even get to see my father, but the wings were pretty cool. A small consolation.

I pulled myself onto a pile of rubble and jumped onto a crumbled pillar. Pulling myself onto it was the easiest way to take in the damage and look for where the box with my sister could have fallen. Things were worse than I originally thought. It wasn't just the castle; it was the royal's village and the great skeletal bridge beyond it. Devastation stretched as far as I could see.

The forest was flattened, and smoke filled the sky beyond it, thick black columns rising into the blood-red night. Nikola had no reason for it, but he took down everything with him. Things had been bad enough; I didn't know how we would recover now. A small smile came across my face when what looked like a shooting star came from the sky. It brought with it the twinkle of a small black and white box, falling straight toward us.

"Coy!" I shouted, "There!"

He took off running in the direction I pointed. He picked up the box and tossed it at me. I was unprepared and didn't catch it. It hit the ground and bounced off of a few rocks, my heart stopping with each impact. Why did he toss it to me? He was the only one of us that had broken a seal.

I picked up the box and looked at all of its sides. I didn't see a button or a keyhole, just smooth, intricately carved surfaces. I shrugged and released blood magic from my fingertips. It was a failure, too, the magic sliding off the box like water off wax.

"I don't know how to get this open," I groaned back at Coy, frustration building.

Yes, I did. I jumped up with excitement and realized quickly I needed to pull myself together. I held it up and thought hard. My eyes shook in response, and I was using the power of time to roll the seal on the box back until she was released. The box seemed to age backward, its materials becoming newer, its edges sharper, until it cracked open.

"Has it been another hundred years?" Hesperia cried, her ghostly form spilling out of the box like mist.

"No," I laughed, relief warming my voice. "Not even close."

Coy ran up behind us, breathing quickly but sounding nowhere near as out of shape as the rest of us. "I found your body!" He smiled, excitement lighting his face.

He ran his hand over the lock on the coffin, and it dropped to the ground with a metallic clang.

"How do we get her back into it?" I asked, looking between them.

My words were ignored by both of them. I wished I could have ignored them as easily. They were babbling like children to each other, lost in their own world. I felt my lips sag down at the sight. They were making me far more uncomfortable than I had ever been. Their reunion was touching but also awkwardly intimate.

I could have sworn I heard rubble shifting. I was happy to take any distraction from the two of them. I turned back around to where Nikola's body had been. The only remains still in place were of sloughing skin, like a snake's discarded husk. I shifted to see Riven, but when I did, an emerald viper, larger than anything I had ever seen, was swallowing Riven whole. Nikola wasn't dead; he had changed. Horror froze me in place.

Nikola was using his tail to slap and hit anything within range. He was cautious before but only had rage now, his massive body whipping through the air with deadly force. The closer he got to me, the harder I wished that I knew how to use anything he was so sure I possessed. He called me a goddess, but I felt more vulnerable now than as a mortal.

"Even if I have to change my plans, I'll still end with your heart out of your body," Nikola hissed, his voice a rasp that seemed to come from everywhere at once.

His tail came crashing into me, throwing me from the rubble I stood atop. He showed me no mercy. The air in my lungs escaped with such force I struggled to get enough air when I could inhale again. I had landed with my ribs on the corner of a stone. I rolled onto my back with a groan, still holding the ribs, pain radiating through my chest.

"Even if I have to trap us together for eternity, I'm not handing you my heart," I groaned, defiance giving me strength.

I knew I wasn't getting up yet, so I didn't try. I watched him from where I lay, his body slithering closer, scales gleaming in the moonlight. I knew what I wanted to do. I wanted to rip one of his fangs from him and use it for his death. I closed my eyes and held my hand over my rib, hovering just above. They shook, and I felt the hands of the clock turn back. What hurt was feeling my ribs snap back in place. When they did, I could breathe normally again, though the memory of pain lingered.

He was so close now I just had to wait a little longer. I needed his head as close as it could be. I left my eyes closed and counted his breaths, the hot, putrid air washing over me. When the heat from those breaths became unbearable to lay under, I shot my eyes open and wrapped my body around the fang closest to me. He slung his head back, but I pulled the dagger hidden on the thigh out and started stabbing.

I stabbed and dug at the skin, uncovering more of the tooth until it started to move back and forth. Blood and venom sprayed across my face, burning wherever it touched. Nikola didn't slow his resistance, and it took all of my strength to hang on. I had to stop digging at him when he shook his head, but I started again as soon as he stopped. It was so close. I locked my feet together and used both hands to slice up his gum line, the flesh parting beneath my blade.

He gave me another good fling, and this time, I did get slung out of his mouth, but the fang came with me, torn free with a sickening rip. Being slammed into the ground under the fang hurt, but it didn't take away my joy. I rolled onto all four limbs and spat blood; enough, it had me concerned about where it was coming from. Nikola used his tail to slap my back to the ground on my stomach, the impact driving what little air I had from my lungs.

I tilted my head, which was covered in sweat, to see a wolf come running in, snarling and showing teeth, but not at me. He stood in front of me, growling at Nikola, hackles raised and muscles tensed for battle.

The crimson and black wolf shifted into a man I knew. It shifted into Koa. He was covered in markings the same color as his wolf, intricate patterns spiraling across his skin. I hadn't seen them before. I looked at him enough; I would never have missed them. There's no way they were always there. I coughed blood and spit it beside the rubble I was lying in, trying my best to pull myself together.

Koa cracked his neck and balled his fist. When he shoved his fist into the ground with a strength I could only wish to have had, a pulse of red energy shoved Nikola backward like he had been hit by hurricane winds. The ground cracked beneath his knuckles, power radiating outward in visible waves.

"You're going to bring Whiskers back yourself," he said, not looking back, his voice a low growl of determination.

Caym and another man, as large as Coy, stood on each side of Koa. Coy held out his hand and helped me to my feet before he stood in front of me with the three other men, a wall of protection.

"Coy, this is Onyx. Onyx, this is Coy," Koa said. "That's all the introduction you get for now."

The wave of relief that washed over me was shameful. I was confident enough at the sight of them. I sat on the rubble beside me, if only to catch my breath, watching as the four men faced down the giant serpent, my rescuers at last.

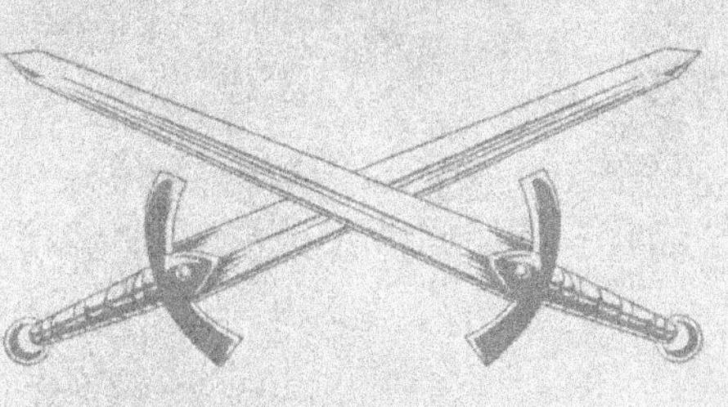

CHAPTER THIRTY-EIGHT
THE WOLF

KOA

My entire chest ached at the sight of her lying in a pile of rubble. Her clothing was tattered, her body shredded. I couldn't tell what of the blood that covered her was from magic and what was a result of that pile of meat and teeth hurting her. The crimson stains blended together, telling a story of pain I couldn't fully comprehend. I knew I wanted to pick her up, to take her away from here and clean her up. I knew I wanted to eradicate everything in this realm that could have helped hurt her. The rage inside me burned hotter than any flame.

The blood moon in their sky was close enough that there was no lack of light, casting everything in an eerie red glow. A storm was raging in the background. Thunder, rain, lightning. Gusts of wind that whipped debris through the air like deadly projectiles. She was underplaying how bad things were here. The destruction stretched for miles, buildings reduced to rubble, bodies scattered like discarded dolls. I moved as fast as I could. I came as soon as I found a way that worked. It took many of us working together to get us here. It took the power of the Goddess of space, every Nola that Caym had in Merripen, and all of the tourmaline stones we could find. The desperation fueled our determination.

I wanted to go to her first and make sure she was alright, but the marks I acquired pulled me to Nikola instead, burning with purpose. I felt her pain and panic. I heard her heart, and when I did, even from my realm, a transformation happened. Vein-like markings were burned into my skin by something beyond even my knowledge. They came with an increase in power that I merged with, energy coursing through me like lightning. I was confident it helped in our ability to travel to her realm. The marks pulsed in time with my heartbeat, guiding me forward.

The one thing I'd never consider a downside of the curse I carried was being able to extend my claws while in a man's form. I listened to the pulling and dived into the side of Nikola. When we made contact, I dug my claws into meat. Ripping as far as I could before the tug on them was too much for me. The resistance of his flesh gave way with a sickening tear, warm blood coating my hands. When I removed them from him, the hissing that came from Nikola was as loud as the shake of the ground around us, pain and rage mingling in the inhuman sound.

I'd also not complain about the new abilities I had since the markings on my skin appeared. Caym had the markings, too, but none of us thought too hard about it. Maybe we should have. We were all beginning to think there was a lot more going on than met the eye. I lifted my hands and used the magic brewing inside of me to summon my leopard. Power surged through my fingertips, manifesting in a flash of crimson light. I had hoped once Nikola was dead, we could all sit down and, without interruption, fully exchange knowledge. The mysteries were piling up faster than we could solve them.

I sent my leopard to Nikola, the beast's muscles rippling

beneath its spotted coat as it leapt. Caym and Onyx followed him, their movements synchronized as if they'd fought together for centuries. I would come to help them soon, but first, I dropped the illusion Juniper left on the cat that had been with Shivani. With no illusion magic, Vero could be her true form. The small housecat shimmered and grew, transforming into a majestic white tiger with blue markings along its spine. The Goddess of Fall had done well keeping an eye on her when she had no magic in Shivani's realm. It was something we needed to test, and she didn't want to part from her. She bonded with her from the moment she saw her, just like I did. The connection was instant and undeniable.

When we could find a way to wake Ruri again, when the problems in our own realm were solved, she would be overjoyed to hear about Vero. She spent all of her time wandering without a purpose. Always whining and crying at the tree, her loneliness palpable. We tried everything we could, but she only craved the sunlight garden. It wasn't until this that she found happiness. Seeing Vero in her true form, powerful and free, filled me with hope.

I unclasped a button on my hip, releasing the grip it had around the hilt of my sword. Onyx spared no trick on it. Ironic he molded the jaw of a wolf into it, the metal teeth glinting in the bloody moonlight. I flung my hand down to my side, and the motion released its blade. Thick and oversized, it covered itself in flames that danced along the metal, hungering for combat. Vero dived, talons first for Nikola's eyes. She gave no mercy with every chance she had to scrape the sensitive whites of Nikola's eyes, each attack drawing shrieks of pain. Step after step, I walked to him, filling with rage, each footfall deliberate and heavy.

"Nikola! Show me what you've got," I yelled before I positioned myself, blade held high above my head, challenging the serpent god.

His body moved to me with a speed I would expect from a

serpent, but I was ready, muscles tensed for impact. I craved feeling my blade dig into his flesh. I yearned to see his blood sit with the rest of the crimson scattered on the ground around us. The need to protect her was stronger than even the need to eat had ever been. It consumed me entirely, driving my every movement.

Nikola lunged at me with only one fang, and I slashed the top of my blade across his mouth. It only grazed him, drawing a thin line of dark blood. He was large, larger than even the building left in sight. I hadn't encountered anything yet that made my blade look small in comparison, but he was succeeding. His massive form dwarfed us all, a mountain of scales and rage.

I gripped the claymore with both of my hands before I took off in a run. I was already using abilities I didn't have before these markings, like the speed I developed. I was quick as a wolf, but not without shifting. The speed I was able to run at now matched my wolf, the world blurring around me as I moved.

Bright red puddles appeared in front of me, forming a stairway to Nikola's head. When I looked behind me, Shivani was creating them, her hands outstretched, face contorted with effort. Even sitting on death's bed, she was the brightest soul I had ever seen, fighting alongside us with whatever strength she had left. I bolted from puddle to puddle until I was face to face with him and shoved my blade into the roof of his mouth, forcing the flames of the sword to grow hotter, searing flesh and bone.

Nikola howled and dropped to the ground, but not before hitting me with his tail. The impact knocked the air from my lungs, sending me flying through the air. A blood angel with the most beautiful, flamed wings caught me before I could hit the ground, and we landed together, her arms surprisingly strong around me.

"Consider it payment for catching me more than once," Shivani said, a tired smile gracing her lips.

"This feels different in a lot of ways," I laughed, reluctant to let her go even as my feet touched the ground.

Our feet hardly had time to hit the ground before Fennic's body floated in the same way Hesperia had. I could see through him, but it wasn't just him there. Dahlia stood in front of him, not as a tree but as a woman this time. Her presence radiated power, ancient and vast, making the air around her shimmer.

"Why am I here again? I thought I died," Fennic asked, confusion evident in his translucent features.

"You did, but I am giving you a chance to go out, as you put it, heroically. I can't give your body power and run it all on my own. I command you to stay and do half the job. You do not get out of our deal," Dahlia answered, her voice melodious yet stern.

"I remember telling you no," Fennic said, crossing his arms in defiance.

"I told you, yes," she responded, unmoved by his resistance.

Fennic shook his head, resignation settling over him. "So now what?"

"Now I give you the power of the creator, and you save my daughters before your next death," she said, her hands beginning to glow with golden light.

"How many times will I have to die?" Fennic sighed, running a hand through his spectral hair.

"Until you listen and die correctly," she answered, the hint of a smile playing at her lips.

Her next movements were to a coffin sitting amongst the rubble. She opened the lid and knelt down, the wood creaking beneath her touch. Both of her hands lay over the face of the body inside. I could not see who it was or what she had done.

I did hear the sounds of gasping and screaming coming from inside, the noise chilling me to the bone.

"It is all I can do for you," Dahlia said before disappearing like morning mist, leaving only a lingering warmth where she had stood.

We stood around, looking between each other and Fennic, uncertainty hanging in the air. Coy only glanced at us all once before he took off for the coffin. Pulling the girl, white as snow, from inside. He gripped her in his arms and held her off of the ground. Her hair was as white as Coy's, but so were her eyes and skin, alabaster and ethereal. It was only a second before they were both covered in white barren tree branch markings. They glowed too brightly to see where the markings began or ended, forcing me to shield my eyes. When I could open my eyes again, the glowing died, but their embrace didn't, the connection between them palpable.

"Hesperia, you have horns," Shivani pointed, her eyes wide with wonder. "On your head."

Hesperia let go of Coy and grabbed her head, running her hands around the newly grown silver horns running back with the flow of her skull, their surface gleaming in the moonlight.

"I do! Are they beautiful!" Her voice was as joyful as it was when she was a spirit, excitement bubbling over.

"I'd love to keep doing this, but the viper is recovering," Caym called, urgency cutting through the moment.

Nikola had recovered enough to lift himself upright again. He greeted us all with a smile, forked tongue flicking out to taste the air. His eyes held a malicious intelligence that made my skin crawl.

"I was just discussing how proud I was of my son. Four of you stand in front of me, fighting together, and my boy looks like he is really one of you," Nikola hissed, poison dripping from his remaining fang.

My stomach turned and sank, ice spreading through my veins. "What did you say?"

Caym locked eyes with me, and I felt a flicker, for the first time, of distrust for him. Something unreadable passed across his face, gone before I could name it.

"I will say no more."

Nikola ended his talking and lunged for us again, his massive form blotting out the blood moon above.

CHAPTER THIRTY-NINE
THE FINAL STAND

SHIVANI

Onyx had his blade into Nikola's side. Coy had half of Nikola's tail gone, but it was making no difference. Caym and Hesperia were working together on something that I didn't understand.

I knew it was the wrong time, but I spoke anyway. "How did you get here?"

Koa tucked hairs behind my ears and gave me a soft smile.

"I traveled the universe." He laughed as if it were so simple. "I used Vero as a beacon to follow, and the Goddess of space in my realm assisted; I actually think it's best we save this story for another time."

"Vesim?" I asked, my voice barely above a whisper.

"She is safe. I asked her to stay." His voice became rushed.

He kept speaking, but I didn't need his reasoning. I grabbed each side of his face and kissed him. Our lips meeting caused a spark. I knew he had to have felt it like I did, but I didn't open my eyes to see. His hands were in my hair, pulling me closer.

When he pulled away from me, I felt like this kiss had

somehow taken so long and yet not long enough. A lifetime and a heartbeat all at once. I opened my eyes, and he was glowing. The markings on his skin turned a deep red and glowed.

When I looked down, there was glowing, too. Red markings started to appear on my skin. One by one, they lit up with the same intensity as his. The air was knocked out of me, and I felt a rush of power before a quake ran through the earth. I felt it even from above. I watched everyone with their feet on the ground shake.

My feet were back on the ground, but I felt different somehow. I could sense the life in everything around me. The trees, the men still clinging to life, Koa. I felt too much at once. The world suddenly seemed both sharper and overwhelming.

"Seems you have found your guardian," Fennic remarked.

"How are you here? I watched you die!" I exclaimed.

"Your mother, we can leave it at that."

Nikola opened his mouth and sprayed venom from one end to the next, and the only thing anyone could do was hide behind rubble. Koa's leopard spared no tooth and kept himself embedded in the viper. Vero proved her skills in flight and showed off the damage her claws could do, but it was not enough. Nikola acted as if he hardly noticed anything was happening to him.

I had confidence in Koa; he was the god of war. I knew he had fought many battles—he had to have. Even if Koa could beat Nikola, it would not be without injury. The thought made my stomach turn, acid rising in my throat.

Koa shifted himself back into a wolf, which still took me by surprise. He mentioned his sister put a curse on him, but I wasn't expecting something like that. He was beautiful. He was beautiful in both forms. It would still take time to get adjusted. I shook myself from the thought. There would be no time to admire him if I let him die.

I didn't have the chance to consider my options when

Nikola used his fangs to pick Koa up and sling him into a pile of rubble. He tossed Coy next. It lit something inside of me that I couldn't ignore or control. Every step I took into the rubble and dirt at our feet left an indent filled with red droplets I could only assume were blood. Did I cut my feet?

I released blood from my fingers and shaped it into a fist much bigger than I. They were a suitable size for Nikola. When the first hit made contact, I couldn't stop. I hit him again and again. I positioned myself in front of Koa, shielding him from anything else that could have come our way before I landed another blow against Nikola. His slithering body collapsed into the rubble and only twitched.

"I'm supposed to protect you," Koa gasped out.

"I'll take it from here," I responded.

It only took me looking back at Koa for Nikola to get up again. He was spraying venom, and I waved my hands in a square to form a shield of blood around us. Fennic used the most ungraceful roll to dodge the venom and get by our side.

Hesperia stood with Caym still. She used her powers to raise every single body that surrounded us. They were alive, gripping their weapons and charging Nikola. It had to have been her who raised the royal family for their crypt to attack the castle, too.

"No, I shall have this." Dahlia's voice sounded through Fennic's mouth.

It scared me enough that I almost dropped the shield protecting us. My heartbeat stuttered, then raced.

"You sound like a woman?" I looked him up and down.

"This is no time for questions!" Fennic's mouth called back.

He wrote something invisible to my eye in the air, and a sigil made of gold appeared, line by line, in the sky above us. It glowed bright enough to light up every piece of land for miles. Beams came down next, like prison bars around Nikola.

Fennic, no, my mother was holding him steady and locking him in place.

The viper's body thrashed and pounded against the glowing golden bars, but it made no difference. Nikola made no change in the strength around him. He was throwing himself against it hard enough that blood came from him. He didn't spare his fang, either.

"Shivani, Hesperia, you must finish it!" She urged.

I knew I didn't have time to think it over. Hesperia and I ran to Nikola and laid both of my hands on him. Hesperia put hers over the top of mine. I didn't know what I was doing or what we were doing. I only knew that we had to do something.

I leaned down and focused. Clearing my mind. When I did, everything stopped around us, and my eyes shook. They vibrated but did not hurt. Dahlia and Hesperia were the only things still moving. It was like the realm, and time stopped.

His size lessened and lessened in front of me until he was just a body again. I did not lift my hands until he was drained of every piece of life I could feel inside of him. His life force drained like emptying water from a pot. Growing smaller and smaller until not a drop remained. He was left unmoving. Nothing more than tightly wrapped skin on bones remained of him.

Hesperia opened his chest and took the root system that sat inside. She used her magic to rot it away until it was nothing but dust.

Fennic's body finished drawing in the air, and the beams closed around Nikola's body. The cage turned into a tiny cube next to the sun god's artifact that dropped from Nikola. Sadness waved over me when my father's artifact was filled with the same sun magic as Caym used. It gave me a sense of closeness to him I almost didn't allow myself to have. My throat tightened with emotion.

Fennic's body stood beside me. His mouth was still speaking with a voice that was not his own.

"He would be so proud of you if he could tell you himself," the voice murmured.

We looked at each other for a moment, and I couldn't decide what to say first. I had so many things to say and so many questions to ask. It was a bit awkward seeing Fennic's face while considering how to ask my mother intimate questions, but it was better than not being able to speak at all.

"You're doing so well, beautiful girl."

Fennic's body dropped to the ground and became lifeless again. A small, quick wave of guilt washed over me for Fennic, but it was beyond brief. It was followed by a rush of sadness for myself. For the fact that, I had no idea how to speak to her now.

At least it was done. Nikola was done.

CHAPTER FORTY

THE RUBBLE

SHIVANI

Koa lay in my lap, and the sound of his breathing filled me with concern. It was the last thing I noticed. I could feel him. I could feel him like he was me. We were tied so closely that I wasn't convinced it was him that I felt. If I didn't focus, it was as if I were dying, too. A part of me was upset that he didn't mention just how badly he was doing. I could see his life roots frayed. It was something I had never seen before, like feeling him wasn't something I could feel before.

I could make out where the pounding heart in his chest should have been, but I didn't see that. There was a seed with such frayed roots. I wasn't a gardener, just as I wasn't a healer. If Vesim were here she would know what to do. If Juniper were around, she would have something to give him. All I could do was guess. I could only hope that whatever direction I picked was the path that would save him. The weight of this choice pressed down on me, heavy and suffocating.

His breath started to sound as wet as he was. He was soaked in sweat and dirt. Every piece of his clothing I moved gave light to another laceration. Every part of him had bruises forming or cuts flowing. I lifted my hand and released my blood magic. The other held his head. I was not a healer, but I couldn't let his death sit on my conscience like Fennic's mother did. I already carried Mori, the farmers. The miners and the animal herders that only came to fight for a better life to hand down to their children.

It was my hands that killed them, no matter who was steering my mind. If he was next, the thought made my heart palpitate. Blood flowed from my fingers into his chest. There was not a single drop from me onto him. It streamed steadily into him. I was giving my best, but it wasn't enough again.

I felt the beating inside of him slow more. It was a feeling that sat in the front of even my own. I hadn't realized I was crying until it was his hand that reached up and wiped them away from my cheeks. His fingers were cold when they made contact. They shouldn't have been that cold. How was I to say that I was a goddess, yet I couldn't save him? How was I to face Dahlia again? What would I say when his friends buried him? That I knew I had the power to stop this but couldn't figure it out until it was too late?

I cut the stream of blood magic off and wiped the rest of my own tears away with my forearm. This time, I put both of my hands on his chest and focused only on the sound of his breath. I felt my eyes start to shake again. It came with a wave of power that set my body on fire. Anxiety still covered me in a layer around it. I unleashed a surge of red into him, and this time, I felt the hands of a clock tick backward, and I could see the roots I had watched before grow lush and full. They grew at an unrelenting pace.

The pace of his heartbeat quickened, and the root took on a white glow before disappearing from my view. Nothing was in front of me now but his chest. I removed my hands and shoved his tattered clothing around. The gashes that should have required needle and thread were closing on their own. The air he was exhaling lost the moisture it was filling with.

"That was close." He groaned.

I couldn't hold back the urge to slap him on the arm, and he let out a cry through small bits of laughter in response.

"Don't you ever do that again! I almost couldn't save you," I scolded him, my voice shaking with leftover fear.

"I never doubted you," he smiled.

My head swam in a shallow pool of fear and joy, panic and relief, tears and laughter. They all flooded out together with a tinge of pride that I had done it. It was me who saved him because I could do it. Doubt filled many corners of me, lurking until it could show itself. Everything I was having a hard time placing boiled over into one motion: a kiss. I kissed him like I'd never get a chance to again.

It was a stupid thing for me to do. We hadn't ever called ourselves close in that way. We never labeled ourselves. What if he had someone in his realm waiting on him, and I was the one who kept pushing? What if he was too afraid to let me down easy? What if he was only kissing me back because I saved his life? The questions buzzed frantically in my mind, even as I pulled away.

"Maybe I will knock on death's door more often," he murmured through a smile.

I watched him get to his feet as if nothing had ever happened. As if he was not just a breath away from never standing again. He moved with the same hidden strength and demand I would have pictured the god of War having. He held out his hand for me to take. I could only look at it at first. It wasn't the right time for me to let my thoughts spill out into the world. There was enough happening, enough to talk about. I gripped his hand, and he pulled me to my feet to join him.

I tried to pull my focus off of him and lay it anywhere else. I wasn't going to ask him any of the things I wanted to. It wasn't the time. I knew I needed to keep my hands to myself.

That kiss was enough. It meant I needed to find something to do that he couldn't join me in.

Vesim created a rift beside us and was finally back before I could find that something. She gave Koa and me a look of silent questioning; she was making sure we were okay before marching to where Riven was handing out commands. I didn't open my mouth, and neither did anyone else. His hands were all over. He was too animated to notice anything else. He tossed out demands as if he still had a full residency of people to do his bidding.

The number of living members of our realm left around us was so small I was positive I could count it on both hands. She took out a blade and spun him around to face her. He gave her a stunned expression before she put both hands on her small blade and shoved it into his chest with a scream. From my view, it appeared she did it with ease, but I knew it couldn't have been true. She gripped it harder, shoving it to ensure it couldn't fit even an inch further before she ripped it down past his belly button.

She let go of the blade when he dropped to his knees in front of her. I looked away. She still had her goal, and I would not interrupt that, but I did not want to watch anymore. Hearing his gasping and the final gurgle was enough to remember forever. I knew she wanted this, and I understood why. It was not my burden to bear, but I would support her all the same.

She made her way to us, tossing a chunk of obsidian in her hand with a smile on her face big enough to start pulling joy from others.

"I knew you'd get him," she smirked.

"I wasn't so sure," I admitted, shoving down the sight I had just witnessed.

"I never doubted you. Nikola is dead. You found your mother. I have Riven's soul right here." She pointed to the obsidian, "What now?" Vesim asked, triumph glinting in her eyes.

"I guess we try and rebuild now," I said, taking in the endless rubble.

"The throne is yours," Vesim declared.

"Now that I have it in front of me, it's the last thing I want," I laughed without joy.

I still wanted my realm to flourish. I wanted the people left to find peace. They deserved to live that. We all deserve to experience it. I wasn't sure anymore that I was the one to bring it to reality for them. I wanted just as badly to find my sisters. To learn who they were, to befriend them. I couldn't stay and do that. I would have to find someone else who wanted peace just as much as I did to take the throne.

I was beginning to realize I didn't have to be alone, and I started to think I didn't want to be alone. I was confident in saying Vesim had things she wanted other than Rivens's soul, too. I was sure if I offered her the throne, she'd deny it. I don't know why I considered her an option to begin with. She never wanted it. It could have gone to Fennic, but he was a casualty of this, too.

"That's something I didn't expect to hear you say," Vesim crossed her arms, "Love gave you reevaluating things?"

"No," I shot the lie at her, feeling the heat creep up my neck.

"How about next we eat something?" Onyx suggested.

"Or we go read those scrolls Cyrus left here?" Caym offered.

"How about a bath!" Hesperia joined in.

"I think we should discuss the comment Nikola made before he died," Coy interjected.

"I don't think I know enough to fully understand," I admitted.

"There are five guardians, four true and one false. We

haven't learned who number five is, but it looks like now we know that one of us is the traitor," Caym explained.

I felt the tension between all of them and thought for a minute that I could be a peacemaker. "I think, all things considered, we can sit that aside for now. I mean, even if he was telling the truth, we all fought today. We should also consider the possibility that he knew it would pull us apart if he didn't live through us," I reasoned.

"She's right; what if he was just trying to plant a seed of doubt? Haven't you all been looking out for each other?" Hesperia chimed in.

"How about we eat while we read the scrolls?" Koa finally spoke, his eyes meeting mine with silent understanding.

"Sounds good!" Hesperia exclaimed.

She didn't miss the chance to start shoving and pushing people inside of the half-standing castle.

Inside, Coy gathered the scrolls while Vesim and Hesperia picked through what they could for rolls and cheese. We did our best to put together several broken tables until we had the space for everyone. This felt as nonsensical as it did joyful.

Even with the uncomfortable silence sitting between us all, I wanted to be with them.

Coy came back with the girls. With hands full, he still stopped to help them bring back food. Even if conversation was hesitant, grabbing for food was not. Koa put a roll in front of me to spare me from having to reach into what looked like a death trap of fingers. As many hands were on scrolls as they were on rolls.

"Do you think we can trust these scrolls?" Koa questioned.

"We couldn't trust the teachings that Yumi gave us," Caym pointed out.

"Cyrus wouldn't keep scrolls that were faked; he takes pride in his job," Onyx argued.

"It makes sense to think they're important," Coy added.

"There are a lot about the types of plants and animals," Hesperia joined in as if she had known them forever.

"The most useful information I found was in the personal journals, not the scrolls. I can recite that from memory," I volunteered.

All eyes looked up and were resting on me, urging me to continue and do just what I said I could.

"You, you actually want me to?" I asked, surprised by their unanimous attention.

"Yes!" Caym pressed me to continue.

I took a deep breath to prepare myself to recite everything I had spent my time reading while in the castle.

CHAPTER FORTY-ONE
THE COLLISION

SHIVANI

I followed Koa to the top of a hill that was far from the castle. He asked me to take him to a place that meant something to me. There wasn't anything to show him here like he had shown me in his realm, but I had only this spot come to mind as something that may be worth anything. It was where I went as a kid to find peace. The only peace I ever did find. It over-looked our ocean. The water was clear enough to see to the bottom.

In everything our realm went through, the one thing that remained untouched was the water. I spent hours as a child thinking that if I could only find a way to become a fish, I might see this realm as something completely different. I painted the view in my mind with trees taller than any we had. They would have been covered in bright leaves, and the view would have actually been breathtaking and not just the best-looking garbage next to a pile of trash.

When I protested and told him we would never make the journey from the castle to the location in a reasonable time before he had to leave, he laughed. He fed me a smirk glowing with challenge. A warrior in a shop just stocked with new blades looking to show that he could make the choice.

He shifted back into the wolf I wasn't yet used to and nudged at me until I was on his back. The speed he could run in that form was terrifying. The fear he invoked in the creatures hiding in our outer territories was enticing. I knew that, in reality, I could defend myself against these creatures now with ease if I tapped into my newly awakened gifts, but something about the idea of him, the god of war, filling them with enough fear they didn't try, it was intoxicating. Overwhelming to think that he would, no, he did defend me against worse.

I alternated between gripping his fur so tightly that I was sure he would develop bald patches to loosen my grip and almost slide off of his back. The scream I'd let out caused him to jolt each time. He didn't say a word, but I felt his body jerk. I was far too close not to notice such a thing. I was sure he regretted making the choice to do this. My heart hammered wildly with each leap and bound he took. I felt foolish when I considered I had wings now. I was so unsure of them; I'm sure I could have flown, but I'd surely not have made it far, right?

The foolishness deepened when I looked to the sky and saw Vero flying above, no longer the small cat I named Miss Whiskers. Why didn't we use those wings? I was unsure how I would remember to call the now huge, very orange and red dragon by her own name instead of the small cat I was sure it was. Did they talk to the dragons? If I flew on her, would she consider me her next snack?

"You can talk to her if you want," Koa spoke in my mind.

"How do you keep doing this? How are we able to keep talking this way?"

I was too unsure how much he could hear or know. I did the best I could to keep my mind quiet.

"Do you think it's a guardian thing?" I asked.

"In my realm, it's a mate thing," he said.

"mate? Is that some wolf thing?" I regretted my words immediately.

"No. It's a soul thing," he laughed.

His voice didn't sound as offended as I thought it would after I spoke.

"It's two souls bonded so tightly that they feel each other. They hear each other. It's two souls whose life and death are so closely tied that they need each other. In my realm, the goddess of love tied souls to each other as her first gift to the realm," Koa explained.

"It can't be what this is, right? I'm not from there?" I said.

"That's not true, though, is it. We're all from the same realm, broken into two pieces. We all come from Dahlia or Yumi. There are traces of blood magic in my realm. You've clearly left marks there; it makes sense to think we left marks here," he said.

We were almost at the location, and I considered it a blessing because I didn't know what else to say.

"Don't think about it too much. I won't pressure you into any such idea, and I'd still pick you even if it weren't true. Even if there were someone else out there that claimed to be my mate. I'd still pick you," he said.

I felt my cheeks heat under my blushing. I was all too happy that he was still a wolf and not looking at me. The warmth spread down my neck as I tried to collect myself.

He stopped us at the top of the hill and lowered himself so I could get off of him. It would have been harder if I were still in a dress. Everything that had gone on tore it apart and I had nothing of it left. Leather pants made life a lot easier today.

His red and white fur shortened place by place before retracting fully into him, leaving the shape of a man in its place. I held his clothes still, but I used my other hand to cover my face. It seemed a bit intrusive and presumptuous to watch him, fully nude, standing in the sunset. I didn't want to-.

"Are you peaking through your fingers?" he asked, leaning his head down to check.

"No!" I snapped my fingers shut.

I listened to the rustle of his clothes, holding my eyes shut tightly. I truly was a fool.

"Good as new," he said.

We walked to the edge of the hill without saying a word. I was too hot from embarrassment, and this time, I knew he could see it. I could see him from the corner of my eye, and he took in the view instead of me, which gave me some relief. I tried to think of anything other than the way his skin glistened in every place the sun touched or the way his hazel eyes filled with more green when he was more focused.

"It's beautiful," he said.

I shook my head, silently I agreed his eyes were, but I knew he meant the view of the land. "You don't need to lie. It's nothing compared to Cylla."

The water was so clear coral could be seen from where we stood. The grass was not green but a dead, endless rug of brown. The trees didn't bear a single leaf. Only burnt branches hardly holding on.

He cleared his throat and cut me off from my own thoughts.

"It's everything to me because it's the first place you thought of as important to you," he took my hand in his, "I wasn't afraid to die when I saw Nikola. I didn't consider for even a second what would happen to me if I got lost in the abyss trying to get here. I was scared of facing a world without you," Koa said. "seeing this, getting to experience, even for a moment, the things that brought you love or happiness. It means everything to me."

His shaky, deep breaths filled me with fear. His words created a lump in my throat and an urge to kiss him, but the way he shook, as if there was something else, scared me too much to fully enjoy the sentiment he was giving. My pulse quickened as I watched him struggle with whatever was coming next. He let go of my hand and reached into the pocket of his black, tightly fitted pants.

"I can not stay long. I have to help in my realm, but before I leave, I wanted to, well-"

He cleared his throat again, and I almost asked him why he kept doing it. I almost stopped him and blurted out that he needed to let me off the cliff of fear and suspense he was dangling me from.

He fidgeted with a small white ribbon tangled from being in his pocket, and I felt like clearing my newly dry throat, too. He tied it around my wrist in the most perfect bow I had ever seen. With every movement he gave the ribbon, his eyes shifted to me. The green in them took over the brown. He glanced for approval to continue, and my response was instant each time. We were silent but so loud.

"I know it's not a good time, but I may not get another chance to ask you to be with me," he fidgeted with the end of the ribbon, his eyes seeking mine.

I didn't hesitate, wrapping my arms around him in a clear yes. I was thankful we could put a title to us, and I could stop my mind from doubting what my heart felt.

If we had to take away anything from all of the death and destruction we were still surrounded by, it was that he was right. None of us knew when we would get more time with each other. We didn't know if we'd see another sunset like the one around us or have the time to take a wolf back ride again.

Vesim and Juniper moved from the trees at the side of the hill, clapping and yelling as they made their way to us. My first thought was attack, and it was clear, by the blood already forming strands from my fingers, that I'd have to face the reality of what marks the current events left on me. My heart jolted before I recognized them, adrenaline surging through my veins. Not today, though.

"I knew she'd say yes," Juniper said.

"I'll pay for drinks then," Vesim grumbled.

"You two knew? And you bet against me?" My jaw hung open.

"You were trying to marry Riven while torn between like or lust with Fennic. Your taste in men hasn't been the best," Vesim crossed her arms.

"I'll remember this!" I pointed.

The rest of the group came from the same spot where the two were hiding.

"If It helps, I knew you'd say yes, too. I never doubted Koa's charm," Caym said.

"It's even worked on me a time or two," Onyx said.

"So, what is going on in your realm?" Vesim asked, turning away from the jokes.

"Yumi has lost her mind. She's a lot different than we've ever seen her," Koa said.

While Koa gripped my hand and they all kept talking between each other, it suddenly hit me. Nikola had been trying to find my sisters. My sisters. It hit me that the same thing that destroyed their life was the reason for mine being lost, too. The realization washed over me like a cold wave, making everything else seem small in comparison. Trying to save my small corner of realms felt like a child's dream compared to this bigger picture blooming in front of me. What we had done here felt like the tiniest win compared to what still needed to be done for us all to be whole again.

"It feels like we have a long way to go, still," I said.

Hesperia nodded in agreement. "We aren't even fully ascended yet. Our sisters need a lot more than we do. There's a guardian in hiding. Yumi needs taken care of, not to mention the other counters."

"Okay, on second thought, let's not keep going. I'm already feeling stressed," Vesim said.

The air was thick and full of thought. It didn't matter

because before we could finish talking out the full reality in front of us. Before we could openly discuss how much danger we were truly in standing in front of Nikola as we had just done, our world began to shake again.

Worse this time than any other. The shaking turned into rumbles, and the ground beneath us started cracking open around us all. I wrapped them all in a blood shield again, Pulling Vero from the sky to keep her safe, too. I could only hope she didn't want to eat me after all.

It was a move made just in time because a beam of bright white light came from somewhere I couldn't make out into the ground around us. I could feel the heat from the shield, and I was using every piece of myself to keep up. Sweat beaded on my forehead as I strained to maintain protection. The beam of light grew wider and brighter before it erupted my realm into pieces.

Pieces of castle rubble, pieces of rotted dirt, and creatures wound together floating in the darkness around us were all pulled into the beam and pushed out of the other side, slamming into bright green grass and trees. The chunks of castle stone slammed into the trees, taking them down and creating craters everywhere.

"What just happened?" I asked, lowering the shield.

Koa stood and looked around, "We're back in Cylla?"

Branches broke and snapped from behind us, and I raised my hand, ready to pull every drop of blood from whatever came next.

"You didn't think you could get rid of me that easy, did you?" Fennic groaned as if he were an elder, coughing and heaving breath.

"How many times can you die and come back?" I exclaimed in disbelief.

"I didn't ask for any of it," he said he still had not recovered from the sudden and rough travel.

"Looks like all that stress fixed the part of our problem that got us all in the same realm," Onyx said.

"Mhm," Coy agreed.

CHAPTER FORTY-TWO

ALL THINGS COME TO LIGHT

ONYX

The presence of the blood guards had become more of a nuisance than a true threat. They were strong but brainless. If Helia had been smarter, then she would have given them more brains over strength. They were meant to keep us away from Yumi, but they had not done much for that yet. I put my palm to the wall in the shape of a blood print and listened for the click of the lock. The sound was satisfying—a small victory in my larger plan.

Doors pulled themselves open in puzzle piece segments. I did not wait for them to finish before I stepped inside of them. Yumi was paced on her knees, still chained. My favorite part was how the red of her blood dried into her white gown. It was beautiful once, but now it was as filthy and stained as she was. The sight of her brought a dark pleasure I didn't bother to suppress.

"What do you want now?" She mumbled.

It took her too long to lift her head. When she did, her eyes met mine, and they were filled with life. I watched the wave of hope wash over them and pink flush to her cheeks. The transformation was delicious.

"I knew you'd come for me. I knew you hadn't forgotten. If I were just patient, you'd find a way to get me out of here." Her voice was filled with so much joy that I nearly wanted to let her continue so that I may keep swimming in how deep her betrayal would go.

I lowered myself and knelt down on one knee in front of her. I took my time moving the hair from her face and breathing in the relief on her face. The moment was perfect— suspended between her hope and my truth.

"Yumi, Who do you think ensured the details were sorted so that you would be here?" I questioned softly.

The speed at which her cheeks paled forced a smile onto my face. I couldn't resist. The moisture that filled her eyes and the questions waiting to pour from her lips made my patience worth it. Her realization was everything I'd waited for.

"It was I that ensured your angels were busy. It was I who ensured you would not take Caym seriously and try to fight against him. It was I that allowed Caym enough time to punish you how he saw fit. I do still have hope that he will side with me in the end. He would do anything for Ruri's safety. I think I'll be able to use it." Her lips quivered, and it made my smile grow. "I'm only here to ask you a question. I want free access to your room, but you've got it locked down well."

"No!" She screamed, desperation edging her voice. "Give me my freedom, and then I'll help you."

I shook my head. "When my father gets into the realm of the gods, we can talk about your freedom. I can't risk you doing anything foolish until then."

"My daughter will come; when she does, I'll come for you first!" Yumi yelled, but her voice cracked. Her confidence was as low as it should have been. The hollow threat lingered in the air between us.

"Sahir? If she were still alive, she would be helping Nikola.

You'll sooner be released by me than her," I taunted. "I'll come back soon to see if you change your mind."

I lifted myself back to my feet and marched out of her cage. The walls shut behind me, and I stepped through the vines to Cosima, Deimos's realm.

"I've been waiting for you, brother," Deimos crossed his arm, irritation evident in his stance.

"Don't call me that," I shivered, revulsion crawling up my spine.

I was many things, but his brother was not one. Yumi and Nikola claimed their children were with each other, but that was only another lie. Sahir and Deimos were siblings. They were Yumi's children, whom she created with pieces of Olexei, the sun god. The two of them had nothing to do with me. I was Nikola's son, and my sister was the worst of them all. Juniper thought she could fit in with Dahlia's side and the mortals, but when I was finished, I'd show her otherwise. Her betrayal would be repaid in full.

"I only came for an update. I need to get back to the guardians before they notice how long I've been absent," I insisted.

"I'm doing what I can, as fast as I can," Deimos growled.

"Maybe you would try harder if I added a bit of pain to motivate you," I pointed, contempt dripping from every word. "I cannot keep killing Sage to buy you more time."

"Don't start with me. You haven't done any better. All you had to do was get a desperate girl to fall in love with you. You couldn't even do that after the spider attack you and Sahir helped set up on Erebus," he countered.

I looked at his gloved hand, which was now made of mist and smoke. The look on his face said we were both thinking the same thoughts. He talked a lot for someone who lost such a valuable body part to Caym. The memory of that fight still brought me satisfaction.

Movement was at the vines, and both of our eyes shot up to see what it was.

"Boys. Bickering back and forth like this won't help you. In the end, it's my punishment you should fear," Nikola declared as he moved further into the room until he stood in front of us.

I turned and placed my hands behind my back in silence. My father did not need to make threats to me. I had done nothing since my awakening but followed his word. His presence filled the room, making even the air feel heavier.

"What is the plan then?" Deimos challenged.

His tone filled me with anger. The disrespect he had for my father would catch up to him.

"The plan is to wait until the girls start piecing themselves together and release Dahlia. While they do, we will weaken their counters. Helia can not be allowed to continue gaining power. The power belongs to us. When they start killing their counter gods, we will start killing their guardians until they have no protection left," Nikola explained, his voice calm but laced with authority.

"Why don't we take them out together? One of us can take the guardians, and the other can take the girls," Deimos questioned.

"This is why you'll never be better than me. You lack patience and brains. You haven't seen power like the power they've been blessed with. If you'd like to die, by all means, proceed how you see fit," Nikola's tone dripped with sarcasm, his eyes glittering with dangerous amusement.

"I do not require you to tell me twice, father. Send word, and I will kill them," I vowed with unwavering conviction.

I bowed and left Deimos's realm to go back to my own. I needed to blend back in, and soon. The time for patience was running thin, but the reward would be worth every moment of waiting.

CHAPTER FORTY-THREE
THE NEXT STEP

HESPERIA

I tried my best to settle into a land. To find one that felt warm enough, but it hadn't worked out yet. I drifted from inn to inn as I was needed. There were many beautiful places in Cylla, but there was no Golden City. There was no forest of sprites or mother to greet me. The absence left a hollow ache that never quite faded. I had hoped seeing me would give Ruri what she needed to come back to us, but that hadn't worked, either.

Our list of failures only grew since we arrived in Cylla. The island we landed on was turned into ruins. The buildings were nothing but rubble now. The greenery was lost. Only leafless trees stood, still covered in signs of fire. It was named the cursed forest after several groups traveled to it and never made it back. They were turned into creatures the realm had never seen before. Mortals were sure a curse had been laid on the island. Some days, I agreed that we felt like a curse. Some nights, the guilt of what we'd brought with us kept me from sleep.

I knew it was only the monster from our realm being sent

here with us. When we thought we had cleared them, somehow, we were alerted that more had shown up. We searched for a reason, a rift, anything, but we also came up emptyhanded.

When we landed, part of Nikola's soul came with us. It attached itself to the other half we brought back, too. The golden glowing soul shard we couldn't sense was all a part of Nikola's plan. He was here, the same as us, but we couldn't find a single trace of him since the souls combined and disappeared. We played into his plans. He appeared weak, and we cheered on our perceived victory. In the end, he was waiting for us to bring him back with us.

He was waiting for the realms to merge back together and his chance to get back to Mother and my sisters.

Trust was thin between many. The groups of us were close at first, but they became even smaller as more time passed. I could feel the bonds we'd forged beginning to fray at the edges. The breaking point was when someone broke Sage's mind. We found them after Helia killed them both, and the two made it quite some time, but before Sage could become a young lady, she was pushed too far and died again. She was reset.

A fight beyond any I had seen between friends was the next event.

Suggestions of killing Ruri so they could restart together entered the discussions. Caym rejected. We learned Sage could not be reborn until Ruri was, as well. The discussion became a demand. Onyx wanted Sage back; Vespera wanted her, too. The two of them were adamant they were her guardian, and the other was false. Caym didn't care who the false guardian was with the idea of Ruri's next death on the line. He called the Nola and the dragons to protect her.

Caym was consistent in the idea that he rejected every single suggestion. He created a life with Ruri again. They were beyond happy. They had a home, a wedding, and a child. Koa tried for years to convince Caym he could not stay living that way. He was shut off from us all. They lost their second child, and he lost her. Their first child was murdered while he buried his second. He became the darkest of us all. The light in his eyes extinguished like a candle snuffed too soon. He thinks someone in the group killed them to bring Sage back. I agree.

Both girls came back again. They were able to grow enough that Ruri attended Orest to become a temple dragon guard, and Sage became the leader of an assassin's guild called the Daughters of Steel, which she formed herself.

I've sided with Caym. I spend my time training and looking after Ruri. Shivani and Vespera spend their time looking after Sage. Shivani is certain she remembers Vespera as a traitor. She uses her free time to try and find a way to free the vampires from Helia's hold and catch Vespera. The vampires are Shivani's children, who resulted from a curse when Helia used Shivani's blood magic with alterations.

Koa tries his best to help Caym and Shivani, but he is knee-deep in a land of shifters still trying to get their bearings in the realm. I use my free time to help the witches who made it to this realm. I used their bones from the collision to bring them back, and they have flourished in the dark. Their gratitude sustains me when little else does.

Ruri left the Goddess of Spring in charge of her temple and the Seere people that reside in Ashbell. She left everything that was needed for her clerics to thrive in the absence of her presence. Ruri was more prepared than even our mother.

I was having good luck bringing Sage's sprites back from the dead as well. She would have a lot of work to do when she was awake again, but it was better than the alternative.

Life was busy but empty. A constant pattern of motion that never quite filled the void within. Helia was progressing in finding a way to pull souls from the stars without help, and Deimos still focused on his nightmares. I knew that he was waiting, like Nikola was waiting for Dahlia to fully unlock us so that he could show what hand he held to try and take our powers.

Our side was no closer to getting Mother free, but many steps closer to exactly what Nikola left as a backup plan.

We had to start working together and moving again soon. I could feel the shifts in the land and the dead. We were running out of time before something else moved on us. The clock was ticking, and the hands moved faster each day.

Yumi
goddess of starlight

Kyrell
god of life

Helia
goddess of time

Astra
goddess of space

Minna
goddess of fate

Thann
god of rebirth

Caym
god of death

Amaris
goddess of beauty

Ekron
god of sin

Orla
goddess of night

Ivory
goddess of pride

Crystal
deity of love

Ruri
goddess of magic

Sage
deity of nature

Nesrin
goddess of healing

Koa
god of war

Aero
god of justice

Juniper
goddess of wrath

Sahir
goddess of chaos

Morticia
goddess of envy

Drimos
god of dreams

Onyx
god of pestilence

Amari
deity of truth

Izaria
deity of water

Kyra
deity of storm

Vespera
deity of plague

ALSO BY HARLEIGH KNIGHT

COMING SOON...

Sunlight and Shadow, Book Three

Rage of Gods and Dragons, Book Four

***

THE BLOODBORN INHERITANCE

A Prophecy of Ruin, Book One

Hourglass of Blood, Book Two

Shadow of the Last Born, Book Three

***

Keep up to date with the latest news and release dates by following
on social media.

Find Harleigh Rose Knight on all platforms.